T0208020

CAN THESE BONES LIVE?

*A Novel of the Armenian Massacres
of 1915 and of ISIS Today*

TOM FRIST

 iUniverse®

CAN THESE BONES LIVE?
A NOVEL OF THE ARMENIAN MASSACRES OF 1915 AND OF ISIS TODAY

iUniverse books may be ordered through booksellers or by contacting:

iUniverse
1663 Liberty Drive
Bloomington, IN 47403
www.iuniverse.com
1-800-Authors (1-800-288-4677)

ISBN: 978-1-4917-6848-8 (sc)
ISBN: 978-1-4917-6847-1 (e)

Library of Congress Control Number: 2015907763

Print information available on the last page.

iUniverse rev. date: 5/20/2015

I dedicate this book to the memory of Dr. Stephan Tchividjian. It was his friendship and his family history that initiated my interest in this subject.

"The hand of the Lord was on me, and he brought me out by the Spirit of the Lord and set me in the middle of a valley; it was full of bones. ² He led me back and forth among them, and I saw a great many bones on the floor of the valley, bones that were very dry. ³ He asked me, "Son of man, can these bones live?"

I said, 'O Sovereign Lord, you alone know.'" Ezekiel 37:1-3

Contents

Appendix

Notes to the Reader

The image on the cover is used with the permission of Thomas K. Horton © 2005 Tom Horton, Further to Fly Photography. It is of the "Resurrection Column" rising from the bones of Armenian martyrs at the Armenian Memorial and Church in Deir ez-Zor, Syria. ISIS destroyed the column, the memorial and the church in September of 2014.

Can These Bones Live? is a story involving many different places and five generations of an Armenian family. In order to help orient the reader, I have included a U.S. Government map of Turkey and surrounding countries, a rough drawing of Peter Johnson's route in southeastern Turkey and northeastern Syria, as well as a family tree of Peter Johnson and Ashti Kaya. They are at the back of the book together with disclaimers and acknowledgments.

Prologue

In southeastern Turkey, not far from the modern city of Elazığ, the Euphrates and the Tigris Rivers begin their long separate journeys until they join at Al-Qurnah, Iraq, and then flow into the Persian Gulf as one. The land between the two rivers, Mesopotamia, is considered to be the site of the Garden of Eden and the Cradle of Civilization. In this region, city-states first developed, and their inhabitants made important advances in agriculture, irrigation, language, writing, law codes, mathematics, architecture, astronomy, and religion.

But also in this area, political powers and ethnic groups have constantly battled to establish their dominance—Sumerians, Akkadians, Babylonians, Assyrians, Hittites, Persians, Greeks, Romans, Ottomans, Mongols, Germans, French, British, Americans, Kurds, Arabs, Turks, Armenians, and Syriacs.* This, too, is the region where Abraham was born and where he first declared his faith in the One God. From his loins and from his faith emerged not only different nations but also three major world religions—Judaism, Christianity, and Islam—and the many different sects associated with them. Sometimes these Children of Abraham have lived side by side in peace, and sometimes they have killed each other.

Just as today, the late nineteenth and early twentieth centuries were times of killing. The supreme authorities in the Muslim Ottoman Empire, by then having long been in control of what had once been Christian land, no longer viewed Turkey's many Christian subjects of Armenian and Syriac ethnicity as being loyal citizens who had played an important role in the development and prosperity of the empire. Instead, they saw them as potential traitors—collaborators with their former Christian subjects in the Balkans in the West who had rebelled and declared their independence from the Ottoman Empire. They also considered them allies of their Russian and Armenian Christian enemies in the East whose presence blocked the creation of Turan—a greater Muslim Turkey stretching all the way from Europe to China. In 1915, based on these suspicions, the Triumvirate of the Committee of Union and Progress, which now ruled what was once the Ottoman Empire, developed a policy of arrests, killings, and deportation to the desert and towns of Mesopotamia of the vast majority of these Christian citizens.

Many individuals, organizations, and governments have called this policy "the first genocide of the twentieth century" because specific groups of people—the Armenians and Syriacs—were officially targeted and killed by decree or died because of the harsh conditions of the forced deportation they had to endure. Most agree that the total number of Armenians who perished because of the implementation of these policies in the next few years was around 1,500,000 souls and the number of Syriacs approximately 300,000. April 24, 1915, is the day it all began in Istanbul with the arrest and then killing of prominent Armenian intellectuals and leaders by the authorities.

The Turkish government and most Turks vehemently deny the charge of genocide. Their position is that the actual death figure was much less, and that most of those who died did so, not because of an official extermination policy of the central government, but because of local decisions and animosities and the terribly harsh conditions of World War I in Turkey. Furthermore, they feel it is unjust to speak only of the Christian Armenians and Syriacs who perished in those years and not of the Muslims and Turks who also lost their property and lives during that war, the wars of independence in the Balkans, and in the Russian and Greek invasions of Turkey.

Whether "massacre" or "genocide" is the correct term for what happened in Turkey during those terrible years, the fact is that the once thriving Armenian and Syriac communities in the east of the country are no more. Almost all of their 2,500 or so churches and monasteries were destroyed or converted into mosques. Their once-flourishing schools and businesses were closed or taken over by Turks. Whole communities and villages were obliterated and their Armenian and Syriac names erased from memory.

Once numbering in the millions, today the self-declared Armenians and Syriacs who still live in Turkey are less than 100,000, mostly concentrated in

Istanbul. However, many more "hidden" Armenians and Syriacs exist. They are descendents of ancestors who converted to Islam in order to survive, and these may number in the millions. Many of them do not know their family history, or if they do, choose not to reveal it out of fear of discrimination.

Today, most of the descendants of the survivors of the mass deportation of 1915 live outside of Turkey in the small new nation of Armenia on its northeastern border or in the many towns and nations around the world that took their ancestors in as refugees. Our story begins in one of these towns in the United States with a significant population of Armenians—Watertown, Massachusetts.

*In this book, we will use the term "Syriac" to denote the peoples of southeastern Turkey and northeastern Syria who some also call Assyrians, Chaldeans, and Arameans. We will also use the same term for the ancient Aramaic language that some of them still speak, a dialect of the language of Jesus.

CHAPTER 1

The Journey Begins

My name is Peter Johnson, and I have chosen to start my story in the early evening of Monday, March 31, 2014 in Boston, Massachusetts. That is when I arrived at Logan Airport, signed a rental contract for a small economical car, and then headed towards the condominium of my hosts, Aram and Susan Petrosian, who live in the nearby town of Watertown. "Uncle Aram" is my great-uncle, and since he and his wife, "Aunt Susan," are now quite elderly, I did not want to cause them more trouble than I had to by arriving too early and making them prepare dinner for me.

At the time, I lived alone, as I still do, in a rented garage apartment in Black Mountain, North Carolina, about sixteen miles from Asheville where my mother, Mariam, and my stepfather, Bill Daniels, live with my half brother, Frank. I moved out of their house even before going to Warren Wilson College because I have always had issues with my stepfather and have never really felt his approval—especially since his biological son, Frank, was born in 1995 when I was eleven years old.

Mother has often tried to be a mediator between us, but now she has teamed up with him in pestering me "to settle down and get a real job." They want me to join the commercial and residential real estate company started by Noah Ross-Terzian, my maternal grandfather, and now run by my stepfather, Bill. They keep telling me, "You can't be an adolescent all of your life, depending on others. You need to earn your own money so that you can support yourself and a family."

My problem is that I do not want "a real job"! I want to be a writer. In order to get them off my back, I promised them at my twenty-ninth birthday party two weeks before arriving in Boston, that if I had not finished writing my first novel or gotten a position as a full-time reporter by the time I turned thirty, I would accept their offer. I figured that in twelve months time, I will exhaust the inheritances from my grandfather and great-grandmother that I have lived on this past decade, and I will need a full-time job.

The story I most desire to tell is not my own, for my life up until now has not been that interesting. Instead, it is about my ancestors on my mother's side of the family, Garabed and Talitha Terzian and of their descendants through their daughters, Karine and Margarit. Ever since I first read my great-grandmother Karine's account of her early life in Harput, Turkey, and then of the disasters that happened to her and her family and to the whole Turkish-Armenian people, I wanted to understand why such evil had taken place. It was a subject especially important to me as a great-grandson of an Armenian victim of those terrible times, but even more so, because I was also a great-grandson of one of the Turkish perpetuators of those horrors. While I was proud of the first, I was deeply ashamed of the second. I wanted to find out as much as I could about them and hopefully to come to a better understanding of myself.

My plan was to research the novel during April of 2014 and hopefully to publish it by April 24, 2015—the hundredth anniversary of what my Armenian relatives call the "Armenian Genocide." Boston was to be the first leg of a three week journey that would take me from there to Istanbul and then to Elazığ, the modern name for the town in Turkey where the Terzian family lived prior to 1915. From Elazığ, I would drive a rental car and follow the deportation route of Karine Terzian and her mother, Talitha, to the border of Syria. Unfortunately, I would have to end my journey there as the civil war in Syria had made it impossible to follow the final stages of their escape to the United States through Aleppo and Beirut.

Not wanting "to put all of my eggs in one basket," I also planned during the Turkey trip to research and write up some newspaper articles involving current events, especially the demonstrations in Taksim Square and the refugee problems caused by civil war in Syria. I felt that doing so might help me get my foot in the door at some major magazine or newspaper as an international correspondent, if my dreams of becoming a novelist were not to be.

Six months before starting my journey, I wrote to my distant Turkish cousins Dilovan Kaya and his daughter, Ashti, and told them of my plans of retracing the 1915 deportation route in southeastern Turkey of our ancestors Karine and Margarit Terzian. I asked if they would like to join me on the adventure, and to my delight, they enthusiastically agreed.

I also sent a second e-mail to Father Gregory Petrosian, another distant cousin who is an Armenian Orthodox priest now living in Mardin, Turkey, helping Armenian refugees from the Syrian Civil War. I wanted to see if the Kayas and I could meet up with him at the end of our trip and if he would allow me to write an article about his work with refugees. He, too, agreed. While the Kayas are descendants of Margarit Terzian, Father Gregory and I are both descendants of Karine Terzian.

Finally, I got in touch with Dr. Aram Petrosian, who is Father Gregory's father, and told him of my project. He, also, was delighted to help in any way he could. He and his wife live in the apartment they had inherited from his mother, Karine, when she died in 1989. When I spoke with him on the phone about coming to Boston for three days to start my research, he and Susan insisted that I stay with them in their building overlooking the Charles River. "It's the perfect location for you," Aram said. "We have two empty bedrooms, and we won't take 'no' for an answer."

I gratefully accepted his offer because their apartment really was the perfect place for what I needed to do in Boston. It was located near the Armenian Museum of America that I wanted to visit, near the Mount Auburn Hospital where I was born, near the apartments in Cambridge where I had spent my first years, and near the Houghton Library on the Harvard Campus where I needed to start my research.

After successfully maneuvering through Boston traffic, I arrived at the Petrosian's condominium a little after seven in the evening and parked my rental car in the visitor's parking lot. I then opened the trunk and pulled out my one piece of luggage. I like to travel lightly and so had chosen a convertible suitcase-backpack which contained all that I thought that I needed for the trip. I had packed in it a few changes of travel clothes, my laptop computer, a head-lamp, some memory sticks, a camera, battery chargers, small binoculars, a razor and toothbrush, my documents, a detailed guidebook of Turkey, and the memoir of my great-grandmother Karine. I also had a smaller backpack for daily outings. I then entered the ground floor reception area of the apartment building and explained to the concierge behind the desk that I was Peter Johnson and that I would be staying a few days with Aram and Susan Petrosian in apartment 505. He called them to let them know I was on my way.

When I arrived at their apartment, Aram and Susan were at the open front door waiting for me, and they greeted me warmly. Aram had noticeably aged from the last time I had seen him, but he still looked like the distinguished Harvard Medical School Professor that he had been before retiring. Always formal, even at home, he wore the same round steel rim glasses he had always worn and even sported one of his colorful bow ties. His head was still full of thick white hair he groomed carefully and above his mouth was the white moustache that I remembered.

While the skin of Aram's neck was now looser and his face a little more splotched, Susan had hardly changed at all. She still had that refined beauty she always had and still displayed that unpretentious, outgoing, and empathetic personality that made unimportant people like me feel important.

"You're still as good-looking and trim as ever," Susan said as she released me from her welcoming hug. "Thank you for honoring us by agreeing to stay with us." Her bright blue eyes reflected her sincerity.

"You're kind to invite me," I replied. "It's so good to see you both again."

"Why don't you take your things upstairs to your room and then come back down and join us," Susan said. "You know where it is. It's the same room you stayed in the last time you were here."

I did know where it was for I had been in the Petrosian condominium several times before—first as a child when Aram's mother, Karine Petrosian, lived there alone, and then twice as a young adult after Aram and Susan moved in following Karine's death.

It was here in this very apartment that my mother learned of the tragic death of my father, Brent Johnson, and of her brother, Thaddeus

Ross-Terzian. It happened two days after Christmas in 1988, and Karine had invited us to have dinner with her and to pick up the Christmas presents that she had for us. My grandfather Noah Ross-Terzian called us while we were eating and told Mother the terrible news. I was only four years old when it happened, but I do have a memory of my great-grandmother Karine holding us and weeping with Mother.

My father co-owned a small Cessna with some friends of his at the time, and had flown it to Asheville to pick up his old roommate and now brother-in-law, Thaddeus, for a five-day skiing trip to Aspen, Colorado. As they landed later in the evening in the Aspen airport, an upward draft of wind flipped their plane, and it burst into flame as it hit the runway. Fire totally consumed the plane before the emergency vehicles could get there to put it out.

The two other times that I visited the Petrosian apartment were much happier occasions and involved visits with my Turkish third cousin, Ashti Kaya. She had come to the Boston area as a Rotary International high school exchange student from Istanbul, and Uncle Aram and Aunt Susan wanted to give her a welcoming party and to introduce her to our family. My parents could not come because of other commitments, but I did, driving fourteen hours from Asheville to Boston without stopping to sleep so I would not miss too many classes.

I was so glad that I did. Ashti was beautiful, smart, and friendly, and we kept up with each other through e-mails after that first meeting. When she returned two years later for another visit to the Petrosians, I went up again to see her. This was even a more delightful time for me as I was able to stay for three days, hanging out with her in Boston and sharing with her my life and dreams and hearing hers. When I told her of my desire to learn more about the Turkish part of my background and some of the history and language of the country, she suggested that I come over in the summer and stay with her and her parents in their Istanbul apartment. Later, her parents, Dilovan and Fulya Kaya, wrote to reiterate the invitation and even offered to help me enroll in a Turkish class for foreigners in the university where Fulya taught Political Science.

"Are you sure you don't want something to eat?" Aunt Susan asked as I started up the stairs with my bag. "We went ahead and had our dinner like you said, but I can easily warm up some leftovers for you if you wish."

"Thanks, but there's no need. I've already eaten," I replied.

"Well, at least join us for a glass of wine on the balcony," Aram insisted. "We like to have a little before going to bed and to watch the last light of the day turn into night over the city. It will also give us a chance to learn more of what you plan to do in Boston and how we can help you."

"That sounds great," I said. "As soon as I clean up a bit, I'll meet you outside."

In five minutes, I had used the bathroom, returned down the stairs and gone through their well-stocked library and through the glass sliding doors onto the wide balcony overlooking the Charles River. The lights of the towns of Watertown, Brighton, and Cambridge had come on, and in the far distance, the skyscrapers of Boston were in view against a darkening sky. The headlights of cars flowed up and down the boulevards on each side of the winding and peaceful river. Aram and Susan turned in their deck chairs when they heard me, and Aram got up and motioned for me to take the empty chair on the other side of him. "Is Pinot Grigio all right or would you like a Pinot Noir?" he asked.

"Whatever you are having is fine," I said. Aram poured me a glass, and as I sat down, I commented, "It's so beautiful here."

"But with a little more traffic than the mountains of North Carolina, I imagine," Aram answered. "I guess every place has its own character, beauty, and tradeoffs." He then changed the subject and asked, "What are your plans for your days here, and how can we help you?"

"First, I need to get my research credentials at the Houghton Library tomorrow morning," I said. "Then I hope to spend most of the day there looking at their files on the Euphrates College in Harput where Garabed Terzian taught. Since the library research desk only opens at nine, I thought I would leave around seven-thirty and use the time to visit the apartments where my parents and I lived when I was a young kid. On Wednesday, I'd like to visit the Armenian Museum of America in Watertown, and if you are amenable, to see some of the places related to your family—your old homes, your church, work places, and the cemetery where Karine is buried.

I'd also love to talk to you about your memories and insights about Karine and Margarit."

"You better ask him quickly," Susan interjected, joking. "At eighty-five, his memories aren't what they used to be!"

"Don't listen to her," Aram replied. "The one thing we Armenians do remember is our history! And like that of the Jews, it hasn't always been a happy one." He added, "I'll be glad to help in any way I can. While you are at the library, I'll make some copies for you of photographs that Garabed took in Harput of their house and of Euphrates College." He paused and smiled sadly. "If I were ten years younger, I'd invite myself along with you on your trip. It sounds like a great adventure, and I will be anxious to read anything you might write about it. By the way, do you have a publisher yet who is interested?"

"No book publisher, but the editor of our local paper in Asheville is open to receiving some articles from the trip. He even promised to pass them on to a friend of his with the Associated Press if the articles were good enough. He particularly likes the story line of a local boy heading to Turkey in search of his roots in the Armenian Genocide."

Aram nodded.

"He's also interested in any pictures and accounts I can send him of current events like the demonstrations in Taksim Square or Turkey's role in helping refugees from the Syrian Civil War. He wants his paper to move beyond just local stories to international ones. To help me out, he had his secretary prepare for me an official looking document saying that I was one of their independent reporters."

"That should be useful!" Aram commented. "And you will have some great sources to interview. Ashti, I understand, was involved in the Taksim Square demonstrations a year ago, and our son, Richard, is now living in southern Turkey helping Armenian and Syriac refugees from Syria."

"Seeing Father Gregory again will be one of the highlights of the trip for me," I told them, using Richard's religious name. "I sent him an e-mail several weeks ago, and he agreed to meet up with the Kayas and me in Mardin, Turkey, at the end of our trip. Actually, I would love to write a novel on him. He's lived such an interesting life!"

"And a precarious one!" Susan added. "I pray for him many times each day."

I had been fascinated with Father Gregory ever since I first learned his story. Since I am a secular skeptic, I have never really understood his religious motivations and his view of the world. However, I have always admired his courageous and adventurous spirit, his intellect, his integrity, and his compassion. Twenty-five years older than I am, Father Gregory, from his altar boy days as Richard Petrosian, has always been involved in some way with the Armenian Apostolic Orthodox Church. After graduating from Stanford, Richard decided to become a priest. First he went to the Armenian seminaries of Saint Nersess in New York and then to Saint James in Jerusalem where he learned Arabic and Syriac, the latter being the language of Jesus and of the ancient Church of Antioch. After being ordained with the new name of Father Gregory, he served Armenian Churches in Lebanon and Syria where many of the Armenian Diaspora lived. He also taught the Syriac language in the seminary in Etchmiadzin, Armenia, the headquarters of the Armenian Church and was a scholar in early Christianity. It was while Father Gregory was there that I had the opportunity of meeting him for the first time in 2005.

At the time, I was in Istanbul living with Ashti and her parents in their apartment and studying in a summer course for international students at Bosphorous University. When the Kayas told me that Father Gregory was in Armenia teaching at a seminary, I decided to get in touch with him to see if we could meet either in Turkey or Armenia. He e-mailed back that he would enjoy that and suggested that we meet in Turkey at Kars. He could take a week of vacation from his teaching, and as he had always wanted to visit Kars, Ani, and Van, ancient Armenian capitals in Turkey, this would be a wonderful opportunity for him to meet me personally and do the visits together.

I was delighted. When my classes were over, I flew from Istanbul to Kars while Father Gregory came by bus. Because of the closure of the Armenian-Turkish border by Turkey, he had to come by a roundabout route from Yerevan, Armenia through the Republic of Georgia.

For five days, we roomed together in cheap hotels and took dolmuses and local taxis to visit the ruins of Armenian monasteries, churches, and forts of the area, and we even went to the supposed site of Noah's ark on the mountain across the valley from Mount Ararat. Father Gregory was an excellent tour guide, explaining the history and significance of the places we visited, and I was also impressed by his spirit of empathy for all those who had suffered so much in this region—Armenians mainly, but also Turks and Kurds.

After that trip, we corresponded from time to time. In 2010, Father Gregory was called back to the Middle East to represent the Armenian Patriarch of Jerusalem and the Armenian Catholicos of Cilicia in ecumenical talks with other Christian groups of the region. Also, as the Syrian Civil War intensified and church bombings, killings, and kidnappings became more frequent, he was asked to use donated funds from abroad to help the trapped Armenians who wanted to escape from Syria to Lebanon, Armenia, Europe, and the United States, often through Turkey. "You should be proud of him," I said to Aram and Susan, "Father Gregory is a good man."

Aram smiled sadly. "Yes, but good men are often unappreciated and die young!"

"Don't say such a thing!" Susan exclaimed, reaching over to squeeze her husband's arm.

Aram nodded and changed the subject. "Tell me a little about this desire of yours to become a writer," he said. "What is it about writing that's so appealing to you?"

I laughed. "Actually, I don't enjoy the actual writing so much. What I like are the other aspects of a writer's life."

"For example?" Aram asked.

"For example, being a learner all of my life and being free to research whatever topic I want—like this topic of our family history. I also like the notion that successful novelists can work where they want and when they desire, can earn a steady royalty income, and can choose to be anonymous or famous, as few people recognize their faces. Most of all, though, I value the idea that one of my books may survive my death and be a means through which I can communicate with future generations and let them know who I was and what I valued."

Aram nodded and asked, "Have you published anything yet?"

I laughed. "That's the problem. I'm not a successful novelist yet, just a wannabe. I have published a few articles but no novel. When I was the editor at the college newspaper at Warren Wilson College, I had two of my articles printed in the local Asheville newspaper. Then after I graduated, the newspaper accepted a couple more.

"What were they about?" Susan asked.

"One was a piece on my adventures hiking the Appalachian Trail. The other one was a three-part series on the college told through the eyes of three generations of my family: first, through those of my great-grandfather, James Ross, who came as a Presbyterian missionary from New England in the early 1900s to teach there when it was known as the Asheville Farm School for Boys. The second article described the experiences at the school in the 1930's of his adopted son, my grandfather, Noah Ross-Terzian. In the final article, I gave my own impression of student life in the school from 2002 to 2006 when I was there. By then Warren Wilson had morphed from a boy's high school into a small coed college known for its liberal tendencies, environmental emphasis, and its Triad program of Academics, Work, and Service." I paused and then laughed again. "Besides tending hogs on the college farm, learning to play the fiddle, to mountain bike, to question authority, and to become a social activist, I actually also got a good academic education. I particularly liked my creative writing classes, and that is when I decided that I wanted to become a novelist—a teller of the truth in fictional form."

"Well good luck!" Aram said. "I look forward to reading your book when it is finished, especially since it will be about our family." He glanced at our empty goblets of wine and stood up. "I hope you don't mind, but it is time for this old man to go to bed."

"Of course, I don't mind," I replied. "I need to go to bed myself in order to get an early start tomorrow. I also want to re-read your mother's account of her life in Harput and of the deportation before going to the library. Thank you for helping her put it together and for sending it to me. It has been extremely interesting and useful."

"I'm glad," Aram said.

"I'll leave the coffee percolator set up and cereal out in case we aren't up when you leave. You're family, so we won't make a big fuss." Susan added. "It's so good to have you here."

I thanked them again for giving me a place to stay, said good night, and went upstairs to my room. I unpacked my clothes and the memoirs of my great-grandmother Karine Terzian Petrosian and put the memoirs on the table by the bed. After I brushed my teeth, got into my pajamas and into the bed, I reached for the memoirs to read once again.

CHAPTER 2

My Memories of the Massacres and Outrages of 1915

Karine Terzian Petrosian
April 24, 1983

My name is Karine Terzian Petrosian. I am eighty-three years old and I live in Watertown, Massachusetts, where many other Armenian immigrants to America like myself have settled. With the help of the American Board of Commissioners for Foreign Missions, I arrived here in April of 1916 along with my mother, Talitha Terzian, from Turkey. I was sixteen years old at the time. Along with my mother, I took a job at the Hood Rubber Factory in Watertown, and eight years later while working there, I met my future husband, Nigol Petrosian, who was a year older than I was. He was from Yerevan in Russian Armenia and had immigrated to the United States when the Communists took over. Later, he started his own business—a coat factory. We had two wonderful children, Margaret, whom we named after my sister, and Aram, whom we named to honor Nigol's brother. Since Nigol was a member of the Armenian Apostolic Orthodox Church, he insisted that I join that church and raise our children in that faith. My mother, however, remained Armenian Protestant until her death in 1954, although, she often worshiped at our church with us as well as in a Syriac Church in Boston. Her own parents had been Syriac Orthodox Christians.

For many years, you, my children and grandchildren, have asked me to tell the story of my early life in southeastern Turkey and of Mother's and of my escape from the massacres. While I have told you parts of the story, I have not told you all of it, as it was just too painful. I was afraid that telling the truth of what happened back then would bring dishonor to me, to your father, and to you. It was only in 1982, after finally reuniting with my sister Margarit in Istanbul after 65 years of separation that I decided that I had to tell my story with all of its pain. My grandson, Father Gregory, a priest in our Armenian Apostolic Orthodox Church, encouraged me to do so. He said, "An infection must first be recognized, its boil lanced, and its poison and puss let out, before true healing can take place." Since my husband died in 1974, Father Gregory says that I no longer have to protect what I consider his honor. "You did nothing wrong, Grandmother, and Grandfather loved you no matter what," he reminded me. So, as painful as the process is, I am determined to do my best to be truthful and recount what really happened— both the horrors and heroism, the poison and balm—of this horrible time in Armenian and our own family's personal history. I do not want to die before telling the truth of what I myself saw and experienced and what my mother recounted to me before her death in 1954. I also do not want to die before seeing again my son Noah, and asking for his forgiveness. May God then grant me and all of us who have suffered because of those hellish times, deep healing and peace.

Life in Harput

I was born on April 2, 1900, in the American hospital in the town of Mamouret-ul-Aziz, Turkey. We called it Mezire for short. It was a new town compared to Harput and was the administrative capital of the Province of Harput, a vast region of many other Armenian, Kurdish, and Turkish villages. I was the oldest child in our family, two years older than my sister, Margarit, and four years older than my brother, Lazar. The hospital where we were born was an hour by mule from our mountainside town of Harput overlooking Mezire where my father and mother lived.

My father, Garabed Terzian, taught at the Euphrates College in Harput. It, like the hospital, was run by the American Board of Commissioners for Foreign Missions that had its headquarters here in Boston. My father had been such a good student at the college that the American director sent him to Yale University to study, and when he was finished, he came back to Harput to teach Biology and English.

When my father returned in 1898 from America, he married my mother, Talitha Davut. In those days, parents arranged the marriages of their children. Since my mother's parents were both killed in the Hamidian massacre in 1895 in their village near Mardin, my mother's uncle and aunt arranged the marriage with my father's parents. Even though my father's family was Armenian and my mother's family Syriac, they were friends and did business together. My father's parents lived in the village of Hussenig close by to Mezire and Harput. They were farmers and had cows, sheep, and orchards and sold some of their fruit, vegetables, and wool to Mother's uncle who lived in Mezire and owned a store there.

I remember having a happy childhood. Almost all of my friends were Armenian Christians with a few who were Syriac Christians. Most went to the Armenian Protestant Church in Harput although some went to the Armenian Apostolic Orthodox Church. My mother's uncle and aunt and their son and daughter-in-law went to the Church of the Virgin Mary, a Syriac Orthodox church in Harput. The majority of the people in Mezire, Harput, and Hussenig were Turks and Kurds and therefore Muslims, but Armenians and Syriacs owned most of the businesses and were the doctors, lawyers, and teachers. I learned Turkish in school, but we had very few neighbors or friends who were Turks or Kurds other than the ones who were tenant farmers on one of my father's two rural properties. My mother's uncle had many more such friends because of his store and his involvement with the government.

Our family at first lived in the apartments for teachers at the school in Harput, but after my brother was born and my grandfather died in 1912, we moved to my grandfather's bigger house in Hussenig, a village at the foot of Harput Mountain. We needed to take care of my grandmother and the family property, and we needed more room for our own family. Father traveled by mule up the mountain most days to teach his classes but he often spent the night in the teacher's quarters at the school when he had late church or school meetings. When we were young, my sister, brother, and I went to a small one-room school in Hussenig where our pastor was the teacher. Later, my sister and I studied in the school for girls at Euphrates College and slept during the week in the girl's dorms, coming home only on weekends and vacations.

I liked our farmhouse in Hussenig as we had a lot of space. It had a flat roof and five rooms upstairs for sleeping, eating, and entertaining. Downstairs was a pantry and a courtyard where we kept the animals—cows and oxen, a mule, some pigeons, and chickens. I remember that the pantry was where we stored our flour and cracked wheat and other foodstuffs for the winter in big pottery pots. Outside we had an orchard of mulberry and apricot trees, and we would dry the fruits on sheets on the roof for our winter treats.

I guess you could say that we were better off than most as we had land that we rented out to some Turkish neighbors for them to farm and to keep sheep and goats. We also had nice carpets and comfortable chairs that my father had purchased in Constantinople when he returned from America. Our most treasured possession, though, was a beautiful silver cross that my father's family had passed down from generation to generation. My grandfather and grandmother were the first of the Terzian family to leave the Armenian Orthodox Church and become Protestants. My mother also treasured a massive, finely etched, and hammered copper tray that my great-uncle, Boulos Davut, had given to her as a wedding present. She would not allow us children to eat on it. Father's most valued possessions were his camera that he had bought back from America and his violin that he would play at night around the fireplace in our main room. Besides being a teacher, he was also the college's photographer and he played in and sometimes directed the Euphrates College Orchestra.

Sometimes you have asked me what we did for fun in Harput and Hussenig. Life was different then, and we did not do things like go on vacation as people do here in America. We matured early as most of our lives were spent in learning and doing the necessary chores to help our family survive the harsh winters and to prepare for our roles in the future as wives and husbands and guardians of our own families. Still, as young children, we had fun with our games—the boys with their knucklebones and we girls with the dolls that we made from sticks and cloth. I also remember picnics at the Harput Fort with the families of teachers at the Euphrates College, and once we made an overnight visit to Lake Goeljuk, which was some six hours away from Harput by oxcart.

We also celebrated holidays like Christmas, Easter, and the Turkish National Day. Once, Father took us to the American Consulate in Mezire on the American National Day. It was the finest building in the town with its walled gardens and large house. When I asked Father about it, he explained, "The Consul is here to help American companies like Singer Sewing Machines and the hundred or so American missionaries in the Eastern Provinces. He also provides support for people like me who want to go to America to study or work." Many Armenians from our region had done just that. Unlike my father, they had stayed there and become American citizens, sending back money to their families in Turkey. As for the American missionaries in Mezire and Harput, we knew of a dozen or so who ran the American college, hospital, and orphanage. Another handful of French Catholic monks and nuns and German and Scandinavian Protestants lived in Mezire administering their own schools, orphanages, and churches.

Sometimes we had relatives visit our home in Hussenig and that broke our normal routines. Two cousins, Nabila and Lagina Terzian, came from Palu, a town two days journey from Harput on the Murat River, a source of the Euphrates. This same river waters the vast plain below Harput. My father's brother lived there on a farm with his family. My cousins were a little older than Margarit and I, and they stayed several months in our home to learn embroidery and weaving from my mother.

As for relatives from my mother's family, I never met anyone other than her uncle and aunt, their son Varkey and his wife Akka, and their little boy, Poonen. My cousin Varkey Davut, who was 10 years older than I was, often came to Hussenig from Mezire to help with the harvest on our farm. I remember him as very hard working and kind. Later he joined the Turkish Army.

As I said before, my mother's parents died in 1895 along with many others in their village, killed by Kurdish tribesmen and convicts who attacked them on orders from the Sultan in Constantinople. Mother survived because she was studying at the American Protestant missionary girl's school in Mardin when it happened. Later the missionaries sent her to live with her uncle and aunt in Mezire and to study at another mission girl's school in Harput.

While Mother was not as educated as Father was, she was a very smart woman and very good with her hands. She was constantly doing something—cooking, weaving, embroidering, drying fruits, and even volunteering to make bandages for the American hospital in Mezire when they opened it to Turk soldiers who got typhus or were wounded fighting the Russians in the northeast. It was during that time that she became friends with Miss Isabel Ross, an American missionary nurse, who later helped us to escape Turkey for America.

That then is mostly how I remember my early life before the great crime happened. We were a happy and prosperous family. Then our world turned upside down. I was fifteen at the time. My sister Margarit was thirteen, and my brother Lazar only eleven.

Disaster

The nightmare started for our family and for the entire Armenian population of the Harput Province in June of 1915 when my father, Garabed Terzian, was arrested and taken from our house at night. The gendarmes came without warning and took him away in his bedclothes to Mezire. The noise woke us all up, and we were very scared, but as Father left, he assured us that everything would be all right. "Don't worry, I have done nothing wrong" were the last words I ever heard from him. He was a dear, dear, smart and loving man and I wish that you, my children and grandchildren, had known him.

Mother went early the next morning to the prison in Mezire searching for him, leaving us children with my grandmother who lived with us. When she returned, she told us, "The guards pushed me away and told me nothing so I hurried to Uncle Boulos's store. It was closed so I went to their home and found Aunt Rahel weeping. She said the soldiers had taken Uncle Boulos away as well, and that she had heard screaming all night from other houses in the neighborhood."

Desperate, Mother then went to the home of her friend Miss Isabel Ross, the American missionary nurse. She told her what had happened to Father and to my uncle and asked for her help. Miss Isabel agreed to do what she could and passed on to Mother that she had heard that the gendarmes had arrested many other Armenian men as well. Mother asked her, "Why?" Her answer was, "They are being accused by the Turkish authorities of supporting Armenian revolutionaries and of being allies of the Russians who are the enemies of Turkey. They also are suspected of hiding illegal weapons in the school and in their houses and businesses."

While Mother was away in Mezire, the gendarmes returned to our house and searched it, looking for hidden weapons. "We don't have any," my grandmother told them, but they did not believe her. Instead, they gouged holes in the wall with their bayonets, broke our pottery storage pots with their rifle butts, and even dug in the courtyard where we kept the animals. Of course, they found nothing, but they left us terrified. None of us slept that night. We just huddled together, fearful that they would return. Mother tried her best to comfort and reassure us.

The next day, in the afternoon, Miss Isabel showed up at our house in Hussenig on horseback accompanied by one of the Turkish men workers at the hospital. She told us what she had learned from talking with the American Consul in Mezire and to the American director of Euphrates College in Harput. "Hundreds of the most prominent Armenian men of Harput Province, including many of the professors and instructors of the College, the businessmen and professional men of the town, and even the Bishop of the Armenian Orthodox Church, have been arrested and taken away to prison. When the Consul asked the Vali, the highest Turkish authority in the Province, about the arrests, he only said that he had received orders from Constantinople to detain suspected traitors and to deport all the rest of the Armenian citizens of the Province to the desert region south of Urfa and Harran." Miss Isabel added, "The town criers in Harput and Mezire are already spreading the word on every corner that the deportation of all Armenians will begin in six days. Those in Mezire will leave on July 1, those in Harput on July 5, and those in other surrounding villages like Hussenig, a few days later. They say that you will be accompanied and protected by Turkish gendarmes along the way and that any goods that you have that can't be taken on the journey should be left locked in your houses and stores or deposited in government warehouses where they will be protected until you return."

As we waited for the date we were supposed to leave Hussenig, we children had little to do because the Vali had ordered our schools to close. We played with some friends in the street near our house, but when Mother heard us being insulted by one of our Muslim neighbors as children of infidels and traitors, she refused to let us go outside anymore.

While some Muslim neighbors treated us badly, Haydar, the Turkish man who worked on our small farm near Hussenig, came to our house and offered his help in any way that he could. He said he was ashamed and could not understand why the Vali had made such a decree to arrest the men and deport the women and children.

As the arrests of the Armenian and Syriac men continued in the town and the date for the deportation of the rest of us approached, Mother and Grandmother became increasingly frantic. Rumors flew everywhere. For example, we heard that a caravan of oxcarts filled with our beloved fathers, brothers, and sons had been seen secretly leaving the town late at night heading towards Lake Goeljuk. We also heard stories that even Armenians and Syriacs serving in the Turkish Army on road building crews were now being rounded-up and shot. Never allowed to carry weapons by the army, they had no way to defend themselves.

Such terrible stories received confirmation from an Armenian professor at Euphrates College who was released at the insistence of the American Consul because he was an American citizen. He reported that he had been tortured and had witnessed personally the torture and execution of others. It soon became clear that the only Armenian males being spared these horrors by the Vali were young boys, old men, those who were American citizens, or those who had friends among the authorities or had been able to bribe them.

Three days before we had to leave for Urfa and the Syrian Desert, Miss Isabel returned to our house with the same trusted Turk bodyguard who worked at the hospital. Aunt Rahel also accompanied her. Aunt Rahel sobbed as she told us that she had heard nothing from her son, Varkey, who was in the Turkish Army or news about her husband who had been arrested. She held out little hope for their safety or for that of my father. She told us that her daughter-in-law, Akka, was so desperate and fearful for the future of herself and for her small son that she had decided that the only way for them to save their lives and their possessions was to officially convert to Islam at the appropriate government office in Mezire. "I agree with her," Aunt Rahel told Mother. "You should do the same. That way you will be able to stay in your homes. You can still pray in secret any way you want to!"

Mother refused to consider such an option, and Miss Isabel agreed with her. Then, as Aunt Rahel and Miss Isabel prepared to return to Mezire together, Mother asked them to wait and she went into her bedroom and got Father's camera and all of the photographs that he had taken at Euphrates College and of our town and family. She gave them to Miss Isabel and begged her to take care of them. Miss Isabel agreed, and both she and Aunt Rahel were in tears as they embraced Mother and all of us in our last goodbyes. Miss Isabel said that she and some other missionaries had offered to go on the trip south with us to help but that the Vali had refused their offer telling them, "The gendarmes will protect and take care of them." Miss Isabel then made Mother promise to let her know when we got to our final destination. Then they left. That was the last time I ever saw Aunt Rahel.

Those last few days before our time to leave Hussenig, chaos reigned in our village, and from what we later learned from others, in all the towns in the province with large Armenian populations. From the roof of our house, we could see our neighbors hauling what they had to the town square or to Mezire and Harput to sell them for whatever they could get from the Turks and Kurds in order to buy gold. People were also buying food and pack animals. Mother sold one of our cows to an Armenian neighbor who wanted it both for the milk and to carry her family's bundles the long distance. She decided, however, not to sell any of our family's valuables. "Our neighbors are getting almost nothing for theirs, and we risk being robbed on the road taking them to Mezire or Harput to sell," she explained.

Mother finally decided to give Father's violin and the copper tray to Haydar for safe-keeping and to leave the rest of our goods locked up in the house. She implored Haydar to look after them while we were away as she did not trust the word of the government. She also gave him the key to the house, and at his request, a letter saying that she had turned over the house and the remainder of our cows and chickens for him and his family to use and take care of until we returned. She also gave him one of our best rugs as a gift for him and his family.

Later that same night, Mother went out to a special hiding place at the corner of our courtyard wall that only she and Father knew about. She dug up a metal box containing some fifty gold coins that they had hidden for an emergency. I then watched as she secretly sewed the pieces into some of her clothes and veils and canvas tents to take on the journey. With Margarit's and my help, she and Grandmother also made lavash bread and packed as much dried fruit and meat and bulgur wheat as they were able, loading up our oxcart. Mother then took Grandmother to the cemetery to my grandfather's grave so that they could pray and say goodbye. When she came back she told me that she had considered burying our family's beloved silver cross behind Grandfather's headstone but then decided not to as she feared the graveyard would be desecrated as soon as we left. "That's what happened in 1895 in our village graveyard near Mardin. The Turks and Kurds dug it up looking for the gold and silver that they thought Christians bury with our dead," she explained.

"I know a safe place we can hide the cross," I told her. I was thinking of the small crevice cave where I used to play off the canyon trail that Father took from Hussenig to the Euphrates College in Harput. It was not very far from our home and was an excellent hiding place. I discovered it one day playing hide-and-seek with my friends. Behind some bushes and with a small opening, the cave was my secret. After school, I used to crawl in and squat on the ground looking out the narrow opening up to the beginning of the canyon trail at the top of the mountain waiting for Father to appear as he returned home on his mule. I used to hide my favorite doll in a crack in the wall towards the back. "That is where we should hide it," I told Mother.

Mother wrapped the cross in a cloth sack and asked me to go with her and show me where the cave was. So together, making sure no one saw us or followed us, we went up the rocky trail, crossed a small stream, climbed up a hill, and then went through some bushes to the cliff wall crevice hidden from view. I told her where I hid my doll at the back of the cave and Mother crawled in, felt around for some time, retrieved my doll and put the cross in its place. When she backed out of the cave, she said, "It's a good place." Easing our way down the hill to the path, again we made sure that no one saw us.

The long march south to the Syrian Desert

When July the fifth, the day of our departure, arrived, some fifty gendarmes went through the village banging on the doors of all of the Armenian houses, forcing everyone into the mud streets. Most of them had rifles and all of them had sabers or knives. We knew what awaited us because two days before, we had seen from our roof a river of several thousand persons with their possessions from Harput descending the mountain road linking it to Mezire. We had heard they were heading to Urfa by way of Malatia. An earlier group from Mezire had gone another route through Diyarbakir, which seemed to be the route that we were to take since the Turkish gendarmes directed us to leave the town in that direction. I was glad because I knew it would take us by the beautiful Lake Goeljuk where we once went on an outing.

Mother already had prepared us and had assigned us each to our place. Grandmother was to ride in the oxcart with Mother and with all of our bundles of tents, food, clothes, and water. Lazar was to ride on Father's mule behind, tethered to the back of the cart. Margarit and I were to walk alongside the cart, but if we got really tired, we could change places on the mule with Lazar. As I was the oldest, Mother made me responsible for looking after my brother and sister.

As we left our village, we found ourselves towards the front of a long column of people, mostly women and children, but also some older men and boys. Most were from our village of Hussenig, but as we slowly walked towards the lake, other columns from nearby Armenian villages joined us on the road. Our family was fortunate as we had an oxcart and a mule to ride on and to carry our burdens. While a few dozen families were like us, the majority of the people had to walk carrying their burdens on their shoulders or heads. Some mothers carried their babies and Mother offered to help by putting two such babies in the oxcart with her and Grandmother.

Because we were so many and we walked so slowly, it took us about two days to get to the lake. At first, I experienced no great fear but only the excitement of being on a great adventure. Soon my attitude changed. Even before we had gone a couple of hours on our first day, I saw the first body lying by the road. It was that of an old man who must have fallen exhausted and then died. The next day, on the other side of the mountain from Mezire going down to the shores of the lake, I saw a dozen more such bodies. The most gruesome were four naked corpses sprawled out in a grotesque way in a gully. It looked like someone threw them there. The gendarmes ordered us on when we stopped to look.

Arriving at the lake, we followed the road along its edge until we came to a wide-open level area where the gendarmes ordered us to stop and make camp for the night. I remember the place to this day. It was where we had camped and picnicked and had such fun a couple of years before with other families from Euphrates College. There was a grove of mulberry trees and a beach, and across the lake from where we stayed was a small island with the ruins of an old Armenian church and monastery. One day an Armenian boatman from Goeljuk Village, which was near to the island, came across the lake and took us to visit it. At night, we sang Armenian folk songs and hymns around the campfire and sometimes we danced the folk dances we had learned in school. Now I view that same campsite not as a place of happiness, but as a place of unimaginable suffering and evil.

After the gendarmes ordered us to halt for the night, Mother chose a place for us to camp by an isolated tree at the edge of the camp a little up the slope of the hill from the rest because some grass was there for our animals to eat. After we had tethered our animals and brought water for them from the lake, we used some of the tree branches to make a fire for cooking.

The gendarmes, who were guarding us, had set up their tents farther up the hill close by. They also wanted to be in a grassy area where they could graze their horses and mules. After their evening prayers, we could see them eating and laughing around their fires. It was still daylight and Margarit, Lazar, and I were helping Mother put up our two tents for the night when three of the gendarmes came towards us from their camps. The oldest of the soldiers, the one who seemed in charge, said to Mother, "We noticed you on the road, and we want you and your daughters to come to our camp and entertain us with your Armenian songs and dances."

Mother answered that we did not know any songs and dances, and that anyway, we needed to stay where we were to set up our tents, help my grandmother, and watch the animals. Her reply made the officer angry, and he called my mother "kuffar," an insulting name in Turkish for infidel. He then ordered us to come. When we did not move, he slapped my mother on the face and then grabbed her wrist starting to drag her to their tents. The two other gendarmes grabbed Margarit and me as well and started to pull us up the hill. That was when Lazar, my dear young, brave brother, took the tent pole in his hands and swung it as hard as he could at the head of the soldier who was holding on to Mother. The blow stunned and infuriated the man, and he reached into his belt pulling out his dagger, which he plunged repeatedly into Lazar's stomach and chest. As we watched in horror, Lazar fell to the ground writhing, his shirt covered with blood. We tried to rush to help him, but only Grandmother was able to get to him. The soldiers held tight to us and dragged us fighting and screaming up the hill to their tents. My last image of my brother alive was of his jerking body on the ground held in the arms of our wailing grandmother.

That night, I descended into the depths of hell. The soldier who grabbed me pulled me into a tent and then in a fury threw me onto the ground and tore my clothes off me. He bit me on my chest and did things to me that hurt and shamed me so much that I cannot bear to mention them even in confession to Almighty God and to his priest. When he was finished and exhausted, he let me go. At that time, I was just a young girl, and I did not understand the way of men with women. Nor did I yet grasp how their lusts could turn them into blind and ferocious animals throwing aside any human kindness in order to satisfy their desires. That night of horror will always be burned into my brain and my emotions.

Mother and Margarit were also raped that night, but none of us could talk of what happened when we got back to our camp. We could only weep and lower our eyes in shame and despair. Mother hugged us both tightly to her and said over and over, "I am so sorry, I am so sorry." But as great as the shame and pain we felt for what had happened to us, it was nothing like the grief and horror that we experienced at the sudden and violent death of our brother, Lazar. Throughout the night, Mother rocked his lifeless body in her arms and Margarit and I sat on the ground next to her reaching for his hands and his feet or tenderly touching his hair, lost in our pain and incomprehension.

When daylight came, and the morning prayers of the soldiers were over, the gendarmes gave orders all through the vast camp for us to pack up and get moving. The officer who had raped my mother and killed my brother was the one who gave the order to us, acting as if nothing had happened the night before. When he saw the body of my brother lying on the canvas of one of our tents, he went to a campsite below us and ordered two old Armenian men sitting there to come to our campsite to bury my brother. None of us had shovels or hoes, so they dug into the ground with broken branches about fifteen paces from the tree where we camped. While they were digging, Mother washed Lazar's body with the water that we had and changed his bloody shirt. She then wrapped his body in one of our blankets, and the two men laid him in the shallow hole facing the lake and the island with the ruins of the church and monastery, his body just below the ground surface. The grave was so shallow that they went and gathered large stones along the slopes to cover him and protect his body from the animals. Some women from their campsite came to assist them, but Margarit and I were still too dazed to understand or to help. When the grave was complete, one of them prayed for Lazar's salvation and for our own protection. All of us now feared that we could be next.

The two men who helped bury Lazar were in fact the next. The hated officer who had killed Lazar and ordered the old men to bury his body now ordered them and some two dozen other older men among the deportees to return up the road that we had come down to bury other bodies that we had seen along the way. They left with fear in their faces, and we never saw any of them again.

For the next few days we journeyed in a trance. During the day, Mother drove the oxcart carrying Grandmother, our food, water, and cooking instruments while Margarit and I followed behind with the mule and the lighter tents strapped to the saddle on her back. Sometimes Margarit would walk and I would ride, and sometimes she would ride and I would walk. When Mother saw older women or young children particularly struggling, she allowed them to rest for a while by riding in the cart with her. At night, we tried to camp in the middle of everyone, as Mother wanted to keep us as far away from the gendarmes as possible, especially the officer who had killed her only son, our brother.

As we got near to the mountain town of Maden, famous for its copper, the wheel of our oxcart broke as it slipped off the rocky trail winding down the mountain besides the large stream that became the Tigris River. Mother was driving the cart with Margarit and Grandmother in it at the time, while I was riding Father's mule. Mother tried to fix the cart, but as we had no tools or replacement wheels, she said that we would have to abandon it. She released the ox from his oxbow, and then with our help, she did the best she could to load him with the bundles that he had been pulling. Unfortunately, we could not get the ropes tight enough around his belly and the bundles kept falling off. Most of the caravan had since passed us by in their slow march south, and we were alone at the end of the line. As Mother was struggling with the bundles, some men with hatchets in their belts approached us on horseback from behind. Mother saw them and told Margarit to get on the mule with me and for us to run as fast as we could towards the rest of the caravan. I obeyed her immediately, remembering what had happened the last time strange men approached, but Margarit hesitated and clung to Mother. Mother yelled at me to go and I did, leaving them there. Until today, I both regret and am thankful for my choice.

Mother and Grandmother were weeping when they found me later that night in the camp. They said that the men were three Kurds from a village nearby and that they had kidnapped Margarit along with everything we had. "They surrounded us, and looking at our ox and the bundles on the ground, the leader thanked us for all of our goods." The leader then looked at Margarit and asked Mother in Turkish "Is she your daughter?" Mother answered "Yes." He said how beautiful she was and he asked Mother, "Will you give me her as a second wife in exchange for your lives?" Mother pleaded with him not to harm them. They could take what they wanted of our goods but "Please don't take my daughter or harm her." The man laughed and replied, "If I take her as a wife, I will be saving her, instead of hurting her as where you are now headed is certain death." He then ordered his men to pick up the bundles from the ground and take the ox back to their village.

As they dismounted to do so, the chief turned his own horse toward Mother and Margarit, knocking Mother to the ground with his knee and grabbing Margarit with his arm. He then pulled Margarit up in front of him on the horse's neck and galloped off with her up the road as she screamed. Mother and Grandmother ran after him in desperation until they came upon one of the gendarme rear guards of the caravan who forced them to turn back. When Mother told the gendarme what had happened and pleaded with him to go after Margarit, he just laughed. When she offered him the gold sewed into her shawl to help, he took the gold but still did nothing.

A cloud of despair descended on us, as we now understood our destination and the dangers that surrounded us everywhere. Kurdish bands from the villages we passed saw us as easy targets to kill and rob and as a source of slaves or brides. The Turkish gendarmes who were supposed to protect us, did nothing and often profited from our plight, selling us to the highest bidder of those who wanted us as servants or as wives or concubines.

The gendarmes also saw us as objects of their own savage delight. Each night, the gendarmes chose girls and took them to their tents. The same gendarme who first raped me took me into his tent several times more. The only comfort for me was that he was gentler the next three times and refused to share me with the others. Some of the girls were not so lucky and were raped repeatedly in the same night. Thank God, They spared Mother, because many younger and prettier women were available.

Caught in this situation, mothers with young sons did not know what to do to protect them. Since they were male, they were the first on the list to be killed. If their mothers disguised them as young girls, they risked being selected for rape or kidnapping and then quickly killed when the deception was discovered.

What was so hard for me to understand was that all of the evil that was done to us was done with impunity. Our persecutors seemed to have no sense of guilt. It was all justified in their religion. After all, we were Armenians, the enemies of the state. We were infidel Christians, the enemies of Allah. To their way of thinking, forgiveness from the state or from Allah was automatic for whatever atrocities they committed against us—robbery, rape, and murder, because we were "kuffars" or infidels. Indeed, evil became for some, the good.

We not only lost Margarit that day but all of our supplies and the gold that Mother had sewn into her clothes. All that remained now to us were the clothes that we were wearing, our mule, and one tent. We still had the four pieces of gold sewn into the tent, and Mother took two of them and exchanged them with others in the caravan and with sympathetic Turks and Kurds in the villages we passed, for food. Then, the order came from the hated officer that we should hand over to him all of our gold and jewelry for safekeeping, as we would soon be entering the town of Diyarbakir where we could be robbed. "If you do not obey my orders," he said, "you will be shot!"

Thank God, that Mother decided to turn her remaining two pieces of gold over to our persecutor as the next day, they ordered us to strip in front of the gendarmes. If they found any gold or jewelry of worth, they confiscated it and took away the person hiding it to beat and then to shoot or bayonet them to death. Of course, we never saw again those two pieces of gold as the gendarmes never returned anything to anyone. So now, without anything, we had to scavenge from plants or fruit trees along the way what we could find in order to survive.

While water had not been a problem for us in the first weeks of the march as we walked near a lake and then the streams that joined the Tigris River, this changed as we went further south and the land became drier. Then, when we arrived at a well or a muddy stream, fights would sometimes break out. The gendarmes always made sure that they got their water first, and only then would they permit us to drink.

The intense summer heat was also devastating, and the elderly began to falter and fall as malnourishment and dehydration set in. Most of us had diarrhea, and the stench of body wastes filled the camps and our clothes. Those who had started the march with oxcarts and mules no longer possessed them because of breakdowns, animal deaths, attacking Kurds, or the gendarmes themselves. The hated officer took our mule from us saying that he needed it to replace the horse of one of those of his gendarmes that had broken its leg. Without the cart and mule, Grandmother now had to walk besides Mother and me.

We were able to rest and camp for several days in an Armenian cemetery in Diyakbakir. There, our Turkish guards consolidated several new groups of deportees coming from different regions as far away as Sassoun, Moush, and even Erzurum. Despite the horrible smells and danger of diseases because so many of us huddled together in such a small area without any sanitation facilities, I look upon those few days in Diyarbakir with gratitude as we had abundant water. Once, even, the gendarmes brought wagons of bread donated by some good person and distributed it. The best news, however, was that while we were camped there, the hated officer, the murderer of my brother, Lazar, and molester of my mother, finally met his earthly judgment.

What happened was that the officer had chosen a young woman that night from the new arrivals from the east for satisfying his lusts. Like what happened to my mother, he forced her into his tent and ravished her. When he fell to her side exhausted, the brave woman reached for the dagger in his belt, the same dagger that killed Lazar, and plunged it into his heart. If he screamed in surprise and pain, none of his soldiers dared enter, for they had surely often heard him scream in fury and pleasure. The girl hid the knife in her skirts and waited. When no one came to check on things, she slipped out of his tent and returned to her camp spot and told her neighbors from Sassoun what had happened. One of them advised her to flee over the cemetery wall, as she would surely be horribly executed when the day came and the soldiers found out what had taken place. Maybe she could lose herself in the streets and alleys of Dyarbakir and find someone to hide her or help her. Taking this advice, she headed to the wall and a friend helped her to climb it. Before she could jump down to the other side, a shot rang out from the street and she fell back dead into the encampment. A gendarme guard patrolling the street outside the wall had seen her and murdered her.

We learned of what had happened from her friends, and she became a hero for all of us in the camp. Her companions said her name was Sosamma Esmerlian and they told us of what she had suffered in the past. She was the young wife of an Armenian man, Badal Esmerlian, who had been killed earlier in the year resisting those who had come to arrest him. To this day, I praise them for not going like sheep to their slaughter and for resisting the horrible events that happened to them and to so many of their fellow Armenians—the robbing and burning of churches, the rapes, kidnappings, hangings, bayoneting, decapitations, horseshoeing of victims, and even their crucifixion. Those who survived in those terrible times did so through chance, money, friendship, cunning, or physical endurance. Most of us did not fight back, but Sosamma and Badal did, and I honor them for it.

When we reinitiated our journey south from Diyarbakir, the distribution of bread stopped, and we had no more gold to buy what we needed. At the beginning of the march in Harput, people shared. Now, people guarded jealously what they had, and sometimes they tried to rob what others still had. Fights over water and food began to happen frequently among us, but the rape of women by gendarmes diminished greatly because of what happened to the officer that night in Diyarbakir. I was never touched again.

Two days out of Diyarbakir, heading south towards Mardin, Grandmother began falling farther and farther behind because of her weakness. Finally, around noon one day, when the sun was the hottest, she collapsed onto the ground besides the road. She told us that she could continue no longer. Mother and I pleaded with her to go on, telling her that in a few more hours, we would be able to stop and that then she could rest. We warned her that the gendarmes would have no mercy. They would leave her to die of thirst by the road or would shoot her as they had so many other stragglers. We told her, "We won't leave you, but if we stay, then the gendarmes will kill us as well. You have to come with us even if we have to carry you!"

As we were begging her, two gendarmes rode up on horseback and told us to get moving. They were the same two who had come with the officer to our camp by the lake and had raped my sister and me. My mother recognized them as well and pleaded with them in Turkish. "You say that Allah is merciful, so you too must have mercy. Your officer killed my only son and raped me against the commands of your merciful Allah. You both have raped my daughters against the commands of your religion and your merciful Allah. Your fellow believers kidnapped my daughter Margarit and stole all of our goods against the commands of your merciful Allah. Now you threaten to kill an old woman who can no longer walk, against the commands of your merciful Allah. Your Prophet once sought refuge among Christians, and they helped him. Now help us. Take my mother-in-law on your horses to the next camp where she can rest and then continue with us. Please do not leave her to die here on the road or kill her with your sabers or guns. Too many have died already. Have mercy!"

The gendarme who had raped Margarit yelled insults at my mother, calling her "kuffar," an infidel. But the gendarme who had raped me four different times, but protected me from others, got off of his horse and picked up my grandmother in his arms and put her in his saddle. He then walked beside us as we headed towards our next campsite, saying nothing. The other gendarme rode off in a fury. Mother and I were so astounded that we also could say nothing, not even, "Thank you." We just walked behind him carrying our tent, the last belonging that we had. When we got to the camp, the gendarme lifted grandmother off his horse and then left us without a word.

That night, Grandmother died. I do not know to this day if it was by choice or by her body's exhaustion. Many Armenians carried poison as a final remedy when they could take no more, but I hold to the belief that Grandmother died because it was her time and not her choice. We buried her like my brother Lazar, in a simple grave by the road with stones covering her body. I marked it in my mind, as I had Lazar's grave. It was also near a tree but in a flat area near a dry stream two days march from Diyarbakir and a day's march from where we had camped the first night south of the Tigris Bridge.

Grandmother and Lazar were the lucky ones who had someone to bury and say prayers over them. So many others did not. Gendarmes and Kurds killed them in groups and threw them into gulleys, wells, caves, rivers, lakes, and even the Black Sea, far from those who loved them. Some had dirt thrown on them to cover them. Others just rotted in the heat. We saw many such exposed bodies along the way.

As we were burying Grandmother, I observed the gendarme watching us from a distance. When he saw me raise my head and recognize him, he slowly rode his horse over to us. He looked around to see if anyone was watching and then he reached into his saddlebag and pulled out a piece of flatbread, which he handed to me. As he did so, he said in Turkish to both Mother and me, "My name is Altay. I am sorry." He then turned his horse and rode back through the campsites urging people to begin the daily march.

Mother and I shared the bread gratefully but neither of us could understand how someone who had been so cruel could also show kindness. We also knew that we could not trust him. In fact, at this time of our journey, we trusted only each other, no one else, not even God. Like the Jews after us who underwent the Holocaust, we could not understand how a loving Father could allow such a tragedy to happen to his people. The Turks mocked us for our beliefs and asked us, "If your religion is true, why doesn't your God save you?" We had no answer. Having now lost everything, including some of our faith, our worst fears were the loss of each other. Wherever I went, even to the bushes to answer nature's call, Mother was close behind.

Our caravan now consisted of a slow moving herd of bedraggled skeletons, mostly mothers and daughters and orphans. The only pack animals and oxcarts now belonged to the gendarmes, and the only supplies for most of us were the clothes we had on and the shoes we wore, if we were still fortunate to have shoes. After almost a month on the road, and despite the addition of new groups to our column in Diyarbakir, we had easily lost half of those who had begun the march. Only a handful of older men and young boys remained with us. Most of the older persons had died or been killed as stragglers. The gendarmes had sold many of the younger women, and they were now the wives, concubines, prostitutes, and servants of those who bought them or kidnapped them. Some of the more daring or desperate of our group had escaped. I learned later that they tried to return home or to head towards the Caucasus Mountains and Russia. Some mountain Kurds, who were Alevis, helped them find their way.

For the next several days, Altay found us either early in the morning before we began our march or during the day when we were struggling step-by-step down the dusty and rocky roads on swollen and battered feet. When he thought that no one was looking, he always slipped us some bread. Once, a woman from Erzurum saw him do so and commented, "You must be his whores!" Mother spat at her. While what the woman accused us of was a lie, the terrible truth now for me was that I could understand how women traded their bodies so that they and their loved ones could survive. I just wondered when Altay would try again to collect on the down payments that he had already made in gifts of bread and in helping Grandmother.

That time came when we were close to the town of Mardin. Ever since we learned in Diyarbakir that we heading towards Mardin, I saw Mother's hopes rekindled. She had once been a student there in the Protestant missionary school as a young girl, and she knew the missionaries who ran it. She hoped that somehow we could find them and that they would recognize her and protect us.

It was early evening and we had just come down a steep incline from a half-moon range of cliffs into a rocky valley. It was a desolate place with no village. That fact was a blessing and a curse, as villages meant water but they also meant danger from kidnappers and rapists. A sizable stream cut through the valley and on each side of its banks were two green strips that contrasted sharply with the brown rocks and dirt everywhere else. In the distance from where we stopped stood a roofless house of stone and mud brick and a livestock pen beside it in ruins.

The gendarmes made us camp about a hundred meters from the house in a rocky field near the stream. After slaking our thirst at the stream, Mother and I returned to the field to set up our tent. The reason we still carried the tent, despite its weight, was that it shielded us from the hot sun in the day and hid us at night from the eyes of the gendarmes. The gendarme who called himself Altay had not given us any bread that day and we were hungry. That was when we saw him slowly riding his horse through the camp as if looking for someone or something.

It is strange how life is. I found myself hoping that he was looking for us, for the sake of the bread. At the same time, I was hoping that he would never find us because of the fear of once more being taken to his tent. After a short while, he did find us. This time he gave us no bread, but sitting on his horse, he told us firmly, but not threateningly, to follow him towards some abandoned houses. I looked fearfully at Mother but she nodded that we should go. What choices did we have anyway? We were hardly humans anymore.

As we slowly followed him past the campsites of our other miserable companions into the open field away from the camp, no one made eye contact with us, perhaps not wanting to participate once more in the tragedy of another Armenian being led to their execution. Passing the tents of some of the other gendarmes, I saw one or two turn their heads to watch for a moment and then go back to their cooking of their meal. The former sharp spirits of lust, laughter, violence, and terror had now turned into a spirit of sadness and resignation among us all—both those in authority and those of us who were victims. The truth is that we had all become victims.

When Altay arrived at the side of the empty house, he got off his horse and tied her to a scrubby tree. He then reached into his koorge or saddlebag and pulled out what looked like some dried meat. He then motioned for us to follow him through the door into the roofless structure. Inside, he told us to sit on one of the fallen beams that were on the ground. Once we had done so, he gave us the dried goat meat to eat. We grabbed it, and as we devoured it, he said, "I know you fear me, but I will not hurt you anymore. I did an evil thing to you and I wish to make amends."

Even though I could recognize him by his voice, face, and build, I had never really looked at him straight on in the day light. I still could not bring myself to do so out of the fear and the shame that still dominated my emotions and actions. Gradually, however, as we ate the meat, I looked at him from the edges of my eyes. He was a young man in his twenties, tall and thin and with a full moustache. He wore a soldier's cap and a dirty uniform with some type of minor rank medal insignia on his chest and a stripe or two on his sleeves. Perhaps he was a sergeant. He carried a rifle, because the gendarmes always did so, but he had put it down beside him on the ground.

"In two days, we will get to Mardin," he continued. "There the caravan will stop for a few days and food will be brought as it was done in Diyarbakir. There you will wait a decision of the authorities. You may then be taken to Urfa and to the camps of Aleppo, or you may continue straight south by foot through the desert to the camps of Ras al-Ayn and Deir ez-Zor. Both are difficult journeys and many of you will surely die. In Mardin, I will leave you and will no longer be able to protect you."

"Why are you telling us this?" Mother asked, raising her head and looking at him.

"Because I wish to offer you a way of escape," he replied. "Mardin is my home and I can protect you there as my father is an Imam, a respected religious leader in the town. For such a thing to be possible, though, you both must be willing to convert to the true religion and you must give your daughter to me for my wife. That way I can amend for my dishonor and her dishonor."

"How could I permit such a thing?" Mother asked. "It would be much more dishonor to her and to me and to God if we said we were Muslims and in our hearts we did not believe."

Altay was quiet for a moment and then looked sadly at her. "Then there is no other way. I will not force you, as our Prophet has said there is no compulsion in religion. Neither do I wish to bring further shame on me or on you. "Insha'Allah, May God's will be done."

"But there is another way," Mother said, suddenly. She then told him her story of growing up in a Syriac village near Mardin and of the murder of her parents by the Hamidiye, the Kurdish special forces of the Sultan. She told him of going to the Protestant girl's school there and of her certainty that the missionaries would help us if we could get to them. She thanked Altay for his compassion and pleaded with him to help us find the missionaries and school once we got to Mardin.

Altay made no reply. He just said that it was time for us to return to the camp. We walked in front and he followed us on his horse. As we got to the edge of the camp we parted ways, he to his tent with the soldiers and we to our spot among the deportees. Some of them looked up at us now, surprised that we had returned.

The next two days Altay neither spoke to us nor gave us bread as we walked to Mardin. We scavenged from the grasses and plants along the road, eating almost anything to relieve our hunger. It was late in the afternoon when we arrived at the mountain town of Mardin. On its outskirts, they led us to a now abandoned school and they told us we would be there for a few days. Mother recognized the walled-in compound and the now empty buildings as the Protestant school she had once attended as a young girl. She wept as she remembered what had been lost since those times.

From Despair to Hope

We were grateful to be in Mardin, for as in Diyarbakir, we now had food and water, and we were able to rest from daily marches. After we had found our places, in the early evening, a cart came through the front gate accompanied by Altay with bread to distribute. He told us that the bread was from one of the religious schools in Mardin, and so I suspected that Altay's father had sent it since Altay seemed to know the driver of the cart. After the cart stopped and the driver unfastened the oxen and took them away, Altay and several other gendarmes took off the canvas covering the baskets of bread in it, and they began to distribute them in as orderly a fashion as possible, given the fact that we all rushed to get our share. When Altay saw us among the throng of hungry beggars, he pushed his way to us, gave us our portions and motioned us to go to the wall away from the others. There, he told us to stay near the cart until it was empty and darkness had come. "I have a plan to take you to the foreigner's dwelling," he said.

Elated and anxious at the same time, for we dared not hope too much, Mother and I squatted on the ground with our backs to the compound wall eating our bread. We waited for what seemed an eternity watching Altay and the cart until the last crumbs of the bread disappeared, swept up by hungry hands from the tarp on the floor of the cart. By then, everyone had returned to their campsites in the compound and the gendarmes to the school rooms where they were sleeping. It was now dark, and the oxcart driver had come back through the gate with his oxen to hook them up again to the cart and return with it to his home. When he had finished attaching the oxen and had climbed onto his seat, Altay came over to where we were sitting and told us to get quickly into the back of the cart under the tarp covering the now empty breadbaskets. With the body of his horse, he shielded us from any prying eyes of those already lying down to sleep. Only the cart driver was watching as we climbed in as quickly and quietly as we could. Once we were lying down between the baskets, Altay adjusted the tarp so that no one could see us. "Be as still and quiet as you can," he whispered. He then told the cart driver to start and we began to move slowly.

At the gate of the school compound, Altay told the guard that since it was night, he was going to accompany the cart driver to his home and would be back within an hour. The cart then started up again, and Mother, who was lying beside me, squeezed my hand in happiness. Then for about fifteen minutes, we bounced along the cobblestone streets of Mardin hearing at first the night sounds of a main street with its public places and then the relative silence of a smaller residential alleyway. Altay, from time to time, would give the cart driver directions.

Finally, the cart stopped, and Altay came back and pulled the canvas off us. He told us to get out. He said that we were at the residence of Dr. Frazer, an American missionary doctor who had lived in the city for many years. He then pointed to a locked wooden door of the courtyard wall and his last words to us were, "I will leave you now, but if you reconsider my proposal, look for Altay, the son of Imam Aslan. Do not mention to anyone that I have helped you, as it would cause me great trouble." He then gave something to the cart driver and turned his horse back towards the deportee camp at the school.

The cart driver also drove off, not looking back. We were then alone in the narrow cobblestone street. It was an hour or two after dark, and we saw a flicker of oil lamps from a window above the street. Mother decided to knock on the gate and call out in English using the Doctor's name. "Dr. Frazer, we are friends from Euphrates College, please may we speak with you." We heard a noise in the courtyard and then the climbing of steps and voices in the room with the light. Someone came to the window and looked out, but of course, they could see nothing but the shape of two women in the street as it was very dark. Within a few minutes, a guard came to the gate and opened it, letting let us in.

On seeing our condition and hearing our story, Dr. and Mrs. Frazer decided to help us. I can therefore only say wonderful things about them for they saved our lives. In his early seventies, Dr. Frazer was a naturalized American, born in Scotland. He had spent the last forty years of his life serving in this isolated part of the world thousands of sick and hurting people, including Mother as a young student. He said that he remembered her because of the murder of her parents.

The Frazers lived in one of three houses in the missionary compound. The other two were inhabited by the Protestant minister and his family and by the head of the girl's school. The high walls around the compound at the edge of the hill town of Mardin, protected them and gave them a space of privacy they yearned for after long days of teaching, healing, and evangelization. It also provided space for small stables for their horses, gardens for fruit trees and vegetables, and a yard to play in for their children when they were younger. Now there were no children, as all four of the Frazer daughters had long ago grown up and returned to America to study and to marry. The minister and his wife were also old and the teacher was single.

This lack of children now meant that a number of rooms in the compound were empty and available, and the Fraziers graciously gave one of them to Mother and me for our use. Dr. Frazer insisted that we first take a hot bath to kill the lice and vermin that we had lived with now for over a month. Mrs. Frazer prepared the bath for us, and it was the most delicious hot bath that I had ever taken or will ever take again. After we finished and dried ourselves, Mrs. Frazer then gave us clean clothes and led us to the real bed we were to sleep in. When we stretched out on that soft mattress, we both felt that we had gone directly from hell to heaven.

We stayed with the Frazers for three months. Two days after we arrived at his house, Dr. Frazer informed us that he had learned from one of the Turkish government officials who frequently visited him in his office that our convoy from Diyarbakir had left Mardin and was now heading south through the Mesopotamia Plain and the Syrian Desert to Deir ez-Zor, its final destination. He held out little hope for the survival of our companions, as the conditions in that area were much worse than those that we had faced on our journey to Mardin.

Because hiding Armenians was a crime punishable by death, perhaps even for Americans, Dr. Frazer made sure that we were careful never to go outside of the compound during our time with them. In the daytime, we would stay in our back room, weaving and embroidering and helping the Frazers and the Mission in any way that we could. At night, however, Dr. Frazer allowed us to go into the courtyard or up on the flat roof to see the glorious heavens and feel the night breezes on our skin.

A few days after we arrived, at Mother's request, Dr. Frazer sent private correspondence by courier to Mezire to Miss Isabel Ross to tell her that we were with him in Mardin and safe for the time being. He told her of the deaths of Lazar and Grandmother and of the kidnapping near Maden of Margarit, asking her to do anything she could to find and release her. He also asked Miss Isabel to get help from the American Consul in Mezire to furnish us with documents and funds so that we could travel to Aleppo and Beirut and leave for America.

Five weeks later, Dr. Frazer received a reply that Miss Isabel was returning herself to America and that she would come by way of Mardin and try to take us with her. She would be traveling with the director of the German school for Armenian boys in Mezire, Rev. Johannes Kober, and his wife, Hannelore. They had lived in Mezire for almost twenty years but had decided to close the school because there were now no more students due to the deportations and killings. They had offered to accompany Miss Isabel to Beirut and then continue their own way back to Germany. Two weeks later, the three missionaries arrived by horse and pack animals in the company of the German's two trusted Turkish escorts.

It was such a blessing for us to see Miss Isabel again and to find out that she had brought Father's photographs with her. It was also fortunate for us that the Kobers accompanied her, because as Germans, they were allies of the Turks in the war that was now going on in Europe.

Rev. Kober had a document from the Vali, the highest government authority of the Harput Province, giving him, his wife, and their party safe conduct to Aleppo and Beirut. Miss Isabel had also arranged from the American Consul in Mezire an official looking document in English, Turkish, and Arabic, giving Mother and me visas to enter America. He also gave her a letter of introduction to the American Consul in Aleppo and told us to seek his help if we needed it in getting to Beirut.

Rev. and Mrs. Kober knew of our situation from Miss Isabel and agreed to help us as fellow Christians. Together with Dr. Frazer and Miss Isabel, they decided that the safest and quickest route to Aleppo and Beirut for us now was for us to go a two day's journey south by horse to Ras al-Ayn, the last completed stop on the Baghdad railroad that the Germans were building through the Ottoman Empire from Germany to Baghdad. From there, we would take the train to Aleppo and then continue on to Beirut where Miss Isabel's American mission society had contacts. In Beirut, we would wait until we could book a ship to Marseilles and then to America.

They also insisted that Mother and I should dress and act as Americans instead of Armenians for the rest of our journey. They thought it best that we cut our hair, and that we dress in an American style and only speak English and Turkish and never Armenian. As America had not yet entered the German and Turkish war against the Russians, French, and British, the Turks still saw Americans as neutral.

Mardin to Beirut

Four days after Miss Isabel and the Kobers arrived in Mardin, we started early in the morning on our two-day journey by horse and pack animals to the railway station in Ras al-Ayn. Dr. Frazer lent us horses, and he gave us food and water for the journey, saying a prayer for our protection as we left.

Mother fell at his feet and thanked him, and I covered Mrs. Frazer with kisses for their goodness in protecting us.

Mother and I went outside of the compound walls for the first time in over three months, and while I had never seen Mardin, it had once been Mother's home for three years of schooling before moving to Harput. Mardin was a town like Harput in many ways—built on a mountain with a fort at the top, with very narrow streets and many of these with stairs. Christians, Kurds, and Turks lived in separate sections of the town.

The buildings of Mardin were flat-roofed and mostly two-storied like in Harput, but they seemed much more durable and beautiful than the ones in Harput. They were mostly of chiseled stone, while the buildings in Harput were mostly of clay brick. Mardin overlooked the Mesopotamian Plain, which stretched out flat in front of it as far as you could see, and the winding road that we took out of the town now headed towards that plain. As we descended the cobblestone road on horseback, I made sure that my American hat covered as much of my face as possible so that no one would think that I was anything but American. I also kept a fearful but hopeful eye out for Altay, but I never saw him again. As much as I will never forgive him for the outrages he did to me, I will always be grateful to him for his last kindnesses to us.

The journey from Mardin to Ras al-Ayn took us a long two days by horse, and along the road we saw dozens of unburied bodies stripped of their clothes and now dried and rotting in the sun. At one well where we stopped, a villager told us that we should not drink the water because gendarmes had thrown corpses into it. I wondered if those corpses were those of neighbors from Hussenig or others we had met on our march. They could have been Mother and me.

We were stopped twice on the road, once by several gendarmes and once by a small band of armed Kurdish tribesmen. Nothing happened to us because of Rev. Kober's explanation that we were German and American missionaries returning home by way of the Baghdad railway and also because we were accompanied by two Turkish escorts. All along the way, we never had to show any documents.

The first night of the journey, we stayed in a filthy khan owned by a Muslim Chechen family who had been expelled from their home by the advance of the Russian army. Mother and I slept on fold-up traveling cots that Dr. Frazer lent us to protect us from the vermin.

When we got to Ras al-Ayn, Rev. Kober inquired of some locals if they knew of any German missionaries or civil servants in the town, and one of the locals led us to the home of a German engineer who was involved with the continuation of the railroad to Nisibis. When he learned that we were German and American missionaries from Harput, he was very kind to us and put us up at his house, giving Mother, Miss Isabel, and me one guest room, and turning over his own room to Rev. and Mrs. Kober. He allowed our Turkish guards and animals to stay in his stables.

The next day, Rev. Kober and our engineer host, whose name I think was Holbein, left early to arrange passage on the train for our party to Aleppo and then on to Beirut. When they came back, Rev. Kober told us that thanks to the engineer and his contacts, we would be leaving the next morning on the train. We would have a night stopover in Aleppo and then would continue the next afternoon to Beirut.

Rev. Kober also warned us again how dangerous the situation was in Ras al-Ayn. "The town is full of Armenian and Syriac deportees and their guards," he said. "It's a major holding zone for the survivors of the long marches from Diyarbakir and of those who came packed in cattle cars from Adana and the west."

After Rev. Kober shared with Holbein what he had seen of misery and death on his journey south, Holbein told him of his own experience in Ras al-Ayn. He had visited camps of thousands of deportees along the tracks that were full of squalor, disease, dead bodies, and desperation. Women and children had pleaded for his help, and he and some other Germans who were disgusted with the sights of desperation and the smells of feces and death, had gone to the German Military Command in the city to demand that something concrete and immediate be done to stop this horror. He said that the answer from the Command was that it was a Turkish issue and not a German one. The Turks were their allies in the war against Russia, and the Turks saw the Armenians as collaborators with the Russians and therefore that they needed to be neutralized. Holbein said that he and a German army medic lieutenant were so traumatized and ashamed that they started writing reports and taking pictures secretly of the horrors. They had to smuggle them out as the Turkish government had forbidden any picture taking of the refugees.

When Mother asked how things had gone at the railway station, Rev. Kober confessed to telling a small lie. When the Turkish official selling the tickets asked for the names of the passengers, Rev. Kober answered, "Two Germans with the name Kober" (he and his wife), "and three Americans with the name Ross." He felt that if he had given our Armenian name Terzian, our safety, as well as that of the Kobers and Miss Isabel, would be in jeopardy. Surely, God would forgive him for the deception. He was only trying to be "as wise as a serpent" as the Bible enjoined. He advised that from now on, until we got to the safety of Beirut, Miss Isabel should do all of the talking for us. If asked about us, she should say that she was Mother's sister-in-law and my aunt and that her brother, who was my mother's husband and my father, was waiting for us in Beirut.

The next morning, Engineer Holbein went with us to the train station and stayed with us until we were safely in the train with all of our goods, which for Mother and me now consisted only of the pictures that my father had taken in Harput. Everything else, including the American clothes that we had on, belonged to Miss Isabel and the Kobers. Thanks to our being women and therefore inferior, none of the Ottoman authorities at the station asked us directly any questions. Whatever questions they had, they asked to Rev. Kober. Because he was a German and Holbein was a respected German engineer known to the authorities in the town, everything went smoothly, and we were given good seats in the passenger car, which was mainly filled with German soldiers and Ottoman officials.

While we got on the train without incident, the trip to the station on our horses with the pack mules was very traumatic for Mother and me. Naked and half-naked Armenian beggars constantly accosted us pleading for food or money or help in finding a lost mother or child or help in hiding them. It was almost more than I could bear. Except for the grace of God and the kindnesses of others, I knew that I could have been the one pleading. I had nothing to give them, nor could I even look them in the eyes for the shame that I felt and the fear that a neighbor or gendarme who accompanied us on the long journey from Harput to Mardin might recognize me.

At the station, the Kobers and Miss Isabel thanked their faithful Turk employees who had journeyed with them so far from Harput. Rev. Kober paid them generously for their service and gave to them the animals that he and his wife and Miss Isabel had used. They thanked him profusely and agreed to return the two horses and travel cots that Mother and I had used to Dr. Frazer in Mardin on their way back to Harput.

The trip to Aleppo on the train was a new experience for Mother and me as neither of us had ever seen a train before, much less been on one. The shrill air whistle, the smoke of the engine, the jerking of the cars, the flying cinders, the speed at which we soon traveled, both excited and frightened us. As we left the station, we could see out of the windows some of the misery that Engineer Holbein had alluded to—rows and rows of tents with hundreds of hopeless and emaciated persons squatting or lying beside them staring at us. Herr Holbein told us that many thousands of these deportees had been brought from Aleppo to Ras al-Ayn stuffed in cattle cars with no water or food. Our train had fifteen such cars that were now returning empty to Aleppo to fill up again. Two other cars were for passengers like us.

The trip to Aleppo took us about eight hours. We sat on wooden seats, the Kobers in front of us facing us. Mother clasped the package of photos Father had taken, and I held on to the package of food that Engineer Holbein had kindly given us for our journey. Miss Ross read her Bible. In the other seats of our car were German soldiers laughing and telling stories in their language. Elsewhere were groups of what I now imagine were Arab and Turkish businessmen or government workers. We stopped several times for water for the locomotive, and we passed over what Rev. Kober said was the Euphrates River. Most of the journey, however, was through desert. We finally arrived in Aleppo in the late afternoon after again passing by hundreds of meager deportee tents outside the city lining the tracks.

I had never seen such a large city as Aleppo—so many buildings and streets filled with people. The station was an impressive building, and groups of huddled travelers filled it, sitting on piles of baggage waiting for trains or for someone to pick them up. We were unsure what to do that night, as the train for Beirut was to leave only the next afternoon. None of us had any personal acquaintances in Aleppo, although the American Consul in Mezire had told Miss Isabel to seek help from the American Consul in the city if we had any trouble. She also said that he had told her that we could also probably get help from one of the orphanages operated by some Swiss and Danish missionaries. Such orphanages were full of Armenian children who had lost their parents.

As Rev. Kober had no personal contacts in the city either, he decided that the safest course for us would be to find a decent hotel nearby and stay in it until the time for our departure by train or to spend the night in the station itself. He found a spot near a wall to pile our belongings, and then he left us with them and went outside to inquire as to possible khans nearby where we could stay. He was gone for an hour or so, and he came back discouraged.

"It's best to stay where we are as the khans have no space," he said. "The city is full of deportees from all over the empire." From what I gathered from him and from others, Aleppo seemed to be a place of limbo for Armenians. Due to the benign policies of a lenient local Vali who ignored the orders of Constantinople, many of the Aleppo Armenian churches and businesses were still functioning in the city and did what they could to help their fellow Armenians who arrived there from the north. The same was true of the American Consul and of the orphanages run by foreigners in the city. While most of the Armenians entering the city from the north lived in the deplorable tent camps by the railroad line and waited to be shipped eastward to the desert camps, more fortunate ones found refuge in the homes and churches of sympathetic local Armenians or in the foreign orphanages. The most fortunate, however, were people like us, who because of the help of others, were able to escape south to Damascus, Beirut, Jerusalem or Cairo.

The next day we did escape, taking the train south to Riyaq and then to Beirut. Unlike the train from Ras al-Ayn to Aleppo which consisted mostly of empty box cars, this train was principally for passengers and was packed—not only with Turks and Arabs but also with Armenians and Syriacs trying to escape the horrors of the massacres. In Riyaq, we changed trains for Beirut.

Beirut to America

Four months had passed between our departure from Hussenig and our arrival in Beirut. There, we parted company with Rev. and Mrs. Kober who continued their journey back to Germany by ship. I will always remember them with gratitude for all that they did for us. To think that in another two years, they as Germans, and we as new Americans, were to be enemies at war is something hard for me to understand.

Miss Isabel, Mother, and I stayed in Beirut for almost five months waiting for authorization from the American government to enter the country and for funds from Miss Isabel's mission headquarters in Boston to pay for our trip to New York. Miss Isabel could have left much earlier, but to her credit, she refused to go back to America without us. While we waited, all three of us lived with her co-workers who ran an orphanage and a school for girls in the city. Because of a huge need, they had also started relief efforts for the thousands of Armenian refugees who had flooded into the city from Turkey. Local authorities quarantined most of these refugees in an area near the port and they all needed food, shelter, and medicines. They also needed help to start new lives in Lebanon or to continue on their journey to other countries like Egypt, France, or America. Generous people in Europe and America sent funds through an organization called the American Committee for Armenian and Syrian Relief, which made it possible for the mission to help so many people.

While we lived in Beirut, Miss Isabel and Mother helped our hosts by providing basic medical care to those in the refugee camps, and the missionaries asked me to teach what I knew of English and Math in the orphanage close to where we lived. The orphanage was packed as so many children had lost both of their parents in the massacres and the marches. Some of the girls there were about my same age and they shared with me their horrible stories. Some saw both of their parents killed in front of them. Some were sold into harems and tattooed or raped before they escaped. Two of those who were raped were now pregnant. I could identify totally with them in their dilemma because I, too, had discovered that I was pregnant with Altay's child. Mother, Miss Isabel, and I decided that I must await its birth and then give it up for adoption.

More sad news came to us in Beirut in a letter that arrived for Miss Isabel in December from missionaries still in Harput. From the letter we found out that Dr. and Mrs. Frazier, our great benefactors in Mardin, were both now dead. The Turkish authorities in Mardin had discovered that they had harbored us and other Armenians and had arrested them and sent them accompanied by gendarmes to Sivas. The American Consul in Harput had tried to get their release, but he was unsuccessful. In Sivas, the Ottoman authorities had allowed Dr. Frazer, still under arrest, to work at the mission hospital there treating Turkish soldiers. There, he contracted Typhus from the soldiers and he then transmitted the disease to his wife. They both were buried in Sivas. In Beirut, we and others of the missionaries who knew and loved the Frazers, joined in a special memorial service to remember their heroism and service.

In late February of 1916, we finally received the authorization and funds from Miss Isabel's mission society in Boston to buy our tickets and leave Beirut for America. We were overjoyed! After hunting around for the best prices and availability, Miss Isabel booked us on a French cargo boat leaving for Marseilles at the end of March. It took us a week to get there because of stops at other ports on the way. Since no passenger ships were going from Marseilles to New York until June, we purchased tickets on the 'Rochambeau' leaving from Bordeaux in northwestern France in the middle of April. That meant that we had to take a train from Marseilles and change in Paris to get there in time for its sailing. All of this was such an adventure for me.

The 'Rochambeau' was a two-master and two-funnel French steam ship, which transported over two thousand passengers, almost all of them immigrants like us seeking a better life in America. Because of Miss Isabel's insistence with her mission, we were in second class instead of third class, and the three of us were fortunate enough to have our own small cabin.

During our nine-day voyage to America, I delivered my son—a handsome, robust boy whom I named Noah. Miss Isabel was the one who thought of the name. It was in English because Noah would be American, but it also reflected his Armenian heritage and the unique circumstances of his birth. Miss Isabel explained, "Your belly was like an ark carrying him safely through the turbulent times that seemed to us like the end of the world." Soon we would all arrive in a safe haven.

Miss Isabel delivered Noah in the privacy of our cabin on April 20, 1916, four days before we were to land in New York. She bathed him and treasured him from the start, but I must confess that Mother and I had mixed emotions about him. We loved him because he was a precious, innocent, helpless baby who came from my own body. We also rejected him because of the great shame and violence he brought to our minds.

Mother came up with the plan as to what we would say about Noah when we got to New York. She insisted that she register Noah as her own son and not as mine with the Ellis Island immigration authorities. She felt that if I, as a young single woman, registered him as my son, I might harm my chances of being allowed into the country and I would certainly diminish my chances of later getting married and having my own family and a happy life in America. Her idea was to put Noah up for adoption and to hide from him the truth of how he was conceived, so that he, too, could have a happy life.

Miss Isabel at first was reluctant to agree to such a scheme as it was untruthful. Later, though, she changed her mind as she thought about the difficulties the baby would cause for me, a sixteen year old. Another factor that made her alter her opinion was a new idea that came to her. While waiting for our ship to sail in Bordeaux, France, she had received a wire that her older brother, James Ross, and his wife, Grace, would be coming by train from Asheville, North Carolina, to New York to meet the vessel and to welcome Miss Isabel home. They had not seen each other in over five years. James was a missionary teacher at the Asheville Farm School for Boys, and as he and Grace were now in their early forties and had been unable to have children of their own, Miss Isabel thought they might be overjoyed at the possibility of adopting Noah. If it all worked out, Noah would have a good family and a good future and Miss Isabel could keep up with him through the years and report to Mother and me on his progress in life.

God must have been with us, as the plan worked without a hitch. Since Miss Isabel was a nurse and vouched for our story of Noah's birth on the ship, the American immigration authorities registered him as Noah Terzian, born April 20, 1916, the child of my mother and father and therefore my brother. The other good news was that Mr. and Mrs. Ross were delighted with Noah and the prospect of having him as their son. Two days after our arrival in New York, Mother and the Ross family went with Miss Isabel to the legal authorities and registered Noah as their adopted son, Noah Ross. They liked the name Noah and so kept it.

We all agreed that the story the Ross family would tell Noah when he turned eighteen was that he was the orphaned son of Armenians who had both died and that Miss Isabel had rescued him and brought him to America to be adopted by her brother and his wife. We also agreed that for his sake and ours, the only future communication between the Ross family and us would be through Miss Isabel, Noah's new aunt. No mention of Noah's birth would be made to the mission or to others in Boston to protect my future marriage prospects. With these decisions, white lies for everyone's good, we parted company. James and Grace Ross returned to Asheville, North Carolina, with their new son, Noah Ross. Miss Isabel, Mother, and I took the train to Boston for our new life there.

My contact with Noah ended in 1942 at Miss Isabel's death when Noah would have been twenty-six years old. While I have often thought about him and prayed for him, to my shame, I never tried to get in touch with him for many, many years. It was only after my dear husband, Nigol, died in 1974 and my encounter in Istanbul in 1982 with my sister Margarit that I knew that I had to do all I could to make contact with him. So far, I have been unsuccessful.

So with this final confession, I am now finished telling you, my children and my grandchildren, the true story of what happened to me in Turkey as a child and as a young woman. I hope that you will learn from this story about the destructive evil in this world and in all of us. I hope, too, that it will not cause you to despair because there is so much good as well in people like Garabed, Talitha, Magarit, and Lazar Terzian; like Haydar, Miss Isabel, the Frazers, the Kobers, Herr Holbein, and the Rosses; and, yes, even people like Altay who repented of his evil. I ask you all, especially Noah, if we ever find you, for your understanding and forgiveness of me for my deceptions. May God have mercy on us all and grant us His peace.

From your mother and grandmother who loves you,
Karine Terzian Petrosian

CHAPTER 3

The Terzians

Tuesday morning, April 1, I was up early but not as early as Susan and Aram. They were already sitting at the table in the kitchen reading the morning newspaper and drinking their coffee when I came down the stairs at seven. I had shaved and dressed and was ready to go.

"Good morning," Susan greeted me. "What can I fix you for breakfast? Cereal or eggs?"

"Just some cereal and some coffee, thank you. It's going to be a full day, and I want to get going early."

As Susan started to get up, I stopped her. "Just tell me where it all is, and I will get it myself."

Susan explained where the cups, bowls, and cereal were, and after I had poured myself some granola and coffee, I came back to the kitchen table and sat down. Aram put down his paper, smiled, and pushed in front of me a $10.00 roll of quarters. "If you are lucky enough to find a parking place near the library, you'll need these for the meter."

I thanked him and reached into my back pocket for my wallet to get a bill to exchange for them.

Aram shook his head. "No, consider it a research grant. After all, we are all interested in what you find out. They are our ancestors, too!"

By seven-thirty, I had finished my breakfast, said goodbye to the

Petrosians, and had driven the short distance from Watertown to the Harvard Business School apartments where my parents and I had lived for the first few months of my life. The apartments were a good distance away from the road on the other side of a sports field, so I took a zoom photo with my digital camera from the car.

I then drove to the house on Maple Street in Cambridge where my father, Brent Johnson, had rented a second story apartment after he had taken a job in Boston as a mutual fund manager. There I lived for five years—three years with Father and Mother until Father's death in the airplane crash, and then two years more just with Mother until she moved back to Asheville to take care of my grandfather Noah. Since I was unable to find a parking place near the house and get out, I again took pictures of the pleasant old three-story gray home from the car.

From there, I went in search of the Houghton Library on the Harvard undergraduate campus. I located it by a quarter past eight, but I still had to drive around for some twenty minutes until I found an empty metered parking place close by. I put in eight quarters for two hours, and at nine o'clock I was at the library entrance when it opened. After showing my identification and getting my photo snapped for a temporary research pass, I entered the reading room and introduced myself to one of the research assistants at the main desk.

"I'm interested in seeing the archives of the American Board of Commissioners for Foreign Missions," I said, "especially those related to Turkey and to the Euphrates College in the town of Harput." I added, "My great-great-grandfather taught there."

The research assistant was very cordial and competent. She first explained the rules of the library and then asked me to wait a few minutes while she searched for an index of their holdings related to the mission society. In a few minutes, she was back with a large ledger. I thanked her and took it to one of the long tables where other researchers were sitting and began to peruse it, jotting down with a pencil what archived material I wanted to see. The librarian made it clear that the use of ballpoint pens was not allowed.

As the amount of material held by the library was vast and I had so little time to go through it, I had a hard time choosing what papers I was interested in seeing. Finally, I decided that I would concentrate first on finding a general summary of the history of Euphrates College, and then look for any mention of Garabed Terzian during the years of 1900 to 1915 when he taught there. I would also search for references to Isabel Ross, the missionary nurse in Mezire, or to Dr. Frazer in the city of Mardin, both of whom had been so important to the survival of our family.

Except for when I left every two hours to feed the meter, I spent the rest of the day until five in the afternoon at the library—either in the reading room or in the basement of a nearby annex. I was so engrossed going through microfilms and folders of fragile and faded personal letters of missionaries, handwritten annual reports, board meeting minutes, budgets, and inventory lists that I even skipped lunch.

I discovered that graduates of Williams College, who felt called to spread Christianity worldwide, founded the American Board of Commissioners for Foreign Missions in 1810. It was not only the first American missionary society but was also the largest one throughout the entire nineteenth century. Its missionary preachers, doctors, nurses, teachers, and administrators had gone alone or with their families to Indian tribes in the United States, to India, China, Ceylon, Africa, and to many of the countries of the Middle East, including Turkey. There they preached the gospel, established churches, high schools, colleges, seminaries, and hospitals.

Their original objective in Turkey was to convert Muslims to Christianity. As that was so difficult because of the severe consequences such converts faced, the missionaries in that country soon began to concentrate on converting to their Protestant brand of Christianity the large communities of Armenian, Syriac, and Greek Orthodox Christians who then inhabited Turkey and other parts of the Ottoman Empire. This strategy, of course, caused much friction with the authorities of these long established historical Christian churches.

One of the principal interests of the American Board of Commissioners for Foreign Missions was education, and so it began to establish seminaries for the training of its leaders, and then colleges and high schools for Armenians and other Christians living in Turkey. In 1852, the Board started a seminary in Harput, a historic town in the southeast of Turkey with a large Armenian population. The initial purpose of the school was to train ministers and evangelists for the Armenian Evangelical Church, but in 1859, the school expanded its curriculum and began providing a general education in the English language to non-theological students as well. The name of the school changed several times after that: first to the American Harput Missionary College in 1859, then to the Armenian College in 1878, and finally to Euphrates College ten years later. The Ottoman authorities had specifically complained about the Armenian name and ordered it changed.

Constructed with money from the United States government and United States private donors, as well from local contributions from Christian citizens living in Turkey, the facilities at Euphrates College included not only the college and seminary but also high schools for boys and girls, an orphanage, and a hospital. In 1895, Kurds, in a campaign against Armenians and Syriacs authorized by the Ottoman Sultan at the time, Abdul Hamid II, burned down eight of these buildings. During these attacks from 1894 to 1896, in Harput and throughout Turkey, 80,000 to 300,000 Armenians and 25,000 Syriacs died.

In 1908, the Young Turk Revolution replaced Abdul Hamid II, and many Turks, and especially minority groups like the Armenians, hoped that a constitutional government and more liberal policies would be the outcome and lead to a better life for everyone, including them. In 1913, a new group of three leaders of the Committee of Union and Progress, the political party that had led the revolution, dashed those hopes. Enver Pasha, Talaat Pasha, and Djemal Pasha became the effective rulers of the Ottoman Empire, and their nationalistic policies were a disaster for the large Armenian and Syriac communities of the realm and led to their decimation.

In 1915, Armenian members of the faculty of Euphrates College in Harput, including my great-great-grandfather, Garabed Terzian, were arrested and executed; hundreds of Euphrates students and their families, including my own, were deported, and the college buildings were taken over by the government. These events led to the school's final closure in the 1920s as no teachers or students were left in the region.

After learning this basic history of the college, I spent the rest of the day looking in the mass of records for mention of persons named in Karine's narrative. I found Garabed Terzian, the Frazers, and Isabel Ross in lists of missionaries and teachers, and even found some of Garabed's photographs, but I could find no personal letters written by them. I wish that I could have stayed longer, but when it was five and the library closed, I packed up my spiral notebook now filled with the notes I had taken, thanked the research assistants who had helped me, and headed back to the Petrosian apartment. It had been an exhausting but informative day.

Susan started to cook supper when I arrived, and Aram invited me into their book-lined library to hear about my day. He also wanted to share with me Garabed Terzian's photographs of the college and of Harput. He had made copies of them for me to take with me to Turkey.

"Well, what did you find out today at the library?" he asked me as he motioned for me to take a seat beside him on the sofa.

"First of all how easy it is to get a research pass at Harvard, and second, how hard it is to find a parking place!" I replied joking. "Your roll of quarters saved the day for me!"

Aram laughed.

"Seriously though," I added, "I was amazed at how many different institutions the missionaries set up throughout Turkey—churches, orphanages, schools, colleges, seminaries—and how many people were served by them. Also, how detailed their reports were."

"What's so sad is that today almost nothing is left of that entire enterprise," Aram said. "Neither the institutions nor the thousands of people once served by them. Every time I look at the photographs that Garabed took of the teachers and the students in their diploma ceremonies and in their orchestras, I wonder what happened to this one or that one. Was he shot? Did she die of starvation or typhus? Did they escape somehow to Armenia, Lebanon, Russia, Europe, or America?"

He reached for a folder on the low table in front of the sofa and opened it. "Here, take a look at some of Garabed's pictures that I made copies of," he said.

I noticed that the folder contained some ten pages of xeroxed pictures, and Aram began to show them to me one by one. He started with the faded black and white pictures of the town of Harput, hugging the steep slope of a mountain. In the photograph, most of the structures of the town looked to me to be simple two-storied, flat-roofed mud houses packed along narrow alleyways close to each other. At the highest point in the town, however, were a dozen or so much larger structures of up to five stories, some with slanted roofs and small cupolas on top. Aram pointed at them. "These were the buildings of Euphrates College—its classrooms, dormitories, and eating, bathing and assembly halls. The boys and girls orphanages and high schools were also located there. After 1915, the government took them over for a military installation."

"Is anything left there?" I asked.

"I have no idea. That's what I hope you will find out for us on your trip."

Aram then showed me some more pictures of the college from different angles and in different seasons—one with snow on the ground. In one photo, the Armenian Apostolic Orthodox Church of Harput was featured prominently, and far off in the distance, I could also clearly see what Aram said was Harput Castle, the ruins of an ancient fort that overlooked the plain below.

"Is that the castle where Karine said they sometimes went for picnics as children," I asked, remembering her account.

Aram nodded affirmatively and then flipped through the pictures and found what he was looking for. "Here's a photograph of them at such a picnic."

I looked carefully at the photo of young men and women sitting on a long carpet on the ground and dressed more or less formally in suits and long dresses. They all had serious expressions on their faces. The same serious expression was true of all of the photographs that Aram showed me of school orchestras, of teachers and student class photos, of people outside in the streets or inside the assembly hall, of men and women. The men all wore dark suits with white shirts, high collars, and ties. All had long dark moustaches, and many had full beards and wore fezes. The male components of the orchestra and band with their stringed instruments and horns looked like they could have been photographed in the elegant theatres of Paris rather than in the simple stone and mud brick buildings of Harput. No one in any of the pictures smiled. This non-smiling, formal look was also true for the women in their conservative dresses, buttoned high on the neck, with long sleeves reaching to their hands, and cloth covering all of their legs to their ankles.

I found all of the pictures fascinating, but those of the Terzian family and of their house interested me most. A couple of them had Garabed himself in them, so I wondered who took them. Thin, darkly handsome, and mustached with a well-kept beard, Garabed was standing stiffly with his wife Talitha behind his mother and father who were sitting in straight chairs. Standing beside them were all three children—Karine, Margarit, and Lazar. Aram explained that the photograph must have been taken around 1911 because of the apparent ages of the children and the fact that Garabed's father was still alive and in the photograph.

I saw two other photos of the Terzian home, one taken outside with Garabed's mother and father standing stiffly in front of it. The other, Garabed took inside the house, showing Talitha and the three Terzian children sitting on a divan with a round, etched copper table in front of them. In the background, hanging on the wall, was an Armenian silver cross.

"These copies are for you to take with you to Turkey," Aram said, handing me the folder. "They may help orient you as to where the college and the Terzian house were located when you get to Harput and Hussenig." He added, "It's hard to believe, but as far as I know, you will be the first one of our family to go back there and search for our roots. Not even Ashti, Dilovan, or even Margarit have ever gone back."

Then, as if suddenly remembering something, Aram got up and went again to the bookcase. "And speaking of Margarit, or Zara as her family in Turkey calls her, I also have an album of pictures I took of our meeting with her in Istanbul in 1982. If you see any you like, I will be more than happy to make copies of them for you." He brought a thin album back to the sofa, sat down again, and opened it.

In the album were some twenty faded colored photos taken in Istanbul in 1982. I also noticed a newspaper clipping. I looked through the photographs slowly as Aram explained them. A few were sight-seeing pictures of Hagia Sophia and the Armenian Patriarch's Church, but most were of the two sisters, Karine and Margarit, either sitting or standing together alone or with Dilovan and Fulya, and Aram and Gregory. One had them all in it except for Fulya. "Fulya took that picture," Aram explained.

I immediately noticed two things in the Istanbul pictures. First, unlike the photos taken by Garabed, everyone in the colored pictures was smiling and not serious. Second, I could not help but see the contrast in the conservative black Muslim dress and head covering of Zara next to the colorful dresses and white coiffed hair of Karine. They looked so different, and I would have never guessed that they were sisters.

"How in the world did the two sisters ever find each other after so many years?" I asked.

"Dilovan was the catalyst," Aram explained. "He was always close to his grandmother, and after his father, Diyari, died, the duty of taking care of Zara fell to him. He brought her from Diyarbakir, where she had been living, to stay with Fulya and him in Istanbul. Istanbul is where she lived until her death in 1990."

"Did Dilovan know her Armenian history?"

"He did know it, as Zara had helped raise him and slept in the same room with him when he was a child. Dilovan told me that sometimes as a boy he would hear his grandmother cry out in her sleep in anguish in a language he did not recognize. When he asked her about it, she confessed that she had been born Armenian and that was the language she spoke as a child. When Dilovan spoke to his father about his conversations with his grandmother, Diyari told him that it was true, but that it was important for Dilovan never to talk about his Armenian history openly because many Turks and Kurds would treat them badly if they knew. They felt that all Armenians were "kuffar" or infidels.

"Was that true?" I asked. "Did she still practice Christianity?"

"Not that Dilovan knew of," Aram replied. "He told me that he was surprised that anyone could say that his grandmother was an infidel as she was by far the most pious Muslim of all the family, saying her prayers regularly. As for myself, I imagined that she did so in order to protect her children and to convince her Muslim husband and her Muslim neighbors that she was not only like them, but even more pious than they were."

"When and how did Dilovan decide to search for Karine?" I asked.

"It was after Zara moved in with Dilovan and Fulya in Istanbul," Aram explained. "For some reason she now opened up completely with him about her Armenian heritage. Maybe what motivated this change in her was the fact that her husband had been dead for many years and his commands of silence were no longer valid. Maybe it was learning that some Armenians lived openly and proudly as Armenians in Istanbul and even went to their own churches that gave her confidence. Maybe it was her age and that she now had little to lose by telling her true story. Maybe it was just Dilovan's insistence that she talk about her Armenian family, as he wanted to learn his own history. Whatever the reason, she began to tell her true story to her grandson. She told of her family in Harput and of being raised a Christian. She told of being taken from the deportation caravan and of converting to Islam and changing her name from Margarit to Zara so that she could become Dilovan's grandfather's second wife. She also expressed her desire to try to establish contact with any member of her Armenian family or their children who might still be alive. That's when Dilovan decided to help her."

"How did he go about doing that?" I asked.

"Dilovan said that he first went to the Office of the Armenian Patriarch in Istanbul and asked them the same question—how could he locate his grandmother's Armenian relatives if they were still alive? A priest in the office first checked church archives but only found the baptismal record for Garabed Terzian. He then advised Dilovan to do what many survivors of the deportation had done—to place ads in Armenian newspapers in Istanbul and in Russia, France, Lebanon, Syria, and the United States. So with the priest's help in finding the addresses of such newspapers and in writing the ads, that is what Dilovan did."

Aram turned to the last page of the album to a yellow newspaper clipping under a plastic sheet protecting it. "This was the ad that my son, Richard, I mean Father Gregory, saw in the Armenian Weekly published here in Watertown."

I read outloud the small ad in a box, "Margarit Terzian, daughter of Garabed and Talitha Terzian of Harput and Hussenig, Turkey, seeks any information about them or about her sister Karine Terzian or her descendents." Underneath was Dilovan's address and telephone in Istanbul for contact.

"When Father Gregory drew Mother's and my attention to the ad, we immediately contacted Dilovan and made arrangements for the two sisters to meet. In June of 1982, Father Gregory and I flew with Mother to Istanbul and stayed in a hotel that Dilovan had gotten for us near their apartment. It was a remarkable visit of almost a week with each sister sharing what had happened to them."

"How did they communicate," I asked.

"At first, Dilovan had to translate between English and Kurdish, but later, each of the sisters regained enough memories of their childhood Armenian and basic English to communicate directly with each other. They constantly held hands with each other, laughing and crying. A couple of times, though, they even got angry at one another."

"What about?"

"Mother was upset that Zara would not renounce the Islamic faith that had been forced on her. Zara justified her position saying that Muslims controlled Turkey and that she believed that Christians would always be discriminated against there. She also said that her children were raised Muslims and her return to Christianity would cause great pain and perhaps even violence in her extended family. Anyway, she added, 'Allah was the same whether one was a Muslim, Christian, or Jew. He was merciful and would understand.'"

I thought that her answer was reasonable.

"The other friction between them came after we asked them both to share their memories of the deportation march," Aram continued. "I requested that they go into detail so that I could write it all down. Dilovan translated what Zara said about Lazar's murder and the subsequent rape of the two sisters and their mother. When Mother heard what she had said, she became hysterical and told Zara to stop. She denied vehemently that she had been raped, but Zara insisted that she had. It was only after Gregory and I reassured her that no matter what had happened, it was not her fault and that our love for her would not diminish, that she calmed down. Finally, in tears, she admitted her violation, not just once but several times."

"Did she say anything about the birth of my grandfather, Noah?" I asked.

"Later, yes, and she even confessed to us her mixed feelings about Altay and her guilt about giving up your grandfather for adoption. She wanted Father Gregory and me to help her locate him and ask his forgiveness before she died."

I was astounded. "This was the first time that you had ever heard of my grandfather?"

"The very first time," Aram replied. "When we got back to Watertown, Mother insisted that I try everything to locate him. She became obsessed with the idea. It was not easy. This was before the internet and Google search, and I was unsuccessful. Miss Isabel was now dead. James Ross was dead and the school he taught in had changed its name. But complicating the search most of all was the fact that Noah, too, had changed his own name from Noah Ross to Noah Ross-Terzian."

I already knew that part of the story from both my grandfather, Noah, and from my mother. My grandfather did not know that he was adopted until he turned eighteen years old. On his birthday, his adoptive parents, the Rosses, and his Aunt Isabel revealed this fact to him. They told him that his birth parents, whose name was Terzian, were Armenians who had died in the massacres and deportations of 1915 in Turkey."

"Why didn't they tell the whole truth," I asked, "and tell him that his mother was still alive?"

"I imagine because of Miss Isabel's promise to my mother, that she would protect that secret for the sake of my father and my own family," Aram answered.

The rest of the story I also knew. Completely surprised at this revelation about his adoption and Armenian background, Grandfather threw himself into learning everything he could about his Armenian heritage. He subscribed to Armenian publications and joined Armenian associations. He even changed his last name from Ross to Ross-Terzian to honor both his adoptive and his birth parents. He became very proud of his Armenian heritage and made a big deal of it.

"Finally, it was a quirk of fate or of Providence that we made contact," Aram said, continuing. "We didn't find your grandfather; it was your grandfather who found us!"

"That was 1983?" I said, remembering as best I could what Grandfather had told me.

"It was 1983. Noah had come to Cambridge to bring your uncle Thaddeus to the Harvard Business School where he had been accepted as a student. He decided that since he was so close to Watertown, where so many

Armenians lived, he would see if he could find any with the Terzian name who might be distant relatives of his birth family. He looked through the phone book and visited several of our Armenian churches asking if anyone knew someone with that name. Finally, at our church, Saint James, he talked to our priest who had heard Mother's story the year before and he knew that her maiden name was Terzian. The priest called me, and Mother and I set up a meeting the next day here at the condominium with Noah."

"I bet that was emotional," I said.

"Extremely so," Aram replied. "Mother was overjoyed and so was Noah at first to find each other. But as Mother told her real story and not the one Noah had learned at eighteen, it gradually dawned on him that his father had not been an Armenian professor killed by the Turks as he had been told, but instead had been a Turkish gendarme who had raped his mother. He had a hard time adjusting to this new information, and when he did, he became deeply depressed, as well as bitter and angry at Mother."

"I knew that he was always depressed about being the offspring of a Turkish rapist but why was he angry at your mother?" I asked.

"It was because he felt that Mother had rejected him by giving him up for adoption. He was also angry that she had insisted that Miss Isabel and the Rosses tell him the lie about his birth parents that he had shared widely with his family and friends. Now he was humiliated! His anger at Mother even increased two years later when Mother supported Mariam's marriage to your father, Brent Johnson. Noah was adamantly against it."

I knew this story as well and was about to ask another question when Susan called us to dinner.

CHAPTER 4

Noah Ross-Terzian

After dinner, I decided to skip the evening wine with the Petrosians on the deck and to return to my room and type into my laptop the new information that I had gathered from my visit to the library and from my conversations with Aram. Aram's memories of my grandfather stirred some of my own feelings and memories of him that I will share with you now.

Like my grandfather Noah, I only learned the truth about my own birth circumstances when I was eighteen. Going through some of my mother's family files looking for my birth certificate in order to get a passport, I came upon the marriage certificate of my parents with the date of October 19, 1984, on it. As strange as it might seem, for the first time in my life, I realized that a space of only five months existed between the marriage of my parents and my own birth on March 15, 1985. That must have meant that I was "conceived out of wedlock," as I had had a normal birth. I also noticed in the pictures of their small civil wedding that neither my grandfather Noah nor my father's parents were in any of the photos. The pictures included only a dozen or so people—a few of my father's business school friends as well as Thaddeus, Karine, Aram, and Susan.

When I confronted my mother about these two facts, she admitted to the truth. "Yes, it is true, you were conceived before Brent and I married. I never told you out of embarrassment."

She explained that their wedding was small for the same reason. Both Noah and Brent's parents had refused to come. "The Johnsons thought that I had manipulated Brent into marriage, and after his death, they had nothing more to do with me or with you. Even my own father was cold to us both for several years afterwards." She added, "I loved my father very much, but he was very controlling and traditional in his view of women."

I asked her to explain, because I had only known my grandfather as a very loving and supportive person.

"Father," she said, "felt that a woman's place was in the home. While he supported my brother, Thaddeus, all through his college days at the University of North Carolina and then at the Harvard Business School, he asked me to stay at home after I graduated from high school to help him take care of Mother who had cancer and was bed-ridden. I agreed because I loved my mother. After she died, however, I wanted to go on with my own life and continue my education. Thaddeus was on my side, but Father made me feel guilty by telling me how much he still needed me at home now that Mother had died and how lost he would be without my help. I was twenty years old and completely dependent on Father's financial support, so I felt trapped. Once again, I agreed to stay, but I was not happy!"

"So you stayed at home with him, but what does that have to do about my own father?" I asked.

"I'm getting to that," she said. "In June of 1984, at the end of Thaddeus's first year at the business school, Thaddeus brought Brent to Asheville to visit for a week. Brent was his roommate and friend, and Thaddeus wanted to show him Asheville before Brent headed out to California to spend the rest of the summer there with his own family. During the week Brent stayed with us, I fell in love with him. He was handsome, worldly, witty, smart, and most important, he paid attention to me."

She then told me that Brent and Thaddeus had invited her along when they went hiking and to one of Asheville's nightspots. "Brent seemed attracted to me, and I was flattered by his attentions. On one of our hikes to the top of nearby Greybeard Mountain, Thaddeus left us alone for a few minutes to go into the woods to relieve himself. Brent took that opportunity and kissed me. I didn't resist, and this must have encouraged him.

"Later that same night, after we got home and had gone to bed in our individual rooms, Brent quietly snuck into my room. I should have asked him to leave, but I didn't, and after kissing for a while, he made love to me. It was the first time I had ever had sex," Mother confessed, her face turning red at this intimate revelation to me her son.

"The next night, the same thing happened, but this time we were discovered by Father who heard Brent in my room when he got up to go to the bathroom in the night. Father was livid with anger when he opened the door and saw us in bed together. He yelled at Brent to get his things and to leave the house immediately. Thaddeus was awakened by the shouting and while he was angry at what he felt was Brent's betrayal of their friendship, he was also embarrassed that Brent was being thrown out of our house in the middle of the night.

"Later, Brent apologized to me and to Thaddeus for his actions, and he and Thaddeus made peace with each other when they both returned to school in Cambridge at the end of the summer." Mother started to cry and excused herself to go to the bathroom to get some tissue paper and recompose herself. When she came back, she continued. "In September, I wrote Brent and Thaddeus that I thought I was pregnant. I was scared out of my wits because I didn't know what to do and feared the reaction of Father who was still angry with me and wanted nothing to do with Brent."

I said nothing and gave no sign of disapproval or support to her as she told her story. It was bewildering to me, though, that I had lived for eighteen years without the slightest suspicion that all of this had once happened.

Mother continued. "Brent wrote back that even though we had been together so little, he thought that he could love me, and that we should marry whether I was pregnant or not." Mother cried again. "I have never been so relieved in all of my life. I felt as if a ton of bricks had been lifted off my back!

"He said that if I accepted his proposal, I should call him, and we would set a time on a weekend for him to fly down to the Asheville airport in his private plane and take me back to Cambridge where we would marry. Brent sent the letter to me in an envelope addressed by Thaddeus so Father would not be suspicious and open it. In it, Brent also included a hundred dollars in twenties for any expenses, his new telephone number, and a note from

Thaddeus saying no matter what my decision, he would support me. He also said that he would try to help me mend fences later with Father.

"I immediately went to a pay phone in a convenience store near our house and called the number," Mother continued. "Brent answered and I thanked him for his proposal and the money and I told him that I accepted, as I thought that I could love him as well. We then made plans for when I would take a taxi to the Asheville airport and meet him. Thaddeus, who was in the room with him at the time, got on the phone and congratulated us both. He said that he would take care of telling Father, and that he would also get in touch with Karine, our newly discovered grandmother in Watertown, and would see if I could stay with her until Brent and I were married."

"What did Karine say?" I asked. "Had she ever met you before?"

"No. She had only met Father and Thaddeus," Mother replied. "She was so gracious and said 'yes' right away. I guess she remembered her own past situation as a young, single pregnant girl and was empathetic."

"What about Grandfather?" I asked. "He must have been devastated by the news."

"He was," Mother answered. "He saw my pregnancy and running away secretly to marry Brent, as well as Thaddeus's and Karine's support of me, as personal betrayals. It was just one more disaster in his life for him. First, he was devastated to find out who his birth father was—a hated Turkish gendarme who had violently raped his Armenian mother. Then he discovered that his birth mother had rejected him as a baby. Soon after that, Mother died, and I became pregnant out of wedlock and ran away to marry a person he could never accept. The greatest grief of all, though, was yet to come. When Thaddeus, his beloved son died in that accident with your father, he snapped. He became an increasingly bitter man and started to drink heavily and even tried to commit suicide with an overdose of sleeping pills."

That was news to me. Grandfather told me that Thaddeus's death devastated him, but he had never alluded to his reactions to Mother's marriage or to the fact that he attempted suicide. "When did that happen?" I asked.

"It was right before we moved back to Asheville. I got a telephone call from your stepfather, who was your Grandfather's right hand man in his real estate company. When Grandfather did not answer his calls, Bill went to the house and found him on the floor. He called an ambulance and got him to the hospital in time to save his life. After that happened, I decided we had to move back to Asheville to take care of him." She paused and added, "It was you who brought him out of his depression, though. You gave him purpose for living. Through you, he finally came to the realization that good can come from evil. He doted on you."

I have only good memories of Grandfather, and until then, I never had even the slightest evidence that initially he had rejected me as a baby. After Mother married Bill Daniels in 1991 when I was eleven, and they had their first child together, Grandfather was now the one who cared for me the most, taking me fishing and watching me play basketball and soccer with the YMCA. We became quite close, and his death of a heart attack in 1998 devastated me. He was eighty-two at the time and I was fourteen. Both he and Karine left funds in their wills to give to me when I turned eighteen to help me pay for college and to get me started in life. For that, I am immensely grateful Those funds were now paying for my trip to Turkey. Grandfather also left me this letter:

Dear Peter,

When you read this you will be eighteen, and I may already be dead. I hope very much that you will lead a happy life and that these funds will help you to do so. As a young boy, you brought me joy in my last years. I want to thank you for that and for the love that you always gave to me.

The truth is that I rejected you as a baby because of the circumstances of your birth. How foolish of me, especially as one who also was rejected by his mother for the same reason! I know you will forgive me for that, as I finally came to understand and forgive my own mother. My greatest regret in life was not telling her that before she died.

I guess that the wisdom that I want to pass on to you in this my first and last letter to you, my beloved grandson, is that thankfulness and forgiveness are the foundations of a healthy, fruitful, and happy life. You can do nothing to change the negative events of the past—the lies, betrayals, robberies, murders, rapes—but you can try to change your attitude to them and to those who did them. The truth is that good and evil are in all of us. Sometimes we are the victim; sometimes we are the aggressor. We all need to learn to forgive even the Altays and Brents of our lives— even ourselves. We all also need to ask forgiveness, as I have done to your mother and as I am now doing to you.

My advice then to you is simple. Always be thankful and forgiving. Always do the best you can. From your grandfather who loves you,

Noah Altay Ross-Terzian

CHAPTER 5

The Petrosians

Aram promised to spend Wednesday morning with me showing me the family graves, the houses he and his family had lived in, and other sights important to the Petrosian family history in Watertown. He also arranged with his friend, the director of the Armenian Museum in town, to allow me to visit the collection on Wednesday afternoon. That was a special favor, as the museum was usually only open to the public from Thursday through Sunday. The director quickly granted his request because Aram for many years had served as a trustee of the museum.

At nine in the morning, after a leisurely breakfast together, Aram suggested that we start the day with a walk across the street from their condominium to visit the vast Mount Auburn Cemetery where their family graves were located. That sounded like a great idea to me, as I not only wanted to see the graves, but I also wanted to get my first exercise in three days. I got my daypack, my notebook, and camera and we were off. Susan, however, declined the invitation to come with us.

"At my age, I will be in the cemetery soon enough!" she said laughing.

Taking the elevator to the lobby, we exited the building, crossed over Coolidge Avenue, turned a corner, and walked for several minutes on Grove Street until we came to one of the accesses to the cemetery. Entering, Aram pointed to the right. "Our family plot is about a hundred yards from here overlooking Willow Pond."

I had never been in the cemetery before, although it was a well-known landmark in Boston because of the graves of famous people interred in it and because of its beautifully landscaped shaded walks under ancient trees amid a wide variety of flowers and bushes. "It's like a little paradise here," I noted.

Aram seemed pleased. "It's really an arboretum as much as a cemetery—the first landscaped cemetery in the country. I sometimes spend entire mornings here just strolling under the trees, meditating at the graves, or just sitting on one of the benches by a pond. I like to watch the birds and squirrels and feel the peace of the place. It's a welcomed relief from the busy bustle of Boston."

We quickly came to the Willow Pond, aptly named because of the weeping willows, lazily drooping their branches over the dark water surrounded by rhododendron and azalea bushes. As we got there, a great blue heron was searching for a fish in the shallow water among the reeds. Just twenty yards away from the pond on a slight incline, Aram pointed to two modest granite tombstones. We headed towards them, and when we got close to them, I read the inscriptions carved in the stones under Armenian style crosses. The smaller of the two stones read: Talitha Terzian, Born February 12, 1882, Died March 25, 1954. The larger stone had two names on it: Nigol Petrosian, Born June 20, 1899, Died May 16, 1974 and Karine Petrosian, Born April 2, 1900, Died November 20, 1989.

"We have one more plot next to them for Susan and me," Aram commented. After a short pause he added, "It is strange how Susan and I are so alike in so many things and so different in others. I love to come here and think of the mystery of death and of the afterlife and have my little conversations with my parents and grandmother. Susan, however, wants to banish any thought of death from her mind and will never come."

"I guess that I'm more like Aunt Susan," I said. "I tend to think that it is all over when it is over. No heaven or hell to look forward to or fear, just the present time to enjoy to the utmost!" I then reached in my daypack that was hanging from my shoulder and took out my camera. I snapped several close-up pictures of the gravestones and then a wide-angle view with Aram and the pond in the background.

After putting the camera back in my pack, I asked, "What were they like? I have only the faintest memory in my mind of your mother, Karine, and never met the others."

Aram nodded. "Grandmother Talitha lived with us until her death. I remember her as being very serious and rarely laughing. She was a good woman, though, and worked hard all of her life—both inside and outside our home. She was always sewing, cleaning, cooking, babysitting, or doing something to help others and to carry her weight in the household. She went to her own Armenian Evangelical Church in town and volunteered there as well."

"Did she ever talk about the massacres to you?"

"Rarely, but she often talked about her life in Mardin and Harput before the murder of her parents and husband. She said that the deportation and the massacres themselves were just too painful to talk about. Once, as a young boy, I saw her in her room alone crying. When I asked Mother later about it, she said that she was probably remembering the killings of her husband and son and the kidnapping of her daughter."

I could imagine her pain. I would not want to talk of such horrors myself, I thought. "And your father? What was he like?" I asked.

Aram took off his Oxford style round glasses and wiped them with his handkerchief. "He was a hard worker and a good provider, but the taciturn type. He rarely showed emotions except for his hatred for the Communists. For example, I never saw him kiss or even hold hands with my mother. He was pro-American but identified heavily with his Armenian identity and always spoke English with a strong accent. He was also a workaholic and very tight with his money so that he could save enough to send my sister and me to college and medical school. He was uneducated himself, but he put great value in my sister and I getting as many degrees as we could. He was very proud of our accomplishments."

"And your mother, Karine, what was she like to you?" I asked.

"Mother was a good woman who had suffered a lot. For most of her life she kept her defenses up and her feelings tightly under control. She told us later that she feared daily that my father would one day find out about her rape and reject her. I think that she also felt tremendous guilt that she gave up Noah for adoption and then never sought him out. It was only in her last years that she became more empathetic, open, and vulnerable."

"So your father, Nigol, never knew her true story?"

Aram shook his head. "Certainly not about the rape and Noah. Father was already dead when we learned that."

"Would it have made any difference in his love for her?"

Aram pondered that question for a moment and then answered. "I honestly don't know. He was a very private and an autocratic person. I loved him for the sacrifices he made for us and respected him for his entrepreneurial talents, but I never felt close to him."

"I will always appreciate the fact that your Mother left me money in her will," I said. "It has meant so much to me, helping me pay for my education and even for this trip."

"Well, it was the right thing for her to do. I hope this new project of yours is successful, and I certainly look forward to reading your book one of these days. If I can help you in any way in completing it, let me know."

"You've already done that! Helping me now and providing me with the basic document that got me started on this entire project—Karine's memoir about those times in Turkey. What a treasure!"

"I'm glad it has been useful. Mother only agreed to do the memoir if I would help her write and edit it. I interviewed her numerous times and then wrote up what she said in narrative form. The story and impressions are hers, but I tried to make it flow better."

"That's kind of what I want to do with my novel. Of course, it will be fiction because it will be about persons, places, events, and a time I know little about. But I hope that it will also be truthful at a deeper level, helping us to understand what happened in those terrible times and why it all happened, so that we don't ever repeat such events."

"Good objectives," Aram said. "Dilovan's and Ashti's perspectives as Turks should be particularly helpful to you when you interview them in Istanbul. We all see things somewhat differently." Aram affectionately patted the two family tombstones as if saying goodbye to them and suggested, "Speaking of seeing things from different angles, why don't we walk over to the Washington Monument Tower which is close by. There you can climb up and have a full view of the cemetery from above and even see Cambridge and Boston. It is good exercise and a magnificent vista."

When we got to the round tower at the top of a hill, Aram waited below as I ascended the steps to the lookout levels. The view from the top of the tower was indeed rewarding as I could see the treetops, ponds, and lakes of the vast cemetery, and interspersed among them the white tombstones and monuments to so many people who had lived, made their mark, and died. In the distance, I could see Cambridge with its church and university steeples, Harvard Stadium, and Boston with its skyscrapers. A soft wind caressed my face as I took pictures from different angles. It was a place of beauty and of peace. When I got down, I thanked Aram for his suggestion.

"There's one other grave I want to show you. It, too, is part of the history of what happened in Turkey in 1915," Aram said. "It's not far from where we came into the cemetery."

I was curious as to what Aram meant, but I said nothing as we descended some steps and then walked along the curving paths towards the entrance. Soon we came to a small trail called the Cardinal Path and walked down it. Just off it, Aram stopped in front of a simple gravestone with a flowery Armenian cross carved into the top center. The dates of the birth and death of two people, who were obviously husband and wife, were engraved on it. I noticed no names above the dates, only initials.

Aram explained to me why he had brought me there. "This is the grave of an Armenian patriot who, just like Mother, was born in Harput, Turkey, died in Watertown, and was buried here. He was sixteen years older than Mother, attended the same Euphrates College in Harput where Mother's father, Garabed Terzian, taught, and went to the same church here in Watertown that Mother and our family attended. In his later years, he was mostly a recluse, but for much of his life he had a very important role to play in Armenian politics. You should take a picture."

I took out my camera and snapped another photo. "But what was his name and what did he do that was so important?" I asked.

"His name was Hagop der Hagopian, but he went by other names as well like John Mahy and Shahan Natalie. When he was eleven years old, the Turkish authorities killed his father and many others of his family in Harput in the first massacre of our people. Their deaths and the deaths of so many other Armenians politicized him and caused him to join and later become a leader in the Armenian Revolutionary Federation. Most Armenians in Turkey went to their deaths like sheep to the slaughter, but he was one of those who took up arms in what he claimed was self-defense. He also sought justice for the victims by executing the perpetuators of the massacres."

I asked him to explain.

"At end of World War One and the defeat of the Ottoman Empire, many of the Turkish officials responsible for ordering the 1915 massacres were put on trial in Istanbul as war criminals and were condemned to death by their own people. Their sentences, however, were not carried out, and many of the top leaders escaped to live in countries like Germany, Georgia, and Turkmenistan. Natalie and his organization later tracked them down and executed them.

"The most infamous and powerful of the Turkish officials, Talaat Pasha, Natalie ordered to be killed by another Armenian named Sorghomon Terhirian. Natalie advised Terhirian not to run or resist arrest once he had carried out the killing, as he wanted Terhirian's trial to spotlight the reasons for the assassination—the Armenian massacres organized by Talaat Pasha and his political party the Committee of Union and Progress.

"It happened just as Natalie predicted. Even though the Germans had been allies of the Turks in the war, once the German jury learned what Talaat Pasha had done and of his death sentence in the war crimes trial, they acquitted Terhirian. Natalie's tactics, however, divided many in the Armenian community, and some saw his violent actions as hurting their cause more than helping it. In his last years, Natalie withdrew from politics, and he died peacefully here in Watertown in 1983 at the age of ninety-nine."

"Amazing," I said. "So many parallels exist in the lives of Karine and Natalie, yet also such profound differences! Karine was the silent victim and Natalie the militant seeking justice or revenge. Do you agree with what Natalie did?"

"That is a hard question for me to answer," Aram replied. "We have to defend ourselves and those we love, yet taking up arms and assassinating our enemies without the cover of law is not the right way. That makes us no better than our enemies. Revenge just leads to more destruction, as our enemies will want revenge as well. The Turk perpetrators of the violence against the Armenians justified their actions on the revolt of a small number of Armenians against their rule. Natalie's actions, no matter how understandable, just confirmed the suspicions of Turk nationalists. The cycle of mistrust and violence has to be broken at some point, or it will continue on forever."

"I think you're right," I said. "Reconciliation and not revenge, is the better way. Just look at the fundamental changes that Gandhi, Martin Luther King, and Nelson Mandela brought about in the last century through non-violence."

"And in contrast, look at the pain, fear, and hate our own Boston Marathon Bombers, the Tsarnaev brothers, created with their violence," Aram added.

"That's right," I said. "I had forgotten that it was right here in Watertown that the youngest hid out and was captured."

"On Franklin Street," Aram added.

"It is just one more example of revenge killings for political or religious reasons," I said.

"Yes, but Natalie would have said that one crucial difference existed between his action and theirs," Aram said. "The killing of Talaat Pasha was a targeted killing—the carrying out of a death sentence imposed by a legitimate court where no innocent bystanders were hurt. In the case of the Boston Marathon Bombers, they disabled and killed innocent people in an act of revenge and as a political statement. No legitimate court sanctioned their action."

Agreeing on that point, we turned away from the grave and walked towards the entrance and then back to the visitor's parking space at the condominium. We got in my rental car, and Aram guided me through the residential and business areas of Watertown pointing out to me the different houses Karine and her mother Talitha had lived in after their arrival in the small town in May of 1916—almost a hundred years before.

"Their first dwelling was a room in a boarding house on Arsenal Street that the American Board of Commissioners for Foreign Missions paid for until Talitha and Karine found employment at the Hood Rubber Company," Aram explained. "Hood ran a giant factory in Watertown that made everything from rubber boots to boats. They were the town's biggest employer, and as many as 500 Armenian immigrants worked there at one time. Mother met my father there some years later."

"Could we drive by the buildings?" I asked.

"Unfortunately, the boarding house burned down a few years after Karine and Talitha left, and the Hood Rubber Factory was demolished. It's now a shopping center."

The other houses in Watertown that the Petrosians had lived in, however, were still there. First, we stopped at the modest rented house on Melendy Avenue where Nigol and Karine had lived with Talitha and then the much bigger and fancier Victorian home on Porter Street that Nigol had purchased after he started his own company making coats for men and women. In 1972, Nigol sold both this house and his business and with that money, he purchased the Charles River apartment and retired.

"Unfortunately, nothing is left of the Petrosian coat factory either," Aram lamented. "It was demolished to make room for an office building."

As we drove around the small town, Aram pointed out other sights with ties to the Petrosians and the large Armenian community of Watertown. He showed me the headquarters of an Armenian newspaper and foundation, an Armenian men's club he had once been part of, and the four story modern brick and glass Armenian Museum of America, where he had served many years as a board member. He pointed out the Armenian Memorial Church, the small Protestant church that Talitha and Karine attended when they first arrived in Watertown, and then not far from it, the much larger Saint James Armenian Apostolic Orthodox Church that Karine became a member of after she married Nigol in 1925. It was in this church that their children were baptized.

At each building, I pulled over and took pictures. When I did so at the Saint James Church, Aram asked me to park, as he wanted us to get out of the car so that he could show me the church's memorial to the genocide of 1915.

The memorial itself consists of a rectangular stone about six feet tall located within a half-circle of shrubs to the right of the church. "We Armenians call these stones 'khachtars,' and they are very important in our culture for marking graves and commemorating important events," Aram explained. Pointing to the top of the gray stone where the date April 24,

1915, was written in the unique Armenian script, he said, "It's the date we use to commemorate the genocide, as it was on that day that the first wave of arrests took place of prominent Armenian intellectuals and religious leaders in Istanbul."

Below the elaborately carved Armenian cross in the middle of the stone, I read these words: "In memory of the Armenian martyrs who perished in the Genocide of April 24, 1915." At the base of the stone, the same dedication was written in Armenian script. Aram and I stood there respectfully for a moment, and I took some pictures before returning to the car.

On the way back home, Aram asked me to stop at an Armenian delicatessen on Mount Auburn Street to get some Armenian wine as well as some sweets for the special meal Susan wanted to cook for me on my last night in Watertown. Inside the delicatessen, the owner greeted Aram familiarly, and after Aram introduced me and explained to him that I was on my way to Istanbul the next day, the owner pointed to another man who was shopping in the store. "He's one of our Turkish customers who lives in Brighton. He comes over here a lot to shop, as our food is the same as theirs although sometimes with different names."

Aram bought some special bread, Armenian wine, and some nuts and sweets in plastic containers, and we headed back to the apartment. There, I let Aram out at the front entrance of the building with his bag of groceries and then I headed back to the museum for my appointment at noon. After getting a sandwich at a carry-out on Arsenal Street, I found a public parking place nearby the museum and got there right on time.

CHAPTER 6

The Armenian Museum and Library

As instructed by Aram, I stood at the front door of the museum and called the director on my cell phone with the number Aram had given me. Since the director was waiting for my call, it only took a few minutes for her to come down the stairs from her office to unlock the door for me.

"Welcome," she said shaking my hand. "Aram tells me that you are researching a novel for the hundredth anniversary of the genocide."

"I am, and he tells me this is the place for me to start," I said. "Thanks so much for opening for me, as I don't have time to visit tomorrow."

"Someone's always here throughout the week even if it is closed. We just have to have some down time to change exhibits and to have our meetings."

As she led me inside, the director explained the layout of the building with its two bottom floors for museum exhibits and a store and its upper two floors for offices and research libraries of photos and books. She suggested that I start in the museum and then go to the libraries afterwards. "You have the exhibits all to yourself," she said. "If there's anything you need, just call me on your cell phone or come upstairs to my office."

I thanked her again for her courtesy, and as she climbed the stairs back to her office, I entered the museum. The plan I decided on was to walk quickly through its two levels in order to get a feel for its displays and then decide where I wanted to spend most of my time.

After my walk through, I discovered that the exhibits included sections on Armenian architecture, miniature painting, music, embroidery, metalwork, and stone carving, as well as on Armenian history and the genocide. I decided that, as interesting and tastefully arranged as the other sections were, what I really needed to concentrate on were the Armenian history and the genocide displays. I also decided that instead of spending my time taking notes, I would take close-up digital pictures of the exhibits, which I could look at and read later.

The display I started with was quite useful to me as it showed the extent of the territory of Armenia at different times of its history. The Armenians are an ancient people who claim the area around Mount Ararat as their ancestral home. Starting as early as 321 B.C., there were many Armenian kingdoms, and in 70 B.C., under Tigran the Great, Armenia's territory included most of eastern Turkey, northern Iraq and Iran, most of Azerbaijan and Syria, stretching from the Mediterranean to the Caspian Sea. After that high water point, Armenian land holdings continually diminished because of invasions and military defeats at the hands of the Romans, Persians, Byzantines, Seljuks, Mongols, Ottomans, and Russians. Finally, Armenia ceased to be a nation, and it was only in 1991, that it regained its independence from the Soviet Union. Today, the Republic of Armenia lies to the east of Mount Ararat and is a small country of approximately three million people, not much bigger in territory than Massachusetts.

Other informative displays told of Armenia's history as a Christian nation and of its unique alphabet, two special characteristics that have held the Armenian people together through centuries of disaster and persecution by its neighbors. According to tradition, Jesus' disciples Bartholomew and Thaddeus first brought Christianity to the country, but it was in 301 A.D. that it became the first official Christian nation when its king was baptized by Gregory the Illuminator and accepted Christianity as the state religion.

The Armenian Apostolic Orthodox Church, the national church of the republic, belongs to what is known today as Oriental Christianity, along with the Coptic Christians of Egypt and Ethiopia and the Syriac Christians of the Middle East and India. This ancient branch of Christianity only recognizes as legitimate the decisions of the first three ecumenical councils of Christianity in comparison with Eastern Orthodox churches, which recognize the first seven and the Roman Catholics and Protestants, who recognize more. While most Armenians belong to the Armenian Apostolic Orthodox Church, sizable numbers of them also are Armenian Catholics and Armenian Protestants.

The Armenian alphabet and script were also important factors in the development of the cultural unity of the Armenian people. In 406 A.D., Mesrop Mashtots, a priest and linguist invented a script and alphabet of 36 letters that captured the unique sounds of the Indo-European language spoken by Armenians. Two more letters were added in the early Middle Ages to handle new sounds coming from other language groups, which Armenians had come into contact with after they were conquered or dispersed. The fact that the Armenian people had their own written language became a strong foundation for the development of an extensive body of both religious and secular Armenian literature. According to what I saw in the display, the earliest Armenian text still in existence is an Armenian Bible dating from the sixth century.

When I finished visiting the displays on the first floor, I went upstairs to immerse myself in the largest exhibit in the museum—the one devoted to the Armenian Genocide. Like the Holocaust for the Jews, this was the one event in modern history that has most profoundly marked the character and politics of the Armenian people. I wanted to spend as much time in this section as possible as I hoped it would help me understand the Armenian view of what happened and why it happened.

What I learned was that the Armenians who lived in what is now the modern nation of Turkey were subjugated by many peoples, including the Christian Byzantines and the Muslim Seljuks and Ottoman Turks, militant invaders coming from the steppes of Asia who had converted to Islam. The Muslim conquest of the region was gradual, but with the fall of Constantinople in 1453, the Ottoman Turks began to consolidate earlier advances. Soon their empire included not only the traditional homeland of the Armenians in eastern Anatolia, but also a good portion of what is today Eastern Europe, the Middle East, and North Africa.

While the Ottomans allowed the Armenians to continue practicing their

Christian religion, they clearly viewed them as second-class citizens and saddled them with special religious taxes as well as with severe limitations on their civil, judicial, economic, and political rights. The Armenians were also often targets of periodic killings and confiscations as 'infidels.'

Despite these limitations and periodic persecutions, many Armenians thrived under Ottoman rule and rose to positions of wealth and importance in the empire as doctors, teachers, lawyers, architects, artists, factory owners, and businessmen. Many credit this success to the Armenian entrepreneurial spirit and to the importance they attach to education.

In the middle of the nineteenth century, two parallel movements occurred that influenced greatly the fate of the Armenians in Turkey. The first of these was the slow disintegration of the once vast and powerful Ottoman Empire following a war with Russia in 1877. In this war, the Ottomans were defeated and lost much of their western territory in Europe. Romania, Montenegro, and Serbia were granted independence, and Bulgaria was given autonomy. In the east, the Ottomans also lost parts of what had once been Armenia to Russia and had to pay Russia an enormous indemnity as well.

Another movement of great importance in the nineteenth century that had a big effect in Turkey was the growing trend in Europe towards a constitutional style of government and away from autocratic rule. Both liberal Turks and minorities within the empire such as Armenians, Greeks, Jews, Kurds, and Arabs, who saw themselves as oppressed, demonstrated for the adoption of such a constitutional government within the empire. At first, they were successful, but then Sultan Abdul Hamid II, who was the ruler of the empire and the supreme authority of Islam at the time, in 1878 decided to suspend the recently approved constitution and parliament in order to counter the defeats he was experiencing on all sides.

Activists from these different groups, however, did not give up and continued their protests. As part of their push to claim equal rights and defend themselves, Armenians established two political parties: one was the Social Democrat Hunchakian Party and the other the Armenian Revolutionary Federation or Dashnaktsutiun, the party of Shahan Natalie, whose grave I had just visited.

Faced with this defiance of his authority, which was supported in a large part by Russia and the Christian nations of Europe, the Sultan became suspicious of the loyalty of his Christian subjects, especially that of the Armenians who were so numerous and influential. Trying to reestablish his authority, the Sultan in 1894 unleashed a special force of Kurdish Muslim fighters called the Hamidiye who were armed by him and loyal to him, to teach the Armenian and Syriac Christians a lesson they would never forget. Between 1894 and 1896, as many as 300,000 Armenian and Syriac Christians were massacred and more than 50,000 were left orphans, including my great-great-grandmother, Talitha Terzian.

In 1908, a wide coalition of liberal Turks, nationalists, Muslims, Christians, and Jews and sections of the Ottoman army under the leadership of the Committee of Union and Progress overthrew the government of Sultan Abdul Hamid II and reinstated the constitution and parliament that he had suspended. This coup generated great hope among the Armenian and other Christian communities of Turkey, but this hope was short-lived. In 1909, Muslim supporters of the Sultan and of the Caliphate succeeded in a counter coup, which resulted in reprisals against the Christians who supported the first coup. In the important city of Adana and its surrounding district, more than 4,300 Armenian homes and dozens of their churches and schools were destroyed, and as many as 30,000 Armenian and 1,300 Syriac Christians were murdered by Muslim mobs.

The attitude of Ottoman Muslims to the large minorities of Christians living in their midst was also negatively impacted by the Balkans War from 1912 to 1913 in which the former Ottoman states of Greece, Bulgaria, Serbia, and Montenegro joined forces to soundly defeat the Ottoman army once again. This defeat led to a huge inflow of Muslim refugees into Turkey and great resentment towards Christians.

In 1913, another coup took place in Turkey, putting into power a triumvirate of members of the Committee of Union and Progress called the "Three Pashas"—the Minister of the Interior, Mehmed Talaat, the Minister of the Navy, Ahmed Djemal, and the Minister of War, Ismail Enver. These three persons allied the Ottoman Empire with Germany in the First World War and led the empire throughout the war until its defeat.

These three persons also had the dream of creating "Turan," a greater Turkey that would extend to China, uniting all Turkish-speaking peoples in Asia. In order to promote that vision, they launched an attack against the Christian Russians and Armenians who stood in their way on their eastern border. Soundly defeated yet again by the Russians, the "Three Pashas" sought a scapegoat, which turned out to be the Armenians living under their rule.

On April 24 of 1915, the triumvirate ordered the arrest and killings of prominent Armenian intellectuals in Istanbul and then later extended their orders to include other Armenian and Syriac Christian males throughout Turkey. They also ordered the deportation of their wives and families to the deserts of northern Syria. All of these killings and deportations eventually led to the deaths of 1,500,000 Armenians and 300,000 Syriacs according to most estimates. Once a stronghold of Christianity, Turkey now was transformed into a land almost exclusively for Muslims.

After spending an hour reading and taking pictures in this section of the museum, I then took some forty-five minutes more to look at horrific black and white photos of the deportations and killings taken by German soldiers and foreign missionaries, travelers, and aid workers. To take such photos was illegal at the time and so most of the photographs had to be smuggled out of the country. The photographs showed Turkish gendarmes herding long lines of Armenians out of their towns to their death, the misery of the refugee camps, dead bodies piled in ditches and on the ground, emaciated women, and Turks teasing begging children with bread. They showed the heads of decapitated Armenians on a table with the proud decapitators behind them, Armenians hanging in the public square, tattooed Armenian girls captured and sold into prostitution, and pictures of thousands of orphans. Because of these pictures and the reports of diplomats, missionaries, and German soldiers, the world soon became aware of the terrible events happening in Turkey.

In one exhibit, I also watched the silent movie *Ravished Armenia* based on the memoirs of Aurora Mardiganian, a young girl who, like Karine and Margarit, came from near Harput, was raped, and witnessed the killings of her family. Unlike Karine, she was sold into slavery, and she witnessed crucifixions and the burning of churches with Armenians within them. While Karine escaped Turkey through Aleppo, Aurora escaped through Tiflis in Georgia to the United States.

It was four o'clock when I finished looking at the exhibits in the museum and went upstairs to the research library on the third floor. I introduced myself to the scholarly looking man in charge and explained my purpose in being there, "I'm writing a novel about my family's experience of the genocide, and I would like to get a feel for what is available on the subject."

The gentleman welcomed me and took me into the stacks and showed me dozens of books written in different languages. After pulling out several and showing them to me, he asked, "I'm curious. Why is someone with the name Peter Johnson interested in the Armenian genocide? That's not a very Armenian name."

I laughed. "No, it is not, but I have relatives who were Armenian and Syriac who were deported, raped, and killed during those years. And I also have a great-grandfather who was a Turkish gendarme who was responsible for some of the raping and perhaps killing," I answered. "I hope that researching and writing a book about them will help me understand what happened and why it happened. I hope it will help me reconcile these two sides of my ancestry in my own mind. Also, by actually attempting to put it together in a novel, I want to see if there's any hope for me as a writer!"

The man nodded appreciatively. "I know exactly what you mean about wanting to write. I guess all of us have that desire in us somewhere. In my case, I tried it, and I found out that I'm a much better reader than writer." Both he and I laughed.

"My family was from Harput, Turkey," I said. "Do you have any first-person narratives about what life was like there in the early 1900s?"

"We do." The man took me to another shelf and drew out the book by an American Consul and another book by a Danish missionary who lived there. "These might help. You can also find a number of photographs of Harput in the files of the *Project Save*. Unfortunately, their office downstairs is closed today."

I thanked the librarian for his help, and as he went back to assisting another person looking at Armenian art for a mural she wanted to do, I perused the books that he had given me. For the next half-hour, I also looked through many other books and took pictures of their covers in case I wanted to consult them later. Then at a quarter to five, I thanked the librarian and went downstairs to express my gratitude to the director for her kindness in letting me in. I got back to the Petrosians at half-past five.

By the time I finished my shower, Susan had a special Armenian dinner ready for us on the table—Harput filled keuftas named in honor of the town that Karine was from in Turkey. It consisted of finely ground lamb and a bulgar shell stuffed with parsley, pine nuts, spices, and onions floating in a tomato broth. A dish of yogurt was at the side as well as a basket of lavash or stiff flatbread and a salad plate of cucumbers, diced green onions, chopped peppers, celery, parsley, and chopped tomatoes. For wine, Susan served the bottle of Armenian red wine Aram had bought at the delicatessen, and for dessert, the baklava.

As we ate, I complimented Susan on the meal. Aram agreed. "She now knows more Armenian recipes than Mother ever did."

Susan smiled. "I had to make my in-laws happy!"

Aram then asked me about my day at the museum and library.

"It was fascinating and I took a lot of pictures and notes. I just wish that I had had more time to read some of the books I saw there. One that the librarian showed me looked especially interesting, as it was a neutral report on what happened in Harput between 1915 and 1917 by the American Consul who lived and worked there."

"*The Slaughterhouse Province,* by Leslie Davis," Aram said. "I have it in my library." He got up from the table and went into the other room returning with the slim volume. "You are welcomed to keep it," he said as he handed the book to me.

"Are you sure?"

"Of course, Susan and I are downsizing, and it should be very useful to you."

"Thanks so much. I will read it on the plane tomorrow."

"Now I have a couple of favors that I would like to ask of you," he said.

"Please do," I said.

"One is to take two Boston Red Sox baseball caps to give to Ashti and Richard... I mean Father Gregory, as gifts. They are small and light and should bring smiles to them both."

I laughed and said, "Sure thing!"

"And the other is to ask you to go on a small treasure hunt when you get to Hussenig."

"A treasure hunt?" I had no idea what Aram was talking about.

"Do you remember from Mother's memoir that she and Talitha hid in a small cave the most valuable possession of our family—an ancient silver Armenian cross that was on the wall in one Garabed's pictures?"

"I do."

"Well, Mother also left me detailed instructions on how to find it in case Gregory or I ever got to Harput. Unfortunately, neither of us has had the opportunity, so I want you to try to find it." He added, "I know it is a long shot after so many years, but if by some miracle you find it, I want you to give it to Gregory. Of all the family, he will know what to do with it."

"Fascinating!" I replied. "You just upped the excitement of my trip tenfold by making it into a treasure hunt as well." I reassured him, "Of course I will give it to Father Gregory. There's no one in the world I admire more!"

"Also, I hope that you can find and take pictures of the family residence in Hussenig if it hasn't been torn down. From what Mother said, it was one of the best houses in the town. The pictures Garabed took of it should help you locate it."

"If the house is still there, would you ever try to get it back?" I asked.

"It would be a useless effort. Many former property owners or their descendants have tried to reclaim their property in Turkey but to no avail. The truth is that the land on which the United States Incirlik Air base in Turkey is located was confiscated from Armenians, and even the official house of the President of Turkey in Ankara once belonged to an Armenian named Kasabian."

"What if you had a clear deed or proof of ownership?"

"It doesn't matter. The deportations of the Armenians and Syriacs by the Ottomans and later of the Greeks by Atatürk led to a huge transfer of wealth in Turkey and helped create a new Turkish middle class. I think that one of the main reasons that the present Turkish government won't admit to the genocide is that they fear that such an admission would open them up to massive lawsuits by Armenian descendents trying to claim lost property."

"I can see the government's practical point on that even though it doesn't sound very ethical," I said.

After the meal was over, the three of us continued to sit around the table for another half-hour talking about politics—mostly about Turkey's attempt to join the European Union and the barriers it was facing from them, but also about the mess Aram thought the United States government was making in the Middle East and especially in Syria. As Aram got more agitated, Susan finally got up and started cleaning off the table. I offered to help and after rinsing the dishes and putting them into the dishwasher, I thanked them again for all the trouble they had gone to for me and for the special meal. With that, Susan hugged me, said good-night, and we all went to bed.

CHAPTER 7

The Kayas

Thursday, April 3, was a leisurely day for me as my Swiss Air flight for Istanbul left only that night. After a late breakfast, the first thing I did was to call Ashti by Skype to confirm with her my arrival at the Atatürk International Airport. I offered to take the tram and metro and then a taxi to the Kaya's apartment in the Besiktas neighborhood of Istanbul, but she insisted on meeting me at the exit of passport control and customs. She also gave me her cell number in case we missed each other.

For most of the rest of the morning and afternoon, I sat in the Petrosian's library or out on the deck reading *The Slaughter House Province, An American Consul's Report* by Leslie Davis, the United States Consul in Harput from 1915 to 1917. I also wrote up some of the things that I had learned at the Armenian museum and reviewed some Turkish grammar and phrases I had not used since my last stay in Istanbul nine years previously. Susan washed some of my clothes for me and while they were drying, Aram and I took one more walk in the Mount Auburn Cemetery to get some exercise.

After a light dinner, I said my goodbyes to the Petrosians, thanking them once more for their friendship through the years and especially for their hospitality and help these past few days with my project. I promised to keep them informed, and I joked, "I'll make a special acknowledgement of you at the beginning of my book."

I then drove to Logan Airport, returned my rental car, and caught my 9:45 P.M. overnight Swiss Air flight to Zurich and then to Istanbul. I slept most of the night on the plane, but after breakfast, I once again took out my reading material—a Turkish grammar and phrase book.

After a stopover in Zurich, where I purchased some chocolate for the Kayas in the duty-free shop, I arrived in Istanbul at the Atatürk International Airport at around five o'clock in the afternoon on Friday, April 4. I quickly got through the passport control and customs since I had gotten my visa on line and just had carry-on. Coming out into the public area, I scanned the many faces of those waiting for arriving passengers, and then I heard someone call my name. Turning to my right, I saw Ashti Kaya smiling at me.

The truth is that I had always had a crush on Ashti since meeting her for the first time in Boston at the welcoming party the Petrosians had given her as a Rotary Exchange Student. My admiration for her dark beauty, good humor, and independent spirit only grew through the years, especially during the six weeks I spent in the Kaya's home in Istanbul studying basic Turkish language and history at the Boğaziçi or Bosphorus University. At the time, Ashti was taking courses at the Etiler Otelcilik Lisesi as she wanted to go into the tourism industry. Later, she also studied at the Bosphorus University to get her degree as a translator.

The Kayas and I got along very well, and after my six weeks with them, we kept in touch with e-mails and occasional Skype calls. Even so, I was surprised at Dilovan and Ashti's enthusiasm about my invitation to them to accompany me as I followed the deportation route of the Terzian family through southeastern Turkey. I was particularly pleased, not only because I enjoyed their company, but because their knowledge of the Turkish and Kurdish languages and culture would make a huge difference in my ability to get around and to understand.

Our plan was to take a flight on Sunday from Istanbul to Elazığ, the new name for the city of Mezire where both Karine and Margarit Terzian were born. There we would rent a car at the airport and after visiting Harput and Hussenig, the nearby towns where the Terzians had lived, we would drive south to Diyarbakir where Dilovan had grown up and where his sister still lived, and then on to Mardin. This was the same deportation route walked by Karine and her mother, Talitha, and thousands of other Armenians.

In Mardin, we would meet up with Father Gregory and visit the village where Talitha Terzian grew up with her Syriac family. While Dilovan and Ashti spent a few days in nearby Urfa and Harran where Abraham lived, I would stay on with Father Gregory doing interviews and taking pictures for the article I wanted to do on the refugees created by the Syrian Civil War. I hoped that the article would be good enough to help me gain credentials as an international correspondent. When they got back to Mardin, we would return together to Elazığ to leave the car and fly back to Istanbul.

"Thanks for picking me up," I said, greeting my third cousin with two quick pecks on the cheek and a squeeze of her hand. I was always sensitive about how much public display of affection to show my female friends in Turkey.

"You look great!" I added appreciatively. Ashti was dressed in a long black skirt and a sky blue blouse that modestly showed but did not emphasize her curves. She could fit in just about anywhere with her black hair and olive skin as a Turk, a Kurd, an Armenian, a southern European, or even a Brazilian.

Ashti smiled her warm smile, which always made me feel appreciated. "No other bags?" she asked. She spoke English perfectly but with a very slight accent.

"No. I'm ready to go!"

I followed her as she led the way to her white Renault Megane parked on the second level of the parking garage. Before we got into the car, I remembered the Boston Red Sox hat. I reached into my pack and pulled it out, presenting it to her. "It's a gift for you from the Petrosians," I explained.

Ashti laughed and put it on. "I still don't understand a thing about baseball, but I love Boston, and as a Muslim woman, I guess I'm supposed to keep my head covered!"

The trip from the airport to the Kaya's apartment in Besiktas took us almost an hour because of delays caused by people returning from work in this enormous city spread out over two continents. The Kaya's building was on the European side of Istanbul on the third floor in a very pleasant upper middle class area of five story structures. Dilovan had bought the apartment in the late eighties and it had proven to be an exceptional investment, as the population of the city had doubled in size to almost fifteen million since then.

Their home was close to Dilovan's job in Maslak, where he worked at the Turkish headquarters of the German Bosch Company, and close also to the Bosphorus University where Suna taught. It had also been a convenient location for Ashti for her high school years at Roberts College and her later studies at the Etiler Otelcilik Lisesi and Bosphorus University.

When we got to the apartment a little before seven in the evening, Fulya Kaya welcomed me enthusiastically, apologizing that Dilovan was not at home. "He called this afternoon and said they had a production problem at the Bosch factory in Bursa. It is three and a half hours away, and he thinks he will only be able to get back by dinner tomorrow night. He's so sorry," she added. "He wants so much to see you."

Both Fulya and Dilovan Kaya, like Ashti, spoke fluent English as they had met in the early eighties at Bosphorous University where English is the official language of instruction. At the time they met, Dilovan had enrolled in the engineering school there, and Fulya was an undergraduate student in political science. After Ashti had gone to high school, Fulya returned to the university and finished her doctorate. She now was a lecturer there.

I already knew both of their stories from the six weeks I had spent in their home. Dilovan, like many other Turkish and Kurdish young men, had left Turkey for Germany to seek work when he was nineteen, and he eventually got a job in one of Bosch's factories there. He had so impressed his employers with his ambition and competence that they offered him a full scholarship to Bosphorous University if he would commit to working with them in Turkey after he graduated. Counting Dilovan's employment with Bosch in Germany as a simple factory worker, he had now been with the company for almost thirty-five years. His current position was as an engineer and production manager in the manufacturing of washing machines.

Fulya's father had been a coronel in the Turkish Army and was a convinced secularist who held Atatürk in high esteem. He raised Fulya with the expectation that in the new Turkey she could do just about anything she wanted to, even though she was a woman. Unlike Dilovan, who was raised as a Sunni Muslim, Fulya was more comfortable in the Sufi traditions associated with her mother's home town of Konya. All three of them now, Dilovan, Fulya, and Ashti, were secular Muslims who seldom obeyed dietary and dress rules and did not even say the customary "bismillahi" before eating.

They were also liberal in politics, enthusiastically supportive of Turkey's entry into the European Union and of women's and minority rights, especially those of the Kurdish and Armenian communities whose ethnicity Dilovan and Ashti shared. Yet, while they expressed openly their criticisms about many aspects of Turkish history and current politics, they also were proud of Turkey's many accomplishments and saw their country as a bridge between East and West, just like their city of Istanbul.

"You are in your same room at the end of the hall," Fulya said after welcoming me. "When you get settled, come back and have something to eat."

Their apartment was just as I remembered it. It had three bedrooms and three baths with a wonderful balcony view of the Bosphorus, the channel of water connecting the Black Sea to the Mediterranean. Pictures of family and friends from Turkey, Germany, and the United States were in frames on the walls of the hallway connecting the bedrooms, as well as in their private rooms. I was thankful that my own picture was one of the more prominent ones.

When I came out of my room, Fulya and Ashti were waiting for me in the living-dining room sitting at a table with dishes of fruit, yogurt, sheep cheese, ekmet (flatbread), and fried vegetables on it. Before sitting down, I presented them with the box of Swiss chocolates I had purchased for them in the Zurich airport for which they were grateful.

I ate very little, as the Kayas wanted to hear about the Petrosians and my own family in Asheville as well as about my new research project. I told them of what I had done in Watertown and Cambridge and about my idea of using the trip to Turkey to gather material for a novel and for some possible newspaper articles. "But the best part of the trip is seeing you and Father Gregory again!"

"Father Gregory was here just six months ago and stayed with us for a couple of days," Fulya said. "He came to get the support of the Armenian Patriarch for his work in Midyat with the refugees."

I nodded. "By the way, his father gave me some copies of Garabed Terzian's photographs of Harput. They include several of your great-grandmother, Zara, as a young girl. Would you like to see them?"

"I'd love to see them," Ashti said, and Fulya agreed.

After getting them from my room, we spent some fifteen minutes going through them one by one. Both Fulya and Ashti were delighted and when we finished, Ashti asked, "Can we get copies of them to keep?"

"Of course," I answered.

"I could make the copies tomorrow morning at the university," Fulya suggested. "I need to go to the office anyway as I left my brief case there by mistake with documents I will need to be working on this weekend. Our department is sponsoring a symposium next week." She paused and then asked, "Speaking of tomorrow, what would you like to do here in Istanbul before you leave on Sunday for Elazığ?"

"I guess the main thing is to get more of a feel for the Armenian presence here in Istanbul and maybe learn a little more about Zara and your own family history. I would also like to visit Taksim Square again as my editor wants me to do an article on it. Finally, if it is possible, I would like to make a quick visit to Bosphorus University to say hello to any of my old professors who might still be there."

"Why don't we go with Mother early in the morning to the university and then visit Taksim Square and some of the other places you are interested in afterwards," Ashti suggested. "I've taken a leave from my job for the next two weeks to do our trip together, so tomorrow I'm free."

"Good," Fulya said. "After your visit to the university, I can drop you off at the metro station and you can go where you need to go. You don't want to have a car in the center of Istanbul and have to look for parking."

Ashti must have noticed how tired I looked, because she said, "You've been traveling for sixteen hours now. It's time for us to let you go to bed."

I was glad for her suggestion, and after we agreed that we would have breakfast together the next morning at half-past seven, I said goodnight and went to my room.

CHAPTER 8

Bosphorus University

The next morning happened just as Ashti had suggested. After a good night's sleep and breakfast, Ashti, Fulya, and I got in the Renault and in ten minutes we were at the university.

I already knew the history of Bosphorus University from the summer I studied there nine years before. Like Euphrates College in Harput where Garabed Terzian had taught, Bosphorus University was founded by an American Protestant missionary sent out by the Boston-based American Board of Commissioners for Foreign Missions. Dr. Cyrus Hamlin, a remarkable visionary, established the college in 1863 with the name of Robert College, honoring a wealthy American merchant and philanthropist who gave much of the early money to finance what was to become the first American school of higher learning outside of the United States.

At first, Robert College focused on educating foreigners living in Istanbul and students of Armenian and other Christian backgrounds. In 1923, with the ascension of Atatürk to power, the school adopted an entirely secular model, but its instruction continued to be in English. In 1971, another big change took place when the college's Bebek campus and faculty were turned over to the Republic of Turkey to become a public university. In the turnover, it was renamed Boğaziçi in Turkish, or Bosphorus University in English.

The high school programs of Robert College continued under the same name on another campus. Today, both Bosphorus University and Robert College are among the top educational institutions of Turkey, and they have trained prime ministers, Nobel Prize winners, and other important persons from Turkey and from many other countries that were once a part of the Ottoman Empire.

Because it was Saturday, ample parking was available on campus near the majestic building where Fulya had her office. While she went to get her briefcase and make copies of Garabed's pictures, Ashti and I decided to walk around the campus. I wanted to rekindle some of my pleasant memories of my six weeks of study there and to see if I could locate my favorite professor, Dr. Polat, who gave such fascinating lectures on Turkish history.

Meandering among the historic gray stone buildings perched on the hills above the ancient Rumelihisar Castle and the Bosphorus Strait, I pulled out my digital camera and took pictures of the campus quadrangle and of the ships in the distance passing under the Fatih Sultan Mehmet Bridge connecting the continents of Europe and Asia.

Following Ashti's instructions as to where we could find information about Dr. Polat, we headed down the steps towards the building where the Summer Studies Coordinator for International Students had offices. Students were sitting on the grass either studying alone or chatting with each other. They looked like students on any United States campus.

"This has to be one of the most beautiful and historic locations in the world for a university," I commented.

"And it is also great academically," Ashti added.

"Are you still happy with your career choices?" I asked. I had kept up with Ashti through e-mails and on Facebook and knew that after finishing studying Tourism at the Etiler Otelcilik Lisesi and getting a Masters as a translator here, she was now employed as a conference coordinator in a major international hotel in Istanbul.

"I am, but what I would really like to do is set up my own tourist agency one day. In fact, thinking about our trip next week gave me an idea—to organize return visits of people like you to Turkey—people seeking their ancestral roots here. So many Armenians, Greeks, Syriacs, Kurds, and Turks around the world want and need to come back. The idea would be to take them to the areas where their ancestors once lived and arrange meetings and home stays for them with modern Turkish citizens. My hope is that such visits would increase friendship and reduce mistrust. So many historical animosities and misunderstandings have built up through the years that need healing."

"And what about marriage?" I asked. Ashti wrote often of her male and female friends on her Facebook page but never mentioned anyone special.

Ashti laughed. "You sound just like my parents? Don't you think that a single woman can be happy?"

"I do," I said, "but I would think that a twenty-seven year old woman as attractive as you would be a magnet for potential husbands."

Ashti blushed, and I wondered if I might have overstepped my cultural line.

"Well thank you, Peter, for the compliment," she said, "but in a Muslim society, an independent woman like I am isn't quite as attractive to males as you might think!"

I pondered her response as we walked. In a few minutes, we came to the building on the quadrangle where the Foreign Student Office was located on the second floor of a structure that also housed a small gym and a student canteen. When we got to the office, Ashti introduced both of us to the young woman behind the desk. "Peter was a student here in the summer of 2005 and would like to greet one of his former professors if he is still teaching here."

"Of course," the woman answered in English, "what is his name?"

"Dr. Polat," I answered. "He taught history."

"I don't recall the name," the lady answered, "but I've only been here for the past two years." She stood up, went to a file cabinet, and started to look through its folders. She pulled out one and examined it. "Here is his file. He left in 2010. There is usually quite a turnover in the summer teaching staff," she explained.

"That's too bad," Ashti commented.

"Maybe not," I said smiling. "I would have liked to see him, but he would probably start speaking to me in Turkish and then be disappointed at how little I've improved through the years!"

"It's a hard language," Ashti answered. "But you do pretty well in it."

"Teşekkür ederim. Thank you."

I had immensely enjoyed my six weeks in Istanbul—not only the stay with Ashti and her family, but also the camaraderie with the other foreign students in my classes. When not in the classroom, we regularly went on outings to visit the many tourist offerings of the city. Ashti sometimes went with us, and a couple of times the Kayas graciously invited some of my new friends over to their apartment to eat. One of my British friends took a serious interest in Ashti, but while she was glad to do things together as a group, she refused to go out with him on a single date. She had no such restrictions with me because she considered me family.

After obtaining this information about Dr. Polat, we thanked the coordinator and then went downstairs to the canteen and student center. All sorts of political posters and announcements were on the walls, but what drew my attention was a large handwritten poster with photographs stapled to it imploring students to, "Unite against Facism! Don't forget Taksim Square!" I pulled out my camera again and took a picture of it. "For my article," I explained to Ashti.

As we left the building and headed towards the staff parking lot, Ashti called her mother on her cell phone telling her that we would meet her at the car. When we got there, Fulya was already there, sitting in the driver's seat. She motioned for me to get in the front with her and Ashti got into the back.

"Did you find any of your old professors?" Fulya asked me before starting the motor.

"Unfortunately not," I answered. "The only one whose name I remember, Dr. Polat, left in 2010."

"Dr. Tanju Polat?" Fulya asked.

"I think so. Do you know him?"

"Certainly. He became very politically active after Hrant Dink's assassination. He got into a lot of trouble with the government for his support of the Armenian view that what happened in 1915 was a planned genocide. Later, the government prosecuted him under article 301 for insulting the Turkish Nation. His being a Turkish historian gave his opinion a lot of weight but also made him a lot of enemies among Turkish nationalists."

I was astounded, because I remembered Dr. Polat as very soft-spoken and affable, and certainly not as a political firebrand. "What happened to him?"

"He was given a six month suspended sentence and then worked for a while with the Hrant Dink Foundation as a researcher and writer," Fulya replied, turning on the ignition. "But I'm not sure what he is doing right now."

"Who is this Hrant Dink you keep talking about?" I asked Fulya.

"A great man," Fulya replied. "He was an ethnic Armenian citizen of Turkey who was assassinated by an ultra-nationalist young man in 2007."

"Why did he kill him?" I asked.

"Dink was the editor of an Armenian-Turkish weekly newspaper and published editorials and articles that some nationalists hated because he used the term genocide in describing what happened in 1915. He also denounced modern governmental policies that discriminate against Armenians and other minorities. Another article he wrote, which discussed the possibility that the adopted daughter of Atatürk was really an Armenian orphan, particularly infuriated them. The government prosecuted him and his son with the same law 301 that they later prosecuted Dr. Polak—for insulting the Turkish Nation."

"Do you think he and Dr. Polat were right?" I asked, "That what happened to the Armenians and Syriacs in 1915 was a planned genocide and not just the results of war and famine as the government claims?"

"That will take a long answer," Fulya said. "Do you have time to hear it?"

"Of course," I answered. "It's fundamental to my understanding of what happened to my ancestors and why it happened. It is a major reason for why I'm here."

"Okay," Fulya replied, turning off the motor again and leaving the car in park. "I warn you, however. I'm actually a bit wishy-washy on the subject. On the one hand, I am a proud, pureblooded Turk, directly descended from the Muslim Seljuks who conquered this country. I was even born in Konya, their capital. On the other hand, I am also the wife and mother of two people I love very much who have the blood of Armenians, Syriacs, and Kurds—minority groups who have historical grievances against us Turks."

I acknowledged what she was saying with a nod.

"But to answer your question, from all of the evidence that I've seen, horrible atrocities and massacres were certainly committed against the Armenians and Syriacs by Turkish authorities, Kurdish tribesmen, and other Turks in 1895, 1915, and afterwards. There is just too much evidence to pretend otherwise. Neutral sources of the time, like missionaries, diplomats, and businessmen, and even pro-Turkish sources, like German military personnel who were our allies, witnessed, reported, and photographed the events. But whether these atrocities should be called massacres or genocide, I really don't know."

"Do you think that the government authorities in Istanbul ordered the killings and deportations to get rid of the Armenians?" I asked. "Wouldn't that make it genocide?"

"I do think that the government definitely wanted to get rid of the Armenian men because it saw them as a threat, a kind of fifth column of revolutionaries and sympathizers with their Christian enemies, the Russians, British, and French. On the other hand, I'm not so sure whether what happened to the Armenian women and children should be classified as genocide or massacres."

"What do you mean?" I was not following her.

"What I mean is that if it was the aim of the government to kill off all the Armenians, as in the genocide theory, then it did not do a very good job. Those Armenians living in Istanbul and in the west of Turkey were mostly left alone by the government, and a minority of the deportees survived the march and the refugee camps in the desert.

"If, however, the government's plan was just to deport and not kill the Armenians, then the enormous suffering they faced in their long marches was due more to local animosities and the government's incompetence in feeding and protecting them from marauders instead of to a plan to wipe them out. In this case the term massacres might be more appropriate than genocide."

"Why do you suppose the difference between calling something a massacre or genocide means so much to Turks and Armenians?" I asked. "Aren't both things horrible enough?"

"Calling something genocide is much worse than calling it a massacre. It is a terrible accusation to us Turks. It means that we, or at least our leaders and our ancestors, desired and tried to eliminate by murder and starvation an entire people, including women and children. It means that we wanted to take over their property and destroy their culture. It makes our ancestors—and Turks today by association—into monsters. If admitted, it also makes Turkey liable to huge reparations, including the return of property and citizenship to those who were affected by these policies. It also puts all of the blame for what happened during those times on our Turkish ancestors, when the truth is that many Turks and Muslims were also displaced, robbed, and killed by rebelling and invading Christian armies during those times. My own grandparents were expelled from Bulgaria during the Balkan Wars in the early 1900's. Most Turks believe that what happened during those years was awful, but that it was the result of war, incompetence, and local animosities and not some genocidal central plan."

"And why is the term genocide so important to the Armenians?" I asked.

"Because they believe it is the truth," Fulya said. "They believe it is what actually happened. War and destruction is one thing. The attempt to eliminate an entire people from a country by killing and starvation is another. Tearing down their churches or turning them into mosques, destroying their villages, stealing all of their property, and ignoring their contributions to Turkish history are other parts of the process of cultural genocide that they believed happened then and is still happening today."

"That's why Hrant Dink got into so much trouble," Ashti said from the backseat, entering into the conversation. "He said the events of 1915 were genocide because the fact is that the Armenian nation that had lived on this land for 4,000 years suddenly vanished."

"Do you feel that Armenians want revenge and reparations for what happened?" I asked.

"Sure, some Armenians want revenge and reparations," Fulya answered. "Others even want a return of their property in Turkey or an expansion of the borders of Armenia to include much of the eastern part of our country. I believe that the vast majority, however, just want the truth to be recognized as a first step to reconciliation, renewed friendship, and mutual prosperity between Armenia and Turkey."

"They don't understand why the Turks cannot be like the Germans who recognize today the evil of their past leadership in trying to exterminate the Jews and other unwanted minorities," Ashti added. "The Germans moved on and are now respected leaders in the world."

"So what do you think is the solution?" I asked.

Fulya thought a minute and then said, "I believe that our government should admit to the terrible atrocities that were committed by our leaders and others against the Armenians and Syriacs in 1915 and then allow each individual to make up his or her own mind as to whether this was genocide or massacre. Calling what happened genocide certainly should not be illegal as it is now! A lot of evidence supports that view. Second, I believe that our government should then ask for forgiveness for the sins of our ancestors and for reconciliation with those who were terribly harmed in those times. I believe that while the return of property is no longer viable, that a substantial fund should be established by Turkey to help the new nation of Armenia and to facilitate the return of those Armenians and Syriacs who want to come back to Turkey. We should be helping them instead of impeding them as they seek to reestablish their own churches and schools in what was once their country as well as ours."

I pondered her answer and then asked, "And the Armenians? What do you think their attitude should be to all of this? Do you think there can ever be normal relations between Armenia and Turkey?"

"If our government asks for forgiveness, I would hope that the worldwide Armenian community would try to forgive us. If they cannot forgive our ancestors, maybe they can forgive us their grandchildren and great-grandchildren. I would also hope that they, as well as Russia, and the West would also admit and ask for forgiveness for the crimes they committed against us back then."

I turned to Ashti sitting in the back seat. "Do you agree?"

"I do," she answered. "I respect Hrant Dink just like Mother does. He was an Armenian but also a loyal citizen of Turkey. While he criticized Turkey, he also criticized the international Armenian community for trying so hard to humiliate Turkey with their constant lobbying to have foreign governments make statements recognizing and condemning the Armenian genocide. Dink wanted to recognize the truth but not to rub our modern Turkish faces in it. He wanted to move forward in a positive way and establish good relations between Armenia and Turkey and an open border between the two countries. He wanted to bridge the gap between us Islamized Armenians and those who maintained their Christianity. He was a peacemaker and that is what I would like to be too."

Fulya then turned on the motor, began to back out of the parking place, and then drove down the winding shaded road to the gate of the university. As she did so, she asked with an ironical smile on her face, "Now that we have solved the Armenia–Turkey problem, where should I leave you off?"

"What about the Gayrettepe subway station?" Ashti said. "It's the one nearest our apartment, and we can take the subway directly to Taksim Square from there." She then turned to me. "If you want, we can also stop to see the spot in Osmanbey where Hrant Dink was killed. It's a section of Istanbul with a sizable concentration of Armenians."

"I'd like that," I replied. "How many Armenians are now left in Turkey?"

"The most reliable estimates I've seen is around 70,000 with most of them living here in Istanbul," Ashti said. "But there are many more hidden Armenians like Father and me—some estimate as many as two million. They are Muslim Turks and Kurds with Armenian ancestors like Great-grandmother who were adopted into Muslim families and forced to convert to Islam."

"Most don't realize they are descendants, however, and probably would hide the fact even if they knew," Fulya added.

"You don't hide the fact, though." I said to Ashti.

"Of course not. Father and I are proud of our ancestry, but we have friends and relatives who would never want theirs revealed. They feel that doing so would put them and their children's future at risk."

"Why so?" I asked.

"They fear being discriminated against as non-Turks and as suspected Christians. As some say, 'Once an infidel, always an infidel!'"

CHAPTER 9

The Armenian Remnants

Within a few minutes of leaving the Bebek campus of the Bosphorous University, we arrived in front of the Gayrettepe Metro Station in a newer section of Istanbul surrounded by tall modern banks and company offices. As we got out of the car, Fulya said, "Call me on my cell phone to tell me what time you want me to be here to pick you up in the afternoon."

We thanked her, and then we descended on a series of escalators into the station, which impressed me with its cleanliness and modernity. Passing through the turn-style using Ashti's metro card, we were soon on our way to our first stop at Osmanbey where Hrant Dink was killed.

As we rode, I observed the other passengers in the car. Most seemed to me to be university students—young men and women in European dress. Some sat down, looking at their smart phones and typing messages with their thumbs, and others stood up hanging on to the bar to steady themselves with one hand and listening to music or talking to each other. Just as at Bosphorous University, none of the younger women wore scarves over their hair. In contrast, an older Muslim man with a bushy beard and wearing a skullcap and robe sat across the aisle fingering his chord of brown prayer beads and staring at me. The trip was a very short one and in two stops, we were at Osmanbey.

Coming out of the metro station at Osmanbey, I felt immediately the vibrant life of the neighborhood. Unlike the sterile banking and office center at Gayrettepe where we entered the metro, here people milled, window shopped, and sat in cafes talking animatedly. Cars and buses full of people passed by in the boulevard. Buildings of five or six stories lined the wide street on both sides making the area look like a European city.

"The Hrant Dink Foundation and Agos offices are just across the street," Ashti said, pointing to an older building a block up the boulevard on the other side. "Wait just a second, I want to get something before we cross."

She went to a flower stand nearby on the corner, and I watched her as she purchased one red rose. When she came back to where I was waiting, she explained, "Whenever I come here, I like to leave a flower in Hrant Dink's honor. He was a peacemaker."

We crossed the busy street at a stoplight and then walked up a block to the building where the Agos offices were located on an upper floor. In front of the entrance to the building embedded into the sidewalk was a simple black plaque marking the spot in Turkish and Armenian where Hrant Dink fell on January 19, 2007, shot and killed by an assassin.

I took out my digital camera and took two pictures of the plaque. While one woman stopped to watch me, all of the other pedestrians kept moving without even noticing the marker. Ashti then bent down, touching the head of her rose to the plaque and then leaving it a few feet away beside the steps to the building where it had a chance of surviving longer.

"Unfortunately, it is Saturday and the offices are closed today. Otherwise, I would suggest that we go up," Ashti said. She added, "One of the most moving moments in my life was when Father, Mother, and I joined around 200,000 other Turks, Kurds, and Armenians in 2007 for Hrant Dink's funeral. Muslims and Christians as well as non-believers filled all of these streets. Whether Turk or Armenian we held up little black signs saying 'We are Hrant Dink,' protesting the intolerance that led to his murder."

"What happened to the killer?" I asked.

"He was arrested. Some pictures of him caused outrage because after his arrest they showed him posing with smiling supportive policemen in front of a Turkish flag. But in the end he was sentenced to a long jail term," she said. "Also, posthumously, the charges against Hrant Dink for slandering the Turkish Nation were dropped by the government. Maybe, his death was a turning point for us."

I nodded and then took two more photos of the building and of the rose by the step. When Ashti saw that I was finished, she turned to head towards the entrance of the metro across the street and I followed. We descended once more underneath the earth and one stop later, we were at Taksim Square—the heart of modern day Istanbul.

The sky was overcast when we emerged, and the square was much as I remembered it from my student days in Istanbul—vast, busy, and dull. At its borders, tall hotels and office buildings stood separated from the square by wide traffic corridors filled with vehicles. The once modern but now abandoned Atatürk Cultural Center looked gloomily down upon the concrete open space and towards the Monument to the Revolution where a group of schoolchildren listened to their teacher explain its significance. The monument always seemed so modest to me when compared with the massive and ostentatious Atatürk Mausoleum in Ankara.

While the square was sterile overall because of the gray of the sky, the pavement, the buildings, and the avenues nearby, a huge red and white Turkish flag waving majestically above it all brought some pleasure to the eye. I also saw some color in the trees, the grass, and the flowers of the small park in the distance which ten months before had witnessed such bitter battles between demonstrators and the police. Now, as I looked around, I could see no political groups, signs and banners, or riot police anywhere. The most chaotic activity on the square was that of hundreds of pigeons rushing to peck at the corn being scattered for them by children with their parents.

"What happened to the demonstrators and the police?" I asked, surprised.

Ashti pointed to a long high metal wall at the western side of the square. "Some police are hidden over there with their water cannons, ready for action if needed. As for the demonstrators, they were all cleared out of here long ago."

I was disappointed as I was hoping for something more current for the article that I had promised my editor. Still, I took out my camera and made some pictures as we headed towards Geki Park, the small green space that was the initial focus of the demonstrations ten months before. "In your view, what were the reasons behind the confrontations?" I asked Ashti as we walked.

"Initially, they were to protect Geki Park from the government's plan to get rid of it and completely remake Taksim Square," she said. "Their project was to channel all the arteries of traffic in tunnels underneath the square, tear down Geki Park, and build a huge building based on the design of the Ottoman Military Barracks that used to be here until the 1930s. The building would house a shopping center, mosque, and maybe a theatre—the government was never clear as to just how it would be used.

"When the big machines started to uproot the trees, a few dozen environmentalists gathered here to stop them and protest the demolition of their beloved park. It was one of the few green spaces left in the city. The government sent in the police to evict them, but the demonstrators would not leave. They camped out in the park and started planting more trees. When people like us learned of what was happening, more and more of us started to join them."

"What made you personally decide to go?"

"At first, it was just the image on social media of peaceful demonstrators, people my own age, being gassed and waterhosed by the police for protecting a park. Afterwards, it became the authoritarianism and megalomania of a government ignoring the will of the people that kept most of us involved. Gradually, all types of Turkish citizens who felt persecuted by the high-handedness of the government—opposition political parties, feminists, secularists, ethnic minorities like Kurds and Armenians, homosexuals, religious minorities—came here to protest. We all wanted more trees and fewer shopping centers, but even more important than that, we wanted also the freedom to be who we are and to express our views. The protest spread to all of Istanbul and to cities throughout Turkey."

"Were you arrested?"

Ashti laughed. "No, a thousand were, but I wasn't. I was sprayed by water cannons and tear-gassed, though! My parents insisted that I not go to the camp city again after the police burned down the tents, but they allowed me to support the demonstrators in marches by beating pans, flickering lights at night, or handing out carnations to the police."

After we got to the park and sat down on a bench under one of scraggly trees, Ashti continued. "Never have I seen so much life and freedom in one place. People supporting this cause and that cause were everywhere. Demonstrators plastered the Atatürk Center with banners as they took over the abandoned building. We sang and danced and listened to speeches until the police came in with their water cannons and tear gas. As demonstrators retreated into neighboring streets, they built barricades of paving stones and trash bins to protect their positions from the police riot vehicles, but they were eventually unsuccessful."

I looked around to take in the scene now and imagine the past. In a nearby playground, children enjoyed themselves as their parents watched, city employees swept sidewalks, male retirees sat on benches talking to one another, and another group of high school students toured the park with a professor explaining the events of the year before. A few policemen, scattered here and there, observed what was going on."

"It looks like you won," I said. "The park is still here."

"Yes, the park is still here for now, but we are all still very concerned about the direction our beloved Turkey is going," Ashti said. "Can it be truly democratic and Islamic at the same time, or will we return to the time of autocratic rule and the repression of minorities and of individual freedoms?"

"What do you think?"

"I truly don't know," Ashti said. "So many conservative Muslims in Turkey support the government in its Islamization efforts and are fearful of the economic and social disorder that freedom often brings. To the government's credit, in recent years, Turkey has advanced greatly economically, and our people want that progress to continue."

"Would you mind if I quoted you in my article and took a picture of you for it?" I asked.

Ashti thought a moment before answering. "You know, my first reaction is to say 'Yes, I do mind,' because I fear getting on some government list as an enemy of the Turkish Nation. I am going to resist that fear, for if people like me do not stand up for the freedoms they believe in, then they might all be taken away. So yes, you can quote me and take my picture, although I don't think Father will be very pleased."

"Maybe, I won't use your last name or show your face too closely."

"Now that's a good cowardly compromise," Ashti replied laughing.

I got up and said, "We might as well move on as there's not much here to see anymore. I would like to visit the Armenian Patriarch's office next if that is possible."

"Your wish is my command," Ashti said as she got up and we headed back to the subway station. As we walked, she said, "One other bit of information that might be interesting to you about Taksim Square is its Armenian connections. This whole district of Istanbul used to be heavily populated by Armenian and Greek Orthodox Christians. As a matter of fact, well before this land under our feet ever became a park and a square, it was an Armenian cemetery, the largest non-Muslim cemetery in Istanbul."

"Fascinating," I said.

"But like most things Armenian, it was destroyed and covered up by the authorities in the years following the massacres. Numerous Armenian gravestones were discovered in the initial excavations for the government's development plans here."

"Can we see them?"

"They aren't here anymore. They've been taken to a museum to study," Asti replied. She then added, "Perhaps another fact you might find interesting is that every year on April 24, a Turkish human rights organization, DurDe, commemorates right here the Armenian genocide. One day they hope to build a permanent memorial here, but so far Turkish nationalist groups have vehemently opposed them and stopped any action."

As we got to the edge of the park, I convinced Ashti to let me take a picture of her hugging a tree with the Atatürk Center and the red and white Turkish flag in the background. I also took another one of her in front of the Memorial to the Revolution and got her to take one of me in front of it as well. I then brought a large pretzel from one of the food sellers near the metro entrance and split it with Ashti.

Afterwards, we descended the stairs to get on the funicular car from Taksim to Kabatas. From Kabatas, we took the sleek tramway that carried us over the modern Galata Bridge spanning the busy and beautiful Golden Horn bay into the heart of ancient Constantinople.

I had often come here during the six weeks I lived in Istanbul, visiting its many tourist sites. Here were the walls, cisterns, and commemorative monuments of the Byzantine capitol. Here was the glory of all

Christendom—Aya Sofya or Hagia Sophia Basilica, whose sheer size made one feel insignificant. Here were the splendid buildings of the Ottomans—the vast and luxurious Topkapi palace from which the caliphs ruled, the great Blue Mosque, the Islamic twin of its Christian sister nearby.

The history of Aya Sofya has reflected that of the nation from the time it was built in 537 A.D. First, as a magnificent Christian basilica, it served as the site for the crowning of Byzantine rulers and for other elaborate ceremonies. Later, in 1202 A.D., Latin soldiers of the Fourth Crusade looted it and the rest of Constantinople, and in 1453 A.D., the Ottomans conquered the city and transformed the glorious church into a mosque. In 1935, the secularizing Atatürk, the founder of the new Republic of Turkey, transformed it again into a museum. As the tram passed by it, I wondered what the future would be for the structure, so I asked Ashti what she thought.

"I really don't know," she answered. "Under the present prime minister, Turkey is becoming more Islamic, and more and more devout Muslims are calling for Aya Sofya to be turned once again into a mosque."

"I certainly hope not," I replied. "That would be just one more nail in the coffin of reconciliation."

Several stops later, we got off the tramway at Beyazit-Kapali in front of the labyrinth of the Grand Bazar where I had spent many hours as a student wandering among eating places, carpets, leather goods, beautiful clothing, finely worked decorative pieces and jewelry in silver, gold, and copper. This time, instead of visiting the bazaar, our destination was downhill towards the Sea of Marmara and the district of Kapali where the offices and church of the Armenian Patriarch of Turkey were located. This was a much poorer and older area of the vast city than where Ashti lived, and the streets were narrow and the houses and stores simpler and at times dilapidated. It was full of life, however, as cars, pedestrians, and pushcarts dodged each other in constricted transit corridors. Satellite dishes spotted the walls of the old constructions, many of which, Ashti pointed out, were built in an Armenian style with an extended room on the second floor overhanging the street. Clotheslines secured drying garments outside windows and sometimes even stretched to buildings across the street. Political banners were everywhere with pictures of candidates and little triangular flags in the colors of the many political parties. "Elections were last week," Ashti explained.

The Armenian Patriarch's headquarters was on a small unimpressive street that we had a difficult time locating even though Ashti had been there a couple of times in the past. In contrast to its neighborhood, the actual house and offices of the Patriarch were quite impressive—a three-story, dignified looking building with a white iron fence in front of it. Several policemen stood outside a white fiberglass guardhouse at the gate of its driveway smoking.

"Nowadays, police are assigned to guard Christian sites in Istanbul, as they are at risk for being defaced or of having worshippers harassed," Ashti explained.

Across the street from the Patriarch's headquarters was a high wall of stone. The tower of the Holy Mother of God Armenian Orthodox Church and the top floors of an Armenian school rose above the wall. A sign on the wall by the school still identified it as one of the voting locations for the national election the week before.

As the police across the street observed us, we entered the church compound through an open door in the wall. The only persons in view inside the courtyard were a woman in a glassed-in information center and ticket office and a stonemason repairing parts of the wall. Some blooms of tulips in flowerbeds in the courtyard and brightly colored posters advertising upcoming concerts cheered up the monotone brown of the area.

The woman in the ticket office smiled when she saw us and asked in Turkish if she could be of any help.

"I am Turk and my cousin is American," Ashti answered, "but we both have some Armenian blood in us. I have been here before, but my cousin hasn't. He wanted to see the church."

"Welcome," the woman greeted me in English. "When were you here last?" she asked Ashti in Turkish.

"About five years ago," Ashti said.

"Well, things have greatly changed since then with all of the restoration work. The sanctuaries are slowly regaining their former glory. Unfortunately the benches and carpets in Sourp Asdvadzadzin have been removed for the time being, and I apologize for the construction noise."

The woman, who appeared to be in her middle forties, went to a stand and got two brochures to give to us. "Just to orient you, the main cathedral,

Sourp Asdvadzadzin, the Holy Mother of God Church, is the building in front of you and is used for special Liturgies. The chapel to the right is for regular services. Since we don't have many Armenians living here anymore, it is also used for concerts for the general public. The ticket sales help with maintenance." She added, "Please come back and have some tea when you are finished visiting, and if you have any questions, I will try to answer them."

Ashti and I thanked her, and as we entered the Patriarchal church, Ashti repeated in English what the woman had said in Turkish, in case I had not understood it all. I was glad for that, because while I could easily follow simple conversations, I had more trouble when people spoke of subjects with which I was unfamiliar.

The Holy Mother of God Cathedral was indeed empty of its benches and rugs due to the renovation, but it was still beautiful. Several gold-painted chandeliers with hanging cylinders of glass, looking like weeping willow branches, dropped down from a high blue ceiling supported by blue and gold columns. Elaborate gold also was used in the altar, the pulpit, and the throne of the Patriarch but in much more modest ways than in the Catholic churches, which I remembered visiting in Italy, Spain, and southern Germany. We walked around, and as we did so, I took digital photos of the throne, the altar, the paintings, the chandeliers, and the tombs. When I finished, we went outside past some other tombs with Armenian carvings and then entered into the chapel-concert hall.

The interior of this building was also modestly impressive but less so than the Patriarchal church. It too had a long apse, but in contrast to the main church, it had furniture. Some 200 cushioned maroon chairs arranged in neat rows faced a marble table with a painted golden crucifix at the front. Behind the crucifix, a scarlet curtain hid the altar of the church. As I wandered around the chapel taking pictures from different angles of the soft blue and orange chapel, Ashti sat down on one of the chairs on the first row.

When I finished, I joined her on the chair beside her. The chapel was empty and silent except for the sound of the stone chiseling outside. I noticed that Ashti was staring intently at the crucifix, so I asked, "Did you ever think about re-converting to Christianity once you learned of your Armenian background?"

Ashti seemed surprised at the question. "Of course, I've thought of it, but I almost immediately reject the idea."

"For what reasons?"

"For all kind of reasons, it just makes no sense," Ashti said. "First of all, one either believes something or one doesn't. It has little to do with who your great-grandmother was or what your great-great-grandfather believed. It's who I am and what I believe that determines my religion and not who they were and what they believed."

"So, are you a convinced Muslim?" I asked, probing deeper.

Ashti laughed as she looked at me. "I'm not a totally convinced anything. I am a Muslim, because I was raised as a Muslim. I believe in Allah and I believe that Mohammed was Allah's Prophet. I believe in prayer, and I believe in almsgiving and other righteous signs of personal commitment to Allah. However, I don't believe in ridiculous clothing and food rules that have little or nothing to do with one's heart. I don't believe in the inequality of the sexes, of one rule for males and another rule for females."

She then looked back at the crucifix and added, "I also believe in Jesus as the Koran teaches—his virgin birth, his miracles, his teachings. While I don't believe that he died on the cross and resurrected and is Allah as Christians profess, I think he is the greatest man whoever existed. The truth is that I am much more attracted to him than to our own Prophet."

"What about him attracts you so much?"

"Everything about him inspires me—his life of self-sacrifice to Allah and to others, his power over sickness, nature, and even death and evil, his teachings on love, forgiveness, mercy, compassion, and humility. Most of all, I hope that Jesus' description of Allah as a loving Father is the ultimately true one. I want to worship Allah out of love instead of out of fear. I guess you might say that I am more a Sufi Muslim in my beliefs than Sunni or Shiite." She paused and then asked. "What about you?"

It was my turn to laugh. "I guess you might say that I'm an agnostic. That is the safest answer. I really cannot figure it all out. I depend on science to do that for me, but science itself seems to make so many mistakes. One day this is true, the next day that, but I do like the fact that at least, science is honest and tries its best. I guess you could say that I really believe that all will end in death. Allah has never revealed himself to me, but if I am wrong, then I desperately hope that Allah is good and merciful and will forgive me for my mistakes."

Ashti nodded in agreement and kept her eyes fixed on the large crucifix on the table in front of her and the symbol of a lamb on the blue ceiling above it. After a moment, she changed the subject. "Should we go get something to eat? I know of some excellent seafood restaurants nearby that aren't very expensive."

I looked at my watch and saw that it was a little past one. "Sure, I've seen most of what I wanted to see today, but if it is okay with you, I would like to ask the woman in the information booth some questions about the history of the Patriarchate that I don't understand. I'll need your help in translating."

"Of course."

We got up, and when we got back to the information office, the woman was still alone. No other tourists or worshippers were in sight. Ashti told her how much she had been impressed by the progress of the renovation since the last time she had visited and asked if the woman had time to answer a few questions that I wanted to ask.

"Certainly, but please come in first and have some tea." She motioned to some empty chairs by a wooden table.

Ashti thanked her, and we sat down as the woman went to another side table to pour hot tea from a thermos bottle into three gold-rimmed, tulip-shaped glasses that she took from a shelf. She brought them to the table together with a small dish of sugar cubes and tiny spoons. She then sat down.

"Thank you," I said in Turkish, but then quickly changed to English. "I'm writing a novel about Armenians in Turkey, but I really don't understand very well how the Armenian Patriarch relates to the remaining Armenians here and to the Turkish government. Is he just a religious figure or does he have some other function?"

Ashti translated my question into Turkish, and the woman nodded her head and then answered.

"As you probably know, Sultan Mehmet II conquered Constantinople and the Byzantines in 1453 A.D.," she began. "After that, he had to set up a system for governing his many non-Muslim subjects. Since most of them were Byzantine Orthodox, Armenian Orthodox, and Jews who were dihmmis or 'People of the Book' to be protected according to the tenets of Islam, he allowed each of these groups a certain degree of freedom to manage their own internal affairs. As these nations, or 'millets' as they were known, were based on religion and not ethnicity, a religious leader was put in charge of each and this leader reported directly to the Sultan. In 1461, the Sultan appointed the first Armenian Patriarch as the head of the Armenian millet, which was one of the largest in the land. Since then, there have been eighty-four Armenian Apostolic Orthodox Patriarchs. Later, other oriental Christian groups like the Syriacs and the Copts, who were at first subject to the Armenian Patriarch, gained the right to have their own administrations. The same was true for the Armenian Catholics and Protestants who later split off from the Apostolic Orthodox Church."

"How much freedom were the millets allowed?" I asked, after Ashti translated for me her answer.

"Each millet had its own legal and taxation system, but all were finally subject to Ottoman restrictions. Non-Muslims in the empire were definitely second-class citizens. For example, non-Muslims had to pay a special tax of 10% to the government called a 'jizya,' which Muslims did not have to pay. Also, any case involving a Muslim could not be handled in the millet courts, but had to be handled in the Muslim Ottoman courts according to Muslim Sharia law. Non-Muslims also had to wear certain types of clothing to identify which millet they belonged to, and they had to live in separate neighborhoods from Muslims and were restricted in the jobs they could have. While Christians could readily convert to Islam and escape the financial tax and other restrictions on their lives, Muslims could not convert to Christianity. Nor were Christians allowed to evangelize them."

Ashti added an aside in her translation for me. "All that is true, but probably less discrimination against Christians and Jews existed in the Ottoman Empire than against Muslims and Jews in the European nations at the time."

"What about now?" I asked the woman. "Are Armenians still second-class citizens in Turkey?"

I thought that the woman looked at Ashti and me with a little unease before she answered. "Things are so much better today. Our Patriarch is invited to government events, and as you can see, we are even getting help from the government to restore our church. We have more freedom now to speak our minds, and as you see, we can now have a few of our own schools to teach our language and culture. But we still face many problems."

"Like what?"

"It is impossible to get permission to build or open new churches or to evangelize and baptize Muslims. Another problem is that job opportunities for Christians in the government are severely limited. Also, while we can have our own directors of our schools, our assistant directors have to be ethnic Turks."

"Why is that?" I asked.

"I imagine it is to make sure that what we teach about Armenian and Turkish history follows the government's orientation," she answered. She took a sip of her tea and then continued. "Another problem is that our Patriarchs have to be Turkish citizens, yet the government doesn't allow us to have seminaries here to train our priests. This is not only a problem for us, but a much greater one for our Eastern Orthodox Christian brothers whose Patriarch Bartholomew lives here in Istanbul. He is not only the leader of Eastern Orthodox Christians in Turkey, but is the Ecumenical Patriarch of several hundred million Eastern Orthodox Christians of all nationalities around the world. If they and we have no seminaries to train Turkish Christians, where will our future Patriarchs come from? It seems as if the government wants active Christianity in Turkey to fade away. They want to preserve Christian sites as museums to draw tourists and their dollars, but don't seem to have much interest in making it easy for Christians to actively practice their faith here."

While Ashti was translating, her cell phone rang. She excused herself and went outside in the courtyard to answer it. As she took longer than expected, I finished my tea and used my limited Turkish to thank the woman for her hospitality and for taking the time to answer my questions. I also asked some basic questions about her family and discovered that she and her Armenian priest husband were both from Istanbul and that they had two children who attended the Armenian school next door. When she returned, Ashti looked flustered.

"Bad news?" I asked, as I got up from the table.

"Not good," Ashti replied. She then smiled at the woman and apologized in Turkish again for the call and having to leave so abruptly. She thanked her for the tea and for her information. The woman was very understanding and invited us back any time.

After we left the compound and got back to the street, Ashti stopped by the outside wall of the church and explained. "That was Mother calling telling me that we have a serious problem about our trip tomorrow."

"What kind of problem?" I asked.

"Father can't go with us. He has a production snag at the Bosch factory in Bursa involving software, and he has to fly to company headquarters in Gerlinger, Germany, tomorrow to try to resolve it. He fears he might have to spend a few days there and then next week at the factory in Bursa."

"That's unfortunate," I answered. "Maybe he could join us when the problems are resolved."

"There's more to it than just that," Ashti said with embarrassment. "If he can't go, he doesn't want me going either."

"I don't understand," I said.

"Father is very liberal in some things, but not in others," Ashti explained. "He doesn't think it is right for me as an unmarried female to travel alone with a male other than him." She paused. "Mother argued with him that you and I are relatives, but Father didn't agree that that was enough. He thought it would hurt my future chances of marriage, and his sister and her husband in Diyarbakir would be horrified if they saw us traveling and staying in the same hotels together. He wonders if you could delay your trip for a week or so. Maybe he could go then."

I did not know what to say, I was so taken aback. Finally, I mumbled, "I already have my return tickets, and they're non-refundable."

"Actually ours to Elazığ are, too," Ashti said. "Anyway, I can't wait as I only have these two weeks for my vacation so I couldn't put it off even if you could."

I just stared across the street at the Patriarch headquarters as if in a daze. "I guess the only solution is for me to go by myself," I said finally.

Ashti did not say anything for the moment, but I could tell that she was angry. "I'm so sorry," she finally said. "This is absurd. I am an adult woman. Mother and I will talk to him when he gets home this afternoon from Bursa, and we'll try to get him to change his mind." She then suggested that we go immediately back to the apartment to talk with her mother and wait for her father to get home.

After we walked back to tram and got on, Ashti called her mother again and purposefully spoke in English so that I could understand. She explained my situation and that I would lose too much time and money if I waited another week to go. She said that she could not wait either. It was not fair to ask me to wait she said as I had planned this trip for so long and was counting on them as translators in Turkish and Kurdish. Finally, she told her that we were on the way home and should get to the Gayrettepe station at a quarter past two in the afternoon, but that she would call her again when we got on the metro at Taksim.

"Mother said she would call him again and try to talk some sense into him," Ashti assured me as she ended the call.

CHAPTER 10

Dilovan Kaya

W hen we got to the Gayrettepe station, Fulya was waiting outside in her car for us. Driving back to the Kaya apartment, she told us that she had spoken again with her husband by phone and explained our inability to wait another week to start the trip. She had asked him to reconsider his refusal to let Ashti go alone with me as both she and his daughter thought his concerns were ridiculous.

Dilovan Kaya got back from Bursa at six in the evening. After greeting me with enthusiasm and lamenting his inability to go on the trip with me the next day, he suggested that just the two of us go out to eat to catch up. I agreed, and after Dilovan had taken a shower, we both went in Dilovan's Volkswagen Polo down the hill from the apartment to a restaurant on Arnautkoy Avenue bordering the Bosphorous. Being a Saturday evening, it was almost full, but the headwaiter who knew Dilovan, found us a table with a great view of the waterway and of the many private boats tied up to their moorings across the avenue.

During my six weeks with the Kayas, I had come to know Dilovan quite well, and I had always liked and respected him. Dilovan was a hard worker, and unlike many Turkish men, had an egalitarian attitude towards the women in his life—Fulya and Ashti. Frequently, I saw him help with the meals in the Kaya house, and he always respected their points of view on things, even when he disagreed with them. Dilovan had also impressed me with his love and care for his grandmother, Zara, and his key role in reuniting her with Karine after so many years apart. Now 64 years old, he was looking forward to retiring and spending more time pursuing his favorite hobbies of travel and language study.

After ordering some seafood and after some catching up on the Petrosians and on my research so far, Dilovan finally raised the problem that I knew was the reason for our eating alone without Fulya and Ashti. "I am really sorry that I have had to back out of this trip of yours," he began. "I was looking forward to it ever since you first suggested going. So was Ashti. Unfortunately, I'm in charge of the production of our washing machine line and a major glitch has occurred in our software that we have to get to the bottom of immediately. I've got meetings at company headquarters in Germany tomorrow night and may have to stay there or in Bursa for a week or so to get everything up and running again."

"I understand," I assured him, "but I really can't delay going as you suggested. I've got a tight schedule and limited finances."

"You were counting on us for translating, weren't you?" he asked.

"It certainly would have been useful," I answered. "My Turkish is really basic, and my Kurdish is nil. More important than even that, however, your historical, cultural, and political insights would have been valuable."

Dilovan shook his head acknowledging the truth of that. "Do you understand my reluctance to let Ashti and you travel alone together?"

I took a sip of the Efes beer I had ordered before answering. "At one level, yes," I said. "You are a Muslim father worried about appearances. You fear that your family and maybe your friends and even a future suitor of Ashti would question her modesty and this would damage her reputation and chances of being married."

Dilovan nodded affirmatively again, looking me straight in the eye.

"But at another level," I continued. "I don't understand. You call yourself a secular Muslim, and you are quite liberal on women's rights and minority rights and on dress and drink and all sorts of other things. I don't understand why all of a sudden you make such a big deal about this."

"Because Ashti is my daughter, my flesh and bones, that's why! She is not an idea or a cause or someone I don't care about!" Dilovan said.

"But she is also a very smart and mature adult woman who relishes her independence," I answered. "She is also my cousin, and you know me very well."

Dilovan laughed and took a drink of the water that he had ordered. "That's the problem. I know you, and me, and every other male, very well! I know that sometimes it seems that our brains are not located in our heads but much lower down." He paused and then continued. "The truth is that Ashti is a very beautiful and desirable woman. Don't deny it, I've got the watchful eyes of a father, and when you lived with us, I saw you look at her in ways that no brother or father or close relative ever would."

I knew that Dilovan was right, but I defended myself. "I would never intentionally hurt Ashti."

"I know that's true," Dilovan said. "But the problem of this trip together is that you might unintentionally hurt her by hurting her reputation."

"Neither you nor I can control what people think. And I doubt that Ashti wants to live her life based on that criteria," I reasoned. "You let her come to the United States alone while she was only nineteen. You let her study and find work as an independent woman. You even let her take part in demonstrations that could have turned violent and led to her arrest. You have been a wonderful father to her because you have believed in her and in the choices she makes. I don't understand why all of a sudden you don't want to continue to allow her that freedom."

"You don't understand because you have never been the father of a young unmarried daughter in a Muslim society."

The waiter then delivered the meals we had ordered. Dilovan had ordered levrek or sea bass and potatoes and I had requested shrimp scampi with butter sauce. We were silent as we began to eat. I finished off my beer but decided it would be unwise to order a second. Finally, Dilovan broke the silence.

"You know, both Ashti and Fulya are angry at me for all of this. They think that I am being a male chauvinist trying to control the life of a mature female who can make her own decisions. They say it shows that I don't trust Ashti."

"Or me," I added.

"Or you... So what do we do?" Dilovan pondered. "I don't want to mess up your and Ashti's trip. I know how useful she would be to you as a language and cultural interpreter, and I know that she has been looking forward to this for a long time and can't change her vacation time now. I love my daughter, and I guess that I need to show that by respecting her choices and not worry so much about what others might think."

I listened and felt for Dilovan as he struggled. I wanted to say "I totally agree with you!" but I held my tongue.

"I know that while you are attracted to Ashti, you also are very respectful of her and me and Fulya, and as you said, you would never do anything to intentionally hurt her or us," he added.

"That is true," I said. "I can give you my word on that."

"Will you also promise me the following: that you will not try to have sex with her or even sleep in the same hotel room with her on this trip?"

The question embarrassed me, and I nervously laughed, countering with a joke. "You know how cheap I am. To pay for two rooms instead of one will be heavy on the pocketbook."

"I'm serious. Will you promise?"

"Of course, I'll promise."

"Then I will give her my blessing to go with you tomorrow."

"Thank you!" I said, enthusiastically, reaching across the table to shake his hand.

"You're welcome," Dilovan replied, with a half-smile. "But remember that not only Allah is watching, but also a very protective father."

I laughed.

For the rest of the meal, Dilovan spoke no more about Ashti but answered my questions about his grandmother, Zara, and about Turkish politics, especially about the reasons for the government's opposition to President Assad of Syria and support for the now deposed President Morsi of Egypt. We also talked about Turkey's stymied efforts to join the European Union because of very different cultures and views on human rights issues.

It was about half-past eight when we got back to the apartment from the restaurant, and Fulya and Ashti were sitting in the living room reading. Dilovan motioned for me to sit down and after I did so, he announced, "Peter and I had a man-to-man talk in the restaurant, and based on his assurances that he would be sensitive to and protect the honor of Ashti, I have given my permission for Ashti to make the trip with him as his interpreter. I will call my sister to explain the situation."

Fulya smiled from the sofa where she was sitting and patted Ashti's leg. "It is a victory for women's rights! Thank you!"

Ashti got up from the sofa and kissed her father on the forehead, thanking him as well.

Dilovan was pleased. "But just be careful. Where you are going is a very conservative area and everyone is ready to jump to conclusions."

With this major decision behind us, we made plans for the next morning. We would get up early and have breakfast and then Fulya would take all three of us to Taksim Square. There we would take separate airport buses to our respective airports. Dilovan would fly to Stuttgart from the Atatürk Airport on the European side of the city, and Ashti and I would catch our flight to Elazığ from the Sabiha Gökçen Airport on the Asian side. We then said goodnight and returned to our rooms to pack.

When I got back to my room, I used Skype to call my mother in Asheville and was able to get her on her cell phone. It was early afternoon there, and she was on the way to take my half brother, Frank, to a doctor's appointment. Because of a car accident a few years earlier, Frank was now disabled and confined to a wheelchair. Mother now spent a lot of her time transporting him in the adapted van they had purchased to school and to other places that he needed to go. We talked for some fifteen minutes.

I then stayed up another two hours writing up the draft of an article on my visit to Taksim Square. My main focus was on the environmental issue since Asheville is a very environmentally conscious city, but I also related what Ashti had told me about Taksim's Armenian roots. With the article, I included a picture of myself at the Monument to the Revolution and a picture of Ashti hugging the tree. I did not mention her last name or that she was a relative. At midnight, I went to bed.

CHAPTER 11

Harput

Sunday morning, we were all up early as Dilovan's flight to Stuttgart left at 11:10 A.M. and Ashti's and my flight from Istanbul to Elazığ left at 11:45 A.M. All three of us needed to depart at least three hours earlier to get to our respective airports with plenty of time to check in. I had set my alarm for six in the morning so that I would be able to review my article for the Asheville paper before sending it in to the editor by e-mail. I worked on it for about an hour and sent it and then wrote a thank you e-mail to the Petrosians and copied the article to them.

After a quick breakfast, by a quarter to eight, we were all in Fulya's car with our bags heading to Taksim Square to catch our airport buses. Both of the buses left from the same side street near the square every fifteen minutes on a first-come, first-served basis. Because parking was so difficult, Fulya pulled up in the drop-off area of a hotel nearby and kissed both her husband and Ashti, telling them to call when they arrived. She gave me a motherly pat on the shoulder.

Fulya waved once more, and all three of us rolled or carried our bags down the sidewalk to the line of buses alongside the curb. When we got to the next bus leaving for the Sabiha Gökçen Airport, Dilovan waited with us until we got our receipts from the baggage attendant who loaded our bags underneath. Then, right before we boarded in the rear door, Dilovan embraced his daughter and handed her a roll of Turkish lira to put in her money belt. "So you can pay your own way," he said.

Ashti smiled at him in gratitude but shook her head. "Thank you, but I don't need it. I've got my own credit card and ATM card with plenty in my bank account to cover my expenses. Don't worry so much," she added still smiling, "It's going to be a great trip!" She hugged her father tightly and started to climb up the steps to the upper level.

"Don't forget to call your mother daily," he reminded her. "I will follow what is happening through her when I call home from Germany."

"I will." She turned once more and threw her father a kiss.

Dilovan then embraced me and looked at me half sternly. "I am entrusting her to you. Please realize that you are not in the United States. You are in Turkey, and what one culture accepts as normal, the other doesn't. And also, be sensitive, especially with my sister's family in Diyarbakir."

"I will," I promised. "Thanks so much for letting her go with me. It will make a huge difference to me."

After I got on the bus, Dilovan waited for me to get to the front window seat that Ashti had reserved for me. When he saw that we were situated, he waved once more and then went to catch his own bus up the street to the Atatürk Airport.

Within five more minutes of waiting, our bus was completely full. As I watched the other passengers arrive and board, it seemed to me that about a quarter of them were foreign tourists heading to the airport to catch their international charter flights home or to take the more inexpensive internal flights to the interior of Turkey. When the collector came by to get their ten liras for the bus journey, I started to pay for Ashti's as well as my own. Ashti shook her head and paid her own way.

After the bus left Taksim Square heading towards the Sabiha Gökçen Airport, it descended a street to the Bosphorus, and as it followed another avenue alongside it towards the Black Sea, it passed by the elaborate Dolmabahçe Palace that I recalled visiting when I was a student. This was the home of six Sultans, the administration center of the Ottoman Empire, and the final residence and office of Atatürk. This, in fact, was where he died. I was always struck by the irony that this national treasure was designed by a family of Armenian architects—the Balyans. I mentioned this to Ashti.

"Actually," she replied, "Armenian architects like them and Mimar Sinan, designed hundreds of other Ottoman public buildings, palaces, military academies and even famous mosques as well, not only here in Istanbul but also in the rest of the country."

We also passed near the restaurant where I had eaten the night before with Dilovan, and not long afterwards, we crossed over one of the two majestic suspension bridges linking the European part of Istanbul to the Asian part. Ships and private vessels spotted the blue water below us and few sights could be more striking than the city of Istanbul with its domes and minarets on both sides of this historic waterway. On the Asian side of the city, we got on a toll highway, beautifully landscaped with colorful flowers and green bushes laid out in intricate designs. Alongside this immaculate highway, I could see massive new developments that had sprouted up. Futuristic looking skyscrapers clustered together, new shopping centers, apartment buildings and mosques had been built recently, and they all showed the wealth, creativity, and expansion of the new Turkey.

Within an hour, we were at the Sabiha Gökçen International Airport, itself a sprawling modern facility with a curved canopy roof. After getting our bags from underneath the bus, we entered the vast central lobby filled with passengers heading this way and that. Our flight was on Pegasus Airlines, a low-priced carrier that charged an inexpensive fare but then added costs for food, baggage, special seating, and other privileges. Both Ashti and I were within the weight limits for our carry-ons, and the attendant assigned us two seats together.

After we had gone through the screening area and were settled in our appropriate waiting area, Ashti took out a book and began to read. I spent my time looking around at the different passengers already sitting there and imagining their stories. As far as I could make out by dress, bags, and features, I was the only foreigner on the flight heading towards Elazığ.

I also checked to see if the flight was on time on the airport electronic board over the check-in counter. It occurred to me as I did so that I had no idea who the woman was that the airport was named for, so I asked Ashti, "Who is Sabiha Gökçen?"

Ashti put down her book. "She was the adopted daughter of Atatürk, a sort of model of the modern secular woman that he wanted to promote in the new Republican Turkey. They named the airport after her because she was Turkey's, and maybe even the world's, first woman fighter pilot."

That surprised me, as I really knew very little about the private life of Atatürk.

Ashti then added, "There's something else interesting about her that's related to your research on Armenians in Turkey. Before Hrant Dink was assassinated, he wrote an article in *Agos*, his newspaper, that he had interviewed an Armenian woman who claimed to be a relative of Sabiha. She said that Sabiha was really an Armenian orphan whose parents had been killed in the genocide and that she had actually visited with some of her Armenian relatives in Beirut."

"Is that true?"

"I personally have no idea. From what I understand, Sabiha herself said that her birth parents were Turks. What is so disturbing, though, is the vehemence with which the claim that she was Armenian was dismissed by ultra-nationalists. Their prejudice against Armenians could be measured by the anger level in which they denied even the remote possibility that a national Turkish heroine might have Armenian blood. To them, such an assertion was close to sacrilege."

I nodded, and Ashti went back to her reading. Thirty minutes later, the airport announced the boarding for our flight to Elazığ.

When we finally got on the fully booked plane, Ashti insisted that I take the window seat, just as she had insisted on the bus. I was grateful, as I wanted to see Istanbul as the plane ascended into the sky as well as to lean against the window and catch up on some sleep. I was also glad that it was Ashti, and not I, who for much of the hour and a half flight, had to talk to the verbose woman in the aisle seat beside her.

I finally woke up when the pilot made the announcement that we were going to land in fifteen minutes. I slid open the window shade and looked out the window. It was a cloudless day and I could see clearly below me the brown broken terrain of Eastern Turkey with patches of green near the rivers and dams of the area. In the distance were some mountains with snow on their tops. I tried to identify in my mind exactly where we were from my frequent referrals to Google Earth in my planning of the trip. I could see to the left in front of us the sprawling city of Elazığ and southeast of it was Keban Lake, the biggest artificial lake in Turkey, fed by the Murat River, a source of the Euphrates. A little south of the city, on the other side of a mountain range, was a smaller lake that I thought must be Lake Hazar, the source of the Tigris. Both sources of these major rivers were only about fifty kilometers apart.

The airport terminal at Elazığ was small but modern with a flat roof and glass windows reaching up two stories high. Once we descended from the plane, we immediately went to the Europcar rental desk where I had reserved on the internet our vehicle for two weeks. I listed both myself and Ashti as drivers, and when Ashti showed her identification with a different name and nationality from mine, I thought that the male clerk smirked a bit.

The car we were assigned was a Renault Clio diesel with unlimited miles. After we had checked for dents and learned how to operate the GPS, Ashti, who was in the passenger seat, put into it the address of the hotel she had reserved, and we headed north towards it.

The city of Elazığ, the Mezire of Karine's narrative, was now a metropolis of 600,000 people and the boulevard that led from the airport to the center of town was impressive with its four lanes divided by a median with plants and flowers. It was a little after three o'clock when we arrived at the hotel.

Our rooms were in a moderately priced business hotel on the north side of Elazığ at the foot of the mountain where the town of Harput was located. Ashti had made the reservation for three nights for three persons in separate rooms, but the desk clerk was happy to cancel the third room without charge. After getting settled, we agreed to meet in the small lobby in fifteen minutes to begin our visit to Harput.

When we returned to the front desk, I asked for a map of the city and directions as to how to get to Harput and Hussenig. The two young clerks, one of Kurdish background and the other a Turk, had no idea where Hussenig was, but readily explained how to get to Harput. The road up to it was just a couple of blocks away. We thanked them, and Ashti and I went across the street to the vacant lot where we had parked our car. We then headed up the mountain to Harput, the town so intimately connected with the history of both of our families.

The road to Harput started near our hotel, just as the clerk had said. Turning onto it, we went past a large gendarme base with a stone statue of a soldier with his rifle near the entrance and guards at the gate behind sandbags. This was the first mention of gendarmes that I had seen in Turkey, and it immediately reconnected me with Karine's account of the deportation and to my great-grandfather, the gendarme rapist. What surprised me most about the base were the prominent guns and sandbags because I knew of no internal threats in Turkey now that the government was in dialogue with its Kurdish minority.

The drive up the mountain to Harput was lovely, and every now and then, we saw places provided for citizens to pull over, park, and have picnics at tables overlooking the city of Elazığ spread out on the plain below. When we reached the small town at the top of the mountain, the first building we saw looked like a new construction but built in the old Armenian style with second floor windows overhanging the street. There, we turned right and immediately saw a boutique hotel in the same style. Nearby was a park with children's recreational equipment, some restaurants, and a concrete monument of warrior on horseback with a large Turkish flag waving above it.

"Why don't we park here and ask someone at the hotel or restaurant if there is a tourist information kiosk or history museum where we can get some information?" I suggested.

Ashti agreed, and after we parked the car, we crossed the cobblestone street to the small hotel. The man at the desk welcomed us, and Ashti explained that we did not need a room but that we were looking for where the American Euphrates College used to be located in Harput.

The man at first thought they were talking about Firat or Euphrates University, the large public university of Elazığ, and told us that the main campus was down the mountain in Elazığ, although there were some university offices in Harput overlooking the Harput Fort. He told us that the only other college in the town was a madrasa for the teaching of the Islamic religion. None of these, though, were American or Armenian colleges.

"What about Christian churches?" I asked in Turkish. "Are there any in Harput?"

"Some ruins of churches are near the fort and one of them is being restored," he answered. "The main tourist attractions here are the 2,500 year old Harput Fort and some mosques and graves that date as far back as the twelfth century. You might also like to visit the Balak Ghazi monument up the hill. Next to it are some good restaurants with splendid views of Elazığ."

Ashti and I thanked him and decided to leave our car where it was and walk around the small town. First, however, I wanted to get my daypack out of the car with the pictures of old Harput and of the Euphrates College that Garabed had taken more than a hundred years before. I hoped that they would help orient us as to where we were in the modern town.

For the rest of the afternoon, we explored the town. Except for the Muslim monuments and mosques, the ancient fort, and a few collapsed stone, mud, and wood houses, old Harput was no more. In its place were some new public buildings built in the Armenian style of stone and wood windows jutting out from the top, and many large restaurants overlooking Elazığ. Some streets were lined with what looked to me like summer vacation homes.

What struck me most by our visit to Harput was that no one we talked to, from gendarmes to restaurant owners, from tourists to teachers at the madrasa knew anything about the old Euphrates College that had once dominated and served the town and region for more than fifty years. No maps that we saw showed where it was located, and we could find no historical markers or tourist bureaus where we could go to get information about it. Even the small museum of the town had been indefinitely closed. That meant that we had to try to locate the site of the former Euphrates College buildings by using Garabed's pictures.

I knew from my research at the Houghton Library in Cambridge that the buildings of Euphrates College were in Upper Harput at the top of the old town near a Muslim cemetery, and I knew also that the buildings had been taken over by the Turkish government. Given these two facts, I thought that the probable site of the college might be the gendarme headquarters in Harput and the mostly empty lots right above it. They were in a location that looked similar to the location of the college in the pictures that Garabed had taken. Supporting this theory was the fact that the lots were filled with rubble and the remains of old stone and wood houses that reflected the style of that time and they were not far from a major Muslim cemetery. I was not totally sure that I was right, but I took some pictures of the location and picked up some rubble hoping that it was from a former classroom where my great-great-grandfather Garabed Terzian had taught.

As I did so, I thought how sad it was for Turks, Armenians, and for me that this rubble was all that was left of an institution that had once touched so many lives. Not only had the majority of its Armenian teachers and pupils been wiped out in the executions and deportations of 1915, but also the traces of the houses where they had lived, the buildings where they had studied, and the churches where they had worshipped. Not only were they gone, but as far as I could tell from the people we met that afternoon, so was the memory of them in the minds of the local population.

Wanting to visit at least something that remained in Harput associated with our Armenian ancestors, I suggested to Ashti that we walk over to the Harput Castle and see it and the church that the desk clerk at the hotel said was being restored. Like most things in Harput, it was not far. She agreed.

Our first view of the Harput Castle or Fort was impressive. With its walls rising high above cliffs and canyons on three sides, it offered a formidable defensive position and a point from which it was easy to monitor the wide plains below where so many Armenian, Kurdish, and Turkish villages once thrived, watered by the Euphrates or Firat River.

When we got to the entrance of the fort, we were alone. No one was selling tickets, and the gate leading into the huge structure was open. Here, as well as at the mosques and tombs we had passed getting here, signs in Turkish and English explained the significance of the structure.

One metal sign explained that Urartians built the fort in the eighth century B.C. I remembered from my visit to the museum in Watertown that the Armenians considered the Urartians their ancestors, as they were initially from the region around Mount Ararat and Lake Van. Their early kingdom, which included much of eastern Turkey, formed the basis for later Armenian kingdoms.

The Urartians had dug a cistern in the limestone thirty meters down to supply the fort with water. While access was closed now, a hundred stone steps led down to it and to the cave beside it that was used for a prison. The fort was later conquered by the Byzantines and then by the Selucids, Artuquids, and Ottomans. I also learned that from 1122 to 1123 A.D, Barak Gazi, the Artuquid Muslim ruler of Harput and much of this area of Turkey at that time, had held hostage in the cave the Christian Crusader rulers, Baldwin II, the Latin King of Jerusalem, and Joscelin of Courtenay, the Count of Edessa.

The ground inside the fort was hilly and mostly barren, and at its highest point, a large Turkish flag waved proudly in the slight breeze. For a half-hour, Ashti and I walked around the rubble of former mosques, schools, homes, and soldiers quarters and read the rusty signs explaining what we were seeing. Then we went to the top of the ancient walls of the former fort to look down on the canyons on both sides and on the wide plain in front.

On the side of the fort facing Elazığ and the plain below, I stopped to take a closer look at a small community of tin roofs at the mouth of the canyon running up to the right side of the fort. I was excited and immediately exclaimed to Ashti, "I think that village down there is Hussenig where the Terzians lived." I took out my pages of Garabed's photographs and flipped through them and then came upon the one taken in front of the village facing the Harput Mountain and the fort high above. I showed it to Ashti. "See, we are here," I said, pointing to the wall of the fort. "And Hussenig is here," pointing to the village.

Ashti looked at the roofs below and back at the photograph. "I think you are right!"

"And that must be the trail that Garabed Terzian followed as he rode his mule up the mountain each day to teach at Euphrates." I pointed to the path starting from a rock barrier dam at the village far below, winding up the sides of the canyon until it reached the top of the mountain across the gully from us. "It couldn't have taken all that long to get to the college on horseback."

"Our hotel, I think is over there," Ashti said, indicating an area of the city to the right of the cluster of houses that we thought was Hussenig. "It looks to me that we could easily find our way there by going about a kilometer east off the Harput highway. When we run into that housing complex and park, we turn north." She pointed to a large green area with what looked like children's recreational equipment. "That should bring us to Hussenig."

I agreed. "It's too late today, but we could go there first thing in the morning." After taking pictures of the village and the trail up the canyon with my zoom, I added, "I'd also like to follow the trail up to Harput that Garabed took." I did not mention my reason to Ashti, but I wanted to look for the cave where Karine and her mother had hidden the Terzian Cross.

"I'll let you do that alone," Ashti said. "I could drive the car back up and meet you here in the parking lot of the fort, so you don't have to walk back."

"Great idea!"

We continued our walk around the ramparts of the old fort to its eastern wall. Looking down into the canyon, we could see scattered stones and several crumbling walls on the hills below and beyond us. I pulled out my folder of Garabed's photographs and compared the view to the one he had labeled "Syriac Quarter of Harput." It showed an area of densely packed houses clinging to the canyon on the other side of the fort from where the trail from Hussenig climbed to Harput. I was sure that his picture showed the very place I was looking at.

I showed the picture to Ashti and told her what I thought. "Maybe the church they are restoring is there." I pointed to a small courtyard set alongside the massive walls of the fort where two men were carrying a bag of cement down some stairs and a third was repairing a wall. "Why don't we go down and see if we can find it."

Ashti consented, and so we returned to the gate of the fort where we had entered and walked over to the eastern wall. On the way, we saw a sign indicating the 'Syriac Virgin Mary Church,' so we knew that we were right. Going down the steps to the courtyard that we had seen from the castle rampart above us, we passed one of the workers. Ashti asked him where the entrance to the church was. He pointed to a low rectangular stone structure against a blank stone wall decorated only with a mosaic of fish jumping and a bird flying under a symbol of the sun.

It was a strange entry to a church. First, we had to go down a few worn stone steps to a blue metal door, which thankfully was open. Then, we had to duck down, as the entrance was so low and tight. I actually felt like I was entering a building through a small refrigerator door. When we got inside the church, I was surprised to see that this really was an ancient worship center. I could make out a vaulted stone roof of great age, some dozen carpets covering small sections of the stone floor, and colorful images of saints and the virgin and child on the rough stone. The sanctuary inside was very dark as its only light sources were a high window near the altar and the light of simple chandeliers. In one corner, however, a spotlight illuminated a wall. Two men were working there, taking measurements.

One of them, middle-aged, nicely dressed, and obviously the person in charge, came over to us when he saw us and said in Turkish, "I'm sorry, the church is closed. We are doing restoration."

"Could we not just visit for a few minutes?" Ashti asked. "My cousin has come all the way from America. Our ancestors were from here."

The man hesitated for a couple of seconds, and then said, "Okay, but just for a few minutes."

We thanked him, and as we walked together with him towards the altar, Ashti asked him in Turkish, "How old is the church?"

"We have dated it back to 179 A.D.," the man replied. "It's one of the oldest churches of Christianity. It's now a world heritage site."

The building indeed looked to me like it could have been that old. In fact, parts of it appeared to have originally been a cave. "Are there still services?" Ashti asked.

"Only on special occasions. The Syriac Christian community in Elazığ is now tiny. A hundred years ago, it was a different story. This whole area of Harput was a thriving Syriac community."

"Can I take some pictures?" I asked.

"You can, but without a flash," he said. He followed behind us, as I took my photos. When I finished, we thanked him and he went back to work.

As we left through the small entrance that we had come through, I commented to Ashti, "The way to heaven truly is straight and narrow." She laughed. My guess was that the entrance had been designed this way by its original builders so that worshipers would have to bow low in humility as they entered or exited such a holy place.

Walking back to our car in upper Harput, I felt a great disappointment. Other than this church and perhaps the Harput Castle, where our family sometimes picnicked, nothing remained in today's Harput that linked Ashti and me to our relatives. In less than a hundred years, almost all traces of Euphrates College, other Armenian and Syriac buildings, and Christian cemeteries had disappeared. A people and culture that had once thrived here were no more.

We got back to our hotel at a quarter past six in the evening and had an early dinner in the hotel's restaurant. While the food was decent, the cigarette smoke and the stares of the businessmen in the restaurant made us feel uncomfortable. I imagined that they were curious as Ashti was the only female in the room, and we were the only ones speaking English.

Before going to our rooms, we asked for the Wi-Fi password of the hotel. I wanted to see if I had received any response from the editor of the Asheville paper to my article. Ashti, for her part, wanted to call her Mother and let her know about our first day of travel. Before saying goodnight, we agreed that we would meet for breakfast at eight and then visit Hussenig and look for the Terzian house there.

At ten o'clock, I turned off the lights and went to bed. I had checked my e-mail and had letters from Aram, from my mother, and from the editor of the Asheville paper. The latter said that he had received the article, had liked it, and would be publishing it in the next Sunday's edition. I was elated.

CHAPTER 12

Hussenig

On Monday morning at eight, Ashti and I met in the hotel's restaurant for breakfast and then left soon afterwards for what we thought was once the Armenian village of Hussenig at the bottom of Harput Mountain. We had little trouble finding it as we easily recognized the park where we were to turn left towards the mountain. After parking the car in what looked like a safe place, we went into a convenience store to make sure we were where we thought we were and to buy some small bottles of water.

After getting the water, Ashti asked the man behind the counter if this was the old Hussenig Village. After confirming that it was, he looked at her and then at me and asked in Turkish, "Are you descendants of people who used to live here?"

"We are, but how did you know?" Ashti replied.

"I heard you speaking English to each other when you came in, and the only foreign visitors we have ever gotten here was an American couple last year looking for their roots just like you." He smiled and stuck out his hand to me. "Welcome."

I shook it. Encouraged, I took the folder of Garabed's pictures out of my daypack. "Are there any houses left from that time a hundred years ago?" I showed him several of the pictures of the village that Garabed had taken, including the one showing the front of the Terzian house. "This was our great-great-grandfather's house. His name was Garabed Terzian. Do you think the house is still here?"

The man looked carefully at the picture and said, "Maybe." He looked again. "It looks like the house of the Ozan family. It's one of the oldest in the town, and the family has lived in it for several generations."

"How would we get there?" Ashti asked.

"Take the road next to the store and just follow it up the mountain about 200 meters. It is a house on the left, across the street from an old fountain. Next to it is a walled-in area for animals."

We thanked him for the information and then started to pay him for the bottles of water. He, however, refused to take it. "It is my gift to you," he said as he put his hand to his heart.

Expressing our gratitude once more, we left the store and turned up the narrow road paved with rectangular cement blocks. The street wound between simple houses in poor repair with unpainted, cracked mudwalls, rotting timber, and tin roofs. Clothes attached to lines along the walls facing the sun brought some color to them. A few houses had old cars in front but not many. The town, if it still was a town now and not just a neighborhood of Elazığ, was obviously old and poor.

When we got to the small square and the broken fountain that the storeowner had mentioned, we both were convinced that we had found the Terzian home. Except for its slanted tin roof and a newer addition on the ground floor, it had the same look as the photo with protruding second story windows held up by weathered wooden beams. Behind it was a waist-high wall of stones piled on top of each other. Within the wall's enclosure, ducks and chickens hunted for insects to eat and an ancient red car without tires sat rusting by a shed.

As we stood staring at the house and comparing it to the pictures, three young girls in school uniforms passed us in the street and started giggling. Ashti smiled back at them and greeted them. She then turned to me and asked, "Should we knock on the door and say who we are?"

"Of course," I said.

We crossed the street, and I knocked at the door. Someone pulled the white curtain in the window near the door and peeped out. Soon after, a barefoot woman wearing a long dress and a bright yellow covering over her head opened the door. She looked to me to be in her forties.

"I am sorry to disturb you," Ashti began in Turkish, "but my American cousin and I would like to ask you some questions about your house. We think that it once belonged to our great-great-grandfather."

The woman became flustered. "No, it is not this house. It has belonged to my husband's family for many generations," she replied.

I opened the file folder to the picture showing Garabed's parents standing in the same doorway that all three of us were standing in now. I pointed to the house and to the picture and said in Turkish, "Same house."

"It is our house, and it always has been," the woman repeated.

Ashti reassured her. "Oh, we know it is your house now, and we are certainly not trying to claim it. All we want to learn is its history since my cousin is writing a book about our family."

"My husband is not at home. Maybe you should come back later and talk to him."

As she started to close the door, I heard a man's voice in the background saying in Turkish. "Kismet, invite them in and offer them some tea. I want to talk with them."

The woman hesitated, but then opened the door and motioned us in with her head.

Ashti thanked her, and we both took off our shoes and left them right inside the door as we entered. The room was light, as the morning sun came through the white curtains. A white haired man sat barefoot and cross-legged on a worn Turkish rug fingering prayer beads in one hand in a corner of the room. He was leaning against some red pillows, and a tulip glass of tea was on a white plastic tray beside him.

"Please forgive me if I don't get up," he said. "I am an old man." He motioned for us to sit on a vinyl sofa facing a television set on the other side of the room. As we sat down, the woman went into a side room to get more tea. "And please pardon the lack of politeness of my daughter-in-law. It is true that my son is not here, but I am. It is our duty as Muslims to be gracious to guests. I am Ismet Ozan."

Ashti thanked him and introduced herself and me again. "My name is Ashti Kaya, and I live in Istanbul. This is my American cousin Peter

Johnson. Our great-great-grandparents were an Armenian couple named Garabed and Talitha Terzian who once lived in Hussenig and we think this might have been their house. My cousin is writing a book about them, and I am helping him as his interpreter. Do you know anything about the Terzians?"

The man smiled. "I know about them from my grandfather Haydar Ozan."

"Haydar?" I exclaimed excitedly when Ashti repeated what the man had said. "That was the name of the Turkish tenant farmer whom Talitha entrusted with the keys of the house and some of their valuables."

When Ashti translated what I had said, the man nodded. "Yes, my grandfather Haydar was the same man to whom your family entrusted this house. Your ancestor left a letter for him saying that he was to be in charge of the property. Because of that letter, our family was able to keep it all of these years. My grandfather Haydar told us the story of what had happened and said that one day you might return to reclaim your property."

"Oh no, we have no intention of reclaiming the property," Ashti assured him. "It has been almost a hundred years!"

"That is good to hear," the man said. He then added, "My grandfather kept for many years a violin and an etched copper table that your family left in his care. As children, we were never allowed to touch them."

"Do you still have them?" Ashti asked.

"No. After so many years of waiting for your return, I decided five years ago to donate them to the museum in town. My son and daughter-in-law wanted to sell them, but I thought that was wrong."

"Could we see them?" Ashti asked

"I imagine so," Ismet replied. "You would have to ask at the museum. It's now a part of Firat University."

After Ashti translated what Ismet had said, I pulled out my folder and went over to where he was sitting, kneeling down beside him on the rug to show him the pictures I had of the house and of the family. Ismet put on some old style glasses he had in a case in his shirt pocket and slowly looked at each one. I pointed out the copper tray in the family picture, and he nodded in recognition. "Yes, that is it." He then looked closely at the family picture and pointed to Lazar. "This must be Lazar," he observed. "My father, Ediz, told me stories about him. He and Lazar were the same age and they were friends. They would play together when your family came to visit the farm where our family lived."

"Lazar was murdered by a gendarme just a few days after leaving Hussenig," Ashti said.

"It was a horrible time," Ismet replied, shaking his head. "My grandfather and father were terribly ashamed, and so am I." Ismet then looked again at the photo taken of the Terzian family inside the house. "I think that the rug in the picture is this very rug," he said, pointing to the rug on which he was seated.

I looked at the swirl design featured in both and agreed, taking the picture over to show Ashti, still sitting on the divan.

"As it is the only thing left of your family here beside the house," Ismet said, "I would like for you to have it."

"Oh no," Ashti replied. "It was a gift to your family."

I said to Ashti in English, "I would like to get some pictures of it, though, and of him and of the house. This is fantastic!" Finally, I had found a bridge to our past.

After Ashti translated, Ismet smiled and said, "As you wish."

As I took my pictures, the daughter-in-law returned from the back room with three glasses of hot tea and sugar cubes. She was still reserved and quickly left the room again. Sipping the hot tea, we asked Ismet questions about what was left of the Armenian presence in the town.

"Some of the houses are still here," he replied, "but like this one, they've been modified some. Where we are sitting now used to be a storage area, but we made it into a sitting room as it was so hard for grandfather to climb the stairs when he got old. We also added a bedroom."

"Is there a cemetery or church in the town?" I asked.

"Not that I know of," he said.

"What about the path up the mountain to Harput?" I asked. "Garabed Terzian used to take it daily to teach at the college."

"It is still there as it always has been. It starts just a little way from here. Follow our street until you come to a little park and a small dam that was built to protect our houses from flash floods coming down the canyon from the mountain. The trail starts on the other side of the dam."

Finally, after about an hour together with Ismet, I suggested to Ashti that we leave so that I would have time to follow the trail up the mountain. We could then eat lunch in one of Harput's many restaurants and afterwards try to find the location of the former American Consulate in old Mezire and visit the museum to look for the Terzian violin and copper table. Ashti concurred, although she thought that the museum probably would be closed today because it was Monday.

As she stood up from the couch, Ashti spoke to Ismet for herself and for me. "We are so grateful to you for your hospitality and kindness to us today as well as for the integrity and loyalty that your family has shown to our ancestors." She got out a piece of paper and a pen from the bag she carried and wrote down her telephone and e-mail address and after giving them to Ismet, asked for his contact information. "We would love to keep in touch and send you copies of the pictures that Peter took today."

"I would like that," Ismet said. He then gave Ashti the information that she had requested, and she wrote it down. With some difficulty, he got up from where he was sitting and accompanied us to the door. "It has given me great pleasure to learn that some of the Terzian family survived those terrible years and that in your kindness, you are not wanting to reclaim our house. It has been in our family for such a long time."

The daughter-in-law was nowhere to be seen as we put our shoes back on and left, but I imagined that I caught sight of her staring at us from behind the flimsy curtains of the upstairs room.

Getting back to the car, I commented, "What a gentleman Ismet was, although his daughter-in-law certainly wasn't friendly."

"I'm sure that no matter what we said to reassure her, that she still fears losing her house," Ashti replied.

I looked at my watch, and it was ten-thirty. "Why don't you drive me to the start of the trail leading to Harput," I suggested. "We'll meet in the castle parking lot at noon and then have lunch."

Ashti agreed and got into the driver's seat. When we got to the trailhead at the dam, and I got out with my daypack, Ashti insisted that I take her bottle of water with me. "If the climb is hard, you might be glad to have a second bottle."

I thanked her.

"If you aren't there by 12:15, I'll start coming down the trail looking for you and yelling your name."

I smiled. "I'll be there!"

CHAPTER 13

The Treasure Hunt

After Ashti had driven off, I sat down on a boulder that was in the shade of one of the few trees in the area and unzipped my daypack. In one of the three folders I had inside it, I found the copy that Uncle Aram had given me in Watertown of the instructions my great-grandmother had provided for finding the Terzian silver cross. It was in her shaky handwriting but still very legible. This is what she said:

Instructions for finding the Terzian Cross

As a young girl, I used to play with my sister and friends in the big rocks and stream alongside the trail leading from Hussenig to Harput. Father would take his mule, leave our house when it was daylight, teach all day at Euphrates College in Harput and then return home in the early evening before dark. Sometimes I would go by myself or with Margarit to meet him on the trail coming down. While waiting for him, I explored the areas off the trail, and my friends and I had some favorite spots. One was sitting under a huge boulder held up like a roof of a cave near the stream where a small spring emerged from the ground. It was always cool there. Another place was higher up. A huge flat boulder leaned against a cliff and left just enough space for three or four of us to walk through to a grassy patch on the other side. My most favorite place, though, I shared with no one—not even Margarit. It was a small cave in the cliff wall to the right of the stream with its opening hidden by bushes so no one could see it from the trail. I found it while playing hide-and-seek with my friends. Though the cave and its entry were small, I could stand up inside. I could also look out through the branches of the bushes to the start of the trail from Harput to watch for Father. What I liked most about the spot was that I could see but not be seen. I hid my doll in a crevice in the back of the cave and often came to play and wait for Father when I was by myself.

When I heard Mother talking to Grandmother about the danger of hiding our family's cross in the cemetery as it might be dug up and found, I told her of my little cave where I was sure it would be safe. She asked me to show her where it was, so I took her there. She crawled in and after a little while returned with my doll. She said it was a good place. She put the cross wrapped in cloth where the doll had been and put some loose rock in the cranny to hide it even better. She told me never to forget where the cross was, as one day, we would want to retrieve it.

I never have forgotten, but at my age, I will never get back there to retrieve it. Maybe, you or Father Gregory can do so. To find the cross, you follow the trail for about 300 yards from Hussenig. You will see the big boulder cave over the spring that I just mentioned. On the other side of the boulder, you will climb a steep bank to a clump of bushes near the cliff. You will have to make your way through the bushes to find the entry. It is easy to orient yourself because my cave is directly below the corner of the closest outside wall of the Harput Fort to Hussenig. For a child, the entrance was already a tight squeeze, and for an adult it will be even tighter. Once you are inside, the cave widens and gets high enough so that even an adult could probably stand up. Mother hid the cross in the very back of the cave in a crevice. You will not be able to see the hiding place from the entrance, but if you feel with your fingers along the wall, you will come to the crack where it is hidden. Mother said that she put some pebbles on top of the cross to hide it even better, so just feel around.

If the cross is ever found, I want it to be given to Father Gregory as he, more than anyone, would know what to do with it.

I started up the trail to Harput, for that was all it was—a trail and not a road, not even wide enough for two people to walk on side-by-side. No one else was on it, but I kept my eyes peeled for any signs of people in the town or even high up in the fort of Harput who might be observing me. As I slowly climbed, I focused on the last wall of the Harput Fort high above the canyons. Underneath it was where I hoped to find the Terzian Cross.

It was a beautiful day and I tried to imagine what it was like in the old days. From the pictures Garabed had taken, the hills and canyons between Hussenig and Harput were once spotted with Syriac and Armenian houses. Now only briars, bushes, and stones remained.

I did not have to walk far before I recognized the boulder cave over the spring that Karine had mentioned in her instructions. It was to the right of the path and a trickle of spring water still emerged from underneath the heavy stone supported by another boulder. I slid down the gravel to the spot, and peeking underneath into the cool damp shade, I could almost see in my mind's eye the little girl Karine squatting on the dirt floor giggling with her sister, Margarit, and their friends.

I then climbed up the embankment on the other side, slipping back several times until I got to the clump of bushes some fifty yards higher at the base of the cliff. Although I was in reasonable shape, I felt the exertion from the steep incline and loose gravel. I looked around again to see if anyone was looking, but no one was in sight on the path or on the mountain. Because of the huge boulders and the jutting out of the cliff, I was unable to see Hussenig or be seen by anyone from there. Remembering Karine's instructions, I looked up high above my head and saw the last brick walls of Harput Castle built on the top of a sheer cliff. It was then that I was sure that I was in the right place.

Pushing my way carefully through the bushes, which thankfully did not have any spines, I came to a small open ground space in front of a cleft in the rock about four feet high and a foot and a half wide. "This is it!" I said to myself and perhaps to Karine and Aram, who had confided in me. I squatted down in the open space and looked up through the bushes to the top of the mountain where the trail from Harput to Hussenig started. I imagined that I saw Garabed Terzian starting to come down on his sure-footed mule after a long day of teaching, anxious to get home to his family. I then looked above and around me and was pleased, as it was impossible for others to see me in this secret spot.

I now turned my attention to the cave to see if I could get through the opening and how best to do it without getting stuck. If I could not, I had no plan B, other than to send Ashti or a child in. I took off my daypack and rummaged through it for my small headband flashlight. I then read once more Karine's instructions. Afterwards, I got on my knees, turned on my flashlight, and entered. Both my back and my shoulders touched the edges of the cave as I crawled through the narrow opening. If the entrance to the Virgin Mary Church the day before required humility, this entry required abjection!

Unfortunately, once I was halfway in, I realized something. *What if an animal were in there? I could be blocking its escape.* Not wanting to be clawed, I quickly backed out. I then looked for a long branch to poke into the cave, but finding none nearby, I picked up some small stones and threw them inside. I hoped to scare whatever was there and cause it to come out. I waited at the entrance listening for any sound of movement. Since I heard none, I gathered my courage and crawled inside again.

This time, when I got about two feet inside the cave, I saw that it widened and heightened just as Karine had said. I pulled over to one side and sat down with my back against the cool wall looking out the entrance. As my eyes adjusted to the dark, I was able to see what Karine said she saw, the top of the trail at Harput Mountain.

With my flashlight on, I then began to examine the cave walls, especially the back wall, some six feet away from me. At first glance, I could see nothing of interest, only the jagged rocks of the walls of the cave. I then scooted over to the back wall and started to run my hand over it looking for deep cracks where something as large as a doll or a cross could be hidden. In the first crack, I felt nothing, but in the second, I felt loose stones and pulled them out. I then reached in deeper and felt the softness of crumbled cloth and underneath it the hard smoothness of something. The moment that I realized that it was the cross, I let out a "Halleluia!" as fervent as could be delivered by the most convinced Christian. I do not think that I had ever felt so happy and fulfilled in my entire life! I just sat there for several minutes in the dark caressing the cross that I had discovered.

I decided I wanted to see the cross in the daylight so I turned around and squeezed out of the cave's entrance. When I got to the open space outside between the bushes and the cliff, I leaned against the cave entrance and examined my treasure. It was about a foot high and ten inches across and was made of heavy silver. Elaborately etched, two floral clovers of the Trinity were on each end of the crossbars. While I had no idea how much it might be worth for its silver, craftsmanship, and antiquity, I did know that it was priceless in its significance to me and to our family—especially to Father Gregory.

Taking the water bottles out of my daypack so that there would be space, I replaced them with the cross. I drank the water from the plastic bottles and then crunched them up to put them back inside the pack. I then took more pictures both inside and outside the cave.

The return trip through the bushes, down the slope, over the streambed, and up to the path took a few minutes. When I regained the trail, I took more pictures of the spot on the other side of the stream where I had found the cave. I then started up the mountain to the parking lot of Harput Castle to meet Ashti. I was smiling every step of the way and kept repeating, "Thank you, Lord; Thank you, Lord," even though I was not a believer. I had to thank someone!

When I finally got to the Harput Castle parking lot, I was ten minutes early. Despite the detour to find the cross, it had taken me only an hour and ten minutes to climb from Hussenig to Harput. For the most part, it had been a gradual climb other than the detour to the cave.

I immediately recognized our red rental car below the fort's imposing walls in the dirt parking lot. It was parked next to a pick-up truck. Ashti was standing near the pick-up talking to someone. As I drew closer, I recognized her companion as the man in charge of the Syriac Church restoration whom we had met the day before.

"You made it!" Ashti said when she looked up and saw me coming towards her. "But it looks like you rolled down one of the dirt banks," she added, as she saw the dirt on my clothes and shoes.

Because of the presence of the government official, I did not want to explain the real cause of the condition of my clothes. Instead, I sheepishly said, "I guess I slipped and fell a few times. The good news is that I didn't hurt anything."

Ashti nodded and then introduced me formally to the man standing beside her. "This is Mahir Yilmaz, the man who helped us yesterday at the church. He arrived here in the parking lot just as I did, and we have been talking about his work. It turns out he is employed by the museum at Firat University in their restoration department. I told him about the Terzian copper table and violin that Ismet donated, and he thinks he knows which copper table it is. They have it on display."

I shook Mahir's hand and thanked him again for allowing me to take photos of the church the day before.

"He also has volunteered to call the director of the museum to assist us if we want to visit this afternoon, but he wants to make sure that the copper table on display is the same one Ismet donated," Ashti said. "Could you show him the pictures that you have?"

I was unsure what to do. The picture was in a folder in my daypack but so was the cross. I dared not take the pack off my back and open it in front of them as they would see the cross and I would have to explain how I got it. Doing so in front of Mahir, I faced not only the risk of losing the cross, as it could be categorized as a national treasure, but also possible arrest, as I would be suspected of conspiring to take it out of the country. I had to take out the picture folder in a place where they would not be able to see the cross.

"Of course, but first let me put get some wipes from the car to clean up a bit. Could I have the car key?"

Ashti gave it to me but said, "I didn't know we had any wipes in the car."

I did not answer her but went quickly to the driver's side of the car, which fortunately was on the opposite side from where Ashti and Mahir were standing. I took off my pack carefully so that they could not see how heavy it was and then removed the folder of pictures from it and put it on the car roof. I then secretly withdrew the cross from the bag and slipped it under the driver's seat. Afterwards, I pretended to look for the wipes, which I knew weren't there. First, I looked in the container between the seats and then I opened the glove compartment. Finally, I looked under the seat. I shook my head in disappointment, closed the door, and locked it. Stooping down to look at myself in the side-mirror of the car, I ran my fingers through my sweaty hair and wiped my face with the front tail of my shirt, trying to make it look like getting cleaned up was the reason that I had gone over to the car. After I re-tucked my shirt into my pants, I retrieved the folder from the roof and came back to where Ashti and Mahir were waiting.

"I hope I look a little better now, but you were right about the wipes. I must have been mistaken." I then removed the picture of the copper table from the folder and showed it to Mahir. "This is it," I said in Turkish.

Mahir looked carefully at the designs on the table and said, "Yes, I'm sure that this is the one now on display in our museum."

"What about the violin? Have you ever seen it?" Ashti asked."

"No, but it may be in storage with thousands of other artifacts that were gathered years ago when the Keban and Karakaya dams were built. So many items haven't yet been catalogued—most of them much more ancient and valuable than a violin."

"Would it be possible to visit the museum this afternoon?" Ashti asked.

"Certainly. I'll call the director and tell them you are coming. What time?"

I looked at my watch and then at Ashti and said to her in English, "It's almost twelve, so why don't we have a bite to eat at one of the restaurants up here and then go to the hotel for me to clean up and change? Around two, we could visit the museum and then spend the rest of the afternoon in Elazığ? Would that be all right?"

"It sounds good to me." Ashti told Mahir of the time we expected to be at the museum.

"What about things to see in the rest of Elazığ?" I asked Mahir, beginning in Turkish but switching to English for Ashti to translate. "Is there anything left like the old American Consulate Building or the Missionary Hospital from 1915?"

"I know nothing of them," Mahir answered. "I'm aware of a few crumbling buildings in the center by the market, but most of the buildings from that time are mosques and tombs and one or two public buildings. Elazığ is a thoroughly modern city."

Ashti and I again thanked Mahir for his help and information, and he gave us his card. "If you need any more help, feel free to call," he said and then turned towards the Virgin Mary Church to return to his work there.

Ashti and I got in the car and headed up the road towards upper Harput with its restaurants that overlooked Elazığ. Once at the place where we had parked the day before, I found a spot at its edge, away from the other cars. As Ashti started to get out of the car, I placed my hand on her shoulder to stop her. "No, wait. First, I want to show you something. But promise me that you won't tell anyone about it yet, as it could get me into a lot of trouble."

Ashti gave me a curious look but said, "Okay, I promise."

I again looked around to see if anyone was watching. Seeing no one, I reached under the seat and pulled out the silver Terzian Cross, handing it to her. "Look what I found!"

Ashti was astounded as she took it in her hands. "I don't understand."

"Do you remember in Karine's memoirs of how she and her mother hid the family cross in a cave before starting their journey from Hussenig to America? Well, this is the cross," I explained. "Aram gave me Karine's directions as to how to find it. That's why I wanted to climb up the mountain—to look for it."

"But you never said anything to me about it."

"I didn't because I didn't want information to be getting out until I had found it."

Ashti looked at me as if her feelings were hurt. "You didn't trust me?"

I did not know how to answer that. "That's not the way I would put it," I said. "I just thought that the fewer people that knew about it the better. And anyway, I'm telling you now." I also explained my recent behavior in the parking lot. "And certainly, I didn't want Mahir to find out, as nice as he was to us. The government might try to take it away from us saying that the cross was a national treasure. It's our family's property, and I want to honor Karine's and Aram's request to give it to Gregory."

Ashti nodded and said, "I was wondering why you were acting so strangely back there at the fort."

"That's right."

Ashti looked at the cross again. "It's so beautiful. Look at the etchings on it." She lifted it. "And it is so heavy. It must be made of pure silver."

"I think it is."

Ashti thought a minute and then smiled, "Okay, I forgive you. You are probably right, the fewer people who know about it for right now the better. You need to keep it hidden until you can talk with Father Gregory—maybe locked in the car trunk. You certainly don't want to be carrying it around with you or even leaving it in your hotel room. Who knows if maids go through our things?"

We both looked at the cross again, admiring it. I then put it back into my daypack. Going to the back of the car, I popped the trunk and put it in the corner behind the car tool bag. After making sure the car was locked, we walked across the parking lot to the monument to Barak Ghazi—the hero of Harput, the Muslim conquerer of Latin Christian Crusaders in the twelfth century.

After taking some pictures of the rather amateurish concrete sculpture, we entered the restaurant alongside it. As it was not even a fourth full, we were able to get a choice table looking out from the mountain over Elazığ. In the far distance, we could make out the airport we had arrived in and the edge of the Keban Lake behind the dam. Beyond them was a mountain range.

I pointed it out to Ashti and what I thought was the deportation route that the Terzians and all the other Armenians from Hussenig were forced to take. "They left Hussenig under guard, walked across the plain to those mountains, crossed them, and then came to Lake Hazar. Then it was known as Lake Goeljuk," I explained. "That's where Lazar was killed and the Terzian women were raped. If we can finish here today in Elazığ, I would like to check out of our hotel tomorrow and find a place to stay near the lake to explore it more."

Ashti consented. "It's your trip. Whatever you want to do, I'm okay with it."

The waiter returned and took our orders. Ashti ordered a kebab while I ordered the Harput specialty that Susan Petrosian had introduced me to in Watertown. While we were waiting for our food, our conversation centered on my adventure in finding the cross, our good fortune in meeting Mahir and Ismet, and on the fear of Ismet's daughter-in-law that she would lose her house if we Terzians came back to claim it.

"Justice is hard to determine," Ashti said. "Yes, it was wrong to take property from the Armenians, but it is also wrong to take it away from people who had nothing to do with the crime, and who have been living on that property now for generations."

I added, "Muslims complain that the Jews took away their land in Palestine. That is true, but they forget to say that they took it away from the Christians before them. It is the same all over the world. We see our own ethnic or religious group as the victim but rarely as the aggressor."

CHAPTER 14

Elazığ

It was one o'clock when we got back to the car, and the first thing that I did was to open the trunk to make sure that the cross was still there. Now with such a treasure to protect, I felt very nervous. We then drove down the mountain back to our hotel, and each of us went to our rooms to clean up. A half-hour later, we met again in the lobby.

Ashti arrived before I did, and she had already talked with the desk clerk and found out how to get to Firat University and the Archeology and Ethnology Museum there. We went outside to the car, and I discretely wrapped the cross in a tee shirt and put it into a plastic laundry bag that I had brought from my room. It was good to get my daypack back for carrying other items.

We drove to Firat University and arrived right at two as we had earlier planned. The university was obviously new and very large, and the Museum of Ethnology and Archeology, a modest building, was located right at the gate. The museum was empty of visitors, but we did see a woman sitting at an information desk and a uniformed guard standing nearby. Ashti and I went over to her and introduced ourselves, and Ashti explained that Mahir Yilmaz had said he would call to the director about our desire to see one of their displays—an etched copper table that had belonged to our ancestors.

"We were expecting you," the woman at the desk said in Turkish. "If you can wait a few minutes, one of our directors would like to meet you. She dialed a few numbers and I heard her say, "The American is here."

The director appeared within a minute, a distinguished looking man with black hair and a moustache, dressed in a blue suit. He welcomed us in English but then switched to Turkish. "Mahir tells me that he met you in Harput and that it was your ancestors who once owned one of our treasured exhibits." He smiled. "I certainly hope that you only want a picture of it and not to take it back! That would be very complicated."

Ashti also smiled and replied, "Paying for all the legal work would probably cost more than the worth of the table. We would just like to see it, as it is a link with our personal history."

"Mahir said that you have a picture of it. Would you be willing to show it to me?"

"Of course," I replied, and reached into my daypack to once again show the picture.

He looked carefully at it. "Yes, it is the same table, I'm sure. Would you allow us to make copies of it to put beside the table in the display?"

"Of course," I said again.

"We would also appreciate if you would identify the people in the picture by name," he added.

"They were Talitha Terzian and her children Karine, Margarit, and Lazar. The person who took the picture was Garabed Terzian, a professor at the original Firat, or Euphrates College as they called it, in Harput."

"I know of its history," the director replied

"You do?" Ashti asked. "It seems that few others know of its history. In Harput we saw no historical plaques, and we could not even find anyone who could tell us where it was located."

"You are a Turk?" the director asked Ashti.

"I am a Turk with Kurdish, Syriac, and Armenian blood as well," Ashti answered. "I live in Istanbul."

"Then you know the dilemma we historians are in. The events of 1915 were a very painful part of our national history, and many Turks don't want to be reminded of them." He paused. "But I promise you, I will put the picture of your ancestors with their names and the fact that they were

Armenians besides the copper table in the display. I will also note that your ancestor taught in the original Firat College, an American Christian college in Harput."

Ashti translated for me in case I did not understand what the director had said, and we both thanked him. The director then gave my picture to the woman at the desk to make copies, and he wrote down on another piece of paper the correct spellings of the Terzian family names that I gave to him. He then suggested that we go see the copper table for ourselves.

As we walked through the museum, we passed tastefully arranged exhibits, mostly in glass cases on two floors. In the archeology section, I noticed memorial stones written in Cuneform and Latin dating from Hittite and Roman times, as well as displays of ancient cylinder and stamp seals. The Ethnology Room contained displays of jewelry, clothing, weapons, kitchen and household items of pottery and copper. Several period displays showed mannequins weaving, cooking, and resting on a divan.

The Terzian copper table was in a glass case by itself, and I instantly recognized it by its six circles of fine etchings. I really wanted to take it out of its case to pick it up and feel its weight, but I was reluctant to ask for permission. Instead, I just took numerous photos of it. When the director offered to use my camera to take pictures of Ashti and me beside it, I accepted. He then invited us into his office to have some tea. That offer we also accepted.

After the tea, the director gave us our photo back as well as his calling card and promised that he would take a picture of the copper table with the names of the Terzians printed beside it and send it to us. We both gave him our addresses and e-mails.

While Ashti continued to talk with him about her own family history, which seemed to fascinate him, I walked back to the display one more time. Standing alone there, I tried to see in my mind's eye Garabed and Talitha Terzian and their three children sitting around the table on the second floor of the Hussenig house with the cross on the wall behind them. I was so glad that in one day that we had found the Terzian house, Ismet Ozan, and both of these precious items. They all were bridges to my past.

Returning to where Ashti and the director were talking, with Ashti's help, I got directions to how to get to the oldest part of Elazığ, the old

Mezire, where the American Consulate and the hospital had been located. We thanked the director again for his receiving us so well and asked him to pass on our thanks to Mahir. We then left for the downtown of Elazığ.

I was very impressed with Elazığ. Modern and dynamic with well-kept boulevards and prosperous apartment buildings, it was a model city for the confident new Turkey. As we got closer to the old center of the town, the streets became narrower and parking was harder to find. Finally, Ashti suggested that we leave the car at a parking lot and walk around for a while to get a feel for the place. I felt a little uneasy handing the keys to the parking lot caretaker because of the cross, but Ashti quieted my fears.

For about an hour, we took in the vibrant life of the city, walking in the parks, observing the old men sitting on benches, and the middle-aged businessmen having their shoes shined. We meandered through the old markets with their many fruit and vegetable stands and clothing shops. We became part of the pedestrian flow of office workers and shopkeepers on the main thoroughfares, hurrying past imposing banks and office buildings, hotels, and restaurants. No one whom Ashti asked had ever heard of the former American Hospital and Consulate buildings in the town, but we did discover two streets with the ruins of clay brick and wooden buildings that we both felt were surely from the time of our ancestors. I took more pictures and wondered if one of the houses that I snapped had been the house or the store of my Syriac relatives.

At six o'clock, we got something light to eat on the street and then returned to get our car, and the first thing I checked was the cross in the back. It was still there. When we got back to the hotel, we told the day manager that we had decided to cut our stay short by one day so that we could spend more time visiting Lake Hazar. In preparation, I gave Ashti the book of the American Consul to read before going to bed, and then I went back to my own room to write down my impressions of the last two days and to check my e-mail.

CHAPTER 15

Lake Hazar

At breakfast the next morning in the hotel's restaurant, Ashti filled me in on what was happening with her family. Dilovan was going to be stuck for at least three more days in Germany dealing with the software problem. On the other hand, her mother's conference at the university was going quite well.

Ashti said that she had recounted everything that had happened to us in Elazığ and Harput, except for the most important—the discovery of the cross. "I understand your concerns about too many people knowing about it, but I still feel badly about not being allowed to confide in my own mother!"

After paying separately for our rooms with our credit cards, we left the hotel around nine o'clock. I put our two bags in the trunk of the car after again making sure the cross was still there. As I wanted to follow the entire deportation route of the Terzian family to Mardin, with Ashti's approval, I drove back to the square in Hussenig near the convenience store and parked. I then typed Lake Hazar into the car's GPS and discovered that it was twenty-four kilometers from the square.

The night before, I had looked up on the internet any information that I could find about Lake Hazar, or Lake Goeljuk as Karine and Talitha knew it. It was a rift lake, twenty-two kilometers long and six kilometers wide, whose waters were always clear because of a lack of sodium. Its most important characteristic was that it was the source of the famous Tigris River. I also discovered several possibilities of accommodation at hotels on its shore.

After navigating through the streets of Elazığ, we got on the boulevard that connected the city to the airport and which then became a four-lane highway heading straight towards the mountains and lake. There, the highway continued along its northern shore towards Diyarbakir.

"This must have been the same deportation route that the Terzians followed," I commented to Ashti. "It probably was not too bad at first. The land is flat, they had food, and they rode in an oxcart and on a mule. Also, they knew nothing yet of the nightmares that awaited them."

"Speaking of nightmares, I had them last night after reading the book you gave me," Ashti said. "It took me to midnight, but I finished it. As a Turk and a Kurd, it is horrifying to think that what Davis recounted was actually true."

"Do you doubt him?"

Ashti thought a minute before she responded. "Leslie Davis was an American Consul and a Christian, and so I imagine that those characteristics influenced his opinions. But on the other hand, he seemed very honest and factual, and he recounted only what he himself saw."

"Which was horrifying!" I said.

"Yes, especially around Lake Hazar, or Lake Goeljuk as he called it."

Leslie Davis's book, *The Slaughter House Province, An American Consul's Report*, gave a firsthand account of the terrible events that took place in Mezire and Harput and the rest of southeastern Turkey from 1914 to 1917 when Davis was the American Consul in the region. Davis had been assigned to this isolated outpost in Turkey to look after the interests of the hundred or so American missionaries working in schools, hospitals, and orphanages in the area and the business interests of American companies like Singer Sewing Machines. He was also there to facilitate the comings and goings to and from the United States of the many Armenians and Syriacs who had emigrated there after the massacres of 1895 and become citizens or had gone there to work or study. Garabed Terzian had been one of the latter.

Living and working behind the imposing walls of the large American Consulate in Mezire, Davis was in a unique position to observe and report the details of what was happening in the Province. Because of his status as the representative of a then friendly country, he had both official and social contacts with the highest Turkish authorities in the region and was often able to intervene with them personally to protect the lives of Armenian-Americans or those related to them. A risk-taker and humanist, he hid as many as eighty Armenians in the consulate helping some of them to escape northeast through the mountains to Russia with the help of sympathetic Kurdish tribes.

Davis was also a horseman and outdoorsman, and he often rode with his bodyguard to visit neighboring Armenian villages and the camps of Armenian deportees on their way to the Syrian Desert. There, he saw first-hand the destruction and misery that they faced. He reported to the American Embassy in Constantinople what he had seen—dying women and children, thousands of unburied, rotting, and stacked bodies of Armenians he had come upon, and the destroyed houses and churches of the villages he had visited. These reports were important catalysts to galvanizing international support for the few Armenians who survived and made it to safety. He even accompanied his reports with some photographs.

Ashti pulled out the book from her bag and flipped through it its pages until she came to the place she was looking for. "This is part of his report of his ride around Lake Hazar with Dr. Atkinson, the doctor at the American hospital in Mezire. It's on page 87. It was particularly upsetting to me." She read it aloud as I drove.

> We estimated that in the course of our ride around the lake, and actually within the space of twenty-four hours, we had seen the remains of not less than ten thousand Armenians who had been killed around Lake Goeljuk. This, of course, is approximate, as some of them were only the bones of those who had perished several months before, from which the flesh had entirely disappeared, while in other case the corpses were so fresh that they were all swollen up and the odor from them showed that they had been killed only a few days before. I am sure, however, that there were more, rather than less, than that number; and it is probable that

the remains which we saw were only a small portion of the total number in that vicinity. In fact, on my subsequent rides in the direction of Lake Goeljuk I nearly always discovered skeletons and bones in great numbers in the new places that I visited, even as recently as a few weeks before I left Harput.

Few localities could be better suited to the fiendish purposes of the Turks in their plan to exterminate the Armenian population than this peaceful lake in the interior of Asiatic Turkey, with its precipitous banks and pocket-like valleys, surrounded by villages of savage Kurds and far removed from the sight of civilized man. This, perhaps, was the reason why so many exiles from distant vilayets were brought in safety as far as Mamouret-ul-Aziz and then massacred in the "Slaughterhouse Vilayet" of Turkey. That which took place around beautiful Lake Goeljuk in the summer of 1915 is almost inconceivable. Thousands and thousands of Armenians, mostly innocent and helpless women and children, were butchered on its shores and barbarously mutilated.

Ashti put down the book and looked outside as if contemplating something. We had begun to ascend the mountain on the Elazığ side of Lake Hazar. To our left was a small farming village of mud brick houses on the hill with a gravel road from the highway leading to it. "I wonder if that was one of the 'villages of savage Kurds,' Davis talked about?" she said. "It is painful to hear phrases like 'savage Kurds,' or 'fiendish purposes of the Turks' written about your own people."

I nodded in agreement. "I know what you mean."

Just about a kilometer farther on as the highway rounded the mountain, we had our first view of Lake Hazar from its western most edge—a deep blue body of water stretching out between mostly barren mountains on either side. Snow peaks glistened in the sun on the southern side of the lake. I wanted to take a photograph of this beautiful scene, so I pulled over to the side of the road and got out. It was the first of many such stops for taking pictures that I would make on our way to Mardin, and Ashti was always patient with me.

Getting back into the car and descending the mountain towards the lake, I saw that the highway split. One road led to a small town called Sivrice at the western end of the lake while the main highway continued left along the lake's northern edge towards Diyarbakir. This would be the route that the Terzian's would have taken, so we followed it.

"As I said yesterday, I would like to find a hotel on the lake and use it as a base for exploring the area," I suggested. "So many important and horrible things happened here to our family. We have the time as we aren't due at our hotel in Diyarbakir until tomorrow."

"It's your trip," Ashti replied. "Except for its past history, the lake is a beautiful place to stay."

Nothing in the guidebook that I was using, mentioned either Elazığ or Lake Hazar, as neither were on the normal routes of international tourists in Turkey. However, it was easy to see that Lake Hazar was a favorite place of middle-class Turks wanting to spend their vacations with a beautiful view and enjoy water sports. Clusters of hundreds of mostly identical vacation villas in residential developments spotted the hills on this side of the lake. As it was not yet summer, almost all of the houses looked empty. So did the lake. We could see no boats or swimmers. Most of the hotels and restaurants we passed on its shores also seemed empty, but a particularly nice one, with a couple of cars parked in front of it, drew my attention. I turned into its driveway to see if it was open.

Ashti and I both got out of the car to look it over. We climbed the steps to a reception area attached to a large lobby with sofas and chairs. No one was at the desk, but a well-dressed man in a suit sat in the lobby reading a newspaper and smoking a cigarette. I saw a bell on the counter and so pressed it, and within a few seconds, a young thin man with a white shirt and a tie came out of an office and greeted us.

"What is your price for a room for one night?" I asked in Turkish.

"Ninety lira for one person and a hundred forty for two," he responded. "It's our off-season rate and includes breakfast and Wi-Fi."

I turned to Ashti and asked her in English if that was all right, and she responded, "A little expensive but doable."

"Are you British?" the man asked in English.

"No, I'm American and she is Turk," I responded.

"Welcome! Would you prefer a double bed or two singles?"

"Actually, we would like two separate single rooms," I answered. "We are cousins."

The man seemed surprised, but he nodded and asked us for our documents. We gave them to him, and after we had filled out the forms and given him our credit cards, we went back to the car to get our luggage. The desk clerk called a young man from the restaurant to help us and show us to our rooms, which were on the second floor next to each other. Each room had its own bathroom, a TV, refrigerator, and a balcony looking out over the lake to the snow-covered mountains on the other side.

After we were settled, I returned to the desk where I had agreed to meet Ashti. Assuring the young clerk that the rooms were fine, I asked in English, "My cousin and I are interested in seeing any sights in the area related to Armenians. Are there any old villages, churches, museums, or historical markers around the lake associated with them?"

"Armenians? I'm not sure what you mean," the clerk answered. "I've only been here a short time."

The man, sitting in the chair in the lobby, was obviously listening to our conversation, as he put down his paper, snuffed out his cigarette, got up and came over. He stuck out his hand and introduced himself to me in English. "I'm Bayar Demirci, the owner of the hotel. I understand you are American. I lived in the States for almost a year in Carlisle, Pennsylvania, when I was an officer in the Turkish military. We don't get many Americans here, so welcome."

"Thank you."

"I couldn't help but overhear your question about Armenians. May I ask why you are interested?"

"We are curious because my cousin and I are descendants of Armenians from Harput. They said that they used to come here in the summer to the lake to camp and picnic across from an island with the ruins of an old Armenian church and monastery. We would like to see the spot."

"Actually, it might have been here or near here that they camped. You can see the island right across the lake. As for the church, all that remains there now are stones. Some say they are from an ancient town now under the water, some say they are from a fort, and others claim they are from what you say is a church."

"Could we get a boat to visit it today?" I asked.

"It would be hard on such short notice. This is off-season and most of the boat operators are closed down."

"Is there anything else around here that is Armenian?" I asked. "Remains of villages, churches, or graveyards? Are there any museums or markers that memorialize the thousands of Armenians who were killed here?"

"Where did you hear that from?" the hotel owner asked me. His tone changed and took on a slight edge.

"From the reports of the American Consul at Harput in 1915, who saw the bodies and the bones. He said they were scattered in the mountain gullies and on the beaches of the lake."

"He must have exaggerated what he saw. You Americans have always been friends and protectors of the Armenians, even back then." His voice now took on a tone of anger. "No massacres happened here, and therefore we have no markers or museums to commemorate them. Lake Hazar has always been and always will be a beautiful and peaceful place for families and sports. Like you said, this was a place where your ancestors came to relax and have fun."

At that moment, Ashti came down from her room with a small bag and entered the reception area. I introduced her in English. "This is Mr. Bayar Demirci, the owner of the hotel. He studied in the United States as a Turkish military officer and speaks good English."

Mr. Demirci bowed in acknowledgement.

"He says that the camping spot Karine talked about in her memoirs might have been here or near here," I added.

"Good," Ashti replied.

"But other than the island across the lake, which might have been the site of an Armenian church and monastery, there's nothing else Armenian to see. He says that no massacres of Armenians happened here and so there are no historical markers to remember them."

I then turned to Mr. Demirci. "I believe otherwise. One of our relatives was killed here at the lake, and three of our ancestors were raped here. We know that to be true."

"By Kurdish bandits that used to roam here, I imagine."

"No, by the Turkish gendarmes who were supposed to protect them," I said.

Ashti gave me a warning look and I held myself in check, surprised at my own combativeness.

Mr. Demirci said nothing for a minute, and then he changed to a much more conciliatory tone of voice, "I'm sorry. I should not be talking like this. You are my honored guests. Maybe it is true that some awful things happened here back then. We Turks were at war with the Russians, and the Armenians in this part of the country were Russian allies. We had to deport them out of the war zone to protect our nation. Some passed by here and died in the march from disease or attacks by Kurds. Some were raped by misguided soldiers. But no large-scale intentional massacres by the government ever occured. Such things just did not happen."

This time I said nothing in response, not wanting the unpleasantness of having an argument with the owner of the hotel.

Mr. Demirci continued, though, in his argument. "And even if some ugly things happened a hundred years ago, why should we still dwell on them now? The past is the past. Look around you at all the beauty of this place, the vacation homes, the hotels, the restaurants. This is the reality of today. Your bringing up such images of the past could destroy all of this. Why would you want to do that?"

"We don't." Ashti spoke for the first time. She was polite but firm. "Like you, I'm a Turk, and I love my country. Yet, I don't think that recognizing an historical truth would destroy this place. Instead, establishing a monument here to what happened in the past might actually bring more visitors to the lake instead of fewer."

"That's easy for you to say because you don't have your life savings invested here in this hotel like I do."

"That's true. I don't. But the fact is that my cousin and I came here not to see the beautiful lake and enjoy water sports but to connect to the histories of our ancestors. Others are just like us. You could reach out to them, research the history of the area, conduct tours of sites, and sponsor symposiums for them." She reached into her bag and pulled out a business card, giving it to him. "I'm hoping to set up such historical tours in the future myself. Maybe we could do some things together."

Mr. Demirci took the card and looked at it and then went to the desk and got his own to give to her and to me. "Maybe you are right, but I doubt it. Still, I wish you a good stay here. Even though we don't have a lot of guests right now, in the summer we are always full. And even in the winter, we get a few skiers for the mountains on the other side of the lake."

"Is your restaurant open for dinner?" Ashti asked.

"For breakfast, lunch, and dinner," he replied. "And if you are hungry now, we can fix you something."

"No, we just had a big breakfast, but we will plan to have tonight's meal here," I said. "I think we will just explore the area for the rest of the day. Is there a way to get to the top of the mountains so we can get a view of the whole lake?"

"About three kilometers up the highway to the left is a winding dirt road that will take you to the top. You can see both the Keban Dam Lake from there, as well as Lake Hazar. It's one of the old roads to Elazığ and passes through a couple of Kurdish villages on the way."

"Are there any stores near here where we could get some food and water for a picnic?" Ashti inquired.

"The nearest ones would be in Sivrice about ten kilometers from here, but you don't need to go there. We can supply you with all the food you need from our kitchen."

"That would be great. Maybe some bread and cheese and a couple of bottles of water," I said.

Mr. Demirci gave an order to the desk clerk whom he called Tahir to go back to the kitchen and to bring two bag lunches with some bread, water, cheese and bologna with some fruit and water bottles. When Tahir came back and gave us the bags, I reached for my wallet to get the money to pay. The hotel owner refused to take it. "The rooms and the meal tonight you will pay, but this is a gift."

Considering our somewhat heated exchange a little earlier, both Ashti and I were grateful, and we thanked him for his generosity.

It was a little past eleven when we got back into our car. We decided that what we would both like to do was to find the old road to Elazığ which the hotel owner spoke of, drive to the top of the mountain, and find a nice place where we could have a picnic. From there we hoped that we would be able to see Lake Hazar from one side of the ridge and have a view of Elazığ, Harput, and Lake Keban from the other.

We found the turnoff within a few minutes across the highway from a public picnic area with tables and benches on the lake. It cut through a green cultivated field that contrasted with the brown of the barren mountain behind it, spotted here and there by small, leafless trees. Since no cars were in sight, we cut across the other two lanes of the highway and started up the dirt road. It, too, was empty. I knew little about trees and wondered out-loud if the ones we saw were the mulberries that I had read somewhere that Armenians planted near the lake years ago. Ashti also did not know.

As the road climbed the mountain, I noticed that the gorges by the road became deeper. At each one, I wondered if it was one of the ravines where Leslie Davis had seen hundreds of unburied naked bodies. About halfway up, we encountered a shepherd with a flock of sheep coming down the middle of the road, and we had to stop until they passed. Then, about a hundred yards beyond, we saw an old man in front of us trudging up the road. When he saw us coming, he waved us down.

"Let's pick him up," I suggested. "Maybe he can tell us about the area."

Ashti agreed, so we stopped, and the old man got into the backseat, thanking Allah and us for the ride. He was dirty and smelled, and when he smiled, he showed only a few yellow teeth, but he was very friendly and immediately began to speak in Turkish. He said that he was going to a village about two kilometers away on the other side of the ridge, after visiting his daughter in Sivrice.

While he was explaining his situation, Ashti noticed that he used Kurdish words and expressions. "Are you a Kurd?" she asked in Kurdish.

The man smiled broadly and replied affirmatively, switching to Kurdish, "I am. I was born and have lived here all of my life."

"Are you a farmer?"

"I was before I got too old to do much. Now my son takes care of me. We have a plot of land and some goats, and in the summer, he works in the hotels and residences by the lake. Most of my village does the same. I am still able to take the goats to pasture and watch over them, though."

Ashti explained to the man that she needed to translate to me because I did not know Kurdish.

"Ask him if he knows anything of the killing of Armenians in this area a hundred years ago," I requested. Ashti did so and translated his answer.

The man nodded. "I heard stories from my father. Many people were once killed here and their bodies were left unburied in the mountains. It was before I was born, but as a young boy, I often roamed the hills with him herding our goats. Father would sometimes stop and pick up a small piece of bone on the banks of a gully and say, 'This was once a person,' and then he would put it back on the ground and cover it reverently with dirt."

"Did he and his village take part in the killings?" I asked after Ashti had translated. At first, she hesitated to ask but then did so.

The man seemed unfazed by the question. "My father said that most of the killings were done by the soldiers, but yes, some were robbed and killed by people in our village, too. Our village chief said that the Armenians were infidels and traitors and that the Mufti in Istanbul had issued a fatwa against them. My father, though, said it was a shameful time for our village."

As he talked, we came to a turn off, and I asked in Turkish, "Which way should I go?"

The man motioned for me to follow the main road to the left. "That road leads to the top of the mountain. There's nothing there but grazing land where I take the goats in the summer."

As we came over the ridge, I could see in the distance the sprawling city of Elazığ and the Keban Lake to its right. When Ashti commented how beautiful the lake was, the man nodded. "Yes, but when it was built, many villages were submerged by it, including my grandparents's town."

After a couple of more switchbacks going down the mountain, passing near other deep gullies, we came to a concentration of some fifteen houses made of cement blocks with tin roofs and small plots of farm land behind them. The man told us that this was where he lived and that his name was Bawan. He invited us to come to his house and have some tea and meet his family.

We thanked him but said that we wanted to return to the top of the ridge to have a picnic and get a better view of Lake Hazar. Ashti asked him, "If we keep following this road would we eventually get to Elazığ?"

"Yes, a little after the village of Mollakendi, you come to the highway and then take a left." Bawan got out of the car and said in Kurdish, "May Allah bless you." Ashti returned the blessing. I waved to him and then turned the car around to retrace the distance of about a kilometer to the turn off to the top of the mountain.

"I bet this is the route taken by Davis when he came by horseback to Lake Hazar." I was excited because I remember the Consul mentioning the town of Mollakendi in his account. "It was probably also one of the routes of the deportation." I pulled the car over to the side of the dirt and gravel road, turned off the motor, and reached behind me to the back seat and got my daypack. I unzipped it and pulled out the Consul's book that Ashti had returned to me. Turning the pages to page 80, I came to the place I was looking for.

> At Mollakeuy we left the road and crossed the plain in the direction of the lake. There were several hundred dead bodies scattered over the plain. Nearly all of them were those of women and children. It was obvious that they must have been killed, as so many could not have died from disease or exhaustion. They lay quite near a Kurdish village which was known as Kurdemlik, and I afterwards learned that the Kurds of this village had killed most of these people.

"My guess is that the village where Bawan and his family live is Kurdemlik," Ashti said, interrupting. "The names of villages, especially Kurdish and Armenian ones, have almost all been changed by the authorities to Turkish names."

I closed the book, put it back in my daypack, and started the car again, continuing up the road. When we got back to the turn off, I went left on the smaller road that soon became rockier and more like a trail for shepherds than a road. I thought it best to park so not to damage the rental car and to climb the remaining hundred yards or so to the top of the ridge.

Ashti was game, even though she was wearing street shoes. "I think I will take along Karine's memoirs and the Consul's account, too, so we can try to locate where they went," I said, so I packed them along with our food, water, binoculars, and camera in my daypack.

I parked the car in a visible and safe place and locked it, and Ashti and I began to climb straight up the flank of the hill to the ridge. For the first five minutes, the walk was easy, but as the bank got steeper near the top, Ashti began to slip in the loose gravel and several times fell. She laughed, "We don't have many mountains to climb in Istanbul. I should have brought different shoes for this."

I was used to hiking, and was wearing shoes with soles that could grip. "You're doing great," I said, encouraging her. "Here, give me your hand," Ashti reached out and I took her hand steadying her and pulling her up the steep parts until we made it to the top of the ridge. It was wide, fairly flat and grassy with some small trees spotting it. A slight breeze blew on us, and the view from the top was spectacular. On one side, we could see the Keban Lake, and on the other, parts of Lake Hazar and the snowcapped mountains across the lake. I suggested that we have our picnic on a flat rock next to a small tree looking down at Lake Hazar. Ashti agreed.

As we walked over to the rock, Ashti reminded me with a smile, "I don't need you to pull me up anymore, but you are still holding my hand!"

I laughed. "I certainly am, as no one is up here but you to tell me I shouldn't."

"And I won't."

I stopped and looked at her devilish smile, and encouraged, I kissed her lightly on her lips, the first time I had ever done so. As she did not react either negatively or positively, I dropped her hand and put both of my arms around her and drew her closely to me. This time I kissed her with passion.

Ashti broke away from me with an astonished look on her face. "Peter! I said nothing about kissing like that, only about holding hands. I'm not ready for that!"

"I'm sorry," I said embarrassed. "I thought that you were encouraging me."

Ashti shook her head. "If I was, I'm sorry. I didn't mean to." She then quickly changed the subject as I could see that she was very uncomfortable. "Let's eat. I'm famished!" She went to the big rock, brushed off a spot on it, and then sat down looking down at the lake. "The view here is fantastic," she exclaimed. "You can see from one end of the lake to the other."

I followed her and when I got to the boulder, I took the daypack off my back and emptied its contents of bread and cheese, water bottles, binoculars, camera, and the memoirs of Karine and Consul Davis on the stone. "Rats," I exclaimed as I searched through the pack. "I don't have a knife to spread the cheese. They took it away in Asheville when I went through airport security."

"Blame it on nine-eleven and us Muslims!" Ashti said. "You don't need a knife. You can use your fingers to spread it." She took one of the bottles of water and opened it, taking a drink, and then she picked up one of the triangles of soft cheese the hotel owner had given us, unwrapped it, and spread it with her finger over the bread. I followed suit, and neither of us said anything as we stared down at the lake below and ate our lunch. Ashti finally broke the silence.

"Peter, I trust you and my father trusts you. Neither he nor I am ready for you to kiss me like you just did."

"I'm sorry if I took too much liberty. I just thought that you encouraged me," I repeated. "The truth is that I like you a lot, and not just as my third cousin. I think I always have, even from the first time I met you."

Ashti hesitated a minute before speaking. "And I like you, too, Peter, and not just as a third cousin. From our first time together in Boston, I have felt like you were the older brother that I never had. You were a male version of me who grew up in another culture who could explain it to me; a friend with whom I feel that I can be completely honest, who will teach and challenge me, yet also protect and encourage me and not harm me."

"I was hoping that our relationship might become even deeper than that of a sister and brother," I said.

"Do you mean like lovers? Husband and wife?" Ashti asked. "Peter, although we have so much in common, we also come from such different worlds. To me, holding hands and gentle kissing is possible between relatives and friends as signs of affection. But the way you kissed me the second time frightened me. It almost seemed out of control. To you, in your culture that sort of kissing and even sex between unmarried couples is seen as normal. In mine, it isn't. And as liberal a Muslim as I am, I cannot imagine myself being the lover of someone who was not my husband. It would hurt and shame me and my parents too much."

"Even though they consider themselves enlightened Muslims?"

"Yes."

"You said that you considered me a friend with whom you could be completely honest. I value that a lot. Can I also be completely honest with you and ask you even uncomfortable questions?" I asked.

"You can ask. I may not respond."

"I take it from what you just said that you are a virgin. Is that true?"

Ashti blushed but responded, "Yes."

"I'll also be honest with you. I'm not," I answered. "Nor, to tell you the truth, do I understand why being one is such a big deal. Sex is so natural and harms no one if it is by mutual consent and proper precautions are taken so that a child is not the result. But I respect you, Ashti, and I would do nothing to intentionally harm you."

She smiled and reached out and touched me affectionately on my cheek. "That's one of the reasons that I like you so much. I feel safe with you, even discussing embarrassing things."

"Thank you," I said. "I promise that I will try to control my passion for you in the future, but I would like to be able to continue to show my affection for you with an occasional holding of your hand or peck on your cheek."

"Permission granted," she replied. "But always try to remember when such demonstrations are appropriate here in Turkey and when they are not."

"I'll try." I touched her hand, gave her a light kiss on her cheek, and winked. I then picked up Karine's memoirs from the stone. "Now that we both know the rules, let's get back to the story of our ancestors and to what happened to them here. I flipped through Karine's memoirs until I came to the place in it that she described the arrival of the deportation caravan to the lake. I wanted to see if I could find their camping place from up here. I read aloud what she had written.

> Arriving at the lake, we followed the road along its edge until we came to a wide-open level area where the gendarmes ordered us to stop and make camp for the night. I remember the place to this day. It was where we

had camped and picnicked and had such fun a couple of years before with other families from Euphrates College. There was a grove of mulberry trees and a beach, and across the lake from where we stayed was a small island with the ruins of an old Armenian church and monastery. One day an Armenian boatman from Goeljuk Village, which was near to the island, came across the lake and took us to visit it. At night, we sang Armenian folk songs and hymns around the campfire and sometimes we danced the folk dances we had learned in school. Now I view that same campsite not as a place of happiness, but as a place of unimaginable suffering and evil.

After the gendarmes ordered us to halt for the night, Mother chose a place for us to camp by an isolated tree at the edge of the camp a little up the slope of the hill from the rest because some grass was there for our animals to eat. After we had tethered our animals and brought water for them from the lake, we used some of the tree branches to make a fire for cooking.

I put down the manuscript and picked up the binoculars and began to scan the lake for the island that was situated across the lake from where they had camped. Close to the far shore, I saw one and could make out what might have been the remains of stone buildings from long ago. I then scanned the shore and the hills on our side of the lake directly across from it. "I think where they camped is down there," I said, pointing to a place to the left of the road that we had taken up the mountain. There was a gentle slope of grass and scattered trees with a wide beach at the lake, and it was in direct view of the island where the Armenian monastery and church once were. I gave the binoculars to Ashti to see what she thought.

Ashti looked through them at both places and agreed. "I think you're right." She added, "I see a road that goes around the lake. Since we have plenty of time this afternoon, why don't we drive around it like the Consul did on horseback?"

"Good idea. I would also like to check out some of the gullies and beaches where he described seeing so many bodies. I wonder if there might be any evidence left of the massacres after almost a hundred years." I picked up Consul Davis's book, found the passage I was looking for on page 80 and read it again.

> After leaving the village of the Kurds, we climbed a very steep mountain and then descended into a valley on Lake Goeljuk, in which my predecessors and the American missionaries were accustomed to camp out every summer. It is unnecessary to say that there was no opportunity for camping out during the three years that I was at Harput. Two dead bodies lay on the shore just where they pitched their tents.
>
> We then turned to the north and rode along the lake for about two hours. The banks of the lake for most of this distance are high and steep, while at frequent intervals there are deep valleys, almost like pockets. In most of these valleys there were dead bodies and from the tops of the cliffs which extended between them we saw hundreds of bodies and many bones in the water below. It was rumored that many of the people who were brought here had been pushed over the cliffs by the gendarmes and killed in that way. The rumor was fully confirmed by what we saw. In some of the valleys there were only a few bodies, but in others there were more than a thousand.

I put the book on the rock and looked down at the view. "It's just so hard to imagine," I said. "A place of such beauty and of such innocence and fun—of picnics, singing, and dancing turned into one of the most awful killing fields in the world with thousands of rotting bodies laying unburied in gullies, valleys, on beaches, and even in the water."

"And then turned back again to a place of such beauty and of such innocence and fun as if nothing sinister ever happened here," Ashti responded. "It is astonishing."

I got my camera and then took a dozen or so pictures of the lake with wide angle and zoom lenses. I concentrated mainly on the island and what I thought might have been the campsite that terrible night that so altered the history of the Terzian family. When I finished, I said, "You know, my grandfather Noah might have been conceived right down there that night."

"And my grandfather, Diyari, too," Ashti added. "It is strange to think that we both might owe our very existence as persons to that one night of evil."

I thought a minute about what Ashti had said. "Was it therefore ultimately good that such evil happened?"

"For us, for sure!" Ashti replied. "It gave us a chance to be born." She then added, "For Karine, Talitha, and Margarit, it was total evil, though."

"Not total evil," I argued. "Remember, that while it is true that Altay, my great-grandfather, raped Karine, he also later fed her and her mother, protected them, and helped them to escape from the certainty of death. He was their tormenter but also their savior. Without his help and protection, they could have become some of the thousands of the scattered bones of Armenians along the deportation routes of Turkey and Syria."

"It amazes me sometimes how differently you and I think," Ashti said. "I tend to see things in terms of black and white. You and the other Americans whom I know seem to see things as gray. It is another difference in our cultures."

"You seem to fit quite well into both. Both in America and here."

"Not really," Ashti replied. "I struggle between loving the freedom of your gray world of weighing pros and cons, of respecting reason and arguments, of diversity and change, of individual rights, but I also love the security of my black and white world of clear truths and duties and relationships. To you, I must seem so conservative with my views about sex, about honor and shame. To others here, especially to my relatives you will meet in Diyarbakir, I am hopelessly lost and perhaps on the verge of becoming an infidel. I sometimes feel like a fish out of water. I am a Turk, but also an Armenian and Kurd. I am a Muslim with Christian ancestors and a Western education. I am a woman who wants the same freedom and opportunities of men. I don't know my place, but I do know that I want to find it. I have one life and I want to lead it right!"

"That's what this whole trip is for me, as well," I said. "It's an attempt to not only discover if I have what it takes to be a writer or journalist, but also like you, to find out who I really am as a person." I then added with a smile, "And truth be told, I also wanted to see you. Even your father noticed how attracted I am to you, and he was worried."

"I'm glad he didn't see that kiss," Ashti replied also with a smile. "That would have ended our trip together."

"I agree!"

With relief that Dilovan had not seen my passion, I climbed up on the rock again with my binoculars and scanned the land around the lake. I looked for valleys and gullies near the shorelines described by Consul Davis as places where he had seen the thousands of bodies of massacred Armenians. I also surveyed once again the site where I supposed that the Terzians had camped, where Lazar had been murdered and buried, and where Karine, Margarit, and Talitha had been raped. When I climbed down from the rock, I told Ashti that before we made our trip around the lake, I would like to explore on foot the gully that led down the mountain to what might have been the campsite of the Terzians that night. "It looks like it could have been one of the gullies where the Consul discovered so many bodies."

"You do it on your own," Ashti said. "I'll drive the car down to the bottom and wait for you there."

"It might take me a half-hour or so. You're sure you don't want to go with me?"

"Not in these shoes, no. I'll wait for you across the highway at the picnic area we saw near the lake."

"Okay then, let's go."

We cleaned up our picnic spot on the rock, and I took one more picture of the place with Ashti and me in it. We then climbed down the gravel slope to the car, hand in hand. "It's within the rules," I joked. "No one is looking, and I'm just keeping you from falling."

Ashti laughed, and she did not complain.

When we got to the car, everything was as we had left it. Ashti took the driver's seat, and not far down the road, I indicated to her where I wanted her to let me out. She pulled over and we both got out of the car. I showed her the route that I wanted to take and the place in the picnic area across the highway where we would meet. It looked to be about two kilometers distant. I left my binoculars with her in case she wanted to follow my progress.

"Be careful going down the hill," she said right before getting back into the car. "A broken leg would ruin the rest of the trip!"

The gully that I descended was indeed a steep one, and I slid down part of it on the seat of my pants. When I got to the dry stream at the bottom, I began looking for anything that appeared like a part of a bone, even though I knew that my chances of finding anything were minimal after so many years. Still, I looked.

As I maneuvered between the boulders and the thorn bushes, I tried to put myself back into that time as an Armenian young boy forced into the gully by Turkish gendarmes or Kurdish tribesman who stood with their rifles and hatchets on either side of the ravine. Dozens of us would probably have been ordered down into the gully. Some might be relatives or neighbors of mine, and others strangers from different villages who had joined us on the march outside of Mezire.

From what I had read from survivor accounts, the gendarmes probably ordered us to strip ourselves of our clothes and place them in a pile before they forced us to slide down the steep banks. When that happened, that would have been the moment that I would have lost all hope. I would know that they were going to kill me, as well as my family and friends. In my imagination, I could see the fear in the eyes of my loved ones or perhaps just their resignation after weeks of having survived so much suffering and indignities. Some of us would try to escape down the gulley, but there we would be met by gendarmes with their bayonets or Kurds with their hatchets to be stabbed or hacked to death. Others would try to climb the banks of the gulley and shots would ring out from the ravine's edges to bring them down. Bodies would fall one by one into the gulley, some dying immediately, but most dying slowly. The soldiers or the Kurdish tribesmen would then walk through our bodies, stabbing or hacking those of us still alive until they saw no movement or heard a moan.

Maybe I would be one of the very few who survived, pretending to be dead, hidden under the bloody corpse of another. I would then wait until after the gendarmes or Kurds turned their attention from us to the pile of our clothes that they had made certain would be free from the stain and desecration of blood. They would search among the clothes for hidden gold or jewelry or for pieces of cloth that they might wear or sell. I would then wait until they went away to eat their meals, to say their prayers, or to return with their booty to their villages. I would wait until darkness, and then after checking to see if my father or my uncle or my friend was still alive, I would put on any rags of clothing that were left to hide my nakedness. I would search for water to quench my thirst and to wash my body of the blood and dirt, and then climb fearfully and painfully up the banks of the ravine.

Then I tried to think what I would do afterwards to survive. Certainly, I could not admit that I was Armenian. I would have to pretend that I was a Kurd or Turk and steer-clear of any gendarmes. Perhaps I could find a German, Danish, or American missionary or maybe even the American Consul to protect me and help me escape through the mountains to Russia. Perhaps a Turkish friend would take pity on me and hide me or employ me if I converted to Islam. Perhaps I would become a thief, stealing what I needed to survive until I was captured and then killed. Perhaps, if I were young enough, I would be accepted by an orphanage or be adopted as a servant by a Kurdish or Turkish family. None of the choices were good.

I then tried to put myself in the position of someone like Altay, my great-grandfather who was a sergeant in the gendarmes. My duty was to follow the orders of my superiors. If I did not, I, myself, could be executed. I had been ordered to separate the males from females in the camp and march the men away from the others to an isolated place and execute them.

Arrangements had been made with the head of a Kurdish village nearby for its men to do most of the killing. We were to take the men and boys to the gulley, strip them, and then the Kurds would do the rest. The Kurds would be paid for their actions with the clothes and other goods found on the bodies of the victims. Afterwards they would be allowed to burn the bodies and look for the gold that they thought their victims sometimes swallowed. We soldiers were to use as few bullets as possible, only shooting those too far away to bayonet. This was war and the only way to win was to cleanse the nation of traitors.

I should feel no remorse for killing the Armenians, as the highest government authorities had ordered that we eliminate them because they were rebels and traitors to the nation, plotting with our enemies, the Russians, British, and French to overthrow our government. They, and other Armenians like them, had joined the Russian invaders in the east, killing Turks and destroying our villages. Not only that, the Mufti in Istanbul had declared a fatwa against them because they were infidels who refused to accept the one true religion. Killing them would please Allah, and therefore I could confiscate their wealth with impunity.

I wondered, if I were Altay, would I have had courage to refuse such orders. In all truthfulness, I probably would not have. I might have pretended I was shooting and bayoneting and not really do it, but I would certainly not risk my own life and position to save an Armenian traitor. Nor would I have had the courage even to say to my fellow gendarmes, "This is not right!"

As I thought about these things, I continued my walk down the ravine, picking up a piece of white stone here and there, and digging around a place that looked like it might have been a piece of a skull or a bone. I put a couple of small white hard pieces in my pocket that looked the most promising, but nothing that I saw was certainly bone. If this had been one of the gullies mentioned by the Consul, all remnants of the killings had long disappeared. Still, I took some pictures as I wanted to be able to describe the place in my novel.

Soon the ravine widened, and I came into the much more open grassy valley where the Terzians might have camped on that fateful night. Some two dozen small trees dotted the gently rising slopes and I wondered which one of these had been the place where they had built their campfire and where Lazar had been murdered. I looked for a tree with a pile of stones nearby, the possible grave of Lazar.

Finally, I saw one such promising location. About twenty yards from a particularly old tree, I noticed some medium sized stones that looked like someone had piled them on top of each other. I went over to them and stood beside them, estimating how far they were from the lake and from the tree. I tried to imagine that night—tethering the animals, getting water, and then setting up the tents. In my mind's eye, I could picture the campfires and the tents of the other deportees closer to the lake and those of the gendarmes not far above us.

I looked down at the stones and introduced myself, as if Lazar was there. I commended Lazar for his love and bravery that night. I told him that his mother and sisters had escaped with their lives and that his sisters had married and begat children and that their children had lived good lives. I told Lazar that he was not forgotten and that I was here to honor him.

Since I had no way of making a cross with wood, I took some of the stones near the pile and laid them on the ground in the form of a cross. I did it not because I was a believer but to affirm Lazar's own identity as a Christian. I said an Armenian prayer that I remembered from childhood, and I crossed myself in the Armenian way. As I stood there silently, tears came to my eyes. I was surprised at the deep sorrow within me. For a moment, I felt the full force of my Armenian identity and the suffering associated with it.

I then picked up six of the smaller stones from the pile and put them in my daypack wanting to give one each to Ashti, Dilovan, Father Gregory, and Aram and to keep one for myself and one for my mother, Mariam. Finally, I took pictures of the site, and saying my last goodbye to Lazar, I walked down the hill towards the lake and the picnic area where Ashti was standing outside the car with the binoculars in her hand, waiting for me.

"You must have found something up there. I watched you through the binoculars—even crossing yourself," Ashti said. "I thought you said that you weren't religious."

"I'm not. I thought, though, that it would be what Karine would have wanted me to do for her brother. It might just be a pile a stones, but it might also have been the grave of Lazar." I reached into my pocket and pulled out one of the pebbles I had picked up in the pile. "This is a souvenir for you from the spot."

Ashti looked at it, rubbed it between her fingers reverently and then put it into the pocket of her pants. "Thank you."

I looked at my watch. It was now one-thirty. "Why don't we drive around the lake and then afterwards, I would like to return to the hotel and write up some of my impressions of this morning before we have dinner."

Ashti, as always, agreed with me, and we got into the car again with me driving.

The trip around the lake took us about two hours, as I often stopped to take pictures. The southern side of the lake was much less populated than the northern side, and the road was a rural road and not a highway. We passed by some farms here and there and one or two small villages. We tried to get a boat to go out to Church Island but did not want to wait for the owner to go to Sivrice to buy the gas. At every valley and gully we passed, I imagined what it was like to be the Consul circumnavigating the lake on his horse and finding so many bodies.

One of the most interesting stops we made on the trip around the lake was at its small outlet. Seeing it, I could hardly imagine that this small stream was the beginning of the mighty Tigris River, which would flow by the ancient cities of Nineveh and Asshur before joining the Euphrates in Elam. Along with the Euphrates and two other rivers, the waters of the Tigris were supposed to have originated in Eden. Was this Eden? This place of great beauty and of great evil could well have been.

CHAPTER 16

Confession

It was four-thirty when we got back to the hotel, and Ashti and I agreed that we would meet for dinner at seven in the hotel dining room. I spent the rest of the afternoon writing and a little before seven, I went to Ashti's room next door and knocked. She had changed into one of the two dresses that she brought on the trip and looked stunning. I said so.

She thanked me and explained, "I wanted to freshen up after our climb."

The hotel dining room was mostly empty except for five men, two of whom were sitting together. No families were there, and Ashti was the only woman in the restaurant. The waiter, the same one who had helped us in the morning, brought us menus. They not only had a wide variety of dishes on them but also pictures of old Harput with its castle and some of its surviving mosques and hammams. I saw no pictures of the Virgin Mary Church or Euphrates College, however.

I asked for a beer, and Ashti got mineral water before ordering. Right after the waiter brought the drinks to us, the hotel owner, Mr. Demirci, appeared and came over to our table. "How was your day?" he asked in English.

"Great," I answered. "We followed the road you pointed out, had a picnic on the ridge with a splendid view of the lake, and then we drove around the entire lake. We even did some hiking. The only disappointment was, like you said, we couldn't get a boat to visit the island."

"If you stay tomorrow, I'll make sure you can get there in the afternoon."

"Unfortunately, we will have to leave in the morning. We want to visit some of Ashti's relatives in Diyarbakir and then continue on to Mardin and the Syrian border where I want to interview some refugees from the war."

"Are you a reporter?"

I answered "Yes," although this was only partially true.

"Make sure you report on how your government is making a mess of the Middle East."

I was curious as to what he meant, and so I asked him.

He reverted to his confrontational mode. "Your government is hypocritical and weak. You say that you support democracy but when the people elect governments you don't like, such as Moshi in Egypt or Hamas in Gaza, you support every means to overthrow them. You stand by Israel when it takes over Palestinian land to build their illegal settlements. You say you are Turkey's friend, but you spy on us and support movements that cause instability in Turkey."

"For example?" I asked.

"The demonstrations in Istanbul, the Kurds who want to form their own state just as the Armenians and Greeks did a hundred years ago. You want to break up our country and make it weak."

I was surprised at the passion with which he spoke. He, himself, must have also been surprised because he quickly caught himself once again and apologized.

"I'm sorry. I am a proud Turk, but I should not be saying such things to my guests. America has so many good things, too."

"Don't be sorry," I reassured him. "For me it is useful to hear all sides of the story." This was true, but the schizophrenic nature of our host did bother me.

"Well I do hope that you enjoy your meal and the rest of your stay here in Turkey. Both Diyarbakir and Mardin are beautiful cities. If you need anything, please let me know." He then bowed and excused himself and went over to a table where two Turkish males were sitting to talk with them.

After signing the check for our meal, I suggested to Ashti that we take a walk down to the lake and along its shore. Ashti agreed to the idea, and we went out the back door of the lobby. In the light of the moon, which gave us sufficient visibility to see, we passed by a now empty pool, a soccer field, and playground and came to the deserted beach. On its edge, near some bushes, were some benches where guests could sit and look out over the water. We continued past them over the wide, rocky beach to the edge of the gently lapping water. Both of us bent down to feel its temperature. It was mildly cold, but swimmable.

I suggested that we continue our walk down the beach, but Ashti countered that she was not dressed for that. She suggested instead that we return to the benches and enjoy the view from there. That is what we did. As little traffic was on the highway and few guests in the hotel, the night was quiet. "It's so peaceful here," Ashti said. "and so different from the rush of Istanbul."

Feeling that I was within the rules laid down on the mountain ridge, I reached out for her hand on her lap and squeezed it and then continued to hold it. "It's wonderful being here with you," I said.

Ashti said nothing for a minute, nor did she try to withdraw her hand. Finally, she asked, "How was your writing this afternoon?"

"I'm just taking notes now about what I see and what I feel. I want to be able to have some catalysts to bring up these scenes again when it is time to put them together in a story."

"Have you decided yet on one?"

"Not really. What is so hard is that many readers don't want to hear history or to read a travelogue. They want action and passion. They want mystery, and unfortunately the story I want to tell has little of that."

"Will I be in your story?" Ashti asked.

I laughed. "Of course you will be. At least there will be a fictionalized portion of you."

"Please don't make me someone whom I or my parents would be ashamed of," she said. "Also, please make me wiser, kinder, and more beautiful and successful than I really am!"

I laughed and said, "That would be hard to do!"

She squeezed my hand in thanks and then asked, "How much of yourself will you put into your book?"

"I don't know yet. The book will be about me in the sense that I want to use this trip and the writing of it to help my secular American self examine and somehow reconcile the Turkish Muslim rapist side of my history with the Armenian Christian victim side."

"It sounds like you have already decided to put all of the blame for what happened to your ancestors on the Turks."

"No, not all of the blame. I realize that a few Armenian revolutionaries stoked the fire of hatred and rebellion, and no doubt some Armenians massacred innocent Turkish villagers in the east when they had power for a short time during the Russian advance. But I certainly will put most of the blame on the Turkish government at the time. Nothing that the few Armenian revolutionaries did could possibly justify the murder of ten thousand Armenians in this very valley. Nothing could justify the rape of their women, the enslavement of their children, the leaving of their bones to dry in the sun after their flesh rotted off, the stealing of all of their goods, and the virtual wiping out of their names and culture. Nothing could justify making it a criminal offense to talk about it openly and form one's own opinion about it. War is one thing, what happened to the Armenians and Syriacs is another."

"So you think that what happened was genocide?"

"I do," I answered. "Especially after reading what Consul Davis wrote about what happened right here." I added, "Maybe it was a degree lower and less efficient than the German gathering of the Jews to be sent to extermination camps, but definitely it was an attempt to get rid of the Armenians, at least in this part of Turkey."

"That to me is the problem with the genocide theory. If I wanted to wipe out a people, I would have wiped them out immediately and everywhere—in Istanbul and here. I wouldn't have sent them on long marches where they could escape."

"But then there would have been violent rebellions, and it wouldn't have worked. Most of the Armenians went like sheep to the slaughter because they had the hope that maybe what the authorities said was true—that when the war was over they would be allowed to come back and reclaim their goods and life."

"So is your opinion of Turks today negative because of something that happened a hundred years ago?"

"Yes, but not so much for what happened a hundred years ago. It is more tied to the government's unwillingness to admit the truth today. Compare how the government here has acted with how the German government dealt with its history during the Second World War of trying to exterminate Jews and Gypsies. Turkey stonewalls while Germany admits. Germany tries to make amends, and move on, and Turkey doesn't." I paused and added, "You forget one thing, too. I am part Turk. My great-grandfather Altay watched as his companion stabbed and killed Lazar. He then violently raped my great-grandmother Karine. He probably took part in other killings and cruelties on the march as well. But he later came to his senses. First, he protected Karine from others only because he wanted her for himself, but then he carried her grandmother on the horse in spite of being reviled by his friend; he gave food to them, and with great risk to himself he helped them escape."

"Like all of us, he had good and evil in him," Ashti said.

"Yes, and the good finally won out." I added. "That's what I hope happens with Turkey. It has so many good and wonderful things about it—its location, democracy, beauty, history, economic development, and its kind and smart people. But it also has to deal with the ugliness of some of its past, just like any other nation."

"Like you Americans with your treatment of the Indians and African slaves, your huge prison population, your violence, your abortions, your death penalties?"

"Yes," I said. "We have our sins as well, both past and present."

"Have you personally ever done something for which you were deeply ashamed but couldn't bring yourself to admit to others because doing so would make you look bad?"

"I have," I said.

"Would you share it with me?" Ashti asked.

Her questions caught me off guard, and I was not sure how to respond. "I'm not ready to do that right now," I said. "It's painful, and I don't want you thinking any worse of me than you already do."

Ashti was silent for a while and then squeezed my hand again. "Maybe that is just how some of us Turks feel about the events of 1915." After another moment of silence, she added, "I think it is time that we go back in. I want to call Mother and give her an update. I also need to talk to my uncle and aunt about meeting them in Diyarbakir tomorrow." She stood up still holding on to my hand, and hand in hand, we returned to the hotel. As we climbed the steps to the lobby, Ashti dropped my hand. We then passed through the room and said goodnight to the hotel owner who was sitting there smoking.

When we got to our rooms on the second floor and Ashti had opened her door with her key to go in, I glanced to see if anyone was looking. Since no one else was in the hall, I kissed her lightly on the cheek. "Good night, Ashti, I enjoyed being with you today."

She smiled and gave me a peck on the cheek as well. "And I with you."

"I'll knock on your door for breakfast at half-past seven," I said.

"I'll be ready."

"And please thank your mother and father for letting you come with me. I don't know how I would have managed without you." I grinned and then added. "And tell them that I am behaving!"

She laughed. "I will." She then closed the door.

I went to my own room and after closing my own door, I opened the curtain to the balcony looking out on the lake, the empty swimming pool, and the darkness beyond. I then got out my laptop computer and got on line using the hotel Wi-Fi. After a quick look at my e-mail, including a nice letter from my half brother, Frank, I went to Google Earth. I searched for Elazığ and then found our hotel on Lake Hazar and the roads that we had taken today. I followed them in a zoom mode into the mountains and around the lake, remembering each part of the day, especially what happened on the ridge and now on the beach and at Ashti's door.

I then thought of what could have happened, and what one part of me had wanted to happen. If Ashti had given me any encouragement, I would have passionately made love to her on the ridge, on the beach, and in her hotel room. I would have kissed her deeply, reached beneath her blouse and cupped her breasts, and made love until my lust was satisfied. If she had not pulled away, would anything have stopped me? Would my promise to her father, Dilovan, have stopped me? Would the knowledge of future negative repercussions to her as a young Muslim woman losing her virginity outside of marriage have stopped me?

It shamed me to think that neither reason, nor duty, would have been stronger than fulfilling my own lust. As I remembered Dilovan saying to me that night as we ate together, "I know you, and me, and every other male very well! I know that sometimes it seems that our brains are not located in our heads but much lower down."

Since this was so often true, how could I be so harsh in my judgment of my great-grandfather, Altay, or of even of my father, Brent Johnson? Was I any better than they who considered only their own gratification and not the good of their victim? I had to admit to myself that the only reason I did not fulfill my lust with Ashti was because of Ashti's resistance, not because I had her interests in mind. That realization shamed me. My deepest shame, though, the one that I could not bring myself to share with Ashti on the bench, was tied to something else.

As I said earlier, I have always felt the disapproval of my stepfather and we seem to have disagreements on just about everything. He is conservative, and I am liberal. He is a Baptist, and I am an agnostic. He likes to stay in one place, and I like to travel. He loves team sports like football and basketball, while I like things such as hiking and mountain biking and sometimes hunting. He cares a lot about wealth and material things, while I care mostly for simple living, freedom, having new experiences, and writing. Mainly, he criticizes me all of the time for being too selfish and superior and not thinking of the needs of others. He also resents that he has often had to get me out of minor scrapes with the law involving speeding tickets, unpaid bills, and once even an arrest for possessing marijuana.

In 2011, my stepfather's disapproval of me reached its zenith. What happened was that I was driving my half brother Frank home from an evening basketball game he had played with his school team in Boone, North Carolina. He was the star of the team. Coming back in the dark on the Blue Ridge Parkway instead of on a major highway, we ran off the road into a thirty-foot deep ravine. As I was wearing a seat belt, I suffered only a broken rib and some small cuts and bruises. Frank, however, was sleeping in the back seat without a seat belt, and he was thrown from the car, badly injuring his spine. The result was that he is still confined to a wheelchair. My stepfather's athletic dreams for him were over, and although my brother has forgiven me, I do not think that my stepfather has.

My shame is that this was an accident that could have easily been avoided. What I told the police and the paramedics who rescued us, as well as my parents and my brother, was that I inadvertently fell asleep at the wheel and went over the cliff at a curve. The truth is, however, that I did not fall asleep. Instead, I was texting a message to a friend and I took my eyes off the road at just the wrong time as the road curved in the darkness. In other words, Frank's paralysis, his broken dreams, my father and mother's hopes for him, and the huge expenses they have now been burdened with, were due to a stupid and selfish decision that I made. So far, I have been too cowardly to admit to anyone my guilt.

If I am honest in my evaluation, I have been less honorable than my father and great-grandfather with their own burdens of shame. Brent redeemed himself by marrying my mother. Altay later decided to redeem himself by helping Karine. While passion at first was the victor over honor, at the end, honor won out. I hope that truth and honor will eventually win out in my case as well, and that I will find the courage to leave this confession of mine in my book and seek forgiveness from those I have offended so terribly.

CHAPTER 17

The Kurds

Wednesday morning, after breakfast and saying goodbye to the hotel owner and the desk clerk, Ashti and I got into our car and headed towards Diyarbakir, which was about a hundred and fifty kilometers away. Ashti had spoken with her aunt by phone the night before, and she and her husband had invited us for lunch at a restaurant near their home in the old city. Her aunt also insisted that Ashti stay with them in their home and gave her the name of a modest family hotel within a five-minute walk of their house where I could stay. They had also agreed that as soon as we got to the hotel, Ashti would call them, and that they would meet us there. After a lunch together, Ashti's aunt would take us on a walking tour of the old city.

"They are conservative Muslims," Ashti explained. "Probably, they are horrified that we are traveling together unaccompanied, but they will do their best to be gracious and polite. Please be as sensitive as you can."

I smiled. "I guess that means no more holding hands with you in front of them."

"No," Ashti answered. "And don't be surprised, as I will probably wear a head covering when I am with them."

"Isn't that hypocritical because you don't do that in Istanbul or in other places?"

"I don't think so," Ashti replied. "I see it as a way of honoring them and their beliefs, especially on their home turf." She paused and then laughed. "It is kind of like you honoring me and my family by holding in check your wild passion!"

"That's because you are Ashti, whom I love and respect. That trumps being just a female whose beautiful body I lust for."

Ashti blushed and looked down. "You say things so directly. It embarrasses me." Then she added, "But I appreciate it too."

After we left the lake, we experienced some delays on the highway because of construction projects. "It's like this all over Turkey," Ashti explained. "The government has invested a huge amount of money in improving the nation's infrastructure of roads, dams, and airports."

The new highway we were on wound through the mountains and for a good part of our trip followed alongside the mountain stream, the mighty Tigris in its infancy. When I saw a highway sign that said Maden, five kilometers, I pulled off the highway onto a level dirt area and parked the car. Pointing to an old dirt road hugging the mountain on the other side of the rushing stream, I said to Ashti, "I wonder if that was the road the deportation caravan followed on its way to Diyarbakir. Could it have been near here that Margarit was kidnapped?"

I reached behind me to the back seat and got my daypack as cars and trucks heading to Diyarbakir continued to whiz by us on the winding highway. I withdrew Karine's memoirs, found the appropriate place, and began to read aloud from it.

> As we got near to the mountain town of Maden, famous for its copper, the wheel of our oxcart broke as it slipped off the rocky trail winding down the mountain besides the large stream that became the Tigris River. Mother was driving the cart with Margarit and Grandmother in it at the time, while I was riding Father's mule. Mother tried to fix the cart, but as we had no tools or replacement wheels, she said that we would have to abandon it. She released the ox from his oxbow, and then with our help, she did the best she could to load him with the bundles that he had been pulling. Unfortunately, we could not get the ropes tight

enough around his belly and the bundles kept falling off. Most of the caravan had since passed us by in their slow march south, and we were alone at the end of the line. As Mother was struggling with the bundles, some men with hatchets in their belts approached us on horseback from behind. Mother saw them and told Margarit to get on the mule with me and for us to run as fast as we could towards the rest of the caravan. I obeyed her immediately, remembering what had happened the last time strange men approached, but Margarit hesitated and clung to Mother. Mother yelled at me to go and I did, leaving them there. Until today, I both regret and am thankful for my choice.

Mother and Grandmother were weeping when they found me later that night in the camp. They said that the men were three Kurds from a village nearby and that they had kidnapped Margarit along with everything we had. They surrounded us, and looking at our ox and the bundles on the ground, the leader thanked us for all of our goods. The leader then looked at Margarit and asked Mother in Turkish "Is she your daughter?" Mother answered "Yes." He said how beautiful she was and he asked Mother, "Will you give me her as a second wife in exchange for your lives?" Mother pleaded with him not to harm them. They could take what they wanted of our goods but "Please don't take my daughter or harm her." The man laughed and replied, "If I take her as a wife, I will be saving her, instead of hurting her as where you are now headed is certain death." He then ordered his men to pick up the bundles from the ground and take the ox back to their village.

As they dismounted to do so, the chief turned his own horse toward Mother and Margarit, knocking Mother to the ground with his knee and grabbing Margarit with his arm. He then pulled Margarit up in front of him on the horse's neck and galloped off with her up the road as she screamed. Mother and Grandmother ran after him in desperation until they came upon one of the gendarme rear guards of the caravan who forced them to turn back. When Mother told the gendarme what had happened and pleaded with him to go after Margarit, he just laughed. When she offered him the gold sewed into her shawl to help, he took the gold but still did nothing.

I got out of the car and walked over to the embankment. After snapping some more pictures with my camera, I tried to imagine the scene of the broken cart half-hanging over the bank threatening to slip down to the river, the four women watching the armed horsemen approach, and the terror of what happened next.

Ashti got out of the car as well and stood by me. "It seems so strange that all of this could have happened. That my great-grandfather actually kidnapped my great-grandmother," she said.

"You can look at it two ways. It is true that he kidnapped her against her will. It is also true that he may have saved her life. Since she was young and pretty, she could have been continuously raped along the route. She could also have died. Her kidnapping may have been a blessing, as we don't know the alternative stories."

"All I know for sure is that her kidnapping turned out to be a blessing for me."

"True," I said.

As we walked back to the car, Ashti commented, "It must be fun for a fiction writer—making up new endings for your stories."

"Actually, I think having so many options is daunting. The ending must seem to the reader as having been inevitable, or it will not work well," I said as I opened the car door for her to get in. When I got in the driver's side, I added, "In fiction, anything can happen. In real life, there's only one true ending for all of us—our death."

"Billions of people don't agree with you," Ashti said. "Muslims and Christians believe that our spirits live on in a renewed body. Buddhists and Hindus believe our spirits lives on in another body. Consciousness continues."

"So you believe in the final judgment and heaven and hell?" I asked.

"Of course, I do. Otherwise there would be no justice for all the evil deeds done on this earth."

"But eternal punishment for temporal deeds does not seem like justice to me," I argued.

"One does not question Allah. We must pay for our sins and our unbelief."

"This reminds me of a conversation I had with our cousin, Father Gregory, about the same theme when we were in Kars," I said. "He believes that God's mercy triumphs over his justice. As for paying for our sins and our unbelief, he believes firmly that such a payment was made by Jesus when he died on the cross and that Jesus' plea to his Father to "forgive them for they know not what they do," will be honored by the Father. He says that God the Father uses suffering on earth and after death to purify us from our evil, just as loving parents do when they punish their child. But he doesn't believe punishment is eternal. Once the child learns his lesson and changes his behavior, he or she is once more welcomed back into the arms of the loving Father as the prodigal son was in Jesus' parable. In the end, the very end of all things, Father Gregory believes that all creation, Christians, and even believers in other religions and secularists like me, will recognize and accept who Jesus really is and what his death on the cross and resurrection really mean."

"It is beautiful what he says, but is it the Truth?" Ashti asked.

"Ahh, Ashti," I said. "That is the question. I hope so, but we will have to die and see what happens to find out!"

With that, I started the engine and put the car in gear and eased out on the highway. As we got closer to Maden, I asked, "What do you know of your great-grandmother Margarit's story after she was captured?"

"I never knew her personally, as she died before I was born, but I will tell you what Father passed on to me.

"Good."

"After capturing her, my great-grandfather Egid took her back to his village in the mountains some ten kilometers from here."

"Do you remember the name of it; could we visit it now?" I asked.

"No, I never knew the name, and like hundreds of other Kurdish villages, it was destroyed in 1935 by the army after Atatürk made the decision to move all of the Kurds into the cities from the countryside so that the government could control us better. It was part of his whole policy of Turkification."

"Kind of like the decision to destroy the Armenian villages," I said.

"Actually, a lot of similarities exist between the Armenian and Kurdish people. They are both mountain people from the same regions with their own languages. Both have been persecuted during their histories. The main differences are that the Armenians held onto their Christianity and have their own nation, while most Kurds converted to Islam and have never had their own state."

I nodded.

"Anyway, my great-grandfather was the son of the village chieftain and a man of prestige in the region, although like everyone else in the village, he was a poor farmer and herdsman. He was in his early thirties and married already, but his first wife was barren and had been unable to give him the son and grandson that he and his father so desperately wanted. As he had no suitable young girls in the village to choose from for a second wife, my grandfather decided to see if he could buy a bride in Maden from the market or from one of the gendarmes in the deportation caravans passing through this area from the north and east on the way to the Syrian Desert. The gendarmes often sold some of the youngest and prettiest girls of the caravans in the towns and villages they passed as wives, servants, or prostitutes."

"So Margarit was lucky," I said. "She became a wife."

"She was lucky," Ashti agreed. "She told my father that Egid gave her the choice of converting to Islam, changing her name, and becoming his second wife, or to be sold in Maden as a servant or prostitute. She chose the former and became Zara."

"She was a smart young girl!" I exclaimed.

"After consummating the marriage, Zara lived in the house of her in-laws for a year to work for them and learn Kurdish and the ways of the village, while Egid continued to live with his first wife. Zara quickly won them and her husband over by handing over to them the five pieces of gold that her mother had sewn into her clothes and the tents they had captured, as well as with her hard work and talents. She had learned from her mother how to cook, weave, and embroider and with this knowledge, she was able to transform the wool of Egid's sheep into beautiful rugs that sold well in Maden. She was a great economic asset to the family, but of course the main event that solidified her position in the family was the birth of a baby son, my grandfather Diyari."

"How many other children besides your grandfather did she have?"

"Three other children—two girls and a boy."

"And what happened to them?"

"The two girls died in childhood, and the boy, Sazan, died in his early twenties in Dersim, just north of here in the massacres in 1937. He had gone there to fight alongside other Kurds who were rebelling against the relocation law of 1934 that Atatürk had decreed to assimilate ethnic minorities in the country. The Armenians have their genocide claims, and the Kurds have theirs."

"What do you mean?" I asked.

"I mean that many Kurds saw what happened in Tunceli Province from 1937 to 1938 as an attempted genocide because so many Kurds, including women and children, were killed by the Turkish army. Some estimates are as high as 80,000 deaths, although most historians dispute that number as exaggerated."

"But even 80,000 is nothing near the 1,500,000 deaths of Armenians or the 300,000 number of deaths of Syriacs," I said.

"No," Ashti replied. "And another major difference is that a few years ago the Prime Minister officially apologized for those massacres, but he has yet to do that for the Armenian and Syriac killings."

As we talked, we came to the outskirts of Maden, a town of 6,000 or so inhabitants according to the highway sign. Its houses, tightly packed and clinging to the bare hills all around, were mostly of masonry with rusty tin roofs. It did not look prosperous. The Tigris River, still mostly a shallow mountain stream, flowed alongside the highway.

A huge white building, a copper smelting factory, was at the top of one hill, and the residue from the extraction process tumbled down towards the highway where major construction was going on. We had to wait for some ten minutes as huge trucks removed large stones as they widened the highway into the banks of the hills. As we waited, I turned off the motor because diesel and gasoline were so expensive in Turkey. While waiting, Ashti continued to tell Zara's story.

"After they were forced by the government to leave their village, Egid brought his two wives to live here in Maden. Egid worked in the copper industry because that was where most of the jobs were. The Terzian copper table most likely came from here, as many of the Armenians who used to live here before 1915 were also coppersmiths."

"Did the two wives get along?" I asked.

"I have no idea," Ashti replied. "But Muslim men are supposed to treat their wives equally."

"Can Turks still have more than one wife?" I wondered.

"Officially no, thank goodness!" Ashti said. "Atatürk abolished that practice, but some Muslim men still feel it is their religious prerogative to have as many as four wives, as the Koran allows. Of course, the government does not approve, but some religious authorities continue to draw up contracts for a second marriage. It is a fairly common practice in the Kurdish community."

"Anyway, continue with Zara's story," I said.

"Well, Egid's first wife died here in Maden, still childless, and Egid died soon afterwards. Zara therefore moved to Diyarbakir to live with Diyari and his new wife, my grandmother, Kejal. Diyari had gone there to sell copperwares, first in open markets and then finally in his own store. He then branched out into silver and gold jewelry and did pretty well, allowing him to marry and have a family."

"Maybe his business success was due to the Armenian entrepreneurial genes he had in him," I commented. "In the Armenian museum in Boston, I read tales of how Armenian entrepreneurs used to build round boats of leather here in Turkey and float down the Tigris or Euphrates to sell their goods taking their donkey with them on the raft. After selling their wares in major towns downstream they would fold up the boats and bring them back home on the donkey's back."

Finally, the workers on the highway waved us on, and we continued on our way to Diyarbakir. It took us another hour or so to reach the city and we passed though a couple of major towns on the way. I was struck by how similar the cities and towns of Turkey looked to one another as well as their mosques. Most of the latter were copies in the Hagia Sophia style with a dome and one or two minarets beside it. I guessed that the more the minarets, the more prestigious the mosque, as only the most important mosques had four. From the loud-speakers on these, the faithful were called to prayer five times a day, a constant reminder of Allah in the daily rush of making one's living.

When Ashti and I arrived in Diyarbakir, it was a little before noon. The city was quite impressive and large. According to my guidebook, around a million people lived there, most of them Kurds. Before 1915, Diyarbakir had also been heavily populated by Armenians and Syriac Christians.

Outside of the city, I put the address of the hotel that Ashti's aunt had recommended into the rental car's GPS, but unfortunately, when we got to the spot, we could see no hotel. Ashti asked directions from someone standing on the street nearby, and the nice young man got in the car with us and took us right to the hotel. It is encouraging to see how kind and helpful people can be all over the world.

The street in front of the hotel was very busy, and as I could find no place to park, Ashti got out of the car and went inside the hotel. She came back with a clerk who showed us a place on the street reserved for hotel guests. I was reluctant to leave the car and the cross in the street like that, but I decided to do so as I had no alternative. The clerk assured me that the car would be safe, and he took our bags into the building. At the desk, I showed the clerk my passport and asked for one room, as I knew that Ashti would be staying with her relatives.The clerk, however, misunderstood the situation, and he asked to see our wedding license as he thought that I, an American, and Ashti, a Turk would be staying in the same room.

"We are cousins," Ashti said. "And the room is only for him. I am staying with relatives in the city."

The man nodded and went about filling out the forms. When he finished, he told the bellhop to take my baggage to the fourth floor room.

"I would like to put my bag upstairs with his until my uncle and aunt come to pick me up," Ashti requested.

"It would be best if you kept it down here," the clerk responded. "It will be safer and you don't have to go up and down the elevator with it."

She thanked him and gave him her bag. As for me, I followed the bellhop upstairs.

By the time I had returned, Ashti had already called her aunt and uncle on her cell phone, and she informed me that they would be at the hotel within a half-hour. While we were waiting, Ashti reclaimed her bag and excused herself to go to the restroom in the lobby. When she came back she still wore her same travel pants, but she had put on a long sleeve blue silk blouse and a red and blue headscarf. As she sat down beside me on the sofa by her bag, I complemented her on her looks and asked her to tell me something about her uncle and aunt before they arrived.

"My aunt's name is Rihana and she's my father's younger sister," Ashti said. "Her husband, Bawan Yasin, has a small shop in the old town where he makes and sells simple agricultural tools like rakes, hoes, and shovels. They are fairly poor but very proud, and if they insist on paying for our meal together, just accept with thanks."

"Do they speak any English?" I asked.

"Rihana speaks a little but not much. Our conversation will probably be in Kurdish or Turkish, so I will translate. They are both devout and conservative Muslims. They will be very polite to us, but they are probably scandalized that we are traveling together."

"I will emphasize that we are cousins," I said smiling. "Actually, come to think of it, Rihana is my cousin, as well!"

"Yes, and a few years back, Bawan would have carefully hidden her Armenian history out of fear of stigma. Now, he has become much more open about it."

I nodded. "Do they have any children?"

"They have one son, Loran, whom they love very much. He's two years younger than I am." Ashti paused and then said. "One other thing you should know is that when Loran and I were in our teens, Bawan approached my father about a possible future marriage between us."

"You're kidding! You're first cousins."

"It happens all of the time."

"And…?"

"Father thought it would never work out as we were so different, but he asked me what I thought. I refused, of course! I hardly knew him and he was younger."

"How did your aunt and uncle and cousin take that rebuff?" I asked.

"At first, I think they were hurt. Later, though, when they saw how liberal I was and the difference in our age and educational levels, they realized the wisdom of it all. I now have a very close relationship with them, even though we rarely see each other. And I never see Loran."

"Has he married someone else?"

"No. He is a fighter with the YPG, the Kurdish militia in Syria."

I was going to ask her to explain what that was when Rihana and Bawan arrived at the hotel. When Ashti saw them, she jumped up from the sofa and embraced them with much warmth, greeting them in Kurdish. She then introduced me to them in Turkish. "Peter is our American cousin whom I told you about."

Rihana shyly shook my hand, smiled and said, "Pleased to meet you."

"Good, you know some English," I responded. "Ashti won't have to translate everything."

Rihana shook her head and laughed, saying in Turkish, "What I just said is about all I know!"

I immediately liked her. Dressed conservatively but attractively in a fitted long green outfit with a green scarf over her black hair, Rihana was a female version of Dilovan.

Her husband, Bawan, was also gracious despite the reservations that I am sure he had about me traveling with Ashti. He shook my hand warmly and smiled. Looking older and less refined than his wife, he had beard stubble on his face and wore baggy traditional Kurdish pants with a collarless shirt and sport coat. He had a knitted skullcap on top of his closely cropped hair. I could tell by the dark spot on his forehead that he was a pious Muslim who prayed often, touching his head at least five times a day to the prayer rug.

After they apologized to me for not speaking English, and I to them for not speaking better Turkish and no Kurdish, Bawan turned to Ashti to decide on the program for the day. She then translated for me.

"Uncle Bawan suggests that we go to a restaurant not too far from here to eat and insists that we be his guests. While Rihana will walk with us, he will take my bag to their house on his motorbike and then join us at the restaurant. Afterwards, he would like to show us his shop."

I thanked him in Turkish.

"Unfortunately, this afternoon he has to stay and work," Ashti continued, "but after lunch, Aunt Rihana will take us sightseeing in the old city. He also apologizes to you that his house is too simple and small for both of us to stay there tonight."

"I understand," I said in Turkish.

Bawan asked Ashti for her bag, and then we all went out to the front of the hotel where his Vespa scooter was parked.

"The alleys are just too narrow for a car, and we have no place to park near our home," Bawan explained. He then sat down on the seat of the motorbike, put Ashti's bag between his legs, and started the motor.

After he took off, Rihana asked in Turkish, "Shall we go? The restaurant is only about a ten minute walk from here."

Ashti nodded and said, "It will be good to get some exercise."

Rihana took Ashti's hand and led the way down our busy street as I followed behind. At the first corner, we turned right and I saw what to me was an amazing sight. Rising up before us were the great black basalt guard towers and walls surrounding the old city of Diyarbakir. From what I had learned from my guidebook, they were built by the Romans and then Byzantines, and measured six kilometers in length. Outside the walls, a beautiful park of green grass, trees, and flowers had been planted where families picnicked, children played, and retired persons sat on benches. The contrast of the hard black walls and the colorful park was lovely.

We entered into the old city through the northern Harput Gate along with other cars and pedestrian traffic and headed south on the main thoroughfare towards the southern Mardin gate. The main street of the old city, paved with cobblestone, was bustling with shops and shoppers. The women on the street were conservatively but tastefully dressed in outfits that hid all but their hands and faces but did not hide their female shape underneath. Almost all of them wore bright printed scarves over their hair. Several shops we passed had hundreds of such scarves in the windows and a wide variety of dresses to choose from—all very conservative. Other shops sold gold and silver necklaces, bracelets, and ornaments. I quickly realized that being a conservative Muslim woman did not necessarily mean that one could not be fashionable.

Just as Rihana had said, within ten minutes we were at the restaurant. Actually, it was not just one restaurant, but a magnificent two–storied Ottoman building now filled with restaurants and tearooms. We entered into an open courtyard surrounded by black and white stone arches holding up a second floor at the courtyard's edges. Both in the courtyard and in the balconies above were tables and chairs as well as comfortable and colorful divans where people could eat, drink, and converse. Strategically placed canvas flaps at the open top of the building protected those sitting at tables in the courtyard from the noon sun.

Rihana led us up some steep narrow stone steps to one of the smaller restaurants looking down on the courtyard. The waiter welcomed us and showed us to a table alongside the balcony. Like the others, it had two benches with cushions upholstered in red and gold. He then brought us some large menus to study while we waited for Bawan. Within ten minutes he appeared. When the waiter returned to get our order, Bawan insisted again in Turkish that we get whatever we liked, and that we were his guests. I requested that he order for me a very light meal typical of the region. I wanted to experiment Kurdish food, but I also hoped that a light meal would be less expensive for my generous host of modest means.

"Well, tell me a little about yourself, Peter," Bawan said, addressing me in Turkish after the waiter had left with our orders. "First of all, how is an American like you related to Muslim Kurds like Rihana and Ashti?"

"My great-grandmother was the sister of Rihana's grandmother and Ashti's great-grandmother, Zara. I'm American, but I'm also part Armenian, part Syriac, and part Turk," I explained in my ungrammatical and broken Turkish.

"Too bad, you aren't also part Kurdish!" he replied laughing.

"I agree," I said, content that I had been able so far to hold my own in Turkish.

"Ashti tells us that you are here in Turkey to trace the deportation route of your ancestors and to write a novel about it," he continued.

I nodded.

"What happened in 1915 was deplorable," he said, "and we Kurds bear a lot of the responsibility along with the Turks. Our mayor has apologized and has tried to make some amends by helping rebuild former Armenian churches in the city. After dinner, Rihana will take you to see one of them."

That was when I turned to Ashti for translation. The conversation was getting more difficult and I turned to English. "Are there any other sights to help me get a feel for Armenian life in Diyarbakir?" I asked. "For example, are there any former villages nearby, Armenian museums, or cemeteries?"

"I don't know of any cemeteries," Bawan answered. "They have all probably been paved over in the expansion of Diyarbakir. As for villages, I think Dicle University to the east of the city was built on the site of a former Armenian town, but I'm not totally sure about that either. I do know, however, that one of our women writers restored an Armenian house and now it is open to the public."

"I'd love to see it, if that is possible," I said.

"Rihana can take you. It's near the church," he said. He then added, "Ashti also says that you are interested in the Syrian Civil War and will be heading to Mardin tomorrow to try to interview some refugees."

"That's right," I answered.

"You should get in touch with our son, Loran. He knows a lot about what is going on in Syria and frequently crosses the border. I am sure he would like to meet you, and he could maybe help you. He lives somewhere near Nusaybin, but I don't know exactly where."

Along with her translating, Ashti now entered into the conversation. "How would we get in touch with him then? I would love to see him."

"I have his cell phone number, and I imagine that if you can get hold of him, he would set up some place where you could meet."

"His work sounds a little dangerous and mysterious," Ashti said.

"It is," Bawan answered, proudly. He looked around to see if anyone were listening and then said in a lowered voice, "He works with the YPG, the Kurdish Popular Protection Units in Syria and smuggles Kurdish fighters and supplies across the border. They are defending our Kurdish brothers and sisters and their villages in northern Syria from the Assad government and rival Islamic militia groups. Unfortunately, our government is against his actions."

"Why would the Turkish government be against that?" I asked after Ashti had translated. "Doesn't it support the Syrian rebels against Assad?"

"But not the Syrian Kurdish rebels," Bawan answered. "Our government fears that their real aim is not to just overthrow Assad but to establish a Kurdish state that would unite thirty million people and include not only northern Syria but also substantial parts of Turkey, Iraq, and Iran. Their fear of our intentions is the same fear that the Ottomans had of the Armenians intentions in 1915."

"Is their fear justifiable?" I asked.

"No, I don't think so," Bawan said. "While some Kurds want their own state, many, many more like us and Ashti are content and proud to be citizens of Turkey as long as we have the freedom to speak our minds, use our own language, have our own culture, live where we want, and elect our own officials."

When the meal was served, the conversation turned from politics to the similarities and differences in Armenian, Kurdish, and Turkish food. I enjoyed the meal and at its end, I asked Bawan if he would allow me to help pay. He proudly and generously refused. "You are our guest!"

Following Ashti's previous advice, I did not argue and accepted, thanking him once again for his hospitality.

After our lunch together, we descended to the street, and Bawan directed us to the small business he owned only a few minutes away from the restaurant. We turned off the main street into an alley filled with small shops of grain, spices, vegetables, and fruit and then into another alley with small stores selling shoes, clothes, and hardware. Soon we came to an open shop on the street where a young man banged metal at a forge. On display in the shop and on the street were the products of his labor—rakes, hoes, sickles, pick axes, and shovels.

Bawan introduced us to his employee and apologized that his shop was too small for all of us to sit down. He explained that he had inherited the business from his father, and he hoped that one day Loran would take it over and expand it. After taking some photos, I congratulated him and thanked him again for his hospitality. Ashti and I then left him there to continue down the alley with Rihana for a sightseeing tour of the old city.

Rihana was a transformed person away from her husband. During our meal together, she was careful not to assert herself, and she let Bawan dominate the conversation. Alone it was another matter. She was quite talkative and described different places in this labyrinth of ancient residences that we passed. Many of them she said had once been Armenian homes. Once, the ally we were walking in was so narrow that we had to stop and lean against the wall of an old building so a motorcycle cart with a TV in it could pass. Soon we came to a half-open black metal door at a portal in a high wall. Over the portal was a white marble sign saying Sourp Giragos Ermeni Kilisesi 1376—Saint George Armenian Church 1376. We entered.

The church was a large rectangular building of gray stone inside a spacious courtyard. A spindly bell tower, also of stone, rose high in the sky over it and was crowned with an onion shaped cupola and cross. Scattered at different places in the paved courtyard were a half-dozen square tables with four wooden chairs each. Three people sat at one of them with glasses of tea chatting, and a couple of other visitors milled about. Rihana led us to a portico and then inside the church itself. It was also empty except for two visitors.

The sanctuary was a very large room dominated by three rows of stone columns and arches holding up a flat ceiling of what looked to me to be made up of many round logs. Rihana explained that they held up a roof covered with soil like many of the old houses and churches in the city used to have. Rows of empty pews faced seven different altars in the front of the building. Red curtains with seven white crosses embroidered on them hid the altars. Also brightening up the gray stone floor, walls, and columns were the Turkish rugs here and there on the stone floor, the golden chandeliers hanging from the ceiling, the icons of saints and of the virgin and child on the walls, and the golden and red cushioned throne of the patriarch and lavender cushioned chairs for other authorities. Sun light came in through the many windows on both the sides and in the back of the sanctuary. The church was majestic in its simplicity.

After walking around and taking some photos and enjoying the beauty of the place, I followed Rihana and Ashti outside to the covered portico where Rihana pointed out a display in Turkish, Armenian, and English giving some highlights of the history of the church and of Armenians in the city. All three of us went over to look at the pictures and read the captions. Many of the photographs looked like the black and white ones that Garabed had taken in Harput and they showed small Armenian bands and orchestras, political party gatherings, families, students, businesses, and social gatherings. Here were also pictures of Armenian Orthodox religious figures in their characteristic black robes with pointed hoods. One picture that I particularly appreciated showed the skyline of Diyarbakir before the destruction of 1915 with the bell towers and crosses of the Saint George Armenian Church and its neighbor, the Mar Petyan Chaldean Catholic Church, high above the rooftops. On these rooftops were dozens of beds surrounded by white sheets where families slept in the summer trying to escape the heat of the region.

Reading the captions underneath, I discovered that at the beginning of the twentieth century, around 35,000 Armenians lived in Diyarbakir and that the vice-mayor of the city was almost always an Armenian. Half of the members of the city and provincial councils were also Christians, mostly Armenians. Armenians had government roles as tax collectors, treasurers, fiscal directors, and even were officials in the prison system and police forces. Along with other groups like the Chaldean Catholics, Syriac Christians, and Protestants, Christians also dominated the professional and commercial life of the city as doctors, lawyers, pharmacists, and store-owners. Protestant, Catholic, and Orthodox Armenians each had their own schools as well.

"It was such a thriving community here," I said to Ashti who was also looking at the pictures and reading the captions beside me. "It sounds a lot like Harput was."

"You're right. What a horror it must have been to lose so much, so quickly," she replied.

Other photographs showed the church when it was abandoned, roofless, and with weeds growing on its pavement and the construction work that transformed it into what it was today—the largest Armenian church in the Middle East. When I came to a photograph showing the consecration of the restored church in October of 2011, Rihana stood by me, pointing at it. She said proudly in English, "I was there."

"You were?" Ashti was surprised. "But I thought that Bawan always wanted you to hide your Armenian background."

"Up until a few years ago, he did," she said. "He was worried about the repercussions it might have on his business and on Loran. Then after the mayor reaffirmed the importance of Armenians and other Christians in the history of Diyarbakir, apologized publically for the Kurdish role in the massacres, and committed government funds to restoring some of their churches, Bawan became less concerned. Public opinion here began to change, as well."

"Probably because a lot of Kurds came to see Armenians as a persecuted minority just like themselves and therefore as allies," Ashti said.

Rihana nodded. "Anyway, with the mayor's action, the image of Diyarbakir began to change some from being a hotbed of Kurdish nationalism to a place where reconciliation between different ethnic and religious groups was valued and promoted." She paused and added. "Bawan even came with me to the rededication of the church in 2011. It was a big public event with the mayor and other local officials, along with thousands of Armenians from Istanbul and from all over the world."

I listened carefully, but since I did not get it all, Ashti had to translate for me their exchange.

"Sometimes, I even come here by myself and try to remember grandmother and work out in my own mind what it means to be a Muslim Armenian."

"I know exactly what you mean," Ashti said.

"We Islamized Armenians are much more numerous here in Diyarbakir than the few Christian Armenians," Rihana said.

"Have any of them re-converted?" I asked.

"I know of only a few. One of them later moved away to Armenia," Rihana answered.

I took a few more pictures of the displays and then walked around the courtyard taking more. When I returned to where Ashti and Rihana were talking, Rihana asked, "Are you ready to see the Armenian house? It's right down the street."

I was, and so I followed Rihana and Ashti back out the portal into the narrow alley. A short walk later, we came to another metal door and Rihana rang the bell beside it. Within a minute, a friendly woman with two little girls behind her opened it.

"Is this a good time to visit?" Rihana asked.

"Yes, please come in," she said.

"I've been here a couple of times before," Rihana explained to the woman, but my cousins here have not. Ashti is from Istanbul, and Peter is from America, and we all have a little Armenian blood in us. They want to see how well-to-do Armenians used to live here in Diyarbakir."

"Welcome," the woman said smiling.

I said hello in Turkish to the two little girls peeking at us from behind their mother, and they giggled. The mother shooed them back into their quarters to the right of the house and said, "You are free to wander around at will, and if I can be of help in anyway, just let me know. I just ask that you please not touch anything." She then followed her children into their apartment.

As we passed through the courtyard to the stairs that led to the main entrance of the house, Rihana explained and Ashti translated. "The house was restored a few years ago by a prominent Turkish woman author from Diyarbakir, but it was only opened last year to visitors. Its opening was one more positive step in recuperating the memory of our Armenian ancestors who played such an important role in the history of our city."

As I looked around, I saw that the courtyard was spacious and mostly paved with stone. One section had some soil, however, where a large tree grew. I also noticed that the Armenian family living here must have gotten water from their own well, as a hand pump was sticking up from the ground and dripping water.

The house was a beautiful two-storied gray and white stone, flat-roofed building with arches and windows on three sides of the courtyard. Climbing the stairs on to a covered outside sitting porch with divan, we entered into three long rooms on the second floor, each with high ceilings and indented spaces in the stonewalls to place decorations and personal items. In the main sitting room, chandeliers hung from the wooden ceiling, finely woven carpets covered the stone floor, and upholstered chairs and divans were pushed against the wall for people to sit on. In the center of the room, a beautiful brass brazier kept everyone warm in the cold winters. The walls were decorated with mirrors, framed embroideries, and tapestries—one of them prominently showing a cross. The two bedrooms of the house were similar, but instead of chairs they had only divans, beds, cradles, and chests to store clothes. In one of the bedrooms, fine Armenian nightgowns were displayed.

Downstairs, at the patio level, was the kitchen with its fireplace for cooking and the different pots and pans, plates and dishes needed to prepare a meal. Beside it was a storage room with clay jars filled with grains and other foods. A tiny room acted as the bedroom for the employee who served the house.

As we went through the house, I tried to imagine what was similar and what was different here to the way our own ancestors had lived in Hussenig and Harput. The inhabitants of this house were a more wealthy and urban family than the Terzians, but my guess is that they shared many similarities in their values and culture.

As we finished our visit and were ready to leave, we called the friendly caretaker to thank her. I left her five lira as a donation, which was more than Rihana had suggested. The caretaker seemed pleased and wished us a happy stay in Diyarbakir.

It turned out to be just that—a very happy and interesting stay in Diyarbakir. For the rest of the afternoon, Rihana walked with us through the narrow allies showing us some of the other old Christian churches now being restored. We visited a former Nestorian Church in the Inner Fortress of the city, the Mar Petyun Chaldean Catholic Church, the Armenian Catholic Church, and the third century Virgin Mary Ancient Assyrian Church, which was particularly meaningful to me because of our family's Syriac heritage through Talitha. Speaking with the caretaker in that beautiful hidden jewel of a building with its silver lamps and centuries old icons, I learned that Christians had been in Amida, now known as Diyarbakir, since the first century. They had flourished in the city until the 1915 purges. Today very few Christian families still remained, and were it not for the financial and moral support of overseas Armenian, Chaldean, and Syriac Christians, the churches would be unsustainable. The caretaker was also very grateful to the Diyarbakir municipal government for its efforts at reconciliation and restoration. "It has meant so much to us," he said.

Walking back through the maze of alleys to Gazi Avenue, the main thoroughfare of old Diyarbakir, we were glad that Rihana was with us as it was so easy to get lost. When we got to the avenue, we turned north towards the Harput Gate. While we walked, we began to hear the calls for the late afternoon prayers from the mosques in the city. At the Hasanpaşa Inn, where we had had lunch, people were already entering the large mosque across the street.

Rihana saw me looking at it, and said, "It's called Cami-I Kebir or the Great Mosque. It is the oldest mosque in eastern Turkey and is considered by some to be the fifth holiest mosque in Islam. There used to be a Christian church there called Mar Thoma, which dated from the first century. When the Muslims took over the city in 639, they converted it into a mosque." She paused a few seconds and looked at Ashti. "Actually, since it is time for prayers, would you like to go in?"

Ashti hesitated, looking at me to see what I would like to do.

"You two go in and pray, and I will head back to the hotel."

"Are you sure?" Ashti asked.

"Of course," I replied. "I've got a lot of notes to write up. It will also give you and Rihana some time to be together without having to sightsee and speak English for my benefit."

After ascertaining that indeed that was what I wanted to do, and checking with Rihana, Ashti agreed to meet me at the hotel at half-past eight the next morning and we would continue our journey to Mardin. I thanked Rihana for her kindness in treating us to lunch and taking us on such a useful tour of the city. Since we were standing in front of a famous mosque in a conservative Muslim city, I was not sure whether to say goodbye by shaking her hand, embracing her as a relative, or doing nothing. She solved my problem by giving me a warm smile and extending her hand, so I shook it as gratefully as I could. While I headed up the street to the hotel, they crossed the avenue to do their ablutions before entering the mosque for prayer.

That night, after getting a loaf of bread and some cheese in a small store down the street, I wrote up my thoughts for the day and got on the internet. I reserved two rooms in a hotel in Mardin in the old city for the next few days and replied to an e-mail from Father Gregory. He said that he was looking forward to seeing us, but that all day Friday he would be in Midyat, only getting back to the monastery where he was staying near Mardin in the late afternoon. He wondered if we could meet Friday evening around six o'clock at our hotel in Mardin, have dinner together, and make plans for the rest of the week. I wrote back confirming the meeting. I also gave him the name of our hotel and address and Ashti's phone number if something changed. I then went to bed, satisfied with the day but with my feet worn out from all of the walking.

CHAPTER 18

The Road from Diyarbakir to Mardin

At a quarter of nine on Friday morning, Bawan arrived at the hotel on his motor scooter with Ashti sitting behind him and her suitcase between his legs. Bawan said his own goodbyes and those of Rihana and once again insisted that we give their son, Loran, a call when we got to Mardin.

After Bawan had left for his work, and after I verified that the Terzian Cross was still safe in the trunk, we got in the rental car and made one last visit to the old city entering through the Harput Gate and exiting out the Mardin Gate, south of the city. I knew from what I had read from Armenian deportation accounts, that outside this portal from the city, Kurdish tribesmen sometimes waited for the Armenian deportation caravans heading south in order to steal their goods and their women.

The road we took from the gate followed the Tigris River, which was called the Dicle River here in this area of Turkey. A few kilometers outside the city walls, I stopped the car to take some pictures of the eleventh century Dicle Bridge, which must have been the bridge Karine mentioned in her memoirs. The majestic bridge, with its ten stone arches through which the calm, shallow waters of the Tigris flow, now existed for no practical reason—only to allow pedestrians to walk on it, to give pleasure to the senses, and to honor the past. To me, those were worthy enough reasons.

We continued following the old road a few more kilometers past the bridge and then turned west until we came to the new four-lane highway heading to Mardin, some ninety kilometers south. I imagined that it must have been right around here that Talitha's mother-in-law had died and been buried. As we got on the main highway, I asked Ashti to re-read the section in the memoirs describing the site so that we could be on the lookout for anything resembling it.

Ashti got the memoir from my daypack and after looking through it for the right place, she read:

> That night, Grandmother died. I don't know to this day if it was by choice or by her body's exhaustion. Many Armenians carried poison as a final remedy when they could take no more, but I hold to the belief that Grandmother died because it was her time and not her choice. We buried her like my brother Lazar, in a simple grave by the road with stones covering her body. I marked it in my mind as I had Lazar's grave. It was also near a tree but in a flat area near a dry stream two days march from Diyarbakir and a day's march from where we had camped the first night south of the Tigris Bridge.

"It could have been anywhere around here," I said to Ashti. "We are about a two-day march from Diyarbakir and everything is flat." I decided to pull off the highway and take a picture of an area near a dry stream even though I had no real idea where they buried her. I did so because I wanted to honor her memory, to let her know that she mattered, and that she was certainly worth a picture.

For the next fifty kilometers of the trip, the land continued to be flat and fertile with bright green fields of grain on both sides of the highway. "I wonder if the land was this fertile back then," I said to Ashti. "If so, Karine and Talitha could have lived off some of the grain and grasses in the fields as they marched south."

"Maybe," Ashti said. "But remember that they were more fortunate than the rest because of the bread that your great-grandfather, Altay, gave them each day."

I thought about that for a long time as I drove and then shared my thoughts with Ashti. "We are all such mixed bags, aren't we, Ashti?" I said. "My great-grandfather raped my great-grandmother, but then saved her. The Kurds robbed, kidnapped, and killed our ancestors but now are helping them rebuild their churches in Diyarbakir."

"People can change," Ashti replied. "I saw that in the attitude of Bawan when I was at his home last night. He used to be so dogmatic in his beliefs, and I expected a harangue about us traveling together, but he did not even bring it up once. He's also now much more open about Rihana's Armenian Christian heritage and even allows her to explore it more by meeting other Islamized Armenians like herself."

"What do you think made the difference?"

"My take from our conversation last night is that he has come to recognize the distruction and other evil results that religious and political fanaticism can cause," Ashti said. "Through Rihana, he has also learned how the Armenians and other Christians suffered during the last years of the Ottoman Empire. Through Loran, he has learned first-hand stories about the terrible pain radical Muslims have brought to the cities and people in Syria. They kill anyone who does not agree with them—Christian, Muslim, or Secularist, and often in terrifying ways like burnings and crucifixion."

"I thought religion was supposed to be about compassion and good works," I said.

"To some, though, it is more about doctrine and power, and selfishly making sure that one gets into paradise by following what one think are the shortcuts," Ashti countered.

"I'm glad that compassion finally got the upper hand in the case of Altay and now Bawan," I said.

After about forty minutes more on the highway, the flat green fields ended and were replaced by brown, rocky hills spotted here and there with trees and fields. As we drove through the barren land and got closer to Mardin, I asked Ashti to read once more from Karine's memoirs. I wanted to see if we could locate the spot outside of Mardin where Altay had taken them aside to make his offer to marry Karine if she would convert to Islam.

As before, Ashti found the place and read.

It was early evening and we had just come down a steep incline from a half-moon range of cliffs into a rocky valley. It was a desolate place with no village. That fact was a blessing and a curse, as villages meant water but they also meant danger from kidnappers and rapists. A sizable stream cut through the valley and on each side of its banks were two green strips that contrasted sharply with the brown rocks and dirt everywhere else. In the distance from where we stopped stood a roofless house of stone and mud brick and a livestock pen beside it in ruins.

"This might be easier to locate than Talitha's mother-in-law's grave," I said. "She gives more details."

"When we get within fifteen kilometers of Mardin and start descending the mountains, we should start looking for it," Ashti suggested.

Not long afterwards, we passed a highway sign saying Mardin, 10 kilometers, and soon after that, we began to descend from the high plateau we were on into a long rocky valley with a small river running through it. About halfway down the slope, I looked into the rearview mirrors on both sides of the car and saw the half-moon of cliffs that Karine had described. "I think this is the valley," I said. "The stream is in the right place, it is the right distance from Mardin, and it looks like a half-circle of cliffs behind us."

Ashti turned around and looked out the back window. "I think you're right."

When we got to the valley floor, I turned off the highway onto a dirt road and parked. "Now we have to look to see if there might be any remains of a roofless house and livestock pen," I said. I reached for my binoculars on the back seat and got out of the car while Ashti remained inside. Scanning the area with the binoculars, I saw rocks just about everywhere, but the only place where there seemed to be a pattern in them was about a hundred yards away, farther down the road and to the right.

I got back into the car and drove there, pulling off close to the ruins of what now looked even more to me like the foundation of a house and walled enclosure area for animals. Before getting out again to examine them, I opened Karine's memoir to refresh my memory of what happened here.

When Altay arrived at the side of the empty house, he got off his horse and tied her to a scrubby tree. He then reached into his koorge or saddlebag and pulled out what looked like some dried meat. He then motioned for us to follow him through the door into the roofless structure. Inside, he told us to sit on one of the fallen beams that were on the ground. Once we had done so, he gave us the dried goat meat to eat. We grabbed it, and as we devoured it, he said, "I know you fear me, but I will not hurt you anymore. I did an evil thing to you and I wish to make amends."

Even though I could recognize him by his voice, face, and build, I had never really looked at him straight on in the day light. I still could not bring myself to do so out of the fear and the shame that still dominated my emotions and actions. Gradually, however, as we ate the meat, I looked at him from the edges of my eyes. He was a young man in his twenties, tall and thin and with a full moustache. He wore a soldier's cap and a dirty uniform with some type of minor rank medal insignia on his chest and a stripe or two on his sleeves. Perhaps he was a sergeant. He carried a rifle, because the gendarmes always did so, but he had put it down beside him on the ground.

"In two days, we will get to Mardin," he continued. "There the caravan will stop for a few days and food will be brought as it was done in Diyarbakir. There you will wait a decision of the authorities. You may then be taken to Urfa and to the camps of Aleppo, or you may continue straight south by foot through the desert to the camps of Ras al-Ayn and Deir ez-Zor. Both are difficult journeys and many of you will surely die. In Mardin, I will leave you and will no longer be able to protect you."

"Why are you telling us this?" Mother asked, raising her head and looking at him.

"Because I wish to offer you a way of escape," he replied. "Mardin is my home and I can protect you there as my father is an Imam, a respected religious leader in the town. For such a thing to be possible, though, you both must be willing to convert to the true religion and you must give your daughter to me for my wife. That way I can amend for my dishonor and her dishonor."

"How could I permit such a thing?" Mother asked. "It would be much more dishonor to her and to me and to God if we said we were Muslims and in our hearts we did not believe."

Altay was quiet for a moment and then looked sadly at her. "Then there is no other way. I will not force you, as our Prophet has said there is no compulsion in religion. Neither do I wish to bring further shame on me or on you. "Insha'Allah, May God's will be done."

"But there is another way," Mother said, suddenly. She then told him her story of growing up in a Syriac village near Mardin and of the murder of her parents by the Hamidiye, the Kurdish special forces of the Sultan. She told him of going to the Protestant girl's school there and of her certainty that the missionaries would help them if they could get to them. She thanked Altay for his compassion and pleaded with him to help us find the missionaries and school once we got to Mardin.

Altay made no reply. He just said that it was time for us to return to the camp. We walked in front and he followed us on his horse. As we got to the edge of the camp we parted ways, he to his tent with the soldiers and we to our spot among the deportees. Some of them looked up at us now, surprised that we had returned.

I got out of the car, and this time, Ashti accompanied me. As I picked up some stones, which might have been those of the ruined house where Karine, Talitha, and Altay talked, I tried to conjure up in my mind the scene of a hundred years ago. I imagined the faces and the feelings of my great-grandparents at this pivotal moment—Altay's attraction to Karine, coupled with his sense of guilt; and Karine's fear of Altay, and at the same time gratitude for his food and protection.

Ashti, too, must have been pondering what had happened here so long ago, as she asked me, "If it were not for her mother refusing Altay's offer for her, do you think Karine, by herself, would have accepted it and become a Muslim wife like her sister, Margarit?"

I tried to think like a young Karine and answered, "Alone, without her mother and the hope of finding the missionaries to save her, I bet she would have. People will do just about anything to survive and to escape pain. They lie, steal, betray their friends, prostitute themselves, and even kill others. In comparison with a lot of other things, changing one's religion shouldn't be so hard, if survival depends on it."

"That's what makes the few who would rather die for their religious beliefs than betray them such remarkable people," Ashti said. She then asked me, "Is there anybody or anything that you would be willing to undergo torture and die for, Peter?"

"Wow, that's a hard question," I answered. "I guess that the truthful answer right now for me is 'no.'"

"Not God, not nation, not family, not friends?" she asked.

"I would certainly instinctively fight to protect my family and friends and maybe die in the process of doing so. But I doubt I would have the courage to say 'yes' to being tortured and killed in such a situation." I added, "I wish that I believed in and loved something that strongly, but I don't. I'm too cynical and selfish."

"I appreciate your honesty, Peter. I always have," Ashti said.

I then asked her a question. "What do you think about Muslim suicide bombers? They seek a martyr's death for their religious beliefs. Are they unselfish?"

"Unselfish?" Ashti exclaimed. "They are the most selfish of all people. They have no thought for others, but only in taking what they believe is an easy shortcut to the pleasures of paradise for themselves. They are willing and even anxious to kill others in horrible manners in order to achieve their goals."

"Who then is unselfish? Doesn't selfishness define us all?" I asked.

"I think that Jesus was unselfish, actively choosing torture and death over power and glory for the good of others."

"You sound like a Christian, instead of a Muslim," I said.

"I can be a Muslim and still admire Jesus," Ashti said.

I knew very little about the Muslim view of Jesus other than that they believed in his virgin birth, his miracles, and that he was a great and good man and a Prophet of Allah. But they certainly did not believe that he died on the cross, resurrected, or that he was in any sense Allah or the Son of Allah.

For about ten minutes, I took pictures of the foundations of the house, of the large stream cutting through the barren soil in the distance, and of the half-circle of cliffs in the background. I wanted to preserve it in my memory. After I finished, Ashti and I got back into the car and headed to our next stop, ten kilometers away, the mountain city of Mardin.

CHAPTER 19

Mardin

Ancient Mardin, like ancient Diyarbakir is a beautiful city, yet the two are very different. Diyarbakir, much larger than Mardin, is a walled metropolis on the plain while Mardin is a city with no walls except for those of the citadel at the top of the mountain to which it clings. While the defining characteristic of Diyarbakir is the black basalt stones that are incorporated into its fortifications and buildings, the defining characteristic of Mardin is the cream colored sandstone, sometimes beautifully carved, with which its closely packed houses, churches, and mosques were constructed.

After entering through the modern suburbs of Mardin, Asti and I followed our car's GPS instructions to our hotel in the old city. Because the hotel I had reserved was located on a side-alley off the narrow, one-way main street of the town, we had to stop and ask for directions to it. While I waited in the car, Ashti got out, climbed some steep steps, found the hotel, and returned with a clerk to show us where to park. He took us a long and circuitous route to a parking place above the hotel in front of what I discovered later was the Zinciriye Madrasa, or school. We then descended the street steps from the madrasa to the hotel. I quickly decided that Old Mardin was not the place to own a car.

The hotel, although moderately priced, was a majestic old building of three floors that was the former mansion of a Syriac Christian businessman before the 1915 deportations. Both of our rooms were on the second floor next to each other and although small, they were elegant with their vaulted ceilings and nice bathrooms.

As it was past midday, the calls to prayers were loud and came from the minarets rising above the flat-roofed buildings from all corners of the old town. Ashti decided that since it was Friday, she wanted to go to a mosque to pray. Changing into the long-sleeve blouse and modest dress she had brought with her, she covered her hair with a scarf and climbed the street steps to the madrasa and mosque where our car was parked.

For my part, as we had so little time in Mardin, I decided to get started looking for the former American missionary school and hospital Karine spoke of in her memoirs. I also wanted to see if I could locate the house of Dr. and Mrs. Frazer where she and Talitha had stayed for several months.

Before Ashti left for the mosque, we agreed to meet back at the hotel lobby in an hour and then get something to eat. I also requested a favor from her. "It's a long shot, but if you get a chance and meet some religious authority, ask them if they have ever heard of Imam Aslan, my great-great-grandfather."

"I will," she said.

After she had gone, I descended the courtyard stairs of the hotel desk and asked the clerk, who spoke English, if a tourist office was located nearby where I could get a detailed map of old Mardin and information about a former American school and hospital in the town.

"The tourist office will probably be closed right now because of prayers, but we have a map that you can have," he said. He reached under the counter and pulled out a plan of the old town, unfolding it on the reception desk so that I could see it. "We are right here," he said, "close to the Zinciriye Madrasa." He pointed with his finger to the spot. "I don't know anything about an American hospital or school in Mardin today, but here is a place on the map at the edge of the city showing where the old American mission was." He marked it with a pen. "That might be the place you are looking for, although it is a gendarme headquarters now."

I thanked him and decided that is where I would go first. With map in hand, I descended the stairs to the main street of the old town and turned right heading towards the location the clerk had indicated. During my half-kilometer walk, I admired the exquisite and well-preserved architecture of Mardin and felt like I was walking in an outside museum. The buildings to my right and to my left were beautiful and majestic, constructed with rectangular cream-colored stones that sometimes were chisled with motifs. Whether the buildings were churches, residences, hotels, or businesses, they all fit together in harmony. The most majestic, largest, and perhaps most beautiful building I passed was near the town's Atatürk stature. I read on my map that it was the former Patriarchal See of the Syrian Catholic Church that had been purchased by the government for a museum. I climbed the grand stairs to its entrance but unfortunately found that it was closed for repairs.

Returning to the street, I looked carefully at the faces of the people coming towards me, as well as those sitting at tea tables, shopping in stores, and doing repair work on the carved stone facades and arches. I wanted to see if any of them resembled my Grandfather Noah and might be a distant cousin descended from Altay and Imam Aslan. I felt a certain pride, too, that this fascinating mountain town with so much Armenian, Chaldean, Syriac, and Muslim history, was in a sense my town, as it was where my ancestors lived.

When I finally got to the end of Cumhuriyet Caddessi, the main street that cut through the upper city, I turned down a busy road towards the spot on the map that indicated the former compound of the American missionaries. As Karine had indicated in her memoirs, it was at the edge of town, and like the hotel clerk had said, it was now a large military installation. I approached the soldiers at the entrance, feeling intimidated by their battle gear and the sandbags and concertina razor wire that separated us. This ugly and aggressive sight seemed so incongruous in such a peaceful and lovely place as Mardin. So did their reception of me.

When I got near to the soldiers, I greeted them in Turkish and said that I was an American tourist and wondered if there had been an American hospital and school here at one time. I approached them to show them the spot on the map, but they refused to look at it and waved me off. One of them shook his head. "This is a military installation, and no hospital."

"May I enter and ask someone else?" I asked.

"No, it is not permitted," the same soldier said, while the others beside him and in the guardhouses looked on.

"May I take a picture," I finally asked.

"No, that also is not permitted," the soldier replied. "You must also get away from the gate."

Seeing that I was getting nowhere and wondering why the soldiers were so unfriendly, I turned around and headed back in the direction of the hotel, thinking that I would now try to locate the Frazer's house. Finding a quiet and shady alley off the main street, I took the daypack off my shoulder, retrieved Karine's memoirs inside it and reviewed once more Karine's account of leaving the school compound and arriving at the Frazer's house.

At the gate of the school compound, Altay told the guard that since it was night, he was going to accompany the cart driver to his home and would be back within an hour. The cart then started up again, and Mother, who was lying beside me, squeezed my hand in happiness. Then for about fifteen minutes, we bounced along the cobblestone streets of Mardin hearing at first the night sounds of a main street with its public places and then the relative silence of a smaller residential alleyway. Altay, from time to time, would give the cart driver directions.

Finally, the cart stopped, and Altay came back and pulled the canvas off us. He told us to get out. He said that we were at the residence of Dr. Frazer, an American missionary doctor who had lived in the city for many years. He then pointed to a locked wooden door of the courtyard wall and his last words to us were, "I will leave you now, but if you reconsider my proposal, look for Altay, the son of Imam Aslan. But do not mention to anyone that I have helped you as it would cause me great trouble." He then gave something to the cart driver and then turned his horse back towards the deportee camp at the school.

The cart driver also drove off, not looking back. We were then alone in the narrow cobblestone street. It was an hour or two after dark, and we saw a flicker of oil lamps from a window above the street.

I tried to imagine that night. The Frazer house was some fifteen minutes away by oxcart from the American school. In my mind, I saw the oxcart leaving what is now the military base and climbing the road to the main street of Mardin with all of its noise and activities. Eventually turning off it into a quieter alley, the oxcart arrived at the Frazier's house.

I decided that I would walk down Cumhuriyet Caddessi for about five or ten minutes and explore the side alleyways accessible by oxcart. I would look for a walled compound of several houses with one of the houses having an upstairs window looking down onto the alley. Karine had also later mentioned trees in the courtyard behind the wall in another part of her memoirs, so this was another clue I would look for.

With this information to guide me, I went back to the main street and turned right, keeping my eyes open for a quiet alley off it that an oxcart could travel on and that had residences on both sides. I soon found such an alley and followed its cobblestone pavement for some fifty yards by walled houses until I came upon a place that easily could have been the Frazer residence and compound. Behind a long high wall with an arched stone portal and metal gate, I could see the tops of three trees and three houses. One of them had an upstairs window overlooking the alley. Convinced that this might be it, I took some pictures and then went to the metal gate and knocked, hoping that someone there might know the history of the compound. I waited and then knocked again, the metal making an echoing sound, but no one came. Disappointed but determined to try again later, I returned to the hotel to meet Ashti at the hour we had stipulated.

As Ashti had not returned when I arrived, I spoke with the hotel clerk about his recommendations for places to eat in the town, both for a quick snack right now and a meal later that night. I also asked him about places that he recommended for us to see.

"The best place to start," he said, "is the city museum." He showed me where it was on the map. "There, you can get an overview of Mardin's character and history. Then, I suggest visiting the churches, mosques, public baths, and buildings of the city. Some of the churches date from the fourth century."

"What about the fort at the top of the mountain?" I asked.

"Unfortunately, it is temporarily closed for repairs."

I thanked him and requested that he tell Ashti that I was in my room when she returned from her prayers.

Fifteen minutes later, while I was on my bed typing my impressions of the morning into my laptop, Ashti knocked on my door. When I opened it, she had a big smile on her face and handed me two pieces of paper—one written in Turkish and the other, a faded picture of an older bearded man with a turban seated on an elevated cushion surrounded by a dozen young men. "I think that this is your great-great-grandfather, Imam Aslan!" she said excitedly.

"You're kidding!" I exclaimed. "Tell me everything!" Since the one chair in my room had my clothes on it, I motioned for her to sit by me on the bed.

She shook her head. "No, I'll meet you in five minutes at the lanchonette upstairs on the roof. We'll get something to eat and then, I'll tell you." She smiled. "I remember your passion on the mountain, and I don't want to give you any excuses!"

I laughed.

Within five minutes, we were sitting together at the hotel's small tea and snack place on its flat roof and had ordered some pastries and tea. Another couple sat at one of the other half-dozen tables. The view of the city below, the castle on the cliffs above, and the flat green Mesopotamia Plain in the far distance was spectacular.

"Now that you're safe here in a public place," I joked, "tell me what happened."

"Well, I went to the mosque in the madrasa right above the hotel for prayers. When I got there, I quickly realized that it wasn't really a public mosque. Only a dozen or so people were there, and in fact, I was the only woman. Most of them were students enrolled in Theology courses at the local university along with their professor and a few staff people of the madrasa. I stood in the back, and after prayers, when we had all come out into the courtyard, I introduced myself to the professor who had led them and asked him for advice in how we could go about finding information on your ancestor Imam Aslan. The professor did not know of him personally, but he invited me upstairs to the office of the school. From one of the cabinets, he pulled out a book, some information folders, and picture albums telling the history of the madrasa from its founding in the fourteenth century. Together we went through archives relating to the late 1800s and early 1900s until we found the picture and the caption about Imam Aslan. We also found some written information. He was a respected Imam who taught there for some thirty years—until 1919."

"Wow," I said. I looked closely at the photograph to see if any of his features resembled my grandfather, my mother, or even me. It was very hard to tell given the age of the photograph and the fact that it was not a close-up picture.

"Anyway, the professor kindly offered to make me a copy of the picture and of the page in the book mentioning him. That's why I was a little late in getting back."

"By any chance, did you find out anything about his family?" I asked. "Are any of his descendents still here in Mardin?"

"I asked him, but he said he had no way of knowing. They don't have that type of information. Also, Atatürk did not start requiring last names until later so it would be hard to trace the family."

I nodded and looked again at the picture. "Thank you. This means so much to me!"

Ashti smiled and patted my hand. "I'm so glad."

As we sipped our tea and ate our pastries, I told her of my own adventures trying to locate the American hospital and school and the Frazer's house. I also mentioned the unfriendliness of the gendarmes.

"The soldiers here in the southeast are more hard-nosed than elsewhere, probably because of past Kurdish rebellions," she explained.

When we finished our snack, I suggested that we follow the advice of the hotel clerk and visit the city museum and then some of the churches and mosques of the city.

"You should start at the madrasa," Ashti said. "It's right here, it is beautiful, and it has tie-ins with your family history."

I thought that was a good idea, and so after leaving Ashti's information on Imam Aslan in my room, we climbed the steps to the Zinciriye Madrasa. According to my guidebook, it was also called the Sultan Isa Madrasa after the Sultan who built it in 1385, fought against Tamerlane, and was later imprisoned and then buried in the madrasa.

When we got there, Ashti showed me the magnificent but small rectangular mosque where she had just prayed with its red carpet, high vaulted ceiling, and stone pulpit. She then led me upstairs so I could meet the professor who had so kindly helped her. Since he was giving a class, we were unable to see him, but the person we talked to promised to thank him again for us.

Outside the madrasa again, I checked on our parked car, and we headed towards the city museum. This time we turned left rather than right on Cumhuriyet Caddessi as the museum was at its far end. The walk took us passed other residences turned into boutique hotels, the splendid post office with its grand stairway, an ancient hammam or bathhouse dating to Roman times, and numerous restaurants and tearooms filled with people.

The museum itself, like so many of the other buildings in Mardin, was a work of art. A former army barracks with two long vaulted wings, it now housed exhibits about the history of this ancient city. Some displays told of Mardin's importance because of its location at the intersection of trade routes including the silk route to China; others displayed the coming of the Christians in the second and third centuries; and still others of the conquering Muslims in the seventh century and of their different dynasties after that.

I was impressed with the quality of all of the exhibits about the town's history, architecture, and daily life—including examples of the craftsmanship of its inhabitants in copper, stone, and textile. I was most impressed, however, by the museum's emphasis on the theme of reconciliation between the diverse religious and ethnic groups that had once called Mardin their home— Jews, Christians, and Moslems; Armenians, Syriacs, Kurds, Turks, and Arabs.

Some displays showed examples of the peaceful co-existence of the groups and of their mutual celebration of life events like birth, marriage, and death and of religious events like Christmas, Easter, and Ramadan. One display showed excerpts from documents and pacts purportedly issued by Caliph Umar and Mohammed himself protecting Christians and their property. It also showed a photograph of a recent international conference in one of Mardin's madrasas promoting dialogue and respect between adherents to Christianity, Judaisim, and Islam. The curators of the museum had even videotaped interviews with former Christian inhabitants of Mardin who now lived in exile in other countries. Only in Diyarbakir, another Kurdish city, had I ever seen such an attempt in Turkey to mend fences.

After leaving the museum, Ashti and I decided that we just wanted to walk around the old city and visit some of the ancient churches that we had seen pictures of in the museum. We started with the earliest church that I could ascertain, the Saint Hirmiz Chaldean Church, which was founded in 397 A.D. It was a beautiful structure on the main street of upper Mardin and had recently been renovated. The caretaker told us that he knew of only five Chaldean families left in Mardin, but that a Syriac Orthodox priest presided over the services.

Close by was another ancient church originally built in 569 A.D. Now called the Church of the Forty Martyrs, this lovely Syriac Orthodox Church was still active. Several local men and women were inside lighting their candles and praying when we entered.

From there, we headed for the lower part of Mardin to visit an Armenian Church that we had seen pictures of in the museum. Founded in 424 A.D. as the Red Church, it was now called Sourp Kevork.

We had the hardest time finding it, as it was hidden in a maze of narrow alleys and steps of the old town. We asked several people for directions, and finally a local garbage man, who was picking up trash and putting it into the baskets strapped to the back of a gray donkey, showed us its location. To get to it, we had to enter through a kind of tunnel from the alley into a courtyard. The courtyard itself was filled with weeds, some old chairs, and other junk and rubbish. Some clothes were drying on a line and on the chairs. In contrast with the Chaldean Catholic and the Syriac Orthodox Churches we had just visited, the Armenian Church was totally abandoned and in ruins. Although the doors to the actual church building were locked, we could see through the cracks to an interior of broken columns, bricks and rubbish on the ground, and holes in the roof.

The caretaker, who lived with his wife and daughter in a dilapidated house beside the church, came out to greet us, and when he learned who we were, even invited us inside his house for tea. We thanked him but declined because of time constraints. He apologized for the condition of the church. "Hopefully, now that it is at the top of the list of endangered European cultural monuments, the government will begin to put some money into its renovation," he said in Turkish to Ashti.

"I hope so," I said after Ashti translated. We then thanked him and left.

Since Ashti had not yet seen the house that I thought might have been the Frazer's, I suggested that we visit it before returning to the hotel to meet Father Gregory. She agreed. Fifteen minutes later, after climbing the steep steps and negotiating the narrow allies of this mountain town, we arrived.

Just as before in my previous visit, we were alone in the alley outside the blue metal gate. I knocked again several times, but again, no one came. As we waited for some sound coming from inside, I said to Ashti, "Can you imagine what would have happened to Talitha and Karine that night if Dr. Frazer had not opened the door and let them in? What would they have done?"

"I have no idea," Ashti replied, shaking her head "You figure it out. You're the novelist!"

"My guess is that they would have looked for other foreigners in the city to help them. If that was not successful, they would go to Altay and Imam Aslan," I said. "If they agreed to Altay's terms, today I would be Muslim. If they did not agree, my guess is that they would have been captured eventually and either killed here in Mardin or died in another deportation caravan heading to Deir ez-Zor."

CHAPTER 20

Father Gregory

As we headed back to the hotel through the vegetable and fruit markets of the town off the main artery, Ashti got a call from Father Gregory on her cell phone, saying that he had just arrived at the monastery from Midyat. As he did not know how to get to our hotel, he wondered if we could meet instead at a well-known restaurant on Cumhuriyet Caddessi at around six.

Ashti agreed and wrote down the name of the restaurant. When we got back to the hotel at five-thirty, we found out from the desk clerk where it was located and then went to our rooms to clean up. I returned to our parked car on the street above the hotel, retrieved the Terzian Cross from the trunk and put it into my daypack. Afterwards, I met Ashti at the hotel entrance and we walked together to the restaurant, getting there right on time.

The restaurant was very similar to the one we had eaten in at Diyarbakir, a quiet courtyard off the busy street shaded by strips of canvas held up by ropes overhead. The stone arches around the courtyard gave the place a look of dignity and permanence, like that of so many of Mardin's buildings. When we entered the portal from the street, we looked around for Father Gregory but did not see him at any of the thirty or so tables, which at this time of day were mostly empty.

The headwaiter greeted us and took us to one of the tables in a corner. It was covered by a beautifully embroidered red and light tan tablecloth with benches on each side with matching cushions. We told the waiter that we were waiting for a friend, but that we would order our drinks. Ashti requested tea and I ordered a glass of Syriac wine, as I had never tasted it before.

"I know you want to pay your own way, but this meal is on me," I insisted. "You and Father Gregory are my guests, as otherwise it would be awkward."

"Okay," Ashti replied, "This one time. Thank you."

We did not have to wait long for Father Gregory. Right after I had taken my first sip of the pleasing, rich red wine, he appeared at the portal of the restaurant looking for us. It was hard at first to recognize him as he was bearded, with dark skin, and wore locally made pants, shirt, and coat that made him resemble the Kurds and Turks from the region. He wore no distinguishing clerical garb.

When Father Gregory recognized us, he waved and came over to our table. Ashti and I both got up and welcomed him. He gave me a handshake and hug, and he warmly shook Ashti's hand with both of his hands. In his eyes and smile, I could also see his delight in seeing us again.

"I'm sorry I'm a little late," he said. "I had a hard time finding a parking place."

"I know what you mean," I replied. "Mardin was not designed for cars, only for donkeys!"

Father Gregory laughed the hearty laugh that I remembered from years before when we traveled together in the northeast of Turkey. Actually, he had changed little in the six years since I had last seen him. His hair and neat beard were grayer, but he still had the same joyful eyes and the same slim physique.

Seeing that our friend had arrived, the waiter came back and took our orders. I played it safe and got a salad and Kebab while Ashti and Father Gregory ordered some local specialties like eggplant dolma, kisir, and meatballs that the waiter explained were prepared without cooking. We all ordered bottled water as well.

Father Gregory then asked the question I knew was coming. "I can't wait to hear about your trip. What have you seen and learned thus far?

I quickly went through the whole journey. I told him of the generosity of his parents to me in Watertown and of their love and concern for him. "Here's a gift your parents sent you," I said, as I pulled out the Red Sox cap from my daypack by my feet.

He laughed and put in on.

Ashti then reached into her own shoulder bag and put hers on, as well. "I got one, too!" she said, also laughing.

I then told him of my visit to Istanbul and of the Kayas help, as well as Dilovan's desire to see him but his inability to come because of the problem at the factory.

"Too bad! I had such a good time with all of you in Istanbul," he said to Ashti. "I'll be forever grateful for what your father did to get our grandmothers together. It meant so much to them both and to us."

When I got to our visit to Elazığ, I told him about meeting the family who had taken over the Terzian home in Hussenig. He asked many questions about them, which we both answered, and then I said, "We also have a surprise, a special gift for you from that visit, but I want to give it to you in a more private place, maybe at your car."

Father Gregory was intrigued, but I insisted that he would have to wait to see what it was. We then talked about our visit to Diyarbakir, to Ashti's aunt and uncle, and to the church.

"I'll be going to Diyarbakir in about eight days to take part in the Easter Service at Sourp Giragos," he said. "Maybe I can meet your relatives there. I'd love to, since your aunt is also a relative of mine!"

"That can be arranged," Ashti said. "She often goes to the church to meet other Islamized Armenians in Diyarbakir. It's such a beautiful place now that it has been restored."

"It is," I added. "On the other hand, the Armenian Church we visited here today in Mardin is completely abandoned."

"Yes, I know," Father Gregory said. "It is such a shame, and we are trying to get permission and to raise funds to restore it."

"Fortunately, the Syriac and Chaldean churches we visited were very nice," I said.

"It is all so confusing, these different churches," Ashti interjected. "You have so many—Armenian, Syriac, Chaldean, Eastern Orthodox, Catholic, Protestant. What's the difference?" she asked.

Father Gregory laughed and shook his head. "You mean you want me to give a lecture on early Christianity, when I just want to be with you and visit and hear of your adventures?"

"Not a lecture," Ashti said. "I just want a quick cheat sheet on their basic differences, because I really have no idea."

"A lot is mostly due to language differences," Father Gregory said. "For example, we Armenians worship in Armenian; the Assyrians, Chaldeans, and Syriac's Liturgy is in Aramaic or Syriac, the language of Jesus; and the Copts in the Coptic Egyptian language. The early Byzantine Orthodox and Roman Catholics, who used to worship in Greek and Latin, now use their own languages, just like the Protestants. Also, differences exist in attitudes towards the marriage of priests, church authority, and some cultural things."

"No theological differences?" I asked.

"Some, but the differences seem so much less important and a question of semantics nowadays than in the early years of the Church."

"For example?" I asked.

"For example, beliefs about the nature of Jesus. All of the early orthodox Christians agreed that Jesus was both human and divine. He was the Christ, the promised Messiah of the Jews. They seemed to disagree, though, on the formula for describing just how his human and divine natures were joined. Some described him as being one Person with two separate natures like water and oil that don't mix. This became the doctrines of the Western Church—the Roman Catholics, Eastern Orthodox, and the Protestants. Others described him as being one Person with two natures that do mix, like water and wine. This became the doctrine of the Oriental Church—the Syriacs; the Copts in Egypt, Ethiopia, and Eritrea; the Malabar Christians of India; and my own church, the Armenian Orthodox Church."

"What about the Chaldeans?" I asked.

"The Chaldean Church or the Assyrian Church of the East is a special and complicated case. Their early churches were mostly located outside of the boundaries of the Roman Empire in what was then the Sassanid Empire—the enemy of Rome. They, therefore, did not attend the church councils convoked by the Roman Emperor Constantine to determine official Church doctrine. Given where they were located, it also was not politically expedient for them to accept any decisions coming out of Constantinople other than the decisions of the First Council at Nicaea. Because of this, some in the Western Church saw their view of the nature of Christ as heretical. The Chaldeans always denied this, however, and today their views are seen by most of the other churches as orthodox, only expressed in a slightly different manner."

He added, "What's so fascinating about this branch of Christianity is that for many, many years the Church of the East prospered and spread to a much wider territory than the Western Churches. It eventually had bishoprics and churches throughout Asia, even in places like India, China, Tibet, Mongolia, Saudi Arabia, and Yemen. Some Mongolian chieftans had Christian wives, and the Church's future seemed secure. Then Islam came along, and Tamerlane destroyed just about everything Christian, both people and buildings, in the lands he controlled. Today, the Church of the East is only a small body of Christians, mainly in Iraq and in lands of exile like the United States and Europe."

"All of these theological points are a little hard for me to grasp," I said.

"Exactly," Father Gregory answered. "And we should be more interested in what unites us as Christians rather than the semantics and politics that separate us. Otherwise, it will be hard for us to survive much longer here in the Middle East. Although this is our birthplace, the radical Islamists are doing all they can to destroy us. Christians are afraid and fleeing."

"Your father says that you have been helping Armenians to get out of Syria."

"I've tried to. The Patriarch put me in charge of a special relief fund for those whose lives are threatened. So far, we've gotten hundreds out."

"How did you go about doing that?" I asked.

"At first, it was fairly simple. I just arranged for airplane tickets from Aleppo to Yerevan or for Armenians to go by bus through Turkey to Armenia. Now things are more complicated. The Aleppo airport has closed down, and the Islamic rebels now control some of the border crossings with Turkey that used to be open. Also the Turkish government is cracking down on the flood of refugees from Syria. It is a nightmarish situation for those still inside Syria who feel their lives threatened."

"Like I wrote you, I would like to do some articles on them," I said.

Father Gregory nodded and said, "I plan to introduce you to some refugees and they can tell you their stories. Actually, I have been trying to find a way to get the fiancée of one of them out right now. She is desperate because she is a Muslim convert to Christianity and her life is in danger."

"What about helping them cross the border illegally?" I asked. "Is that against your principles?"

Father Gregory smiled. "Life trumps rules!" he said. "I try to do everything legally, but when it is a matter of life and death, I have no qualms. In the past, I had a contact with a Free Syrian Army commander who helped me do just that. Unfortunately, he was killed last month in a bombing raid by the Syrian airforce. Now I have no accomplice, and I need one desperately."

Ashti spoke up. "Maybe my cousin can help. He lives somewhere near Nusaybin and crosses the border all the time. He smuggles fighters and supplies into Kurdish held territory in Syria. Maybe he can smuggle your people out."

Father Gregory turned to her with a fascinated look on his face. "Your cousin? You're kidding!"

"No, it is true," Ashti said. "I have his cell number and we can try to call him right now if you wish."

"I do wish."

Ashti reached into her shoulder bag for her phone and then looked up his number in her contacts. "What should I say?"

Father Gregory thought a minute and then said, "We can't talk over the phone. Do you suppose you could set up a meeting with him tomorrow or the next day? Nusybin isn't that far from here."

"Explain that we are distant cousins from the United States and would like to meet him," I suggested.

Ashti nodded and put in the number and waited. After about five rings, she left a message in Kurdish. "I told him it was me and that his parents had given me his number and that I was close by in Mardin and would love to see him. I asked him to return my call."

"Great!"

About then, our meals came. As we ate, Father Gregory asked us about our plans after Sunday. "How long are you going to be in the area?"

"Ashti wants to go to Urfa and Harran on Monday. Since Dilovan couldn't come, I would like to accompany her," I said.

"I've always wanted to visit those towns because of their connection with Abraham," Ashti explained.

"Maybe I can set up some more interviews in the refugee camp on the border just south of Harran. Several Armenian families are there that I've helped," Father Gregory said. He then asked me, "When do you plan to return to the United States?"

"The day after Easter," I replied. "Ashti and I need to return to Elazığ to leave off our car and catch our flight on Easter night. She has to be at work the next day, and I plan to return to Boston."

He nodded and then said, "As for tomorrow, why don't we meet at the monastery, and then drive together to Tur Abdin? My idea is to visit Talitha's old village, continue on to Midyat and see the refugee camp and the old Syriac section of the city, and then head south for your interview with some Armenian refugees I've placed with some Syriac families."

We agreed and I thanked him again for setting everything up. After the meal was finished, Ashti and I accompanied Father Gregory to his car, an old Fiat parked on the street two blocks away. "It belongs to the monastery and not to me," he explained.

When Father Gregory opened the door and got into the driver's seat, he smiled and said, "Now just what was that special gift from Hussenig that you said wanted to give me when I got to the car?"

I looked around to see if anyone was watching and then pulled out the Terzian family's silver cross from my daypack.

"You found it!" he said, when he saw the cross. "Father wrote me that you might look for it."

"I did. It was right where Karine said it would be. Your father and all of us want you to have it."

"Thank you, thank you." He took it into his hands caressed it and then kissed it. When he turned towards me, I think that I even saw tears beginning to gather in his eyes. "It means so much to me," he said.

"I'm glad," I replied.

Father Gregory put the cross reverently on the seat beside him and after thanking me again for the meal and the gifts, he said he would be waiting for us at eight-thirty at the entrance to the monastery. He waved and then drove off.

"That was very moving," Ashti said as we walked back to the hotel.

"It was."

I wanted to hold her hand, but I didn't.

CHAPTER 21

The Syriacs

S aturday morning after breakfast, we climbed the street stairs to our car and then drove the six kilometers from Mardin to the Mor Hananyo Monastery to pick up Father Gregory. I had read about the monastery the night before in the tour guide. Founded in 493 A.D. on the site of a former temple dedicated to the worship of the sun, it had been destroyed and rebuilt numerous times after attacks by the Persians, the Mongols, and others. Known popularly as the Saffron monastery, Deyrul Zafaran, because of the color of its stones, it was probably the most important of the monasteries of the Syriac Orthodox Church. Indeed, from 1160 to 1932 A.D. it was the headquarters of the Church until they moved to Damascus because of persecution in Turkey. Ironically, Syrian Syriac families were now moving back to Turkey to escape the war and persecution in Syria.

As we approached the monastery, I saw that it was a formidable building, like a walled fortress isolated among the rocky hills. When we got to it, I parked near the monastery's clunker that Father Gregory had used the night before and saw him waiting for us at the top of the steps of the main building. He came toward us when he recognized us and greeted us.

"Let me give you a quick tour of the building before we leave," he suggested. "It's an active monastery with a few monks and seminary students, but it is also one of Mardin's main tourist attractions. There will be busloads of Turkish tourists coming from Mardin later in the day to visit, so this is a good time to see it while it is still quiet."

He took us up the stairs, past the small ticket office, the store, and café, and then farther up the hill, to the actual monastery. Entering the peaceful courtyard, he showed us the chapel with its gold Patriarch's throne. He then took us below to the former temple to the sun that the monastery had been built on and pointed out its massive stone ceiling constructed without mortar. One small window on a wall faced east towards the rising sun.

Returning to the courtyard and going up to the second floor, we stopped by the Archbishop's office to pick up a packet of documents to deliver to the Archbishop at the Mor Gabriel monastery near Midyat. We then continued on to Father Gregory's room, one of the few in the massive monastery that was now occupied.

His room was simple, consisting of a single bed, a wooden table and chair, a small icon table and bookcase mostly with religious books and dictionaries in different languages. Father Gregory picked up his laptop off the table and put it and the packet of documents into a briefcase. Then he went to the icon table and retrieved the Terzian Cross, putting it in as well. "It will bring hope and comfort to the Armenian family we will be visiting later today," he explained.

On the way out of the offices and sleeping quarters, Father Gregory greeted and then introduced us to a friendly, young French monk who was heading up the stairs from the courtyard in his black robe and distinctive hood with many small white Syriac crosses embroidered on it. His joyful face bewildered me. I could not understand how giving up fame, fortune, comfort, sex, and other pleasures to pursue a relationship with a God who no one knew for sure really existed could bring happiness.

After leaving the monastery, we drove through the modern section of the city of Mardin and then got on the new highway leading from Mardin to Midyat to the east. As on the other highways that we had traveled in Turkey, a lot of construction was going on, so every now and then, we had to slow down or stop. At one such place, Father Gregory turned to Ashti in the back seat and asked, "Have you heard back yet from your cousin about a possible meeting with him?"

"Not yet," Ashti answered. "Do you want me to try to call him again?"

"Maybe a little later. It's still too early in the morning."

After about fourteen kilometers on the highway, Father Gregory told me to take a turn to the left onto a smaller asphalt road heading north towards the town of Savur, a miniature version of Mardin constructed on a mountainside. Not far from Savur, Father Gregory indicated that I should take a right onto a small winding gravel road through the barren hills. At the end of it, we came to a few occupied houses along the road, and on the hill above them, the dilapidated remains of what once must have been a prosperous community. At Father Gregory's instructions, I took a bumpy dirt road that led up to the ruins. Some cows with bells clanking were coming down it, and when they saw us, they gave us a quizzical look as if wondering who we were and why we were there blocking their path. Once we passed them, I parked at the ruins near what must have once been an impressive house. Several structures like it were nearby, unlivable now as their roofs and walls had mostly fallen in.

From the hill we were on, I had a panoramic view of the valley below us and the ruins of what must have been a church and graveyard. Farther east were small plots of land, some with the ancient gnarled remains of vines and trunks of fruit trees, separated from each other by low stonewalls. A small stream ran by the former church and through the middle of the plots watering them. On a hill on the other side of the valley, I noticed young boys tending sheep and goats.

"This was our ancestor Talitha's home village, but I have no idea which of these houses belonged to her family," Father Gregory said. "They were fairly well off as they owned livestock, had vineyards, and plots of land for grain and fruit."

I got out my camera and started to take pictures.

"When Talitha lived here," he continued, "the village was entirely made up of Syriac Christian families. In 1895, Kurdish bands swept down from the north near Diyarbakir and destroyed almost everything, including the Syriac Orthodox and Protestant churches and the nearby monastery. Following the orders of Sultan Hamid II, they killed many people including Talitha's parents. They had hidden in a cave on the other side of the valley and either died of suffocation when the Kurds lit fires at the entrance to smoke them out, or perished from hatchet wounds as they tried to escape. Those few who survived those massacres, however, did not escape the 1915 deportations. Today, no Christians live here. Those houses below belong to Kurdish farming families whose ancestors had no part in the killings."

We climbed up the steps of the former dwelling nearest to us, and as I walked through the roofless rooms now filled with fallen stones, I tried to imagine what life was like when Talitha was a little girl. While I was inside what I guessed was the kitchen because of the fireplace, Ashti's cell phone rang.

After answering in Turkish, she quickly switched to Kurdish and spoke for a few minutes, taking a pen out of her bag to jot down something. When she was finished, she said, "It was my cousin, Loran. I told him about you being with me, and he agreed to meet us tomorrow in Nusaybin. He suggested a hotel-restaurant on the highway outside the city and set the time for one o'clock." She added, "I said that I would call him back to confirm everything after talking with you."

"Wonderful!" Father Gregory said. "Tell him that is perfect."

Ashti re-dialed the last incoming number and passed on what Father Gregory had said, repeating the name of the hotel-restaurant and his directions on how to get to it in order to make sure that she had it right. She then put the cell phone back into her shoulder bag.

"Meeting him at that time will give me a chance to celebrate the Liturgy early tomorrow morning. Several Armenian families come to the monastery from Mardin each Sunday at 8:30 to participate. We could leave about eleven and still have plenty of time to get to Nusaybin."

Happy with the news, Father Gregory led us back to the car and we continued on to the city of Midyat about a half-hour away. On its outskirts, it was an unimpressive city, but in its inner city, the old Syriac Christian quarter, things changed. There we encountered narrow streets and beautiful cream-colored buildings and houses just as in Mardin. After parking on one of the cobblestone streets, Father Gregory suggested going to the roof of a museum nearby where we would have a view of the whole area, including the refugee camp I was interested in seeing.

As we entered the formidable building, he explained that it used to be the house of a prominent Syriac in the city. "After he was killed in 1915, the local government bought it from the family for next to nothing and turned it into a cultural museum."

Climbing up the stone staircase to the roof, we were rewarded with a wondrous view of this heart of what had once been a thriving Syriac Christian community. In front of me were the steeples of several churches reaching proudly above the roofs into the sky—Syriac Orthodox, Catholic, and Protestant—a sight that I had not seen elsewhere in modern Turkey.

He then pointed out far off in the distance the hundreds of white tents of a camp filled with refugees from the war in Syria. "Take a picture with your zoom lens from here," he recommended. "The gendarmes won't allow pictures up close."

"Can we at least drive by it?" I asked after I took my pictures.

"We can," he replied. "Then we will head south for your interviews."

As we were speaking, one of a group of eight or so college-aged Muslim girl students who were also on the roof having fun and enjoying the view, came over to us and asked in English. "I heard you speaking in English. Are you Americans?"

When I explained that Father Gregory and I were, the girl wondered if they could get a picture of us with them. We all laughed and agreed, and Ashti took the pictures with the different cell phones they handed her. I thought how great it would be if Muslim and Christian, Turk, Kurd, Armenian, and Syriac could always relate in that curious friendly manner, delighting in our differences and similarities.

After we descended the steps together with them and said our goodbyes, we returned to the car. Father Gregory then directed me towards the refugee camp. "It's on the property of the Mor Abraham Monastery whose last monk died just this year," he explained.

The monastery itself was a large walled compound at the edge of the Syriac quarter and at the beginning of the vineyards and fields owned by its inhabitants. In front of it was a children's park with swings and slides that Father Gregory said was a gift from the monastery to the town's children. In the open fields behind the monastery was the sprawling refugee camp surrounded by fences topped with concertina wire. As we drove by the entrance of the camp, signs forbade us to stop or to take pictures, and at several barriers, soldiers with their weapons motioned us on.

"The monastery provided the land for the camp because the government initially wanted it mainly for Syrian Christian refugees. Christians, though, do not feel safe in such camps, as they are often harassed for their religion and for being supporters of the secular Assad regime. If you are a young man in such a camp, you also face a lot of pressure to join one of the competing rebel factions who recruit heavily there. That's why I always try first to place refugees like the young man you will interview this afternoon with Christian families or monasteries so that they can avoid such dangers."

From the refugee camp, we headed south of Midyat for Father Gregory to deliver his bundle of documents for the Archbishop at the Mor Gabriel Monastery and then for my interview. About fifteen minutes later, Mor Gabriel came into view.

Like the monastery in Mardin, Mor Gabriel was a splendid complex off by itself in the barren countryside. As we approached, Father Gregory explained a little about it. "It is the oldest Syriac Orthodox monastery in the world, dating from 397 A.D. In its glory years, as many as a thousand monks, both Copts and Syriacs, lived there. Unfortunately now only a handful of monks and nuns are left."

As we approached its gate, he pointed to a new section of the wall that surrounded it. "For the past ten years, the monastery has been in a legal battle with the Turkish government and a Kurdish village about the ownership of that section of their property. Part of the village's claim against the monastery was that the monastery had been built on the site of a former mosque, even though the monastery was founded 173 years before Mohammed's birth! Strangely, the Turkish Supreme Court sided with the village, and it was only because of the outrage of the European Union at the decision and the intervention of the Turkish Prime Minister that the property was restored to the monastery."

"Where's the village?" I asked, not seeing anything near the monastery but barren hills.

"It was that small cluster of houses that we passed several kilometers back," he explained. "So many absurd local property claims are made against Christians that it seems at times as if they are orchestrated by Islamists or extreme Turkish nationalists whose real goal is the eradication of the Christian presence in Turkey."

At the entrance to the walled enclosure, the gateman recognized Father Gregory and immediately let us in. We then drove down a tree-lined road to the actual buildings, parked, and walked through another inner wall into the courtyard of the monastery. A religious service was going on in the chapel when we got there. While we waited for it to finish, Father Gregory showed us some of the well-preserved buildings in the complex built with contributions from Byzantine Emperors dating back to the fifth century A.D. He pointed out the impressive domes, mosaics, and other decorations, as well as the tombs of prominent Syriacs. We then went upstairs to the office of the Archbishop and waited in the long rectangular reception room until he returned from the service. The archbishop's chair was at one end, and chairs lined the walls for visitors. On one of the walls was a picture of Prince Charles standing between two distinguished looking clergy in red robes. Father Gregory saw me looking at it and explained, "The Archbishops of Mardin and of Tur Abdin."

Soon the Archbishop returned upstairs from the chapel looking very dignified in his black clerical garments, with red sash, hood, and white beard. He greeted Father Gregory warmly, and after Father Gregory introduced us to him as his distant American and Turkish relatives, the Archbishop kindly invited us to join him for lunch with two other visitors from Ankara who had accompanied him up the stairs.

Father Gregory gratefully accepted the invitation, and we followed the Archbishop into a very simple room where we took our seats around its one long table. The Archbishop sat next to an older monk and blessed the simple food, which consisted of soup, bread, some cucumbers and water. I was about to ask some questions, but Father Gregory placed his hand on my leg and squeezed, shaking his head, making it clear to me that during the meal, no one was to talk.

Afterwards, however, when we had finished eating and were heading back to the audience room, the Archbishop made a point of inquiring in English about the purpose of my trip to Midyat. After I told him, he graciously wished me the best. We thanked him for the lunch and said our goodbyes, as he and his two guests went into the audience room for their scheduled appointment.

When we got back to the car, Father Gregory called the Syriac family hosting the Armenian refugee I was going to interview and told them that we would be at their house in about forty-five minutes. When he finished, I asked him to tell us some of the history of the Syriac Christians in the area. "Who are they and why do they cling so hard to this barren land?" I asked.

"The Syriacs are the descendents of the original people of Mesopotamia, sometimes called Assyrians and sometimes Chaldeans, who spoke Aramaic, the lingua franca of the Middle East from about the fifth century B.C. The language that Jesus and his disciples spoke was a dialect of that language."

He then went on to explain that after the resurrection of Jesus, his disciples went out from Jerusalem to spread the good news of what they had witnessed to the world. Naturally, they started in places where people spoke their own language, like the important city of Antioch, where both Peter and Paul later lived and taught. Tradition says that the very first Christian church was established there in a cave on land owned by Saint Luke. Syriacs trace their unbroken line of patriarchs to this first Antiochian church and to Peter and Paul.

He also explained that the Syriacs, like the Armenians, also credit the disciples, Bartholomew and Thaddeus for first evangelizing their people. Another disciple they especially venerate is Saint Thomas who they claim evangelized in Mesopotamia and in India where he was later martyred. A merchant later carried Thomas's relics from India to Edessa, today's Urfa, where they remained until Muslim rule forced their transfer to safer Christian lands.

In the early years of Christianity, this whole area was the site of vibrant Syriac Christian schools, hospitals, churches, and monasteries. Important early Christian hymns, teachings, and literature were written here in the Syriac language by great Syriac saints and scholars like Saint Ephrem who lived in Nusaybin and in Urfa and who is venerated as a Doctor of the early church by many branches of Christianity.

"For all of these reasons they cling to this land," he said. "This is Tur Abdin, 'the Mountain of the Servants of God' to them. It represents their history, their culture, their belief, their very essence."

"How many Syriacs are in Turkey now?" I asked.

"Today, only about 25,000 are left. Like the Armenians, most of them are in Istanbul. Not all is bad news, however," he added. "Their numbers seem to be increasing a little, not only because of the influx of Syriac refugees from Syria, but also because of the fact that some Syriacs who left the country in the 1980s are returning because economic conditions in Turkey have improved and hostilities have ceased between the Turkish army and the Kurdish rebels in the area. Most important, the Prime Minister invited them back and has assured them of his support.

"The area we are heading to right now is one of their largest concentrations outside of Istanbul. The region has seven predominately Syriac Christian villages and nine ancient monasteries, which a handful of young monks are now trying to restore and reactivate."

"How has the reception been to those who have come back?" I asked.

"Mixed," he answered. "On the positive side, there has been some help from the government to rebuild a few churches and to return some properties. Another good omen is that a young Syriac Christian woman was just elected co-mayor of Mardin with a Kurdish running mate. Discrimination still occurs, though, not just against Syriac and Armenians, but against all Christians. Three Protestant Christians in Malatya were recently tied up, tortured, and killed by fanatics who accused them of trying to convert Muslims to their faith."

I mulled over this information as I drove and considered the precariousness of the Christian existence in this part of the world. Even in times of peace and reconciliation, Christians living here must always have that fear in the back of their minds that a new bloodbath of persecution, mass killings, and destruction might happen, spurred on by some fanatical hatred and lack of tolerance such as happened in 1895, in 1915, and now was happening again today in 2014 in Syria.

Father Gregory brought me back to the present when he asked me to turn left onto a small paved road leading into the rocky hills. I did so, and not far down this small rural road, we came to a gendarme camp where we had to stop before continuing into the region.

"The government is trying to protect the Syriac villages by having a military presence here," Father Gregory explained.

Within a few minutes more, we came to a dozen or so recently constructed, large stone houses on two streets. Nearby was a small church and a children's playground. Father Gregory directed me to park in front of one of the houses where a group of people were sitting on its covered porch. When they saw us, they stood up and came down the steps to the car to greet us.

They obviously liked and respected Father Gregory, receiving him with genuine fondness. After returning their greetings, Father Gregory introduced Ashti and me to them. He spoke English as he presented us to Natan and Christina Khoury, the owners of the house who had returned from Germany to their homeland to build it. He then spoke in Arabic to Hakob Sarkissian and to his parents, Dikran and Arpi Sarkissian, the Armenian refugees from Syria whom I was to interview. They were staying with the Khoury's and working in construction projects both in the village and in a nearby small monastery.

We climbed the steps to the porch, and Natan invited us to sit down around the table he had set up there and have some juice and pastries that his wife brought out. While Christina poured the juice, Father Gregory told them about the scheduled meeting the next day with Ashti's cousin. "I hope we can make some deal to get Zulehka and your cousin's family out early next week. We need to confirm exactly how many they are and where to meet them, though."

"Why don't we call them right now and find out?" Natan suggested.

"Can you get through?" Father Gregory asked.

"Most of the time," Natan replied. "The land lines still work in the government-controlled area of Deir ez-Zor where Avraham lives. The cell phone and internet connections are less reliable, but every now and then we get through. I always try first on the land line at his apartment or at his produce store."

"Speak in Syriac in case someone is listening in," Father Gregory suggested.

Natan laughed. "I have to anyway as I don't know any Arabic!" He then suggested that Father Gregory go inside with him so that they could call his cousin by Skype on his computer.

After Natan and Father Gregory had gone into the house, I spoke in English to Hakob and his parents. "Thank you for agreeing to talk to me about your experiences. From what Father Gregory tells me, you have an amazing story, and I would like to share it with others."

"Of course, but I prefer to wait and answer your questions in Arabic as my English is not all that good," Hakob replied. "That way my parents can understand and correct me if needed. Father Gregory speaks excellent Arabic and can translate."

"Whatever is most comfortable to you," I said.

While we waited for Father Gregory to return, Hakob asked Ashti and me to explain a little more about our relationship to Father Gregory. After I did a quick summary of our family history, he shook his head in astonishment and said, "You should be writing a story about yourselves, instead of about me."

Right after that exchange, Father Gregory and Natan returned from inside the house and sat down. "We got through on Skype without any trouble," Father Gregory said. "There are five of them and they will be ready any time we can get there. All we need to do is find a way across the border and someone to drive us to Deir ez-Zor."

Natan added, "My cousin warned us that it was impossible right now to get a car into the city from the highway from Turkey as all of the bridges over the Euphrates have been blown up or are too dangerous to cross. Instead, he suggests that you meet them at his farm on the other side of the river. They and Zulehka will take a boat to it tomorrow and stay there until you arrive. ISIS is advancing inside the city and their own building was hit for the first time yesterday by mortar shells."

"How will you know how to get to the farm?" Ashti asked Father Gregory.

"No problem," Natan replied. "I was there five years ago, so I can explain." He turned to Father Gregory. "Actually, I can show you right now where it is located on Google maps." He went into the sitting room again and came back with his laptop computer, turned it back on, and got on the internet connection they had set up for the village. When he got to Deir ez-Zor, he came in for a close-up and showed us first where his cousin lived in the city, where his farm was on the other side of the Euphrates in a place called Al Jnenah, and where his cousin kept his boat to ferry produce from his farm to his store. The farm looked to be less than a kilometer from the boat dock, which was right outside Deir ez-Zor.

"How do we get to the farm from the highway?" Father Gregory asked.

"The farm's name is Palmyra and it is well-known in the area," Natan said. "You come in on Highway 7, take the right fork to Al Jnenah, go about five kilometers, and after you pass through most of the town, you will see a major street on the left. I forgot its name, but it is the biggest street in the town going west. There you will turn left heading towards the Euphrates. Go to the end of the road, and the farm will be there, bordering on the river. If you get lost, you can ask the locals or call him at the farm on his phone."

Father Gregory got a notebook out of his bag and drew a map copying the image and the directions the cousin had given him. Natan also gave him his cousin's landline number at the farm and in the city, as well as his e-mail and cell number.

Before Natan closed down Google Earth, I asked Father Gregory to show me where the Armenian Memorial was located in the city.

"It's in the center, a few blocks from the Euphrates Canal that cuts through the city. He zoomed down on it but the image was blurry. After showing me the location, he asked me, "Have you had a chance yet to inteview Hakob?"

"We were waiting for you to translate."

"It's that I feel more comfortable answering in Arabic," Hakob added.

"Good then," Father Gregory said, "You do well in English, but I'll do whatever you feel most comfortable with."

I started the interview by simply asking Hakob to tell me about himself, whatever he would like. I took notes and the following were his answers as translated by Father Gregory.

"I was born in 1991 and grew up in Ar-Raqqah, Syria," Hakob began. "Our family had roots there for many generations and Father owned a small rug weaving business. We always went to the Armenian Orthodox Church, although there was a larger Armenian Catholic Church in Ar-Raqqah as well."

"Did Christians get along well with the Muslims in the city?" I asked.

"Yes, for the most part. We were about ten percent of the population. Many of our family friends were Muslim including the family of my fiancée Zulehka. Her father, Salim Halabi, was in the cotton and wool business and was a supplier of my father's store. My older brother, Tavit, was the best friend of her older brother, Nadim. Nadim often came to our house."

"So you knew your fiancée from childhood?"

"Yes. We were the same age, and at one stage, we even went to the same state school. But we really did not know each other very well. Our family knew mainly her father and her brother. It was only when we both were living in Deir ez-Zor that Zulehka and I became friends."

"How did that happen?" I asked.

"We both wanted to be medical doctors, and when the new medical university opened up in Deir ez-Zor, we both went there to study in 2012. As we were from the same city, and our families were friends, we often did things together."

"You being a male Christian and she being a female Muslim did not complicate things?"

"Not really," he said. "University students don't think so much about those things, and we almost always met in groups of her friends and my friends who were almost all Muslim. It was only in 2013, right after ISIS took over Ar-Raqqah and my brother was killed, that our relationship began to deepen into something more than friendship."

"Do you mind explaining a little more?" I said as I took notes.

"When Zulehka heard how my older brother, Tavit, was killed and all of the other atrocities that ISIS was committing in Ar-Raqqah, especially against Christians, she was disgusted that they were doing it all in the name of her religion. She could not understand, as all the Christians she knew, including me, were normal people and not evil, and so she started to ask me a lot of questions about what I believed. That's how we got close."

"How was your brother killed?" I asked.

"Tavit was in the Syrian army at their base near Ar-Raqqah and was captured in the fighting when Al Nusra and ISIS took over the city in March of 2013. ISIS executed him and his fellow soldiers in cold blood and dragged their bodies to the main square of the city where they rotted for two days as a warning to others. Later they were thrown into a pit outside the city."

As Hakob talked about his brother in Arabic, his mother lowered her head and brushed tears from her eyes. Her husband comforted her. He then added to what his son had said, "It was Nadim, Zulehka's brother, who found out what had happened to Tavit and later came to our house to tell us and show us where the burial pit was. He advised us to get out of Ar-Raqqah as soon as we could as our lives were in danger. He said ISIS was determined to establish strict Sharia law in the city, make it the capital of their caliphate, and get rid of any Christians or others who opposed them."

"So you took his advice?" I asked the father.

"We did because I had seen for myself what they doing. They had already taken over the main Armenian Catholic Church in town, destroyed its crosses and made it into their headquarters. Christian friends told me that they were instructed that they could choose between converting to Islam, leaving the city without their property, or being killed. We left within a week. I sold the merchandise we had in the store to another Muslim storeowner for a huge loss, but it gave us some cash. I then closed up the store and our house and left by some back roads we knew for Deir ez-Zor."

"Because Hakob was there?" I asked.

"Because Hakob was there, as well as some Armenian friends, and it was still controlled by the Syrian army and other more moderate rebel groups. Our plan was to get out of Syria as quickly as possible, as there really was no safe place in the country. That's when we met Father Gregory at the Armenian Memorial, and he agreed to help us."

"Unfortunately, it took longer than I had hoped," Father Gregory said. "So many of our faith wanted to get out, and I had to arrange for a bus and permissions from Turkey, the Free Syrian Army, and the Syrian government to get them out. I would not have been successful without the help of the United Nations Refugee Commission. We only made it to Turkey in October of last year. Hakob almost did not come with us because of Zulehka."

Hakob nodded. "I needed to escape because I had been drafted into the army even though I was still in medical school. I also wanted to help my parents, but I did not want to leave Zulehka behind. We had come to realize that we loved each other and that we wanted to get married. I gave her a ring and we were engaged."

"Zulehka had also decided that she wanted to convert to Christianity," Father Gregory added.

"Why didn't she leave with you then?" I asked.

"She wanted to finish her medical studies, although it was becoming increasingly clear that the university might have to shut down soon because of the fighting," Hakob answered. "She also felt that she couldn't leave without seeking the blessing of her family. Her idea was to go back to Ar-Raqqah for her father's birthday and tell them of her decision and get their approval. We tried everything to convince her that that wouldn't be wise, but she thought we were wrong, and that they would understand."

"I promised her that when she decided to get out of Syria, I would do everything I could to come back and get her out," Father Gregory said.

"What happened?" I asked. "Did she get their blessing?"

"No. When she got to Ar-Raqqah for her father's birthday party right before it started, she was surprised to find out that her first cousin Mukhtar was also there and that he was now an ISIS commander in the city. She had not seen him in six years as he had gone to Iraq as a young man to fight the Americans for Al Qaeda in Iraq.

"During the party, he bragged to her about his exploits killing Americans and Shiites and escaping from prison in Fajula. He also bragged about his raids in Syria to destroy infidel shrines and to expand the caliphate. Finally, he astounded her with the news that, now that he was back in Ar-Raqqah, he was ready to marry her as both of their sets of parents had planned when they were children. Mukhtar said that he had already spoken with her father about this, and her father had agreed to it. Zulehka should quit her studies and come back to Ar-Raqqah for the marriage. 'The place of a Muslim woman was in the home and not in a school,' he said.

"Wow," I said, looking at Ashti for her reaction. "What did she do?"

"After the party, Zulehka confronted her father with what she had just learned, and he confessed that it was true. He was going to talk with her about it but did not have a chance as she had just arrived. He defended his actions by telling her that Mukhtar had already used his influence, not only to protect Nadim from reprisals because he had been a Syrian government employee in the provincial agriculture office, but had even managed to get Nadim appointed as the director of the office in the new ISIS government."

"I take it that this didn't convince Zulehka to marry him," I said.

"Not at all. Zulehka was in tears and went to her brother. She had always been close to him. Nadim agreed with her that such a marriage would be disastrous for her, but he advised her to buy some time. He said that he would talk to their parents and convince them to speak to Mukhtar and schedule the marriage for six months from then, letting her go back to

Deir ez-Zor to finish the year of her studies. Maybe, by then, ISIS would be defeated or some other solution could be found."

"Did Zulehka tell her brother and parents about her engagement to you?"

"No," Hakob said. "She was afraid that doing so then would cause problems for her family with Mukhtar and ISIS or that they might have forced her then to stay in Ar-Raqqah."

"She was probably right not to do so," Father Gregory said. "We still have a good chance of getting her out of Deir ez-Zor, but if she had been forced to stay in Ar-Raqqah, our chances of getting her out would have been almost zero."

"Anyway, with the approval of her parents and her brother, Zulehka returned to Deir ez-Zor for six months. Several months later, though, the university closed because of the fighting. That's when Natan contacted his cousin Avraham and arranged for Zulehka to go live with them until we could get her out."

Natan, who was listening intently, then jumped into the conversation in English. "Avraham and Elia were glad to help, and they've come to love Zulehka like their own daughter. They have also decided to take advantage of the opportunity Father Gregory has given them to escape for Turkey as well. The situation in Deir ez-Zor has become unbearable as ISIS is advancing. They fear for their lives and those of their children."

"So that is our story right up until now," Hakob said. "We have placed our hope in God and in Father Gregory. We pray fervently that soon Zulehka and the Khourys will all be safely out of Syria, and we can be reunited and go on with our lives. What those lives will be, we do not yet know. At least, we will be together."

"I hope so much it all works out," Ashti said.

"I do, too!" I said. I thanked them for their story, and I promised that after writing it up, I would first let Hakob review it for inaccuracies before publishing it. I got Hakob's e-mail and gave him mine. Afterwards, with their permission, I took some pictures of them.

We continued to talk for another hour on the porch about the Khoury's decision to return to the village that Natan had left when he was a teenager. Despite his good life in Germany, he felt an unquenchable desire to return to his roots. Hearing of the invitation of the Turkish Prime Minister for Syriacs to come back, and overcoming the hesitations of his wife, Christina, he had joined up with other European Syriac families who had similar dreams to return. It had been a great adventure.

As a builder himself in Germany, he had helped supervise the construction of the new houses of the village, the repair of the church, as well as that of some of the monasteries in the area. Theirs was a tightly knit community, but they welcomed not only refugees like the Sarkissians into their homes but also students and others who wanted to spend time in Tur Abin. Their goal was to reestablish the Syriac presence in this land that was so important to their personal identity.

At five o'clock, Father Gregory suggested that we return to Mardin while it was still light. He then opened up his briefcase and pulled out the Terzian Cross. "It's a good sign for the future." He told its story and how I had found it and given it to him and then he said a prayer in Armenian and in Syriac. Both Hakob and his parents kissed the cross, as did the Khoury family.

As we walked with them to our car, Father Gregory said to Natan and Hakob, "I will call you both tomorrow right after our meeting with Ashti's cousin Loran. We will know then if and when we can get across the border and meet them, and you can advise them accordingly by Skype."

They thanked him effusively for his help and told us all goodbye.

On our drive back to Mardin, I made my case with Father Gregory that I wanted to go with him to pick up Zulehka and the Khoury family cousins in Deir ez-Zor, if he could manage a way across the border. "It could be such a great article, and also I would get to see Deir ez-Zor, which is so important in the Armenian deportation story that I want to tell."

"No, it is too dangerous for you to go," Father Gregory said.

"If it is too dangerous for me, then it is too dangerous for you," I replied.

"In my case, it is different. It's my job, and I made a promise to Zulehka and Hakob and to the Khourys."

"In my case, too, it is my job, if I am to be an international correspondent. Like you said, people in the West need to know what is happening here."

"I have a green card for Syria. You have only an American passport, and that is not going to help in Syria except with the Free Syrian Army."

"I also have a document saying that I am a reporter," I replied. "People like to have their stories told."

"What about Ashti and the rest of the trip?" Father Gregory asked me.

Before I could answer, Ashti spoke up. "Don't worry about me. Do what you both have to do. I can wait in the hotel. I would like to see Urfa and Harran when you get back, but my only real requirement is that I don't miss my flight back from Elazığ on the twentieth so I can be back at work the next day."

"Crossing the border illegally is expensive. I have funds to pay for refugees but not for reporters," Father Gregory continued.

"I understand, but I will pay. It's that important to me."

"Well, let's see what happens tomorrow with Ashti's cousin." He was silent for a minute as if thinking. "Could you show me you reporter document?"

"Of course." I asked Ashti to get it out of my folder of papers in my daypack and give it to him.

Father Gregory looked at it and said, "I will translate it into Arabic tonight. Otherwise it won't help you."

When we got back to the monastery, we said goodbye and made plans to pick him up on Sunday at eleven o'clock after his Liturgy for the Armenian families who lived in the area. I thought about asking if I could attend, but I decided that I needed to use the morning to write up the interviews I had just had.

CHAPTER 22

Loran Yasin

On Palm Sunday at eleven o'clock, we picked up Father Gregory at the monastery. He had already celebrated the Liturgy at a small Syriac Church nearby for several Armenian families still living in the city. He had also translated my reporter credential document into Arabic and printed it out. When he got in the car, he took it out of the bag, and he showed it to me. "I think it looks pretty official if I say so myself," he said smiling.

As we left Mardin and headed in our rental car down a winding road through the rocky hills to the Mesopotamian Plain, it occurred to me that this was the route that Karine and Talitha had taken with Miss Isabel and the Kobers to catch the train in Ras al-Ayn. I tried to imagine the mixed emotions Karine and Talitha were experiencing in this last part of their journey—of hope of escape, fear of discovery, and grief at the loss of dear family members, friends, and a way of life.

About a half-hour down the road, Father Gregory suggested that we take a detour off the main highway on a much smaller road in order to pass by the small town of Dara on our way to Nusaybin. The town, he said, was known for its ancient Persian, Roman, and Byzantine ruins and cliff graves. "It's worth visiting and it is not far out of the way," he assured us. "It's only eleven-thirty and don't have to be in Nusaybin until one."

Ashti and I were glad that we accepted the suggestion, as not only did we see some fascinating ruins of this former prominent town at the border of the ancient Roman and Persian Empires, but also had a chance to see a bit of Kurdish culture in the area. As we continued past the ruins, we passed through a small Kurdish village where we heard the sound of music coming from a band and saw a line of young people dressed in colorful Kurdish costumes dancing in the field. Appreciative elders watched them, while young children scurried around and played. We stopped to listen, and soon the village headman came over to find out who we were. When he found out that Ashti was a Kurd, he invited her to join the dancers, which she gleefully did. I recorded the line dance on my digital camera from a seat of honor where the headman had us sit. When it was over and Ashti returned, our host invited us to stay for the meal afterwards, which we had to refuse. I bring this little incident up because it showed me how easily Ashti moved between her Kurdish, Armenian, and Turkish identities, relishing each one. We thanked our gracious host and after returning to our car, continued on our way.

After a few kilometers more on this country road, we regained the four-lane highway paralleling the Turkey-Syrian border. As we drove towards Nusaybin, I was struck by how heavily fortified the border seemed to be with concertina wire and cement fences, watchtowers, and probably heavily mined open fields. Here and there was a Turkish army camp with some tanks and big guns at ready in case there was trouble. The traffic on the highway was heavy with what Gregory explained were trucks heading to and from Iran and Iraq.

Not long after getting on the highway, we came to the outskirts of Nusaybin and started to look for the hotel-restaurant where we were to meet Ashti's cousin, Loran Yasin. We soon found it, an ugly building with a large dirt lot where a dozen or so cars and big trucks were parked. Even with our detour and stops in Dara and at the Kurdish village, we still got to the hotel-restaurant five minutes early. We parked the car as close as we could to the building in order to keep an eye on it, and then went into the multi-purposed building.

To the right was a store full of all kinds of supplies that a trucker might want—from food to electronics, motor oil to blankets. Up the stairs was the lobby of the hotel and to the left was a large restaurant with a buffet. We went into the restaurant, which was about half full with men, most of whom looked like they might be truckers.

"Will you recognize him?" Father Gregory asked Ashti.

"I think so, but I'm not sure. I haven't seen him in over six years," she said. "He will recognize me, though," she said as she looked around the room. "I'm the only woman here!"

Father Gregory led us to a table near the window looking out on the parking lot, and we all sat down. When the waiter came, Ashti told him in Turkish that we were waiting for someone and would eat later from the buffet. He took our orders for some tea and mineral water. Just after the waiter returned with the drinks, Loran came into the restaurant. He was dressed in European clothes except for the red and white Kurdish headdress on his head. He looked around the room, recognized Ashti, and came directly to our table.

Loran greeted Ashti with a kiss on both cheeks, and then Ashti introduced each of us to him. Loran spoke a little English, but after we had gotten our food at the buffet, she began to explain to him in Kurdish why I was in Turkey and what Father Gregory's and my relationship was to him. He listened attentively, and when he found out that Father Gregory spoke Arabic, he began to talk directly to him in that language. With the help of Ashti and Father Gregory translating, I found out the following about him.

Loran was three years younger than Ashti and had not gone to college but to vocational school in Diyarbakir. When the civil war broke out in Syria and different rebel groups and the government began attacking Kurdish communities in the northeast of the country, he and many of his friends enlisted as volunteers in the YPG, the Syrian Kurdish Militia, which had been organized to defend the towns. He did not have a combat role himself, but he facilitated the smuggling of weapons, supplies, and volunteers over the border from Turkey to Syria.

"Could you help us?" Father Gregory asked him in Arabic. "I need to get five people out of Deir ez-Zor as soon as possible. One is a young woman whose fiancé is already here in Turkey and the other is a family of four who have relatives here. Peter and I need to cross the border, drive to Deir ez-Zor, and pick them up. We would need a van for seven people and a driver."

"All of the bridges across the Euphrates, except the one at Ar-Raqqah, have been blown up or are too dangerous to cross," Loran said. "You can no longer get into Deir ez-Zor by car without going through Ar-Raqqah, and you don't want to do that, as it is the capital of ISIS."

"I've heard that," Father Gregory answered. "Our plan is not to meet them in the city but on this side of the river at a farm."

Loran nodded and then looked at me. He asked Father Gregory why we both needed to go. Father Gregory answered in Arabic. "Peter is a reporter and wants to document the rescue in an article for an American newspaper."

"It is possible that I can help you, but I will first have to talk with my commander." Loran added in Arabic. "It will cost you, of course, but I will try to get you a good price."

"Yes, we will pay whatever is reasonable," Father Gregory answered. "We have to get them out."

"How soon do you want to go?" Loran asked.

"Today or tomorrow. It's urgent. They are crossing the river to the farm today and will be waiting for us."

Loran nodded again and then paid attention to his food. While we all ate, he visibly relaxed and conversed in Kurdish with Ashti about her family in Istanbul and about her own studies and job. By his eyes, smiles, and tone of voice, it was clear to me that he had great affection and respect for her. At a little past two o'clock, we finished our meal. Father Gregory insisted on paying for it.

When we got out to the parking lot, Loran told Father Gregory in Arabic, "I will need to make some calls and consult some people." He looked at his watch. "Can you meet me back here in two hours?" After we agreed to be waiting for him in our car in the parking lot at four o'clock, Loran went to his pick-up truck and drove off.

As for us, Father Gregory suggested that instead of waiting here at the hotel-restaurant for the next two hours, that we go into Nusaybin to see the ancient Church of Saint Jacob and the ruins of one of the world's first universities. Ashti and I thought that was a good plan, and so we returned to the car and headed towards the city center.

Father Gregory explained to us as we circled the roundabout on the highway leading into the city, that Nusaybin was the ancient city of Nisibis, another very important center of early Christianity. Today it was divided into two parts—the Turkish city of Nusaybin with approximately 84,000 inhabitants, and the larger Syrian city of Qamishli with 185,000. Both were now predominately Kurdish, although Qamishli also had a highly significant Christian minority population of Syriacs and Armenians. Because of the civil war, the Christian population had dimished from around 40,000 to less than half that now.

As we passed through the modern part of Nusaybin with its banks and stores, I noticed that it looked different in character from Mardin and Midyat, as many people in the street were dressed in more traditional Arabic or Kurdish garb. Following Father Gregory's directions, we soon came to a square where we parked and locked the car and then walked a block to an open place of ruins where the church was. It did not look much like a church to me, as it had no steeple. Instead, it was an ancient cube-shaped, stone building standing proudly inside a chain-fence-enclosed archeological zone of fallen walls and scattered stones.

"Saint Jacob began building it in 313 A.D., and the ruins around it are the remains of the Schools of Theology, Philosophy, and Medicine that his disciple Saint Ephrem founded a few decades later. Some claim that this School of Nisibis was the first university in the world. When the Persians conquered the city in 363 A.D., Saint Ephrem moved the school to Edessa, today's Urfa, where it continued for another 125 years. It was one of the three principal teaching centers of the early Christian Church, along with Antioch and Alexandria."

I noticed that the entire archeological complex was a few feet below the street level, and I could make out the outlines of former classrooms, corridors, and cells in the stone floors and walls that still remained after almost 1,700 years. "Can we go inside the fence and visit the church and the ruins?" I asked.

"We can try," Father Gregory said. "The caretaker lives upstairs above the church. I know him, and if he is there, he will let us in. His family is the only Syriac Christian one that I know of that is left in the Turkish side of the city."

After Father Gregory rang the bell, the caretaker came to his door and immediately recognized Father Gregory. He gladly agreed to unlock the church for us and let us inside the archeological site.

Once we were inside the church, I thought that it was as ancient looking as any building I had ever been in before. Its dome ceilings almost looked like the roof of a cave and the former intricate stone carvings around its doors were now worn and broken. Adding to the cave-like atmosphere was the darkness inside. The church's only light came from a few light bulbs, and its only color was that of a red tapestry of the Last Supper on the altar and a blue painting of a white-bearded saint who looked to be in a state of mystical contemplation. I asked Father Gregory about it.

"It's a painting of Mor Jacob, for whom the church is named," he explained. "According to some, he was the son of an Armenian prince. He converted to Christianity and became a devout ascetic living in the caves of the mountains around here, subsisting on whatever food and water he found in the wild. He was known for his holiness, the power of his prayers, and for his miracles. He and Mor Augin, a monk from Egypt, played an important part in the evangelization of the entire region. After Saint Jacob was named Bishop of Nisibis, he baptized Saint Ephrem, who was one of his disciples. As important as that was, he also participated in the Council of Nicea in 325 A.D. and attended the consecration of the Church of the Holy Sepulcre in Jerusalem in 335 A.D. He died in 338 A.D. and his tomb is downstairs."

After the caretaker turned on some more dim lights, we descended a narrow low-ceiling stairway to the stone crypt where Saint Jacob was buried. It was covered with a red cloth. Father Gregory reverently bent down and touched it, paused in silence, and then made the Sign of the Cross.

After thanking the caretaker and saying goodbye, we visited the Muslim graves and minaret right next to the Mor Jacob Church in Nusaybin's Peace Garden. We then spent the next hour walking around the city—right up to the fences and watchtowers of its border with Syria. After stopping to get some cash from an ATM machine downtown, we drove back to the hotel parking lot to wait for Loran. Within a few minutes, he arrived.

Loran immediately came over to our car and got into the back seat with Ashti. Speaking in Arabic to Father Gregory, he told him that his commander and his contacts on the other side of the border had agreed to help us, but that it would cost us something, as they needed to finance their own operations.

"How much?" Father Gregory asked.

"You and Peter are free, as a courtesy to me," he replied. "As for the other five persons, the commander will charge $2,000 each for the crossing of the border. The one-day rental of a van and driver to take you to Deir ez-Zor and back will cost you another $2,000. The money must be pre-paid. If that is acceptable to you, we can leave at midnight tonight and be back by midnight tomorrow night."

While I thought the price was expensive, Father Gregory did not. He thanked Loran and said to us, "It seems fair, given the risk involved." He then spoke again to Loran. "We need to leave tonight, and I can give you a check for the money."

"I'm sorry, but the commander said it must be pre-paid in cash," Loran said.

"But I can't get that much out in cash today," Father Gregory said. "It's Sunday and the banks are closed. That means we would need to delay going for another day." He then thought a minute and spoke to Ashti in English. "Ashti, would you be willing to stay here at the hotel tonight and go to the bank tomorrow to withdraw the money? I would give you a check for the amount and you and Loran could go together to get it out."

"I'm willing, but would the bank give me such an amount."

"Of course they will. I know the director of the bank in Mardin where we keep our refugee money. I'll call him tonight to make sure that they release the funds to you personally at their branch here in Nusaybin." He then turned to Loran and explained this option in Arabic.

"I will have to call and talk with my commander again," he replied. He got out of our car and got into the driver's seat of his pick-up next to them and made the call. A few minutes later, he was back.

"I told him the situation, and he agreed to it, but he wanted something of value of yours personally to keep as a guarantee until the whole amount was handed over."

"I'm a priest," Father Gregory said. "I have nothing of value. No rings or jewelry and I can't give you my documents, because I will need them in Syria. He will just have to take my word. Please talk to him again and assure him the money will be there. If it isn't, we will be stuck in Syria. You wouldn't bring us back over the border if the money isn't there!"

"That's true," Loran said, "but I don't think my commander will accept that."

Father Gregory thought for a minute. "I have another idea!" he said. He reached into the bag at his feet where he kept his laptop and papers, and pulled out the Terzian Cross. "What about this as a guarantee? It is the most valuable possession our family has. It is made of pure silver and is hundreds of years old. It must be worth thousands of dollars." He gave it to Loran to examine.

Loran held it, feeling its weight and rubbing his fingers over it. He then gave it back to Father Gregory. "I'll try again," he said, going once more to the cab of his truck.

As Loran conversed with his commander, Father Gregory said to Ashti and me, "If he agrees, we will have a lot to do before midnight. We will have to get rooms in the hotel, and then I will need to talk to my superiors in Lebanon, the Bank manager in Mardin, as well as to Natan and Hakob. Natan has promised to pay for his cousin's family, but I need to make sure that the amount is okay with him. He and Hakob also need to get in touch with Zulehka and the others about our coming."

When Loran came back to our car, he said, "He agreed since we are relatives. When I return at midnight to take you across the border, you will leave the cross with me as a guarantee and a check for $12,000.00 with Ashti."

He then turned to Ashti. "I will meet you at ten o'clock tomorrow morning here at the hotel to go to the bank to withdraw the money. When I get the money in cash, you will get the cross back."

"Wonderful!" Father Gregory said. He looked at his watch. "It's now half-past four. We have a lot to do and very little time to do it."

We did have a lot to do. We went with Loran upstairs to the hotel reception to talk with the manager who was Kurd and a friend of Loran's. He assured us that he had rooms available with Wi-Fi, and that it would be a safe place for Ashti to stay and for us to leave our car. Father Gregory reserved two rooms for two nights, one for Ashti and one for both of us. He told the manager to expect us back very late Monday night or early Tuesday morning. He then got the Wi-Fi password for the hotel.

As soon as we reached our room, Father Gregory got on the internet with his computer. He called his superior in Lebanon by Skype getting his authorization for the payment. He then called Natan and Hakob on his cell phone telling them of the arrangements that he had made and confirmed that Natan was ready to reimburse his part of the fees that Father Gregory had agreed to pay and to call Zulehka and Avraham to let them know of our plans. Finally, Father Gregory called the bank manager in Mardin and arranged for the money transfer to Ashti at the bank's branch in Nusaybin for early Monday morning.

At seven o'clock, Father Gregory, Ashti, and I met at the hotel's restaurant to have a meal together and to go over the plans. While at the table, Father Gregory pulled out a check that he had written for $12,500 and gave it to Ashti. "The $12,000 is to give to Loran. The extra $500 is for you to pay for all of our bills in case something doesn't go according to plan."

He then drew out a piece of paper from his bag and gave it to Ashti. "In the small chance that something does go wrong, here are some names and telephone numbers to get in touch with—my superiors in Lebanon, my parents in Boston, and the archbishop and bank director in Mardin. It is always best to be prepared."

"I guess that I should do that, too," I said, and I wrote out for Ashti the telephone number of my parents in Asheville as well as their e-mail address.

Father Gregory and I decided to leave our laptops with Ashti for safekeeping and for her use of Skype while we were gone. We each gave her all the passwords that she needed and then we returned to our rooms to sleep a little before meeting Loran at midnight.

At eleven, we woke up to get ready and then went to Ashti's room to give her all of the things that we did not want to take on the trip. Since we were only going to be gone for one day, I decided to take with me in my daypack only my notebook, documents, camera, binoculars, and a toothbrush as well as the pages of Karine's journal related to Syria. Once more, Father Gregory went over with Ashti what he needed for her to do and then all three of us went to the lobby to wait for Loran.

A little before midnight, Loran arrived at the hotel. He pulled out a cell phone and a charger from his briefcase and gave it to Father Gregory. "This is so you can communicate with me from Syria. He gave him his number, which Father Gregory wrote down on a piece of paper and also on his underarm. "Just in case I lose the paper," he said.

"I will accompany you to the Syrian border, but others will take you across," Loran said. "Your driver in Syria is a Kurd. He's a person of confidence who knows the region well and speaks Turkish, Kurdish, and Arabic and a smidgen of English and French."

Father Gregory tested the cell phone and it was fully charged. He then put it into his shoulder bag and pulled out the Terzian Cross. After kissing it, he gave it to Loran. "It is our guarantee."

Loran nodded, and put it into his briefcase. We then followed him out to his pick-up truck. When we got there, Loran said that he was sorry, but a requirement was that we put on black hoods so that we could not see the place that we would cross. "You will be told when to take them off in Syria."

We nodded in agreement, and he then motioned for us to get in the truck cabin. Father Gregory slid over to the middle. As I started to get in after him, Ashti kissed me on my cheek and squeezed my hand. "May Allah be with you," she said.

"And with you," I replied, unsure just why I said that, since I was not a believer.

CHAPTER 23

Bakur Ahmad

Once we were both inside the truck cabin and settled, Loran gave us each a black hood to put over our heads, explaining where the slits were for our nose and mouth so that we could talk and breathe. We put them on and adjusted them. They were effective because I could see absolutely nothing the entire trip except the lights of on-coming cars and trucks on the highway.

Loran rolled down his window and reiterated to Ashti that he would meet her the next morning at ten, and Father Gregory and I both thanked her and said goodbye once more. Loran then started the motor and turned right onto the highway. I imagined that we were retracing the route that we had come earlier that morning, following the border fence and the railroad line.

We traveled mostly without any conversation, as Loran seemed not to be that comfortable in either English or Arabic. He asked in English if we wanted some water, but as we did not, he said no more. Instead, he turned on the truck radio and listened to a station playing Kurdish music.

After a drive of about forty-five minutes, he turned off the radio and got off the pavement onto a bumpy road or field driving slowly for some ten minutes. He then turned off the motor. Someone spoke to him in Kurdish and Loran got out of the truck. He came around to the passenger side, saying something in Arabic to Father Gregory that, of course, I did not understand.

"We are at the crossing, and we are supposed put our bags on our backs, hold on to a rope and follow the instructions of our guide and not say anything," Father Gregory explained to me.

"Good luck," Loran said in English and patted me on the back. "I will meet you here tomorrow night."

I estimated that we walked for some fifteen minutes on very uneven land in a line of four with one Kurd militiaman leading Father Gregory and then me, and the other Kurd behind me. Several times, I bumped into Father Gregory and several times, I tripped and fell losing hold of the rope. The man behind me helped me up and put it back into my right hand. At two points, we had to get on our knees and crawl, and once, I felt the sharp pain of a prick of concertina wire on the back of my head.

After standing up from the second crawl, we walked for another five minutes or so and then I heard the voice of a third person greeting us in Turkish and Arabic. He helped us get into the back of a van with our two companions and then drove us for some fifteen minutes along what I imagined must have been a gravel road. After it merged into a paved road, we traveled for another twenty minutes or so until we came into a city. My dependence on vibrations and noises instead of eyesight to know where I was and where I was going reminded me of Karine and Talitha's trip under the tarp in the oxcart to the Frazer's compound in Mardin.

Father Gregory and I were silent throughout the trip, but our driver and two guides conversed the whole time in Kurdish, often laughing. At one point in the city, our driver stopped and the two guides patted me on the shoulder, said something in Kurdish, and then got out. "They wished you good luck," the driver told us in Turkish.

When we got to our destination, our driver told us to get out with our bags. He then slid a door open, which I imagined by the sound to be a garage or warehouse door. Once we were inside and he had closed the door, he told us in Turkish that we could now take off our hoods. I did so and was grateful to get back both my vision and to be free from the stuffiness of the hood.

"Welcome to Ras al-Ayn," he said in Turkish, speaking slowly so we could understand. "My name is Bakur Ahmad and I am your driver." He held out his hand to shake ours. In the dim light of the one florescent light hanging from the ceiling, I could see that he was a tall and thin man who was about fifty years old. Like many of the men in this area, he had beard stubble on his cheeks.

Bakur pointed to two mattresses in the corner of what was a small warehouse filled with dozens of gas cans on shelves and sacks of what looked like grain on the floor. "You can sleep there. Some water bottles are on the table and a sink and bathroom are in that corner." He pointed to them. "We will be leaving at six in the morning for Deir ez-Zor. Please don't go outside." He then went through another door into what I guessed were his private quarters.

After he left, I looked at my watch and saw that it was now two-thirty in the morning. That gave us three and a half hours before we were to leave. I did not think I could sleep, however. I was just too excited that I was now in the same town where Karine and Talitha had traveled by horseback with their companions to take the train to Aleppo.

Father Gregory had no such problem with sleeping. After I reassured him that I was fine but wanted to stay up a little longer and write up some notes, he told me good night and immediately went over to one of the mattresses and fell sleep. As for me, I went to the small table and sat in one of the two chairs there, taking from my daypack my notebook and pen and the pages of Karine's memoir that I had brought with me. I then re-read her description of what happened to them in Ras al-Ayn, the same city where I was now.

> When we got to Ras al-Ayn, Rev. Kober inquired of some locals if they knew of any German missionaries or civil servants in the town, and one of the locals led us to the home of a German engineer who was involved with the continuation of the railroad to Nisibis. When he learned that we were German and American missionaries from Harput, he was very kind to us and put us up at his house, giving Mother, Miss Isabel, and me one guest room, and turning over his own room to Rev. and Mrs. Kober. He allowed our Turkish guards and animals to stay in his stables.

The next day, Rev. Kober and our engineer host, whose name I think was Holbein, left early to arrange passage on the train for our party to Aleppo and then on to Beirut. When they came back, Rev. Kober told us that thanks to the engineer and his contacts, we would be leaving the next morning on the train. We would have a night stopover in Aleppo and then would continue the next afternoon to Beirut.

Rev. Kober also warned us again how dangerous the situation was in Ras al-Ayn. "The town is full of Armenian and Syriac deportees and their guards," he said. "It's a major holding zone for the survivors of the long marches from Diyarbakir and of those who came packed in cattle cars from Adana and the west."

After Rev. Kober shared with Holbein what he had seen of misery and death on his journey south, Holbein told him of his own experience in Ras al-Ayn. He had visited camps of thousands of deportees along the tracks that were full of squalor, disease, dead bodies, and desperation. Women and children had pleaded for his help, and he and some other Germans who were disgusted with the sights of desperation and the smells of feces and death, had gone to the German Military Command in the city to demand that something concrete and immediate be done to stop this horror. He said that the answer from the Command was that it was a Turkish issue and not a German one. The Turks were their allies in the war against Russia, and the Turks saw the Armenians as collaborators with the Russians and therefore that they needed to be neutralized. Holbein said that he and a German army medic lieutenant were so traumatized and ashamed that they started writing reports and taking pictures secretly of the horrors. They had to smuggle them out as the Turkish government had forbidden any picture taking of the refugees.

After reading this, I wrote in my journal my own adventure of crossing the border and arriving in Ras al-Ayn. I looked forward to daylight and seeing what the town was like now almost a hundred years later. I went over to the other mattress and lay down hoping to get some sleep like Father Gregory who was now breathing deeply. Unfortunately, it was useless as so many things kept going through my mind.

At five-thirty, Bakur returned with some coffee, bread, and cheese for us and placed it all on the table. While we ate, he opened the door of the garage and started to fetch about a dozen empty gas containers and then tie them to the top of the van. When he was finished, he said in Turkish that we were ready to go. Father Gregory got in the front passenger seat next to him, and I got into the seat behind. It was a new van, similar to a dolmus bus in Turkey with four rows of seats, enough for nine people and luggage in the back.

In the early morning light, the street in front of his house looked empty and quiet. As it was not paved, I thought that we must be at the edge of the city. In fact, we were also near to the Turkish border, and I could see concrete border fences and watchtowers as well as apartment buildings and Turkish flags on the other side.

Looking around, I saw that we were in a mixed-use area of residences, small repair shops, and storage garages. Bakur's house, attached to the garage, appeared to be of better quality and better maintained than most of the other buildings on the street. It had recently been painted and had a neat front yard with grass, bushes, and a shade tree.

Bakur proved to be friendly and talkative, and when he discovered that Father Gregory spoke good Arabic, he switched to that language. I just sat in the back and listened as Father Gregory asked him questions as we drove through the city. When Father Gregory learned something that he thought might interest me, he shared it with me in English.

From Bakur we learned that Ras al-Ayn was a little smaller than its Turkish sister city of Ceylanpinar on the other side of the border. Its population of about 50,000 people were mostly Kurds but with minority groups of Arabs, Chechens, Syriacs, and Armenians. After the capture of the city by Islamic rebels of the Al Nusra Front tied to Al Qaeda, many of the Christians escaped across the border to Turkey. Now that the Kurdish militia, the YPG, of which Loran was a member, had retaken the town, some of the Christians had returned.

While Father Gregory was more interested in the actual situation of the border city and its Christian residents, I wanted to connect it to Karine's story. "If we have time, could you ask him to drive by the railway station where Karine and Talitha took the train to Aleppo?" I asked Father Gregory. "I would like to get a picture of it if possible." Father Gregory nodded and asked Bakur in Arabic about it.

"The railway is closed now and anyway, the station is too close to the border," Bakur replied. "Also, the last thing we want is to be stopped now for taking pictures." He paused and then asked, "Why are you so interested in the railway station?"

Father Gregory answered for me. "Our ancestors were Armenians," he explained. "They escaped the death march to Deir ez-Zor and were able to take the train from the Ras al-Ayn station to Aleppo and Beirut."

Bakur nodded. "It was a shameful time in our history," he said. "Our city was known for its death camps, and they say that 80,000 of your people died here."

I was always surprised that while most Turks and Kurds are said to vehemently deny the massacres, a few others accepted them as something their ancestors really did, and they were embarrassed and contrite about them. "What makes the difference?" I asked Father Gregory in English, thinking that Bakur could not understand.

"My guess is that some people are less egotistical than others," Father Gregory replied. "For most of us, if our ancestors are praised for their past actions, we use that praise to reflect on us. If our ancestors are berated for their actions, such as the massacre or enslavement of others, we of course want to deflect that blame from ourselves. Our first tendencies are to either deny that it ever happened, or to throw the accusation back at the accuser by saying that their ancestors did similar things or worse. 'What about slavery, the inquisition, the crusades?' What is so hard for all of us is to recognize an evil, ask forgiveness for it in the name of our ancestors, and then try to move on. Some can do that but most of us can't."

We soon left the city, and after passing without any trouble through one checkpoint manned by the YPG, we headed south towards Deir ez-Zor.

According to Bakur, we could take several routes to Deir ez-Zor. The one he chose was through the desert as it was quicker and we would be less likely to be stopped. It had only three checkpoints, two controlled by the Kurds and the one at Deir ez-Zor controlled by the Free Syrian Army, which was pro-Western. He normally took this route when he brought oil from the rebel-controlled fields around Deir ez-Zor back to Ras al-Ayn to sell.

It took us about forty-five minutes to get to the second YPG checkpoint at the junction of two roads. It was near a small village with a church steeple similar to the ones I had seen in the Syriac villages near Midyat. The four men who stopped us were courteous and passed us through without any problem, looking only at Bakur's documents and asking if we had enough gas and water to make it to Deir ez-Zor. Bakur assured them that we did.

After this checkpoint, the land on both sides of the highway became increasingly desolate, barren, and empty. As the highway was straight and the scenery monotonous, and since we still had a three and a half-hour trip to Deir ez-Zor and I had not slept all night, I decided to stretch out on the empty car seat. I quickly fell asleep listening to the conversation in Arabic between Father Gregory and Bakur. I probably would have slept the entire trip to Deir ez-Zor had not the van suddenly pulled off the highway onto the gravel bank and come to a stop.

When I opened my eyes and sat up to see what was happening, both Father Gregory and Bakur had turned in their seats and were staring at me. Father Gregory had a big smile on his face.

"You are not going to believe this, Peter," Father Gregory said. "I think that you and Bakur are related!"

I had no idea what he was talking about.

"While you were sleeping," Father Gregory explained, "I asked Bakur about his family. He told me that he was born in Mardin and that he was half Kurd from his father and half Turk from his mother. He and his wife have two children, a daughter who is married and lives in Ceylanpinar and a son who is not married and lives in Ras al-Ayn. His son does computer work for the YPG."

I wasn't sure where all of this was going, or why they stopped to wake me up to tell me, but I kept listening.

"Now listen to this," Father Gregory said with a big grin on his face.

"When I asked about his religion, if he was Sunni or Alevi, Bakur said that he was a Sunni Muslim. In fact, he said, his great-grandfather had been a Sunni Imam in Mardin who taught at the Zincirye Madrasa. Remembering what you had told me of your own background, I asked him the name of his ancestor. When he said, 'Imam Aslan,' I thought this is a God-thing. I then asked him if he also had an ancestor named Altay? He was astounded. He said 'yes, he was my grandfather! How did you know?' I said that we should wake you up, and you would tell him."

Personally, I could not fathom this coincidence. It was like being awakened from a vivid dream and not knowing what is real and what is not. I asked Father Gregory to repeat what he had just said, and he did, this time adding, "I woke you up, because I didn't know what you would want me to say given the circumstances of Noah's birth. It might be a devastating shock to Bakur to learn that his grandfather did such a thing."

Now fully awake, I stared at Bakur to see if I could see any resemblance to my grandfather, and he seemed to be staring at me for the same reason. I decided that the only story that I could recount was the true one, one that did not deny the evil rape, but that emphasized the good of our mutual ancestor as well—his protection, his supplying food, his helping Karine and Talitha to escape. So parked by the side of the highway, in the middle of the Syrian Desert, I told him the story.

As Father Gregory translated, I watched Bakur's reaction. He shook his head at first in astonishment, but then finally in acceptance. "It must be true," he said. "My grandfather told me that he had been a gendarme as a young man, but he never mentioned any of this." He then opened his door and came around to the back door on my side and opened it. He extended his hand to me, and I got out of the van not sure of what to expect. He then embraced me and kissed me on both cheeks, and kept saying "brother" in Turkish. I repeated the same word back to him and kissed him on his two cheeks as well, even though it was so culturally uncomfortable for me. I would give a lot to have a picture of that embrace by the side of an almost empty road in the middle of the Syrian Desert, but I was too stunned to think to ask Father Gregory to take it.

The rest of the trip to Deir ez-Zor was spent mainly telling each other about our lives and families. Father Gregory translated most of the time, but I also spoke several times directly in Turkish for more simple questions and answers. I was particularly interested in hearing about his memories of Altay, and he was glad to tell me what he remembered. He said that Altay eventually married a local woman whom his father had selected for him, had three children, two girls and a boy, all of whom eventually moved away from Mardin. For his livelihood, Altay owned a spice store on the main street of Mardin. After Altay's death in 1969 at the age of 78, Bakur's uncle had taken it over. After some years, he sold it and moved to Istanbul with his family. Bakur remembered his grandfather Altay as a humble and tolerant man, and he offered to show me his grave and that of his great-grandfather Imam Aslan in Mardin if the border ever opened and he could get back to visit.

As for Bakur's own family, he said that his mother was Altay's youngest daughter, Macide, and that she married the son of one of Altay's Kurdish friends whose ancestral home was the twin cities of Ceylanpinar and Ras al-Ayn. Since his Kurdish father's business had been the transportation of people and goods between Syria and Turkey, Bakur had chosen to continue in it. He had lived in both cities and now had family on both sides of the border. He longed for a day when such artificial border separations no longer existed, "perhaps in a Kurdish state of our own," he said.

"I want you to meet my wife and son before you go back to Turkey," he said to me in Turkish. "You can even speak in English with my son. He speaks it very well and he is about your age. He has always wanted to visit America."

CHAPTER 24

Deir ez-Zor

Finally, after the four hour trip—three and a half hours of driving and a half-hour parked by the highway telling our personal stories—we came to the eastern outskirts of Deir ez-Zor. At the crossroads of our highway with Highway 7, we were stopped at a checkpoint manned by militia of the Free Syrian Army or the FSA as they were known. Bakur told the young soldiers at the checkpoint that he ran a van service and that he had come to pick up some passengers and oil to sell. He also explained that Father Gregory was an Armenian priest going to visit the Armenian Memorial in the city and that I was an American going to see it as well and report on the war.

After looking at Father Gregory's documents and my American passport and reporter credentials in Arabic, they passed us through. They did complain to us, however, about the lack of American support for them. "We have to fight both the Islamists and Assad who are much better armed than we are," they said in Arabic. "Tell your government to give us better support!"

Father Gregory translated. I nodded and said that I understood.

From that checkpoint, we continued to a roundabout where one road led to the narrow Siyasim Bridge across the Euphrates to the city center of Deir ez-Zor. As ISIS now largely controlled the bridge, we avoided it and went right on the road towards the towns of Al Hussainiyah and Al Jeneah.

Bakur followed the directions that Father Gregory gave him, but he said that he already knew where Palmyra was from past visits to the region.

When we got to Al Jeneah, Bakur turned left on a road leading towards the Euphrates River. We passed a cluster of houses and then green fields of vegetables, fruits, and grains, which were a great contrast to the desert through which we had just driven. Just as Father Gregory had been told by Natan, at the end of the road were two small houses, a couple of sheds, and fields of vegetables all of the way to the banks of the Euphrates. A sign written in Arabic and in English letters was on the biggest shed saying "Palmyra." I looked at my watch and it was now a quarter to eleven.

A young boy was sitting on the steps of the largest house. When he saw us stop and park, he got up and ran inside. He must have been their lookout, since Father Gregory had advised them that we would probably arrive late in the morning. Soon afterwards, before we had even gotten out of the van, a man in his forties came outside followed by a pretty young woman dressed in European clothes without a headscarf.

"It's the right place!" Father Gregory exclaimed. "It's Zulehka!"

Zulehka smiled broadly and clapped her hands when she recognized Father Gregory. She ran to the van, and as he got out of the passenger seat, she bowed to him and kissed his hand. Father Gregory made the sign of the cross over her and pulled her up. She introduced the man who was with her as her adopted father, Avraham Khoury. She spoke in Arabic with Father Gregory, but when he introduced me as an American reporter, she replied in English, "Thank you for coming!"

We then went into the house where we met the rest of Avraham's family—his wife, Elia, and their two children. The youngest was a little girl toddler still in diapers, and their son was a five year old boy. Elia insisted that we have something to eat and soon brought us out some drinks and food.

As we ate, Father Gregory told them about how excited Hakob and their cousins were about the prospect of seeing them soon. He also told them about our meeting with Loran and finding out that Bakur and I were related. "This whole trip is a God-thing!" he repeated several times.

Zulehka and the Khourys agreed.

When we had finished eating, Bakur excused himself. "I will be back here at seven o'clock to pick you up. That should put us at the border crossing by eleven tonight. It is best to travel at night because it is cooler, and I will be carrying petrol cans on the roof of the van. Remember to take no more than what you can carry across the border on your back—one bag apiece." He exchanged cell phone numbers with Father Gregory in case plans changed, and then he left with the van to meet with his sources and fill his cans with petrol.

After Bakur had gone, and while we were still at their table talking, the telephone rang. It was the Khourys and Hakob wanting to know if we had made it. Zulehka's face lit up when she took the receiver from Avraham and spoke with Hakob. Her excitement at soon being reunited with him was palpable to all of us. Avraham passed on to his cousin Bakur's estimates that we would be at the border around eleven in the evening, and Natan promised to be at the hotel in Nusaybin to meet us at midnight to take them to his home. They would be coming in two cars from the village.

After Avraham put down the phone, Father Gregory asked him if he could use it to try to get in touch with the caretaker of the Armenian Memorial to see if he was all right. Avraham agreed, and Father Gregory then looked through his notebook for the number. When he found it, he called. No one answered.

"Since we won't be leaving until tonight, would it be possible to go over to Deir ez-Zor this afternoon and check on him, or is it too dangerous?" he asked Avraham.

"It's always dangerous," Avraham said, "but still doable. The government controls most of the northern side of the city where we keep our truck, and the FSA controls where the memorial is located. They know me, as I bring fresh vegetables several times a week from our farm to sell in our store, so they won't give us any trouble. Once we dock and get our truck it is only about four kilometers to the memorial."

When Father Gregory explained to me what he was planning to do, I asked to go with them, as I wanted to see the memorial. It was important for my novel and for my articles. He consented and talked over my request with Avraham.

"There's no problem," Avraham said. "We have plenty of time if we leave right now, and the three of us can fit in the cab of the truck."

With that decided, Father Gregory said, "Let's go then." Turning to

Zulehka and Elia, he added, "We should be back in a few hours. Make sure everything is ready to go when Bakur gets back."

Father Gregory and I followed Avraham out the door of the house to the nearby shed. The door was open and inside a middle-aged man, only a few years younger than Avraham, was tinkering with the motor of a small tractor. Avraham introduced him as Tareq Daher, his Arab foreman. Tareq wiped his hand on his shirt and came over to shake ours. Avraham told him that we wanted to make a short trip of a few hours across the river. "Would it be possible for you to get the boat ready and arrange for a couple of boxes of vegetables to take as presents?"

Tareq nodded and went to the corner of the shed where some empty crates were stacked and got two of them. He then put them in a cart that already contained a boat's motor and gas container. He pushed the cart out of the shed heading to the fields nearby to get the vegetables and the then to the boat on the river.

After he had left, Avraham explained, "Tareq will take care of the farm, the house, and our town apartment for us while we are gone. He has been with me for ten years and is totally reliable."

"Isn't he afraid of staying?" I asked.

"No. He is a Sunni Muslim and is not involved in politics. He has never married, so he has no family to worry about. He may have some trouble, though, if ISIS takes over the region. Working for a Christian will not endear him to them. He doesn't seem to be worried, though."

When we came out of the shed, Avraham went back inside his house to get his truck keys and then rejoined us, leading us down a dirt path through his vegetable fields towards the river bank about 200 yards away. Within a few minutes, we arrived at the fifteen feet fiberglass open boat, locked to a metal pole on the bank of the river.

Tareq soon joined us with its motor and with two small crates of lettuce, cucumbers, and tomatoes in his cart. He lifted the motor and attached it to the boat, and he then placed in the hull the two crates of vegetables and the gas container. We all helped push the boat down the muddy bank to the river. After Tareq had gotten in, connected the gas, and started the motor, Avraham, Father Gregory, and I also entered and sat down on the two front boards.

274

As we headed down the river to the dock about a half a kilometer away, I was awestruck to think that I was on the famous Euphrates River, whose historical importance began in the Biblical stories of the Garden of Eden. This muddy, life-giving water had flowed from the mountains and lakes of eastern Turkey, the Armenian homeland. It had passed near Harput, and now was winding its way through Syria on its route to Iraq, bringing green life to the desert wherever it flowed. I reached out over the edge of the boat and put my hand into the warm waters, enjoying the moment. I also took some pictures.

I only saw one other boat on the river as we descended, a motorboat like ours that passed us heading upstream. Father Gregory waved to the lone man at the controls, and he waved back. The river was about 140 yards wide. On its eastern banks, I saw mostly farms, and on its western side, a highway and the buildings of Deir ez-Zor. It took us about five minutes to get to the landing on the Deir ez-Zor side where about ten other boats were docked. We tied up at a wharf and got out. Tareq handed Avraham and me the two crates of vegetables, and as we left with them for the truck, Avraham told him that we would be back in about two to three hours. We all thanked him.

Avraham led us to his old pick-up truck, and we put the two crates of vegetables in the back and got into the cab with him. He started the motor, which ran loudly because of a busted muffler. He told us that to the right was the highway that went to Ar-Raqqah, some 140 kilometers distant, and to the left was the city center of Deir ez-Zor. He crossed the median and turned left into the city.

In order to avoid known checkpoints and non-passable roads because of shellings and bombings, Avraham took us by a circuitous route into the town. As we progressed towards the center, I could see that the damage to buildings increased. He pointed out his own apartment building and store where mortar rounds had opened gaping holes two floors above his third floor apartment. Farther on, the destruction was even much worse. Some of the side streets I looked down were impassable because of the massive holes in the streets and rubble that filled them from the destruction of nearby buildings. Every now and then, I saw burnt-out cars and trucks, some of them on their side. I took as many pictures as I could, but I was always on the lookout for militiamen who might see me, ask questions, and take away my camera.

Not many people were in the streets. I saw a few women dressed in black who walked quickly from one place to another, and some armed militiamen standing at a corner smoking cigarettes. "That's good news," Avraham said. "They must be FSA militia. ISIS soldiers don't smoke. They just behead and crucify!" he added with irony.

When we got to a canal cutting through the city with palm trees on each side, we encountered a little more traffic, but it was clear to me that the city was dying. At what Avraham called the Revolution Bridge that crossed the canal, he turned right, pulled up to the curb, and parked.

As he did so, Father Gregory pointed to the building in front of us. "That's the Armenian Memorial and Church across the street," he said. The caretaker's apartment is next door to it.

We got out of the truck and looked both ways for danger. We could hear the sound of far away booms and occasional automatic weapon bursts but no sounds of fighting near us. Avraham picked up one of the wooden boxes of greens and vegetables from the back of the truck and I picked up the other, and we followed Father Gregory to the two-story apartment building across the street, which so far was undamaged by the war.

When we got there, Father Gregory knocked at the door of the downstairs apartment saying who he was in Armenian. Within a short time, an elderly man, perhaps in his seventies, came to the door and opened it. He exclaimed something in Armenian and embraced Father Gregory, and then something in Arabic and patted Avraham on the back.

Avraham must have explained that our crates were gifts, as he seemed greatly pleased as he ushered us into his house and showed us where to put them on a wooden table in his small kitchen. I looked around and there did not seem to be any other food on the counters or on the open shelves.

After returning to the small living room, he invited us to sit down on the sofa or on one of the three chairs of the room around a worn rug. The only other furnishings were a table, an old TV, and fan. On the walls, he displayed a cheap tapestry of the Last Supper, a cross, and an old framed wedding picture of him and his wife.

Father Gregory introduced him to me as Karim Eminyan, and to my delight, explained that he spoke English, as well as French, Armenian, and Arabic. He then told Karim why we had come to Deir ez-Zor, and he offered him a way of escape tonight with us if he felt that his life was in danger.

Karim laughed. "I'm an Armenian. In this part of the world, my life is always in danger! Thanks, but no. Deir ez-Zor is my home and the protection of the Church of the Martyrs is now my life work after the death of my wife. I plan to die here."

"Would it be possible to see the memorial and the church and take some pictures of it for a newspaper article?" I asked.

"Of course," he answered. "Some of its treasures have been taken away for safety reasons, and we have experienced some damage from mortar shells, but it is still mainly intact so far. We could go right now if you wish."

"I would love that," I said.

Karim got his keys from his bedroom, and after locking his apartment, we all went down the street to the entrance of the memorial. From the street, the building looked like a two-story high wall with six carved arches below and windows above. Karim led us to the second arch and unlocked the heavy molded metal door and we entered. Under the open sky, we climbed up some stairs, and through a stone portal shaped like the front of an Armenian church, we entered into a small courtyard paved in polished stone. Looking around, I could see that the building had been severely damaged by shelling but that Karim had done his best to keep it looking nice by pushing the fallen rubble into one corner of the courtyard.

Facing us in the courtyard was an eternal flame, and behind it was a beautifully carved wall with a large Armenian cross. "This is the Genocide Memorial," Karim explained to me in English. "Everything here has meaning. The steps you just climbed represent the hardships and catastrophes that Armenians have had to overcome, the doves carved on the walls symbolize our hopes for peace. The eternal flame represents our never dying memory of those who perished in the Aghet or Catastrophe, and of course, all of the crosses, our Christian faith, hope, and heritage."

"You are the one who keeps the flame burning?" I asked.

"I do what I can, but in these terrible conditions, it is not always possible to keep it burning and the streams flowing." He pointed two small streams of water emerging from a wall covered with Arabic and Armenian designs. "This is the wall of friendship between the Armenian and Syrian Nations and the streams of water represent life and our hope for the future."

"Do you still get visitors even with the war going on?" I asked.

"We used to have thousands every year, especially on April 24, the date we remember worldwide the genocide. Now, we get only a few as it is too difficult and dangerous to come to Deir ez-Zor. A few local Armenians like me come to worship in the church. One man last week was a Muslim from a village eighty kilometers from here who recently discovered that he had Armenian ancestors. His great-grandfather was an Armenian orphan adopted by a Bedouin family. That was the only way that he survived."

"Father Gregory and I have some Turkish Muslim cousins who survived in a similar way."

"One does what one has to in order to live," Karim said philosophically. He then asked, "Would you like to see the church and the museum?"

"Very much so," I answered.

He then led the way into an octagonal building to our left, the Church of the Holy Martyrs as he called it. In the middle of the stone floor was a circular hole with a beautifully carved column coming up through it from the room below reaching up towards the cupola of the chapel. At the top of the column was an Armenian stone cross. Looking down through the hole in the floor, I saw a circle of bones in a glass case at the base of the column. "We call it the 'resurrection column' because it emerges from its base of recovered bones of Armenians who died here, rising upward through the chapel towards the cupola and sky. It represents hope emerging from despair, the life of a new Armenian nation coming out of so much sorrow, death, and destruction."

Father Gregory crossed himself, and Karim and Avraham followed his example. After a moment of standing silently in front of the column and the recessed altar on the wall behind it, Father Gregory said a short prayer in Armenian.

Karim then led us downstairs to the room at the base of the column, which also served as a museum of pictures, archives, and objects from the time of the genocide. Radiating out from the base of the resurrection column were rectangular rooms with curved stone ceilings and relief carvings on some of the walls—one of a mother and child, others of crosses. Some of the glass cases were broken but those that remained showed photographs of suffering—of Turkish soldiers proudly displaying the decapitated heads of Armenian men or hanging their dead bodies over walls; of mass graves of bodies piled on top of each other; and of emaciated women and children with only a thin layer of skin covering their bones. Other displays showed some of the personal objects and documents of the dead Armenians as well as literature about the genocide. When we came to the pictures on the wall of some of the ancient Armenian towns in Anatolia where the deportees once lived and to the map of the deportation routes that they were forced to take south to the desert around Deir ez-Zor, I asked Karim why was Deir ez-Zor chosen as the final destination.

"I imagine because it was so isolated," he said. "Deir actually means monastery in Arabic and the town was in the desert about as far away as one could get from the eyes of the world." Karim pointed to the deportation map with his finger and traced the main deportation route following the Euphrates River from Jarablus near the border with Turkey through Ar-Raqqah to the town. "The main route of the deportation was along the Euphrates through the desert. It was dotted with open air concentration camps where the deportees were held until they finally got to Deir ez-Zor, the biggest concentration camp of all. At first, the governor of the area, Ali Suad Bey, tried to help the Christians but the authorities in Istanbul soon replaced him. The new governor was a tyrant called Zeki Bey who did everything possible to make sure that he carried out the elimination policy of his superiors. He killed the survivors here or marched them to places like Markada, about ninety kilometers from here, where they were murdered. There's another memorial in Markada to honor those whose bones were found there. It may have already been destroyed, however, as we have gotten reports that ISIS recently took over the town."

"The killing of Christians never seems to end here in the Middle East," Father Gregory said. "Just when we think that maybe we are safe, then persecution starts again. Sometimes it comes from a secular state, sometimes from fanatical Islamists who think they are doing Allah's will to destroy us and take our property." He turned to Karim. "You are one of my heroes, Karim, electing to stay here and defend our heritage despite so many threats."

"I'm no hero, but leaving is just what our enemies want. This is my home and the home of our Christian ancestors. No one has the right to take it away from us. We have to find a way to live together in peace."

After I took pictures of the different displays downstairs, we returned to the courtyard and then descended the steps to the metal door leading to the street. Once outside, Karim locked the door and walked with us to the truck. I thanked him for his kindness in opening the memorial for me to see.

"It is my duty and my pleasure," he replied. "Thank you for writing about our sorrows." He also thanked Avraham for the vegetables and the greens and wished him and his family a safe trip to Turkey.

Father Gregory and Avraham kissed Karim on both cheeks, and Avraham said apologetically, "I would stay, too, but I have to protect the lives of my children. We will return when all of this is over."

Karim smiled. "That may be only when Messiah returns!"

The trip back to the boat was uneventful, but we did hear the sounds of mortar shells and automatic weapons and saw several pick-up trucks with mounted guns racing through the streets to a battle zone. In the government-controlled area where the boat was docked, I saw my first tank.

Tareq was waiting for us when we got to the boat. Avraham parked the truck and locked it, and as he got into the boat, he gave the keys to Tareq. After we all sat down on the benches, Tareq started the motor and we headed up the river to the farm.

At Palmyra, we all helped Tareq pull the boat onto the shore, where he relocked it to the post. He then put the motor and gas container into the cart, and we walked behind him as he pushed it back to the shed. It was around four o'clock when we got there. As the Khoury family and Zulehka packed their one bag apiece and prepared water and food for the journey, I sat outside on the stairs of the house writing in my journal.

At a little after seven in the evening, Bakur returned with the van, the petrol cans on the roof now full. He also came with the news that ISIS was advancing in the east towards the city and that they had taken over some of the oil wells that the FSA had previously run. "It is good we are leaving today," he said. "Tomorrow might be too late."

After he saw that we were all ready, he called Loran on his cell phone and told him the route that we planned to take and his estimation of the time that it would take us to get to the border crossing.

Tareq was there to see us leave, and Elia and her son cried as they said goodbye to him. Each member of the Khoury family embraced him, and he promised them that he would take care of everything until their return. Father Gregory translated for me Avraham's last words to him as we left. "Tareq, my loyal friend, your life is more important to us than these things. If necessary, flee."

His last word to Avraham was, "Never!"

We then all got into the van with our bags—Father Gregory in the front passenger seat, Zulehka and I in the second seat, and the Khoury family in the back two seats. Our bags were in the back or at our feet.

CHAPTER 25

ISIS

It was a little after sunset when we got to the Free Syrian Army checkpoint at the start of the desert highway. This time we saw no militiamen there. While we all felt a sense of relief, we wondered why they had abandoned their post. Bakur thought it was because of the imminence of an ISIS attack on them.

We then settled in for the long journey through the desert. While the Khoury children were soon asleep, Zulehka wanted to practice her English and to ask Father Gregory and me questions about life in America. She was especially interested in the process of getting permission to emigrate there. Studying and living in America was Hakob's and her dream. They wanted to marry as soon as they could in Turkey and then get permission to go to the United States and finish their medical education there and raise a family. "In America, we can live without fear," she told me.

Father Gregory cautioned her about too much optimism. "Your dreams are possible, and I will do everything I can to help you, but your first step might have to be to go to Armenia and then apply from there for a visa for America. It will take some time."

Around nine o'clock, Bakur suddenly turned off his van's headlights and pulled off the highway onto a small dirt trail. He drove down it for about two hundred yards, parked the car behind a hill outside the view of the highway, and turned off the motor. He explained that he had seen the lights in the distance of a small convoy of about a half-dozen vehicles coming our way heading to Deir ez-Zor and he thought that it would be best not to be seen by them. A few minutes later, we could hear the trucks passing. When we could no longer hear them, Bakur said it was safe to leave.

The Khoury children needed to relieve themselves, so we all decided to get out and use the opportunity as well. The women went off into the desert on one side of the car and the men on the other side. As I walked away from the others, I looked up at the glorious sky far from any city lights and felt a deep sense of awe coming over me at the majesty, vastness, permanence, silence, and peace of the desert night. It was no wonder that believers sought the desert to build their monasteries, because there, even an unbeliever like me could feel a sense of the Divine.

When we got back into the van, we drove for another hour, all of us now wide-awake, passing only three single small trucks and cars coming towards us, none of them militia or military. We also began to see some isolated lights as the land became more fertile and tiny farms and villages appeared. Bakur said that soon we would be coming to the junction of our highway with the east-west road that would take us back to Ras al-Ayn. "We should be at the border crossing in another forty-five minutes," he said.

As we slowed down to approach what we thought was a Kurdish militia checkpoint at the junction of the two highways, Bakur let out what I was sure must have been an expletive in Arabic and then the word we all understood, "ISIS!"

From my seat, I could clearly see through the front windshield the black flag of ISIS on the pole where the Kurdish flag had flown when we had stopped here earlier in the day. The lights of several pick-up trucks with guns mounted on the back lit it. Two militiamen dressed in black with AK-47 automatic rifles and flakjackets waved for us to halt and of course that's what Bakur did. What happened next, I saw, but I had to guess at what was said. It was only later that Father Gregory explained to me everything,

A bearded young soldier came to the driver's window and spoke in Arabic. "Who are you and where are you going?" he asked Bakur in a menacing tone.

Bakur was direct in his response. "I run a transportation service between Ras al-Ayn and Deir ez-Zor and am transporting passengers and oil to sell." He gave the young man his documents, and the soldier looked at them with a flashlight.

The soldier then directed his light into the car looking at each of our faces and asked to see our documents as well. Without thinking, I handed the documents of the Khoury family, Zulehka's, and my own passport and declaration that I was a reporter through the window to him. I immediately regretted what I had done when I saw his reaction as he glanced at my American passport. The militiaman called two other soldiers to come over to the vehicle. They talked among themselves for a minute, and then the soldier came back to Bakur and told him to pull off the road and turn off the motor. "I need to show these documents to my commander." He got into one of the pick-up trucks and drove off. The other militiamen remained there guarding us.

We waited quietly and fearfully for some fifteen minutes as the soldier told us we could not talk to each other. When the soldier who had taken our documents returned, he told Bakur that we were to follow him to a village nearby. He then got back into his truck with the mounted gun and headed towards the lights of the village. Bakur followed him, and behind us, another ISIS truck with soldiers followed us.

As we drove sandwiched between the two pick-ups out to the east-west highway, Mrs. Khoury and the children began to cry. Father Gregory prayed in Syriac a short prayer and then told them everything would be all right. We had done nothing wrong.

Within a few minutes, we turned off the highway, and we entered a village and parked in front of the Syriac church whose steeple I had seen earlier in the day. I noticed that the steeple's stone cross was now in broken pieces on the ground. The militiamen came to the van and herded us into the church with their automatic weapons pointed at us.

I was shocked at what I saw inside. In the light of the bare electric bulbs hanging from the ceiling and along the walls, the small sanctuary was a wreck. The walls and ceilings were riddled with bullets, the few pews turned over, and ripped Bibles and pictures were scattered on the floor. Two young girls crouched on the floor in a corner, and not far from them, a wounded Kurdish militiaman held his blood-drenched stomach and groaned. The Khoury children shook when they saw the scene and began crying again.

"Shut them up," a burly bearded man said. He was sitting behind the altar that he was now using as a table with our documents spread out on it besides a revolver. Zulehka let out a gasp when she saw him and immediately put down her head as if hiding. She turned her back to him as she helped Mrs. Khoury quiet the children.

The commander, though, called her by name and told her to come to the table. When she got there, he looked at her in bewilderment. "Zulehka," he said, "I saw your documents. What are you doing in a van with two Americans and a Syriac Christian family."

"I live with the Khourys in Deir ez-Zor. It has gotten so dangerous, they decided to come to Ras al-Ayn. They invited me to come with them."

"I don't understand," he said. "Why didn't you return to Ar-Raqqah to your father's house?" He paused. "Does he know that you are living with Christians and what you are doing?"

"No," she replied. "We left on the spur of the moment. I was going to call him from Ras al-Ayn."

Mukhtar then called me forward and holding up my passport, he asked me in Arabic why I was in Syria. Father Gregory immediately responded in Arabic, "He doesn't speak Arabic, only English."

"And who are you?" Mukhtar thumbed through the documents until he came to Father Gregory's Syrian residency card. "It says here that you are American and a Christian priest. Is that correct?"

"Yes."

"And he is an American reporter," he said pointing to me.

"Yes."

"This makes no sense to me," Mukhtar said to Zulehka. "Why are you traveling with an American priest and an American reporter and a Christian family heading towards Ras al-Ayn?"

"I told you," she replied. "I live with the Khourys in Deir ez-Zor and the Americans are their friends."

Mukhtar then ordered two of the soldiers to go to the van and bring in the bags. They put them on the floor in front of the altar and Mukhtar got up from his chair and came around to stand in front of them and Zulehka. "Which is your bag?" he asked.

Zulehka with hesitation pointed to one of the bags and then asked, "You are not going to go through a woman's bag in front of men are you?"

"Yes, I am. Something here is not making sense to me." He felt the softness of the biggest part of the bag and said, "I don't care about your clothes although you've always dressed indecently." He then unzipped the outer pocket where he felt some books. When he did so, he pulled out a Bible in Arabic, and opening it up, he came across a picture of Hakob inscribed by him promising his love to her.

He was dumfounded and speechless for a minute. He then noticed the silver necklace that Zulehka had around her neck and he reached for it and pulled it out from under her blouse. Dangling from it was a cross and a ring. "You are a Christian!" His face boiled with anger and he slapped her with such force that she fell to the floor. He started to kick her when Father Gregory intervened, putting himself between Mukhtar and Zulehka taking his blows. One of the soldiers hit him on the back of his head with the butt of his weapon, and Father Gregory fell to the floor.

Mukhtar breathed deeply as if trying to regain his calm and then backed up to the altar to get his revolver. "We are going to take the two Americans and the apostate to Ar-Raqqah. The Americans will be held for ransom, and the apostate will be judged." He then pointed to the rest of the bags. "Search the bags and their clothes and bodies for any money or gold or jewels that they are carrying. Take it as a payment for their lives and freedom."

While one of the soldiers pointed a rifle at the Khourys, another soldier searched each of them, except for the Khoury's youngest child still in diapers. They collected wallets, bracelets, and necklaces and some money Avraham had hidden in their bags.

"Put the apostate with the two girls in one truck and the Americans in another. Put their bags in a third and let's go."

"What about the Kurd?" One of the soldiers asked, pointing to the wounded militiaman still quietly groaning by the wall.

Mukhtar went over to him, pointed his revolver at his head said, "Allahu Akbar" and fired. "He is taken care of."

We were all shaking as we emerged from the church. When Mukhtar saw the petrol cans on top of Bakur's van, he ordered them to be taken down and the petrol to be poured throughout the church and on the Sufi shrine in the town and then lit. "Our califate has no room for infidels or for those who help them!" After the soldiers had gotten the cans down from the roof, Mukhtar turned to Bakur. "Go, and take the Christians with you. Getting all of you out of the country is a good thing."

Bakur gave me a helpless, painful look and then helped the stunned Khoury family into the van. He started the motor and drove off, slowly at first, but then when he got to the highway, he sped up. I imagined that he wanted to be far away before Mukhtar changed his mind.

As for us, Father Gregory and I were ordered into the back of one truck, and a heavily armed soldier got in with us. Zulehka and the two girls were put in another truck with a soldier, and our bags and documents went into still another. We sat there crouched against the cab for about a quarter of an hour as the ISIS soldiers poured petrol inside the church and on a Sufi saint's shrine not far away from it. They then lit them both, and flames billowed up and black shadows danced on the empty streets and closed doors of the village dwellings. The only sounds were that of barking dogs and celebrating ISIS militiamen shooting their automatic weapons into the night air and shouting praises to Allah, "Allahu Akbar, Allahu Akbar, Allahu Akbar!"

Our convoy had four vehicles in it. Mukhtar was in the first truck carrying Zulehka in the back with the other two girls, our truck was next, and then two other trucks followed us. Our hands were not tied, as I imagined that the soldiers had no fear that we would try to escape, given the breakneck speed at which we traveled, their bright headlights always on us, and their automatic weapons always at the ready. When I started to say something to Father Gregory, our guard kicked me and told me to shut up.

It took us less than two hours to arrive in Ar-Raqqah. Entering the city, we were driven to a large house that I imagined had been confiscated from a wealthy Christian who had fled or been killed. A large "N" in Arabic had been painted on the outside wall, which Father Gregory told me later signified "Nasarah" or Christian.

The driver of the first truck got out and opened the gate and drove in, and the driver of our truck followed him. The other two trucks parked in the street. We were then taken inside the dwelling to what must have been a reception room. From there, Zulehka and the two young girls were taken down a hall to the farthest room, while Father Gregory and I were placed in what was once a bedroom closest to the main reception area. The room was entirely bare and had bars on the window that looked out at a courtyard wall. It did have a bathroom for which we were grateful.

After the soldier left and locked the door, Father Gregory and I tried to make the best of things. We each got some water from the faucet and sat by each other in a corner away from the window and door. As quietly as he could, Father Gregory explained to me what had happened and been said at our capture. He then prayed for us, for Zulehka and the girls, and for the Khoury family. When he finished, he suggested that we try to sleep. It was difficult for me because the ceramic floor was all that we had to sleep on and we had no blankets to keep us warm in the night. Even if I had been comfortable, my fear of what was to happen would have kept me awake all night. How glad I was that Ashti was safe in Turkey and had not come with us to Syria. If she had come, she would be facing the same terror that Zulehka and the two young girls were now experiencing. What would she and Loran do when they found out that we had been captured by ISIS? What could they do?

CHAPTER 26

Mukhtar Safar

At around seven or eight in the morning, I wasn't sure because I now had no watch as the soldiers had taken it along with my camera and wallet, I heard the sound of the gate opening, a vehicle driving into the enclosure, and then of men talking. I recognized the voice of Mukhtar. Father Gregory was listening, too, and said, "They've come to pick up the girls and take them somewhere else."

"Not Zulehka?" I asked.

"No, I don't think so. Just the other two."

We then heard the girls crying and pleading for mercy, and the young men just laughed.

About a half-hour after the men and the girls had left in the truck, we heard some new voices, one of them very angry and shouting. Father Gregory listened closely and whispered to me. "I think it is Zulehka's father." When we heard a key in the door lock turning, we backed away from the door, and it opened.

It was Mukhtar, and he ordered us to come into the reception room. There kneeling on the floor in front of her father and another younger man was Zulehka. Her eyes were red from weeping, but she was silent now and seemed relieved to see us. Two armed guards were at the door. Mukhtar ordered them to wait outside, and after they left, this is what I saw and what Father Gregory explained to me later.

"She was living with a Christian family and these are the American priest and reporter she was with in the van," Mukhtar said. He picked up a Bible from the table as well as the silver chain with the cross and ring on it. "I found this Bible in her bag and this cross and ring around her neck. She says she has become a Christian and is going to marry a Christian."

"Is that true?" the father asked Zulehka.

Zulehka looked straight at her father and said, "It is true. I have not been baptized, but yes I want to become a Christian and marry a Christian."

The father broke into tears. "How could you do this to your family? You have brought great shame on us. How could you choose to renounce our religion, disobey your father, dishonor your cousin, and even try to run away?"

"Father, I don't want to dishonor you, but I had committed myself to marry someone else before you told me I must marry Mukhtar." She turned to the other man, whom I later found out was her brother. "You know Hakob. He is Tavit's younger brother, a medical student like me and from a good family."

"Hakob, Tavit's brother?" her brother repeated. "But he is a Christian."

"Yes, he is a Christian. We became close in Deir ez-Zor. I wanted to tell you of our plans to marry at your birthday celebration, Father. Before I could, you astounded me with the news that you had already engaged me to this man without telling me anything." She looked at her father with a bewildered expression on her face. "How could you do that to me? Tell me to marry a man who wants to stop my education, who beats me, who kills others in cold blood, and captures young girls to satisfy his lusts and the lusts of his soldiers and justifies it all in the name of Allah."

"Apostate!" Mukhtar was furious with anger and struck her. "You deserve to die."

The brother started to intervene, but the father held him. "Stop!" he said. "We are family. This cannot be." He turned to Mukhtar. "Let us take her home with us and we'll talk sense into her."

"No," he said. "She has gone too far. Allah and our Prophet, peace be upon him, are clear on the matter. Apostates should be killed! She has shamed us all."

"Allah also says in the Koran, 'Let there be no compulsion in religion!'" Father Gregory said, speaking out.

"Shut up, Priest" Mukhtar said, turning towards Father Gregory and raising his hand to strike him again as he had the night before.

"But what the priest said is true," the father quickly said.

That was when Zulehka's brother, Nadim, spoke. "Mukhtar, you have helped us and we are grateful for that. My father and I agree that what Zulehka has done has brought shame on you as well as on us. But just as you are our nephew and cousin, she is our daughter and sister. She is not married yet. Nor is she yet a Christian, as she herself says that she has not been baptized. Allow us to talk to her and reason with her."

"She should be judged by Sharia law and not by you," Mukhtar said. "I will bring the Mufti here to give his sentence. I cannot show my humiliation by taking her to a public Sharia court."

Zulehka's father turned to Father Gregory. "Priest, I don't know you, but I beg you to convince my daughter to renounce her intention of becoming a Christian—for her sake and for the sake of her father, her mother, and her brother. She will destroy herself and her family."

"How can I do such a thing?" Father Gregory answered. "It is her right. How can you possibly kill someone for this? What sort of god would demand this? She would be a hypocrite if she did so. This is pure evil, and she is right to resist your insistence, even at the cost of her life." He then turned to Mukhtar. "If you want blood for your wounded honor, I will gladly give you my life for hers. Let her go with the reporter to Turkey. Keep me if you will and even execute me if you must, but allow them to go. They are young and have full lives ahead of them. They have done nothing wrong."

"I will keep all of you," Mukhtar replied angrily. "A priest and a reporter are worth at least a million dollars apiece in ransom, and this apostate will submit to the will of Allah." He turned to his uncle and cousin. "I will call the Mufti from the Ar-Raqqah Sharia Court to judge her here."

He then went outside and called the guards back. He told them to take Zulehka back to her room and lock her there. He then dismissed his uncle and cousin. "I will inform you of the Mufti's verdict."

After Zulehka's father and brother had left, Mukhtar concentrated on us. "You will have one call each. You have a cell phone." He pointed to Loran's phone on the table with our other personal belongings. "Use it to call one person and tell them the following. The Islamic State must be paid one million dollars apiece for your lives by the end of the week. If not, you both will be killed. You will tell them that we will call again in five days to tell them where to deliver the money." He picked up the phone from the table and handed it to Father Gregory. "And I want it all on speaker phone. Say you are a prisoner of the Islamic State, but do not say where you are."

"It is impossible to get that kind of money," Father Gregory said.

"Call," Mukhtar insisted. "If you don't get two million within a week, you both will die."

"The only number I have is of the person we were to meet at the border to take us across," Father Gregory said.

"Then call him."

Father Gregory raised his arm to look at the number written underneath and then dialed.

I could hear the ringing, one, two rings, three rings, and then the voice of Loran answering.

Father Gregory spoke in Arabic, and when Loran realized who it was, he asked, "You are safe?"

"Peter and I are being held by the Islamic State for ransom. They want two million dollars, a million apiece, for our lives within a week. On Saturday, I am to call you back to tell you where to deliver the money and where to pick us up." He paused and then asked, "Did the others get across the border?"

"We are all together right now with Ashti in Nusaybin. She has already informed your families, and she and they send their love and prayers for your safety."

I heard voices in the background and then Loran asked, "What about the girl?"

Mukhtar grabbed the phone from Father Gregory. "The apostate's fate is different, and she is not your concern, only the two Americans are to be ransomed. You must deliver the money within a week. Do not call back as this phone will be turned off. We will call you on Saturday at this time to give you more instructions. If you don't raise the money, they both will die!" He then hung up and turned off the phone.

Father Gregory shook his head and pleaded once again for Mukhtar to release me. I was a reporter and had only come with him into Syria to write about the war. "He can be useful to you," he said.

Mukhtar laughed. "You are right. He is useful as a source of funds!" He then ordered one of his men to take us back to our room and lock us up again.

The rest of the day, we just sat on the floor, quietly talking together about what was happening, about our concern for Zulehka, and our concern for our families on hearing the news about our capture. As yet, I could not bring myself to think that this would end tragically for Zulehka or for us. At around five or six o'clock, we had our first food since our capture—some leftovers from the meal our captors had eaten. Mukhtar made a point of letting us know that the meal had been purchased with money from our own wallets.

CHAPTER 27

Apostasy

Wednesday morning, April 17, we heard people come and go in the reception room. Father Gregory sat close to the door and listened and then translated to me much of what he heard. Early in the morning, the first ones in the room were two militiamen joking, mostly about the two girls they had captured and were now keeping at another house with some other young women. At about midmorning, however, the joking stopped. Mukhtar entered the house with someone he obviously treated with deference.

"I think it is the Mufti," Father Gregory whispered to me and then got closer to the door to listen. From what he could surmise from the conversations, the soldiers were again told to wait outside, and Mukhtar went and brought Zulehka to the reception room where the Mufti was sitting. He introduced her to him and then made his accusations about her.

"We are first cousins, and many years ago our parents arranged for us to marry. We did not see each other much afterwards, though, as I went to Iraq to fight the crusaders. I killed many of them and their lackeys but was captured and put into one of their prisons for several years. After I escaped, I rejoined my brothers and returned to Syria to fight Assad and form an Islamic State. When we took Ar-Raqqah, which is my hometown, Abu Bakr al-Baghdadi wanted me to stay here to help organize it as our capital.

I then decided this was the time to marry, and I went to my uncle to claim my cousin as my wife. My uncle is a good man but a very lax Muslim and he had allowed his daughter to study medicine in Deir ez-Zor. Of course, I forbade it, but at her brother's request, I allowed her to return there for a few months to settle her affairs. Our wedding was to be at the end of this month."

"Is all of this true?" the Mufti asked Zulehka.

"It is true," Zulehka answered, "although my father never told me before this year that I had been promised to this man."

"Two days ago, I took twenty-five men with me in a raid to expand our caliphate," Mukhtar continued. "We attacked a Christian and Sufi village near Ras al-Ayn and took over a checkpoint from the Kurds at the junction of two highways. Our soldiers stopped a van, and to my astonishment, I discovered that my cousin and wife to be was in it with an American priest and reporter and a Christian family heading to Ras al-Ayn. Later, I found out that they were planning to cross the border into Turkey. While examining their things, I discovered a Christian Bible, a cross, and a wedding ring on a chain around her neck. She confessed to being engaged to be married to a Christian man she was to meet in Turkey. She had said nothing of this to her father."

"Is this also true what he says?" the Mufti asked.

"It is true, except that I planned to tell my parents before marrying my fiancé."

"You know it is forbidden for a Muslim woman to marry a Christian man," the Mufti said.

"Yes, and I also know that the rule is absurd because it is permitted for a Muslim man to marry a Christian woman," Zulehka answered defiantly.

"Show respect, woman!" Mukhtar said to her. "You see what she has turned into!"

"Yes, I see," the Mufti said.

"She confesses now to being Christian herself," Mukhtar continued.

"Is that true?" the Muft asked.

"It is true that I am a follower of Jesus, although I have not yet been baptized."

"So you have not officially become a Christian?" the Mufti asked.

"Officially, no, but in my heart, yes!"

"Do you know the gravity of what you are saying?" the Mufti asked. "According to the Koran, the Hadiths, and the Sira, you are a Kuffar and Murtadd, an unbeliever and apostate. The punishment for the latter is death."

"Yes, I know. But I also know that execution is the fate of a hypocrite as well—one who pretends to be a Muslim, yet is not. If I say I am no longer a Muslim, but I am now a Christian, according to your law, you can execute me. Yet if I pretend to be a Muslim and am not, you can still execute me. Execution is my lot either way. I would rather choose truth over falsehood. You say Jesus is a great Prophet. Then let me follow him. His way is mercy and love."

"I have heard enough," the Mufti said. "She is defiant of Allah, of the Prophet, peace be upon him, of her father, and of you, her betrothed. She should be beaten and then left alone for three days to consider her fate. She should have no visitors other than a Muslim cleric or her family to see if they can convince her of her evil. If after three days she repents, she can be forgiven and freed. If she persists in her errors, she should be executed. That is my ruling."

After the Mufti left, Mukhtar was alone with Zulehka in the reception area. At first, he spoke comfortingly to her. "You heard his fatwa," he said. "I will not even beat you if you renounce all of this silliness and agree to marry me. It is your father's will."

"I am not sure about many things concerning the nature of Allah," Zulehka said defiantly, "but I am sure that I know your nature, and I would never marry someone as cruel and evil as you are."

That was the last remark we heard from Zulehka as from then on all we heard were her cries from the many blows that she suffered from Mukhtar. We then heard Mukhtar dragging her back to her room weeping and then the door being slammed and locked behind her. The only sound after that was of Mukhtar's heavy breathing and pacing.

Neither Father Gregory nor I said anything, as we both were afraid that any noise from us would bring Mukhtar into our room, and we would have to confront his fury. Soon, however, his pacing and heavy breathing ended, and he left the room. We then heard the sound of the gate closing.

About a half-hour afterwards, when I felt that it was safe to talk, I motioned Father Gregory to the other side of the room where I felt that I could talk to him in a low voice and not be heard. I asked him what had just happened in the other room, and he explained. I was astounded.

How could it be that religion means so much? I thought to myself. *How is it possible to kill someone for what they believe or not believe? How can one be condemned to eternal damnation and terrible suffering for believing this and not that? How does one even control what one believes or doesn't? Belief has little to do with the will, but only with reason and experience.* I couldn't understand. *How could basic human rights be so ignored by so many people in the name of a religion?*

Later that afternoon, we were brought our one meal for the day by one of the militiamen. All of them were young men, longhaired and bearded, but the one who brought our meal, his beard looked comical because it was so sparse and shabby. Mukhtar followed him into the room and addressed Father Gregory. "Priest, the Mufti has given Zulehka three days to renounce her intention to become a Christian. If she doesn't, she will die. I have shared his verdict with her father and brother, and they will come tomorrow to try to convince her one last time. They pleaded with me to ask you once again to talk with her to convince her. If you refuse to do so and she continues in her defiance, her blood will be on your hands."

"Her blood will be on the hands of those who condemn her and execute her," Father Gregory replied. "It is you and not me who have that power over life and death over her."

"So you will do nothing to convince her to renounce Christianity?"

"Why would I do that? I believe in the Truth of what she believes."

"You believe a lie. Allah is God, not your Jesus. He is only a human prophet."

"Jesus is the One God of Love incarnate. Your pride, hate, intolerance, and lack of mercy is Satan incarnate!"

"Shut up priest. You blaspheme. In three days, Zulehka will die if she does not ask for forgiveness. In a week, you and your crusader friend will die if your ransom is not paid. Then all three of you will burn in the fires of hell." He slammed the door, and we heard it locked.

Father Gregory went to a corner of the room, and when I asked him what had just happened, he told me, "Please, I will tell you later. Just let me be alone right now with my Lord." He then retreated to the bathroom and closed the door.

None of this made any sense to me, and while Father Gregory was praying in the bathroom, my inner fury grew. I was angry at myself for getting us all into this situation by handing over my passport at the checkpoint. I was angry at the Mufti for his decision. I was angry at Mukhtar for his cruelty and egotism. I was angry at Father Gregory for refusing to try to convince Zulehka to just say she was Muslim in order to save her life. I was angry at God, if God existed, for not making his existence, his nature, and his wishes clearer for everyone involved—for the Mufti, Mukhtar, Zulehka, Father Gregory, and yes, for me!

CHAPTER 28

Nadim Halabi

T hursday, April 18, was quiet all morning. No one opened our door, and no one visited the two soldiers in the other room, so they spent most of the morning listening to the radio and saying their prayers at the appropriate times. Unlike other days, we did not hear Mukhtar's voice at all. Father Gregory surmised from listening to the conversation of the soldiers through the door that Mukhtar and some of his other men had joined a larger contingent of ISIS militia in an attack on another Christian village further east on the Khabur River. It appeared to him that ISIS was gradually expanding its caliphate towards Iraq.

"I wonder how Mukhtar's absence will affect the Saturday deadline for Zulehka to make her decision or for us to call Loran to find out about the ransom money," he said.

While I could imagine that Father Gregory's church could find some way to raise a million dollars to free him, I could not imagine who would do that for me. First, I knew it was the policy of the United States government to refuse to pay ransom to terrorists. Second, Mother and my stepfather could only raise that much money by borrowing against their house and Grandfather's real estate business. Perhaps together, they had that much in them. I cannot imagine, however, that my parents would be willing to jeopardize their entire financial future for me. My impression was that they had had about as much of me as they could take.

"I can't imagine that my family could raise a million dollars to ransom me," I said. "They don't have that kind of money. What do you think will happen to us if they don't get it? Will they really execute us?"

"I don't know. They have certainly executed other priests and reporters before," Father Gregory responded. "Probably, though, they will negotiate a lower amount or maybe arrange a prisoner exchange. It may be a long process."

"I should have listened to my parents and to you about coming. One never imagines that these sorts of things can happen to you. It is what happens to others. I am not ready to die. Are you?"

"I certainly don't want to die. But, yes, I think I'm ready," Father Gregory said. "Life is much fuller when you have something to die for."

I thought about that for a while. It reminded me of my conversation with Ashti near Mardin when she asked me about my own willingness to be tortured or to die for something or someone. I envied Father Gregory and Zulehka, for they both had something I did not—a love for others and Truth that surpassed even their love of themselves.

It was about five o'clock when we heard a knocking on the metal gate outside. A few minutes earlier, the guards had brought us food, and now they were eating. One of them told the other to go outside to see who it was. A few minutes later, he came back and said that it was Zulehka's brother. As the Mufti had suggested, he had come to talk to Zulehka and to try once more to convince her to change her mind.

"Did Mukhtar say anything about that?" one of the soldiers asked.

"I heard him tell the priest that they were coming," the other replied.

"But it is just the brother. The father is not there."

"I guess it is okay to let him in."

Soon, we heard the soldier return with Nadim and Nadim thanking them. They then led him to the room where Zulehka was being kept, and Nadim stayed for some fifteen minutes with her. He later told us what happened.

"I came with two plans," Nadim said. "The first was to convince Zulehka to renounce Christianity and her Christian fiancé and thus escape the death penalty. The second was to free her if she refused to do so and help her get away from Mukhtar and Ar-Raqqah. When I saw how badly Mukhtar had beaten her, I knew that it was the second plan that I had to put into action. I came prepared for it by taping a loaded revolver to my calf and by wearing baggy pants to conceal it. I told Zulehka of what I was going to do in a low voice, and while I have to admit that my original intention was not to free you, as that would complicate our escape, she insisted that you both come with us. I took the safety lock off the pistol, and when I came out of the door, the two guards were eating at the table with their guns leaning against the wall. I pointed my gun at them and told them to free you. One of them leaned towards the wall to reach for his AK-47, so I shot him in the stomach. The other one got the key from the table to unlock your door."

The rest of what happened that night, I can describe myself, because I witnessed it all. From the other side of the door, Father Gregory and I heard Nadim's orders and then the firing of his pistol and the surprised groan of pain of the soldier. We heard the unlocking of the door and then saw Nadim and the straggly bearded guard at it.

"Hurry," Nadim said loudly to us in Arabic. "We have to get to the border crossing at Tel Abiad quickly." He then asked Father Gregory to frisk the straggly bearded guard, which he did, finding a knife and a cell phone in the process. Nadim then locked the soldier in the room that had been our prison, warning him that if he shouted, he would open the door and kill him. When we came out into the reception room, we saw Zulehka, still bruised and battered, bending over the groaning, wounded guard trying to stop the bleeding in his stomach.

"We've got to go quickly!" Nadim said.

"We can't just leave him here like this," Zulehka answered. "He'll die. I don't want anyone killed for my sake. We have to get him to a hospital."

"Zulehka, have some sense. He tried to shoot me, and our own lives are in danger. We have to get out of here." Nadim then turned to us and told us to grab the AK-47s and all of our belongings, which were in our bags on a table in the corner.

I got the guns, and Father Gregory grabbed our bags with the phones, chargers, camera, our wallets, and documents. As he did so, he said to

Nadim, "I agree with Zulehka. We can't leave him to die. We have to get him to a hospital quickly."

"Okay," Nadim replied, frustrated. "Bring him and we will leave him near one, but we have to leave right now. I have a van outside. Pick him up and follow me."

Father Gregory and I picked up the soldier and followed Nadim to the gate. After stepping outside to make sure no one was in the street watching, Nadim opened the back door of the van and we laid the groaning soldier on the seat. While Zulehka got in beside him and continued to try to stop the bleeding, Father Gregory and I went back to the reception room to get our bags and the AK-47s. When we returned, I got in the seat behind Zulehka and the wounded soldier, and Father Gregory sat in the front passenger seat. Nadim started the van, and within five minutes, we were at the city's main hospital. About fifty yards from the emergency room, Nadim stopped the van, got out, and with Father Gregory's help, placed the wounded soldier on the sidewalk. He then told a woman walking down the street with her husband to alert the emergency room to help him. He and Father Gregory then quickly got back into the van, and we sped off. Nadim avoided the main streets, and within ten minutes, we came to a large warehouse at the northern edge of the city. Nadim got out of the van, opened the door of the warehouse, and drove in. He then closed the door behind us.

After Nadim turned on the lights of the large building, I saw bales of cotton stacked throughout it and a truck, also filled with sacks of cotton. He explained his plan to us. "I have prepared a hiding place for you behind the truck cabin in the back of the truck under the cotton sacks. No one will be able to see you there, but you must keep quiet. The truck's tank is full of diesel and we have some spare. My idea is to take some of the dirt roads out of town along the irrigation canals and head across the desert to Al-Hasakah, which is outside the control of ISIS. Mother and Father left this morning in another truck, and we will meet them there at the house of some relatives. Hopefully, we will be safe by the time Mukhtar learns what has happened and tries to come after us. I tried to get him off our trail by mentioning that we would be heading north to Tel Abiad instead of to where we are actually going—west to Al-Hasakah."

"Get the weapons and your personal things from the van and let's get going. Every minute is precious," he said.

While I got the AK-47s, Father Gregory reclaimed our bags. He then reached into his bag and retrieved the cell phone Loran had given him and turned it on to see if it had power. It did. "I need to call someone and tell him we have escaped," he told Nadim.

"Make it quick, or we may be recaptured," Nadim said.

Father Gregory called, but since no one answered, he left a message in Arabic. "I told Loran that we had escaped, but we were still in danger. I asked him to advise Ashti and everyone concerned to pray for us, and that we would call when we got to a place where we were safe."

Nadim put one of the AK-47s in the truck cab, and the other he gave to me. "Do you know how to use it?" he asked me, with Father Gregory translating.

"Of course not," I replied. "I only know how to use a shotgun."

He then explained to me how it worked. "I hope all goes well, and you won't have to use it, but we should be prepared for anything."

He then put on an Arab headdress that he had gotten out of the cab and helped us into the back of the truck with our bags and the gun and some water bottles that he had arranged for us. He showed us where we were to lie down on the bed of the truck in a six feet by six feet space under a three feet high platform roof of boards. He had positioned all around us and above us sacks of cotton in order to completely hide us. "It will be a little cramped," he explained, "as I thought I would only be bringing Zulehka. Just make sure that you are completely still and quiet whenever we stop."

After we were settled, lying down on our sides, Nadim rearranged the bags of cotton so that we were completely hidden. He then turned off the lights of the warehouse, opened the door, and drove out. After closing the door again and locking it, we were on our way. Now with my watch, I saw that forty minutes had passed since escaping.

Within ten minutes, the truck stopped at a checkpoint at the edge of the city and none of us moved as Nadim showed his documents as an ISIS municipal worker and explained that he was heading north to the border to deliver cotton to be exported to Turkey. The guard passed him through without question. Then about ten kilometers up the highway, we felt the truck turn off the paved road and head east onto a bumpy dirt road. We continued for another fifteen minutes or so, and then the truck stopped again. I heard Nadim open the cab door and get out, and then he came alongside us. "We are in a safe place for you to get out and stretch a little and relieve yourselves if you have that need. No one is around," he said in Arabic. Father Gregory translated.

He then got up on the back of the truck untied some ropes and moved some cotton sacks and helped us out. "The bad news," he continued, "is that I just got a call on my cell phone from Mukhtar. He now knows that we have escaped, and he is furious. He and his men are looking for us, and he threatened to kill all of us on sight if he finds us."

I felt my heart sink as Father Gregory translated. I wondered if it would come down to a gun battle in which I would have to use the AK-47 lying beside me.

"The good news," Nadim added, "is that I think he believes that we are in the van we escaped in and that we are heading north towards Tel Abiad instead of in a truck heading northeast to Al-Hasakah. I don't think that he will find us as we only have to get by two other checkpoints between here and Al-Hasakah, and only one of them is controlled by ISIS. I know a way around it, and even if I didn't, I doubt that Mukhtar will alert them or his commanders out of shame that we escaped."

Once I had emerged from our little cubbyhole under the sacks of cotton, I stretched with pleasure. Our hiding place was cramped and stuffy, and at times painful. Some nailheads stuck slightly out of the boards of the bed of the truck, and when the truck bumped, they dug into me. I could imagine how bad it must have been for Zulehka with her bruises.

"I'm okay," she replied in English when I asked her how she was doing. "I'm also extremely grateful to my brother to be free and away from that demon of a man."

"As we all are," I said, and made a point of thanking Nadim again. I then looked around to orient myself as to where we were. The sun had already gone down and it was getting dark, but I could clearly see that we were on a dirt road paralleling an irrigation canal that watered the vast cotton fields around us.

Nadim said that it was now a quarter to eight and in another forty-five minutes of this road, we would come to a secondary gravel highway that would take us to Al-Hasakah and hopefully to safety. He estimated that around half-past nine, we would get to the ISIS checkpoint at another junction of roads. We would try to skirt it. In the meantime, he thought there would be little risk to put Zulehka up front with him in the cab where it would be more comfortable for her. Father Gregory and I should continue to stay hidden in our tomb in the back, as we were Americans and would create suspicions if someone saw us.

For the next hour, the ride was slow and bumpy as Nadim maneuvered around the ruts in the poorly kept dirt road. On the positive side, we both were more comfortable as we had more room now that Zulehka was up front and the outside night air was cooler. When we got to the gravel highway, the ride became much faster and smoother although dustier. An hour and a half later, Nadim slowed down, pulled off the road, and then stopped. He got out of the cab as did Zulehka and they came to the side of the truck.

"We are now about three kilometers away from the ISIS checkpoint at the highway junctions," he said. "It is best that Zulehka get in the back again with you. We will try to skirt the checkpoint by going into the village, but ISIS has supporters there, and they may be curious. I will try to go as quietly as we can without lights, but if we are stopped, be totally quiet. I will attempt to talk my way out of it, but if I shout a curse word like 'Zarba!' it means we will have to fight. So have your gun ready."

Father Gregory translated, but then he reiterated in English, "I don't want anyone killed to protect me."

"Neither do I," Zulehka said.

I thought they were both crazy. I would preferably wound someone only, but I would also be ready to kill anyone trying to kill me.

Nadim then got up on the bed of the truck, pulled aside some sacks of cotton and helped Zulehka climb into the back and get down again into our hiding place. He then replaced the sacks hiding us, took one of the two diesel cans tied to the side of the truck, and poured the fuel into his truck's tank. He then got back into the cab.

Just as he said, Nadim drove very quietly and slowly down one of the dirt roads leading into the small village from the south highway. I was uncertain in my own mind if turning off his lights was a wise decision or not. Yes, the people at the checkpoint down the road would not be able to see the truck turn off the highway if its lights were out, but a truck coming into the small village without lights late at night might cause people to be suspicious. I just hoped that no one would be outside at this hour to notice.

Unfortunately, just what I feared happened. While everything went well for five minutes or so, as we got closer to the small concentration of houses, some dogs started to bark and then follow us. The sound of the truck's motor also amplified as it bounced off the sides of the houses. I became increasingly nervous as Nadim slowed down and then came to a halt. Someone said something to him in Arabic, and I held my breath and clutched the side of the AK-47 waiting to hear what would happen next. I looked at Father Gregory and Zulehka lying besides me. They, too, were tense and listening. Since we had to keep quiet, I had no one to translate for me, so I had to judge by the voice tones how difficult the situation was. I kept my ears attuned for the curse word that I dreaded, "Zarba!"

We must have stopped for only a few minutes, but it seemed much longer than that to me. I felt it was a good sign that Nadim did not turn off the motor or get out of the cab. Other good signs were that I heard no anger in the three different voices, and no one climbed onto the back of the truck to look around or shine spotlights on the cargo. There was only a quick inspection by a weak flashlight. After conversing back and forth with the two men, Nadim put the truck in gear and we started rolling again. I turned to look again at Father Gregory and Zulehka, and as much as I could tell in the darkness, their faces showed relief. They still said nothing. It was only about ten minutes later when we sped up and the ride became smoother on the gravel road that Father Gregory broke the silence and said to me, "I think we made it! Thank you, Lord!"

"What happened back there?" I asked.

"I'm not totally sure, but evidently one of the villagers was in the street and waved down Nadim. He wanted to know who he was and what he was doing driving in the village with his lights out. He was then joined by another man."

"What did Nadim say?" I asked.

"He told him a half-truth!" Father Gregory said. "He said that he was trying to avoid the checkpoint because militiamen always wanted to tax him exorbitant fees on the cotton that he was transporting. One of the men said, 'You are not alone. Others like you do the same. We in the village are supposed to stop and report you to them. We understand your situation, but as we are very poor, we wonder if you could give us each a small token of appreciation for our risks—say 5000 Syrian pounds apiece.'"

"Wow!"

"That sounds like a lot, but it is not that much—around $25 dollars each."

"So Nadim paid them off?"

"He did, and they waved him through, wishing him good luck."

As no truck lights followed us from behind on the highway, I began to relax for the first time, and for the next hour on the journey to Al-Hasakah, we felt free to talk. Father Gregory and I were both concerned about what had happened to Zulehka and the two young girls in Ar-Raqqah, and so we asked her about it.

"The girls were only fifteen and seventeen, the youngest a Sufi and the oldest a Christian," Zulehka answered in a mixture of English and Arabic. "Mukhtar killed the father of the youngest of them because he had tried to prevent the desecration and destruction of the Sufi shrine in the village. The other girl was from the Christian priest's family. Mukhtar did not kill her parents, but he took the girl instead as a payment for letting them live."

"Where were the girls taken?" I asked.

"The soldier who took them said they would be going to a house where ISIS keeps other captured young women. There they would be instructed in Islam and be given as wives to ISIS fighters if they converted, or sold to them as sexual slaves if they didn't."

"How evil!" I said.

"Evil is the exact word," Zulehka replied. "And Mukhtar is the worst of them. He uses what is pure and sacred like family and religion to justify his own egotistical, animal desires. He thinks only of himself. I would rather die than have anything to do with him or his vengeful, merciless beliefs." She paused and added, "In fact, I said as much to the Mufti when he came. I think that is why Mukhtar beat me with such anger."

"Hakob is blessed to have you as his wife," Father Gregory said. "And you are blessed to have him and your own family as well. They seem to have been ready to sacrifice everything to save you."

"You are right," Zulehka said, "I am blessed."

It was past eleven at night when we got to the militia checkpoint outside of Al-Hasakah. Evidently, there was some trouble as Nadim pulled the truck over to the side of the road under a bright streetlight and turned off the motor. Again, I tensed up and held my breath as I heard him get out of the cab and follow the soldier somewhere. It was a good ten minutes before I heard them come back. Nadim came to the side of the truck near where we were and said something in Arabic but not the dreaded curse word that was to signal that all was lost.

Father Gregory responded in Arabic and told me, "It is okay, they are with the YPG, the Kurdish militia. They want to talk to us."

Nadim got up on the back of the truck again and began to shift the cotton bags so that we could get out. I left the AK-47 where it was and crawled out helping Zulehka as well. The highway was lit up and two militiamen in uniforms with Kurdish turbans on their heads motioned us towards the small building with their rifle barrels.

Sitting behind a desk in front of the Kurdish flag on the wall was a uniformed man whom I estimated to be in his late thirties. He motioned for Zulehka to sit down, and the rest of us stood behind her. He looked closely at each of us and began to ask questions to Father Gregory in Arabic.

"This man says that you are Americans and that he just freed both of you and his sister from an ISIS prison in Ar-Raqqah. Is that correct?"

"It's correct," Father Gregory answered.

"Why then do his documents say that he works for ISIS, and why does he have an AK-47 in the cab with him?"

That was when Zulehka spoke up. "He is my brother, and he has two AK-47s—one in the cab and one in the back of the truck. We took them from our captors when we escaped." She then told the man the entire story of how Father Gregory and I had crossed over the border and come to Deir ez-Zor with the help of YPG militiamen and a Kurdish driver to help her and a Syriac family to escape. She explained our capture near Ras al-Ayn and the relationship between the ISIS commander and herself and Nadim. She showed her face and arms where she had been beaten by him.

When she had finished, Father Gregory asked to go back to the truck to get our documents and the cell phone that Loran had given him. "You can call him and talk with him. He will vouch for everything."

The commander called in one of the soldiers who was waiting outside and told him to accompany Father Gregory to the truck and to bring back the other AK-47.

When they got back, the soldier placed the AK-47 by the wall behind the desk where the other confiscated gun was, and Father Gregory put his own bag on the table in front of the commander so he could himself pull out the phone and the documents. The commander looked at the documents and the phone, turning it on. The battery was now dead. He opened a drawer in his desk, and he pulled out an identical phone, asking Father Gregory for Loran's name and number.

Father Gregory gave it to him, and he dialed. This time Loran answered, and the commander spoke with him in Kurdish for some three minutes while we waited. When he had finished, he smiled at us for the first time. "He confirmed everything," he said in Arabic to Father Gregory and even told me that he was a relative of yours. He wants to talk with you." He handed Father Gregory the phone.

They spoke for a few minutes, and then Father Gregory asked Nadim where to send the van to pick us up in Al-Hasakah. Nadim said that he did not know yet and asked if we could call back at nine o'clock in the morning the next day to tell them. Loran agreed.

When Father Gregory got off the phone, he was all smiles. "Bakur will be coming to pick us up at whatever address we decide on. He will then take us directly to the border crossing after dark. Loran will meet us there."

After receiving the phone back, the commander stood up and shook our hands. "I wish you a safe stay in Al-Hasakah and a successful journey back to Turkey." He pointed to the weapons. "But we will keep these here, as you won't have need of them. We will consider them military supplies from the American government, which have often been promised but never seem to arrive!" He seemed pleased with his joke.

The commander then accompanied us back to the truck and helped Zulehka get into the cab. Father Gregory insisted that I get in with them, and he would continue in the back of the truck. I objected because I spoke no Arabic, but Father Gregory countered that Zulehka spoke good English and could translate for me.

Actually, we did not have all that far to go because it turned out that the checkpoint we had just gone through was at the edge of the city. Just beyond it was a roundabout, and we headed north on a four-lane boulevard towards the city center. Zulehka pointed out the university at the edge of town and as we crossed over the bridge spanning a small river she said, "It's called the Khabur River and joins the Euphrates a little below Deir ez-Zor." Other things that I learned from her about the city was that it had a population of about 190,000 people, mostly made of Kurds and Syriacs with smaller percentages of Arabs and even some Armenians. It had grown greatly after government irrigation projects had been completed, and now the region was a major cotton producer. It was for this reason that Zulehka's uncle and aunt moved here in the 1990s to expand the family's Ar-Raqqah business as a buyer and exporter of cotton. Her uncle was a partner with Zulehka's father, and Zulehka and Nadim had visited them at their home in Al-Hasakah several times.

While it was hard to see much in the dark, I was impressed with what I did see of the city's palm tree boulevards, its cleanliness, and its comparative lack of damage from the war. Soon, we were in the commercial center of the city, and Nadim pulled to a stop in front of a nice looking hotel. Zulehka spoke to him in Arabic and they had an animated and at times angry discussion for several minutes. I had no idea what they were talking about until Zulehka told me after Nadim had started to drive again.

"Nadim wanted to leave you at a hotel and to tell your Kurdish contact to pick you up there tomorrow," she said. "In the meantime, he wanted to take me to my uncle's house where my parents are staying. He is determined that I not marry Hakob and that I stay here with them. I am even more determined that I go with you to Turkey to rejoin and marry Hakob. I told him that if you did not come with us to my uncle's house, I would get out with you at the hotel. He finally relented."

"That's a good thing," I said. "Mukhtar took all of our credit cards and money. We would have no money to pay for a hotel."

CHAPTER 29

The Halabi Family

It was eleven-thirty when we finally got to the Halabi house. It was in a prosperous part of the city just off a boulevard with palm trees growing in the median strip and near a park. Nadim pulled up in front of the outside wall of the house, parked, and went to the gate and rang.

While he was waiting, Zulehka explained to me that her uncle was a convinced secularist and a firm supporter of the Syrian government. He had little patience with religion. Having heard from me some of my own ideas, she said, "You will like him!"

Almost immediately, the gate opened and four people came rushing out of the house to embrace Nadim and then Zulehka who had gotten out of the truck with me. The women cried, and they smothered Zulehka with kisses. While that was happening, I climbed up into the back of the truck to help Father Gregory get out. When we both got onto the ground, Nadim told us to follow Zulehka and the others inside. Returning to the cab, Nadim turned on the motor and drove the truck into the compound, parking it behind another truck, also filled with sacks of cotton.

Even though it was very late, all of Zulehka's family were still dressed in street clothes and most of the lights in the house were on. As we entered the main living room of the house, I could see by the numerous used cups and glasses on the tables that they had been waiting for our arrival for some time.

When the two women saw the bruises on Zulehka in the light, they expressed their horror and concern and immediately took her into another room to treat them. While they were gone, Zulehka's father, Salim Halabi, introduced himself and his brother Hasan Halabi to Father Gregory and me and invited us to sit down in two of the chairs of the living room. Hasan, the owner of the house, was obviously a successful businessman, as the room was well decorated and furnished, mostly in a European style. One corner, however, was in the Arab style and had pillows on the floor to sit on around a low table.

Nadim arrived in the room just after we had taken our seats. His father motioned for him also to sit down. "Tell us everything that happened," he said.

Nadim obliged, describing the shooting, the escape, taking the guard to the hospital, being stopped in the village and paying a bribe, and being stopped once more at the Kurd's outpost. He told also of Mukhtar's phone call and threats.

"Mukhtar called me on my cell phone as well," Salim said. "He wanted to know where you were and if I had anything to do with the escape. Of course, I did not answer either of his questions but instead berated him for his treatment of Zulehka. He was furious and said that we were messing with fire and that the punishment for doing what Nadim had done was execution and the confiscation of all of our goods."

"Do you think he knows where we are?" Nadim asked.

"I don't think so. He's my wife's sister's child and has never actually met my brother or has any idea where he lives."

"I tried to get him off our trail by making him think we were heading for the Turkish border at Tel Abiad," Nadim said.

When the women came back into the room with Zulehka, now bathed and wearing the clean clothes that they had given her, they offered us some food. Father Gregory and I gratefully accepted. While we ate, Nadim explained to his parents that Father Gregory and I were to be picked up the next day and taken to Turkey. He said nothing about Zulehka.

After we had finished eating, our host, Hasan Halabi, said that we should all go to bed and that we could talk more in the morning. He suggested that the three women sleep in the master bedroom, the three

Halabi men in the second room, while the third room would be for Father Gregory and me.

"We don't want to run you out of your rooms," Father Gregory said. "We can just sleep out here on the cushions."

"No," he insisted. "You are our guests, and it is no trouble for one night."

We thanked him, and after washing our underwear and socks and hanging them up, we gratefully climbed into the twin beds in the other room that Bahira Halabi, Zulehka's aunt, had prepared for us. I slept well for the first time in several days.

The next morning after breakfast, Father Gregory told Hasan that he needed to get the directions for reaching the house to give to Loran so that Bakur could know where to pick us up.

"Of course," Hasan said.

"We need to talk, though, before he comes," Salim added.

Father Gregory agreed, and after getting instructions from Hasan as to how to find his house, he made his call to Loran. When he was finished, Father Gregory told me, "Bakur should be here sometime in the late morning. The plan is for us to cross the border tonight after it gets dark and then he will take us to the hotel where Ashti and Dilovan are staying."

"How long will it take for Bakur to get here from Ras al-Ayn," I asked.

Father Gregory asked Hasan and then told me, "It's only about eighty kilometers away, so it should take him just a little over an hour." We went to our room to get our bags so that we would be ready.

When we got back to the living room, Salim said, "We need to resolve Zulehka's situation before your ride comes." He suggested that we go with Hasan and Nadim to the garden to talk."

"Shouldn't Zulehka also be here?" Father Gregory asked. "It is her life we are talking about."

Hasan agreed with Father Gregory. "I think the whole family should be involved," he said, "Zulehka, Bahira, and Kamila as well as us."

Salim reluctantly consented. After the women had cleaned up after breakfast, we all gathered in the living room of the house, and Salim took charge of the meeting. "First, I want to say to my son, Nadim, how grateful we are to him for his courage and ingenuity in risking his life to save his sister and the two Americans."

Everyone nodded.

"Second, I want to apologize to our daughter, Zulehka, for even considering her marriage to Mukhtar. Despite his being Kamila's sister's son and helping our family, I had no idea how much he had changed in the last ten years. We are sorry, Zulehka, for making such a terrible mistake."

Zulehka got up from her chair and came over to kiss her father and then her mother. As she did so she said, "I forgive you, and I hope you will forgive me for not telling you earlier that I was engaged to Hakob."

When she sat back down, Salim continued. "Nadim has told me more about Hakob. I do not question that he is a good man just like his parents and his elder brother, Tavit, whom I knew and respected. But we are Muslims and he is Christian, and our religion does not permit Muslim women to marry Christian men, so we cannot support you in this."

"But our religion permits Muslim men to marry Christian women," Zulehka interjected. "Why the difference?"

"Because the man is the head of the house," Salim answered.

"But it is the mother who raises the child," Zulehka retorted. "It makes no sense."

Salim turned to Father Gregory for support. "Christians don't believe in mixed marriages either, do they?"

"Orthodox Christians like me don't," Father Gregory said. "We believe that in a relationship as intimate as marriage, the two partners should have the same belief."

Salim nodded and looked at his daughter as if his point had been made.

Father Gregory then added, "But in this case, Zulehka desires to be baptized and become a Christian."

"To us, that is unacceptable," Salim responded, his voice rising in anger. "We are talking now not only of an affront to her family, but also of her eternal rejection by her people and by Allah. Why would she do that?"

"If Hakob desires so much to marry her, and she to marry him, let him become a Muslim," Nadim suggested. "I could accept that."

"Yes," Salim added, looking at Zulehka. "Your mother and I could accept that as well."

Zulehka was exasperated and shook her head, as if this was something that would never happen. "You think that I want to be baptized as a

Christian just because I want to marry Hakob. That is not true! I want to become a Christian because I love Allah, and I believe that Jesus represents what Allah is really like—just, yet loving and self-sacrificing."

"But Jesus is not Allah, as the Christians claim!" Salim said. "That is blasphemy. He is an honored Prophet but still a man."

"To you, he is just a man. To me, he is more than that. He is Truth and Life. He came to me in a dream with his arms opened wide and told me so."

"A dream?" Hasan said. "You believe that a dream will show you the truth? I had hopes for you that with your scientific medical training that you would be the one person in our family that would come to the realization that all of this religious talk is nonsense—worse than that, is the cause of much of the world's woes."

"To you it may be nonsense, but to me it is not, nor is it to some of the world's greatest minds," Zulehka retorted. "I want to be a Christian because I believe that it is true what the Bible says about Jesus. He claimed to be one with Allah and his miracles and resurrection proved that."

Salim put his hands over his ears as if he did not want to hear any more.

Zulehka, though, continued passionately her defense. "Jesus satisfies both my mind and my heart! His way is the way of peace and not of jihad, threats, and killing. His truth is open to sincere investigation and is not based on authoritarian decrees and rulings. His life and teachings show me that Allah really is Love, as Father Gregory and Hakob have taught me. I wish that you, too, could have the comfort of that knowledge. I pray for you every day now."

"I get no comfort from what you are saying," Salim said, his voice now angry and harsh. "I only feel disbelief, anger, and sorrow that you are rejecting your family and your religion."

"I am not rejecting you," Zulehka said. "I love you and am grateful to you and Nadim for doing all you did to save us from Mukhtar. I believe what I believe, and to pretend differently would make me a liar and hypocrite. Mukhtar and you might think of me as an apostate, but for me, this is the first time in my life I have been able to truly love Allah instead of just fear him."

"Please don't go with them, Zulehka," Kamila begged, crying. "You are my only daughter. I can't bear to think that I won't see you again."

"I have to go, Mother. I love Hakob and we are committed to each other, just like you love Father and are committed to him." She embraced her mother again. "And whether you see me is entirely your choice. I will always want to see you."

At that moment, Salim nodded to Kamila and Nadim to follow him, and they left the room without saying anything more. They headed back to one of the bedrooms, I imagined, to confer. Zulehka was left alone with me, Father Gregory, and her uncle and aunt.

The silence was awkward for a moment and then Hasan broke it. "I don't understand you, Zulehka, or this change in you or what happened just now with your parents and brother. I do want to assure you, though, that no matter what your decision is today—to leave or stay—that I believe it is you, and only you, who has the right to make that decision. You will always be my beloved niece, and I hope you will find happiness whatever your decision."

"I do, too," Bahira said.

Zulehka stood up and went to them and embraced them both. "Thank you. Your support means so much to me."

Father Gregory tried to reassure Hasan and Bahira that this was the right decision for Zulehka. Staying in Syria, she faced a death sentence from ISIS, and she would be a threat to her family. Since the university in Deir ez-Zor was now closed, she could not continue with her medical studies here in Syria. On the other hand, if she left with them for Turkey, she would find safety, a good man who loved her, and possibly, she could continue her medical studies in the United States. As for converting to Christianity, she had made it clear that this was not some hypocritical move so as to be able to marry Hakob, but a true decision for which she was willing to die. It had to be respected.

"Uncle, what Father Gregory says is true," Zulehka said. "I love my parents and my brother, and I love Hakob. I do not want to cause any of them shame, danger, or pain. For the first time in my life, because of Jesus, I now really love Allah instead of just fear him. For the first time in my life, I am not worried about ending in hell for eternity. Allah is too much of a loving Father for that."

Neither Hasan nor Bahira said anything, and their awkward silence was broken only when the doorbell rang. Hasan got up and went outside, returning with Bakur following him. A big smile appeared on Bakur's face when he saw us. He came over to us and embraced us. "We were so afraid for you," he said. "But Allah is good, and soon you will be out of Syria."

Father Gregory introduced Bakur to Hasan and Bahira and told them the story of our discovery that Bakur and I were related. "You might call it a coincidence," Father Gregory said to Hasan, "but as a believer, I see the hand of Allah in it, just as I see his hand in your kindness to your niece."

"I think all of this talk about Allah and paradise and hell is crazy," Hasan said. "When we die, that is it." He then turned to his niece. "Zulehka, this is your moment of decision. What will it be?"

Zulehka was silent for a moment, and tears began to gather in her eyes. "I love my family deeply, but I choose to go meet my husband," she finally said.

Hasan nodded and said, "I will go and tell your parents."

Zulehka fell to her knees on the floor, tears streaming down her face and prayed. I grieved for her. Time passed slowly as she moved her lips silently with her eyes closed. I could hear her mother crying in the back room, but when Hasan returned, he returned alone.

Hasan put his hand on Zulehka's head and said sorrowfully. "They love you, but they just cannot give you their blessing. This is ripping their hearts out." He paused. "But for what it is worth, Bahira and I give you our blessings. You deserve every chance for happiness, and right now, it looks to me like that will only be outside of Syria. We will do all that is in our power to secure the blessings of your family for you, as well. Be patient with them."

As Hasan pulled her up from her knees, Zulehka kissed his hands. "Tell them I love them and will think of them and pray for them every day of my life." She hugged her uncle and then her aunt who had started to cry. "And I will pray for you as well. Thank you."

Father Gregory shook Hasan's hand as did I. "Tell them how grateful we are for rescuing us, and assure them that Zulehka is safe in Hakob's and Allah's hands," he said. He then smiled at Hasan and added, "You are a good man, Hasan, and my bet is that you and Bahira are safe in his hands as well!"

Hasan and Bahira accompanied us to the gate, and right before we got into the car, they both embraced Zulehka again. Hasan reiterated, "Don't worry about your family. They will come around, and it will be all right. They love you very much, just as do we. You have our phone number and e-mail addresses. Keep in touch." He then slipped Zulehka a wad of money. "You are going with only what you are wearing. Bahira and I want you to be able to buy some clothes in Turkey."

Zulehka smiled gratefully, and thanked them again. She got into the back seat with me, and as we pulled away, we waved goodbye. They remained in front of the house watching us until we turned off the street two blocks away.

CHAPTER 30

Mehdi Ahmad

The night before, we had entered Al-Hasakah from the south, and now we exited to the north of the city. The trip to Ras al-Ayn took us about an hour and a half because of stops at two separate road blocks manned by the Syrian government and then by Kurdish forces. No one asked to see our documents, however.

From Al-Hasakah, we took a four-lane asphalt highway mostly following the Khabur River and the ribbon of irrigated fields on each side of it. When we got to the town of Tall Tamr, which Bakur told us had a significant Christian population, he called his wife and told her that we would be there in about forty-five minutes. Putting down his cell phone he explained, "I want my family to meet you. We will eat together, then you can rest, and after it gets dark, we will leave for the border crossing."

When we got to the garage where we had stayed five nights before, Bakur parked the van, and this time, he took us to the front entrance of his house. There waiting for us was his wife and his son dressed in the uniform of the Kurdish militia. To my delight, I could see in the son the clear resemblance of Noah, my grandfather.

"My name is Mehdi," he said, as he shook my hand. "My father says that we are cousins. Welcome to our home." He nodded to both Zulehka and Father Gregory and welcomed them as well. "You are our honored guests."

"It's wonderful that you speak English so well," I said. "Where did you learn it?"

"I really taught myself on the internet." Mehdi laughed. "My father thinks I am what you call a 'computer geek!'" He explained what he had just said to his parents, and they, too, laughed.

We all sat down, and I looked around the room. On the wall were family pictures, and in a corner a prayer rug faced towards Mecca. The furniture was comfortable but simple.

After Bakur's wife brought us some drinks, Father Gregory and Zulehka spoke with them in Arabic, answering their questions about what we had just been through and our escape. While they talked about the war, ISIS, and the future, I observed Mehdi. Like Bakur said, he looked about my age, had a similar height and build, and although he was much darker in skin color than I was, we could easily be brothers. He was my alter ego, the man I might have been if Karine had stayed in Mardin, become a Muslim, and married Altay.

I got to thinking, *If that had happened, would I automatically be and think as a Sunni Muslim? If so, what would my attitude be to the Armenian and Syriac Christians who were my neighbors? Would I be a liberal or secular Muslim and respect their beliefs as Mehdi and Loran, or a fundamentalist Muslim like Mukhtar and find justifications in the Koran and Hadiths for treating them as second-class citizens or even for enslaving, raping, and killing them? After all, Christians are clearly infidels, for as much as they try to explain that they believe in only One God, their doctrine of the Trinity and their worship of Jesus certainly would sound like polytheism to my Muslim mind. Although they insist they do not worship idols, their kissing and bowing down to their crosses and painted images of God, of Jesus, and of their saints certainly would look like idolatry to me. Their immodest dress, their vulgar language, their smoking, drinking of alcohol, and eating pork, would certainly seem to deviate from what the Koran and our Prophet taught. How could I be a respecter of the Universal Declaration of Human Rights if my religion teaches me that men and women, believers and non-believers, have different rights? How would I decide between what my conscience tells me is right and what my religion tells me? Finally, if I felt that the only sure way to paradise was to become an enforcer and martyr for my faith, would I not be tempted to take this route like so many in ISIS had done?*

"Dinner is ready," Mehdi said. That brought me back from my musings and to the table, which was full of with generous helpings of different Syrian and Kurdish foods. After eating, we were served Turkish coffee in the living room, and for the rest of the afternoon we rested and talked. While his wife cleaned up in the kitchen, Bakur, through Mehdi, said that he and his family wanted to present me with a gift. He went into a back room and returned with a package, which he handed to me.

I eagerly opened it and found that it contained two presents. The first was a framed picture of a white bearded old man holding in his lap a young boy whom I estimated to be about two or three years old. The second gift was some type of metal insignia with something written in Arabic script that I could not read.

"The picture is of Father as a little boy with Altay, his grandfather and your great-grandfather," Mehdi explained. The insignia is what he wore on his uniform when he served with the gendarmes as a young man."

I was overwhelmed. This was the first picture that I had ever seen of the man who raped my great-grandmother and then helped save her. He was my own flesh and blood. This was the insignia he wore, which Karine saw each time he raped her, each time he gave her bread, and on the last night that he left her off at the missionary's house in Mardin. "I don't know what to say. They are too valuable for you to give to me," I protested.

"No, we want you to have them," Mehdi said, "We have made you a copy of the original picture, and we have no use for the insignia. For us, it is now a symbol of shame. Please, it is yours, and your taking it is evidence to us that you have forgiven both him and us. Please."

As I said, I was greatly moved. I stood up and embraced both Mehdi and Bakur. "Of course, I forgive Altay, and as for the both of you, I have absolutely nothing to forgive, only to praise and thank."

Bakur embraced me and then turned to Zulehka and addressed her, with Mehdi translating for my benefit. "I also wanted to give you a gift, Zulehka. After learning your story this afternoon and of your bravery and financial circumstances, I want to return to you the money that Loran paid me for transporting you. It is not so much, but it will help you and your new husband start off in life."

All of us were stunned at this gesture, but most of all Zulehka. "Your kindness is very great, but you deserve it for your risks and your own financial losses that night. Anyway, the money is not mine. It was paid by Father Gregory from donated funds."

"The donors, I'm sure, would want you to have it," Father Gregory told Zulehka.

"And don't worry about me," Bakur said. "I was well paid for my efforts by the Khoury family." He smiled. "By the way, they outsmarted ISIS. Avraham later told me that before they herded us into the church to be searched and interrogated, he hid most of their valuables under the van's mats. Nor did the soldiers find the diamonds hidden in their youngest daughter's diapers. No one dared to look there!"

We all laughed.

My cousins were delightful and generous, and for the rest of the afternoon, Father Gregory, Zulehka, and I had the privilege of learning about their lives and their hopes. Principally, they wished for a Kurdish state of their own or at least their own autonomous region. Now that Armenians and Jews had their own countries, they and the Palestinians were the only major groups without their own nations. While describing his hopes, Mehdi also talked about his desire to visit other countries, especially the United States and Silicon Valley, where so much of what he was interested in was happening.

"If you ever get to America," I said, "please come visit me. Unfortunately, I have no contacts or importance to be able to help you much, but whatever I can do, I would love to try."

Finally, when it became dark outside, Bakur told us it was time for us to leave. We would be meeting Loran in an hour at the border crossing, and we did not want to be late. Before we left, I took pictures of Bakur and Mehdi individually and then with his wife as a family. Father Gregory also took pictures of me with them. I promised to send them copies by e-mail, and we exchanged both phone numbers and e-mail addresses. Before getting back into the van, we hugged each of them and I thanked them again for their gracious gifts and hospitality.

After getting out of the city and onto the highway heading east, Bakur pulled over to the side and stopped. He then reached into a bag and got three black hoods. "I'm sorry," he said, "but my orders are for you to put them on again."

We laughed. "It's a small price to pay for our freedom," Father Gregory said.

In another half-hour or so, we stopped again. I knew that we were now at the border crossing when I heard a familiar voice. It was that of Loran.

CHAPTER 31

Reunion

W hen I realized that it was here where Bakur would leave us, I softly
called out his name, and he came over to me. I asked Father Gregory
to translate. "Bakur," I said, "I don't know whether this encounter with you
is of Allah or by chance, but it has made me see my great-grandfather Altay
and my Turkish heritage in an entirely different light. Thank you for your
gifts and for your hospitality. Surely, we will meet again."

I could not see him but I felt his arms around me hugging me. "Yes, we
will meet again," he said. "May Allah protect you."

After Father Gregory and Zulehka also thanked Bakur and said
goodbye, Loran told us what we were to expect as we crossed the border.
As always, Father Gregory translated so that I could understand.

"It will take us about fifteen minutes to get across. You must follow
me exactly, holding onto the rope as before. Twice, you will have to crawl
beneath razor fences so be careful. There will be no talking. I will be in the
front, then Father Gregory, the girl, and then Peter."

This second time crossing the border, I was much less fearful as I now
knew what to expect, and everything went without a hitch. At the end,
Loran told us simply that we had made it, and he led us to a car instead of
a pick-up truck. He opened a door and told Zulehka and me to get in the
back, and he led Father Gregory around the car to get in the front with him.

We rode with our hoods on as Loran asked us questions about our experiences with Mukhtar and ISIS. When he learned the details of our escape, he praised Nadim for his courage and ingenuity.

We then asked him what had been happening on this side of the border. He told us that at the bank, everything went just as planned, and he had returned the cross to Ashti. Monday night, when he met Bakur and the Khoury family at the border crossing and learned what had happened to us, he immediately informed Ashti. She then called the different numbers that we had left her to inform Father Gregory's superiors and our families. She also called Dilovan and Fulya. Dilovan flew into the Mardin airport the next day and Ashti drove there to pick him up. After she learned of the ransom demands, she called everyone for a second time and informed them of the threat to our lives and the conditions for our release. Finally, when the good news came of our escape, she also passed that news on to all of our contacts.

After about twenty minutes of driving, Loran said, "You can take off your hoods now. I'm sorry that you had to wear them, but they are necessary to protect our crossing points."

"As I told Bakur, it is a small price to pay for your help," Father Gregory said.

Loran handed his cell phone to Father Gregory. "Why don't you use it to call Ashti and the Khoury family and tell them that you made it across the border safely and that we will be at the hotel in about forty minutes. Their numbers are in the contacts."

Father Gregory did so, first calling Ashti and Dilovan. I could hear their excitement on the other end. He then called Natan who ran upstairs to tell Hakob the news and to give the phone to him to talk to Zulehka. Zulehka's face glowed with joy even in the car's darkness as they spoke together.

It was ten at night when we arrived at the hotel. Ashti and Dilovan were outside waiting for us at the entrance, and when they saw us, they both rushed over to the car to embrace us as soon as we got out.

Ashti had tears in her eyes but a big smile on her face as she hugged me. "I just got off Skype with your parents and told them you were now safe in Turkey. They sent you all their love."

Dilovan added, "And so does Fulya!"

I thanked them and introduced Zulehka. "You will never meet a braver person, and she even speaks English!" I said.

Ashti hugged her and said smiling, "Your Hakob has called me constantly to find out about you. Have you talked to him yet?"

"Yes, about a half-hour ago on Loran's phone," she answered gleefully. "He says that we will see each other tomorrow morning."

"We were not sure what time you would get here tonight, so we thought it best that you first get some sleep," Ashti said. "If you don't mind staying with me, my room has two single beds. Otherwise, we can get you your own room."

"After sleeping for four days on a cold hard floor, any bed will be like being in paradise," Zulehka said. "Thank you for your offer."

"I also reserved a room with two beds for you and Father Gregory," Dilovan said to me. "My suggestion is that we all get some sleep, and after breakfast we can drive up to meet Hakob and the Khourys." He turned to Zulehka. "They are very anxious to see you."

We all agreed with Dilovan's suggestion, and after thanking Loran once again and saying goodbye to him, we checked in at the hotel desk, got our keys, and then went upstairs to our rooms. When we got to Ashti's room, she said, "Wait a minute. I'll get your cell phone and computers so you can get in touch with your families."

"Would it be possible for me to use one of them to send a quick e-mail to my parents in Syria telling them I'm safe?" Zulehka asked.

"Of course," Father Gregory answered. "Keep my computer tonight, and you can give it back to me at breakfast."

Zulehka thanked him.

"And one more very important item of yours that I need to return," Ashti said, going back into her room, "the Terzian Cross."

Father Gregory gratefully took it from her and kissed it. Turning to Zulehka, he said. "This was the security that allowed us to cross the border and rescue you."

"Please, let me kiss it as well," she replied, and she did so.

With that, we said goodnight and went to our rooms. While Father Gregory took a shower, I called my parents by Skype and talked to them for some fifteen minutes. They were so excited and told me that not only they, but also their entire church had been praying for us. It moved me. When Father Gregory got out of the shower, he used my computer to talk with his parents in Boston as well.

We had a wonderful night of rest, and for the first time in a week, I felt secure. When we got up the next morning and went downstairs for breakfast, Dilovan and Ashti peppered us with questions. When they learned that our driver, Bakur, was the grandson of Altay, they were both stunned. I showed them the picture and insignia he had given to me, as well as the photos on my own camera that I had taken of him and his family at their house.

For our part, both Father Gregory and I were amazed at all Ashti had accomplished in getting the money, advising everyone of our captivity and the ransom demands, and then letting them know that we had escaped. We were also appreciative of Dilovan who paid our hotel bills when we checked out of the hotel.

"I'll pay you back," I promised.

"There's no need. It's a lot less than two million for ransom," he joked. While Mukhtar and his militiamen had taken all of our money and credit cards out of our wallets, thankfully, they had left my license and our passports in our bags. Ashti also insisted on giving back to Father Gregory the extra $500 that he had left her for expenses.

At nine o'clock, all five of us packed into the rental car with our bags. I drove, and Father Gregory sat by me in the front, while Dilovan, Ashti, and Zulehka squeezed into the back. Father Gregory had to put one bag between his legs on the floor, but the rest fit nicely into the trunk. It was tight but the trip to the Khoury home was short—only about an hour.

Our plan was to leave Zulehka off at the Khoury's house, and in the afternoon, continue our journey to Diyarbakir where I would stay in a hotel, and Dilovan and Ashti would stay with his sister and her husband. Father Gregory had accepted the invitation of the caretaker of Sourp Giragos to spend the night at his house. On Easter Sunday, as the only Armenian priest in the area, Father Gregory would celebrate the Liturgy, which all of us wanted to attend. After it was over, Ashti, Dilovan, and I would return to Elazığ and catch an early evening plane back to Istanbul where Fulya would pick us all up at the airport.

From Nusaybin, the highway to the Khoury village followed the path of a swift flowing stream hurtling down over boulders from the mountains to the Mesopotamian Plain. Dozens of small roadside restaurants gave guests the opportunity to sit in comfort on cushioned pillows and enjoy the green vegetation and the life-giving waters in the midst of an otherwise bleak mountain landscape of boulders, dry valleys, and desolate cliffs. Some of these cliffs had caves in them, which Father Gregory pointed out as past dwellings for the ascetics who came here to live alone in the desert with God.

"In the early fourth century," he said, "about the same time the Christian monastic movement started in Egypt, this region of Mesopotamia had its own spiritual heroes. Here they were called 'sons and daughters of the covenant,' and they took vows of chastity and dedicated their entire lives to serving God. While they often withdrew for long periods to caves like these to fight their own personal spiritual battles, they also returned to their communities to help their fellow Christians. Saint Ephrem was one of the most notable of these."

"He's the one you told us about in Nusaybin," Ashti remembered.

"He was. He was born and baptized in Nisiblis, or Nusaybin as it is called today, and withdrew to a life as a solitary in these mountains. At the request of his bishop, Jacob, whose grave we saw in the church, he returned to community life to help others. He was a great teacher, hymn writer, and servant of the poor and sick. When the Roman Emperor handed Nisiblis over to the Persians in 363 A.D. as part of a political compromise, Ephrem and all of his fellow Christians were forced to leave the city. He journeyed north, probably along this same route, to Amida or Diyarbakir. Later he settled in Edessa or Urfa, where he taught and served the poor and sick until dying from the plague."

"You remind me of him," Zulehka said to Father Gregory.

Father Gregory laughed. "In what way could I possibly remind you of Saint Ephrem?"

"You have chosen to help people like me, when I know that you would prefer to be a monk alone in prayer," she said. "You are a modern day 'son of the covenant!'"

We got to the Khoury's tiny village at a quarter past ten. As soon as he saw us approaching, Hakob shouted with joy, ran down the stairs, and was at the gate before I could even turn off the motor. He opened the back door of the car and pulled Zulehka out into his arms. He just held her tightly, half-laughing and half-crying, kissing her on her cheeks and looking at her to make sure that she was real. He then hugged her some more. He seemed oblivious to all of us around him.

The rest of the Khoury household followed him to the gate, also embracing Zulehka and then hugging Father Gregory and even me. The Khoury's neighbors must have heard the joyful sounds in the yard as they came out of their houses and down the street to meet Zulehka and to celebrate our safe arrival in Turkey as well. They told us that they had all been praying for us.

Christina Khoury then invited everyone into the house for food. She and the Sarkissians had put up welcoming posters, paper ribbons, and balloons, and we all felt loved. Although I knew their delight was really for Zulehka and Father Gregory, I very much appreciated that my name was included on all the posters as well.

After the neighbors left, the rest of us sat in the living room. The Khourys and Sarkissians wanted to hear a detailed report from Zulehka and Father Gregory about what had happened during our capture and escape. Both Zulehka and Father Gregory spoke in a mixture of Arabic and English so that all of us could understand. Father Gregory was lavish in his praise of Nadim and of Zulehka's relatives, but mostly of Zulehka herself. "I personally never witnessed anyone braver than Zulehka in her loyalty to our Lord and to you, Hakob. In spite of being beaten and threatened with death," he said, "she remained faithful."

Zulehka shook her head in modesty, "So much praise, Father Gregory. I was just following your example!" She then looked at him with an impish smile on her face. "If I am such a good Christian, then why don't you baptize me right now?"

"And then marry us as well," Hakob added. "It has to be you, and it has to be soon."

"Tomorrow I need to be in Diyarbakir to celebrate the Liturgy at Sourp Giragos," Father Gregory said. "Maybe we could do it next week when I get back to Tur Abdin?"

"Why couldn't you baptize Zulehka and marry them at Sourp Giragos after your Liturgy?" Natan asked. "We could drive them up tomorrow morning. It's only three hours away."

"Yes," Hakob said. "What better day than Easter and better place than Sourp Giragos for an Armenian to be baptized and married?"

Zulehka agreed, as did Hakob's parents.

"Of course it would be an honor for me to do it," Father Gregory said. "But there are serious complications."

"Like what?" Hakob asked.

"First, while I could perform the wedding ceremony after the Liturgy, I would want to baptize Zulehka before it so that she could participate in the Eucharist. That means you would have to be at the church tomorrow by a quarter to nine."

"That's no problem," Natan replied. "We can leave here as early as we need to."

Hakob and Zulehka nodded in agreement.

"The second complication," Father Gregory continued, "is that not only people like Mukhtar oppose the conversion of Muslims to Christianity, even moderate Muslims and the supposedly secular Turkish government do as well. If it became known that Zulehka converted to Christianity and that you as a Christian married her, there could be trouble for you, your families, and the church here in Turkey. It must be done in secret."

"I agree to that," Hakob said.

"I do, too," Zulehka said. "The only approval we really need is from Allah, and we both feel that we have that."

Father Gregory thought a moment and then said, "Okay. God willing, I will do it. Be at the church at a quarter to nine tomorrow morning, and I will have everything ready to start the baptism at nine. After the Liturgy we will perform the marriage ceremony."

With that agreement, the Sarkissians, the Khourys, and Zulehka made plans for the next day with Father Gregory. They decided that they would go in two cars to Diyarbakir, with Natan driving one and Avraham the other, getting to the church in time for the baptism at nine o'clock. They would participate in the Easter Liturgy at ten o'clock and then the marriage at one in the afternoon. After a celebratory meal afterwards, the newly married couple would return to the Khoury home the same day, while Dilovan, Ashti, and I would continue our trip back to Elazığ to catch our early evening plane to Istanbul.

CHAPTER 32

Easter Sunday

At half-past two on Saturday afternoon, Father Gregory, Dilovan, Ashti, and I left for Diyarbakir. I suggested taking the route north through Hasankeyf instead of returning by way of Mardin. This alternative route would only add a few kilometers and about fifteen minutes to our trip, and I was curious to see firsthand some of the archeological wonders of Hasankeyf before they disappeared forever under the waters of a lake to be created by yet another new dam being built by the Turkish government.

It took us a little over an hour from the Khoury's home south of Midyat to get to the town built on both sides of the Tigris River. From the earliest days of antiquity, conquering powers had built and rebuilt important forts on top of its high cliffs and dug thousands of caves into the sides of its hills as dwellings, businesses, and churches. In the next few years, Father Gregory told us that the government had plans to transfer some 3,000 people from the town and 50,000 people from the region into a new city that it was building. He pointed out the ugly buildings in the far distance on a high plain where they would go. Despite the loud protests from locals as well as from important national and international organizations to the plan, the destruction of the town now seemed imminent. Hasankeyf's current dwellings, as well as its twelfth century bridge and other historical buildings, will soon be under water.

After we crossed over the Tigris on a modern bridge, which would also soon disappear, I pulled into a dirt parking lot on the other side of the river to take in the beauty of this historic place before it was gone and to take some pictures of the site. We all got out of the car, and Father Gregory pointed to the ancient minaret on the other side of the river reaching high into the sky and said that the lake's waters would even submerge it to the top. *How sad*, I thought. *How does one balance the good of economic progress in the future with the good of the preservation of the past and of the present?* I decided that I would write an article on Hasankeyf as well.

From Hasankeyf, we continued to Batman, a modern city of 300,000 people. Dilovan told us that it was named after a nearby river and not for the comic book character! A wealthy city because of the discovery of oil in the region, Batman was the home of a Turkish airforce base used by the Americans during the Gulf War. "That sort of cooperation of our country with yours and the fact that we are a strategically located Muslim nation with a secular democracy and strong economy, makes your government very reluctant to offend us," he added.

"You mean by calling what happened in 1915 'genocide' and not just a 'massacre?'" I asked.

"Exactly," he said.

Since we had only about an hour and a half before we arrived in Diyarbakir and I would then have limited opportunity to talk with Father Gregory, I decided to use this last opportunity to find out what would happen with him and with Zulehka and Hakob in the coming months.

"After the church celebrations tomorrow," Father Gregory replied, "I will return to Mardin on a bus and then start the process of getting Zulehka and the Khourys registered with the government. I will also try to get the Sarkissians into Armenia temporarily and then into the United States so that Zulehka and Hakob can continue their medical training. I'm hoping my father can help us with that."

"But what about you?" I asked. "What would you like to do next?"

"Me? I don't really know," he said. "I guess whatever my superiors wish for me."

"Don't you have your own desires?" Ashti asked.

"Of course," Father Gregory answered. "Once these terrible wars end, my greatest personal desire is to help Syriacs and Armenians return to their ancestral homelands as valued citizens with equal human rights to rebuild their homes, churches, and lives. I want Muslims, Christians, and Jews to live together in peace, as we are not so different. We are all sons and daughters of our mutual ancestor Abraham, and 'Allah' and 'Elah' are names that Arab and Syriac Christians used for the One God well before the birth of Mohammed. I hope we will truly treat each other as brothers and sisters, and that one day, all humanity will serve Allah—not only as our Creator and Judge, but also as our Divine Father who loves us and redeems us—full of mercy and grace. For me, Jesus proved that!"

No one spoke, as we pondered what Father Gregory said. It was beautiful, but was it true? Finally I broke the silence and asked Ashti, "What about you, Ashti? What would you like to do?"

"I desire what Father Gregory desires," Ashti said. "I would also like to work for reconciliation and equal rights between all Turks—not just different religious groups but also ethnic groups. If I had enough capital, I would start a tourist agency to bring back to Turkey as visitors all those who have left in the past because of persecution—Armenians, Syriacs, Greeks, and Kurds."

"And you Dilovan?" I asked.

"Ha! I'm not so idealistic as Father Gregory and my daughter," he said. "I would just like to retire and to travel and learn more about the Armenian part of our heritage, maybe visiting Armenia and Boston. Most of all, I would like to see my daughter married to a wonderful man and then to have grandchildren whom I could spoil."

"What if I want to remain single?" Ashti asked. "Or what if I choose someone of a different nationality or religion to marry?"

"What is essential to your mother and me is that you be happy and fulfilled, and if you do marry, that it be to someone who at least is a truth seeker, a good provider, and a compassionate person who loves you."

I silently wondered how many of those categories I fit into. Right now, I certainly would not be a good provider, and I felt too self-centered to be considered compassionate and a truth seeker.

Father Gregory chuckled and said to Ashti, "If you do decide to get married one day, whomever you decide on will get quite a prize!"

"Thank you," Ashti replied. "But the more I know of Zulehka, she is really the prize."

Father Gregory nodded. "You both are," he said, reflecting my own personal thoughts.

When we got to Diyarbakir, I let Ashti, Dilovan, and Father Gregory out of the car in the old city in front of the restaurant where Ashti and I had eaten a week earlier. It was close to Dilovan's sister's house and to Sourp Giragos where Father Gregory was going to stay. I told Father Gregory that I would be at the church at nine the next morning as I wanted to observe Zulehka's baptismal ceremony. Dilovan and Ashti were unsure if they would go to that, but they were certain that they would get to the church for the Easter Liturgy at ten.

I then drove to my hotel, parked my car, registered, and went to my room. After I wrote up my impressions of the day and had a bite to eat, I went to sleep.

The next morning, I had a quick breakfast, checked out of the hotel, and walked over to the Sourp Giragos Church, getting there about ten minutes before the baptismal service was to start. The Sarkissians and the two Khoury families had already arrived from Tur Abdin with Zulehka. The church caretaker showed us to a small school chapel away from the main church where Father Gregory was waiting for us. He was dressed in his full Easter regalia as a priest of the Armenian Church. I had never seen him before in clerical garb and his transformation was profound. He looked like a king in his elaborately embroidered robes.

After welcoming us, Father Gregory explained the solemnity of the moment in Arabic and in English. First, he was going to ask Zulehka some questions regarding her faith. Depending on her answers, he would then baptize her as a symbol of her new life as a Christian and he would anoint her with chrism to symbolize the coming of the Holy Spirit into her life.

Zulehka nodded in acquiescence.

After Zulehka had satisfactorily answered his questions taken from a book of ritual, Father Gregory led her to the small altar in the room where there was a basin of pure water. First he took the cross and ring from her neck and dipped them in the water and then returned them to her neck. Next, he took her hands and placed them in the water, and finally, he cupped some of the water into his own right hand and anointed her head with it three times in the name of the Father, Son, and Holy Ghost. After giving her a clean white towel to dry off with, Father Gregory took some oil from a vial and made the sign of the cross with it on her forehead, ears, mouth, hands, and feet. He then prayed. After the ceremony, Hakob, the Khourys, and Sarkissians hugged her and congratulated her. Zulehka beamed with joy.

While Father Gregory went to another part of the church to prepare for the Easter Liturgy, Zulehka, the Sarkassians, the Khourys, and I went outside to the courtyard where other persons from around the city and Turkey were now arriving. They greeted us with smiles and greetings of "He is risen" in Turkish, Armenian, and English, and the Sarkissians returned their greetings. Near a table covered with colorful Easter eggs, I spotted Dilovan and Ashti talking with Rihana. They had just arrived.

We went over and greeted them and then all of us entered the church together. As Ashti, Rihana, Dilovan, and I sat down on the back row of the church, the Khourys and Sarkissians went to a table and lit some candles in thanksgiving and petition, placing them in the sand along with dozens of others. They then returned to the row in front of us. The sanctuary was now almost full, and the smell of incense permeated the air.

As we waited for the Liturgy to begin, Rihana explained to us that most of the people in the audience were Muslims—Islamized Armenians, Town Officials, or others who had come to the service in solidarity with the few Armenian Christians left in Diyarbakir. A few of those Christians were former Muslim Armenians who had reconverted to Christianity. As their names were never published for fear of reprisals, Rihana was not sure just who they all were.

With the ringing of a bell the service began, and Father Gregory and the four men accompanying him entered from a side door and approached the main chapel in the church. A small choir of mostly women with lace head coverings sang. Now that Lent was over, the chapel's red curtain was open revealing the elaborate wooden and golden altar behind it with a painting of the Madonna and Baby Jesus in her arms in the center. After bowing at the altar, Father Gregory, accompanied by the deacons, walked around the entire congregation, blessing us all with his cross and with his incense—Christians, Muslims, and unbelievers alike. He was dressed in the same magnificent robes I had seen him in at Zulehka's baptism, and the four deacons accompanying him were also dressed in striking garments with large red crosses embroidered on them. The two men leading the procession proudly held metal crosses in front of them high above their heads, and the two following bore giant candles. Father Gregory was behind them with a censer in his left hand, softly swinging it and making music with its bells and sending puffs of sweet smoke like prayers to the Almighty. In his right hand, Father Gregory held the Terzian Cross, blessing us with it.

As he walked by us, Father Gregory smiled and tipped the cross to Zulehka, Hakob, and the rest of us and said, "Krisdos haryal I merelots" Christ is risen from the dead. Hakob bowed his head and touched Father Gregory's robe and replied, "Orhnyal e harutyun' Krisdosi" Blessed is the resurrection of Christ.

From beginning to end, the service lasted about an hour and a half and consisted of scripture readings, the chanting back and forth of liturgical prayers between the priest, deacons, and the choir, much genuflection and bowings and swinging of the censer, and a short homily on new birth and reconciliation by Father Gregory translated into Turkish by a deacon.

His text was II Corinthians 5:17-19:

> Therefore, if anyone is in Christ, the new creation has come: The old has gone, the new is here! [18] All this is from God, who reconciled us to himself through Christ and gave us the ministry of reconciliation: [19] that God was reconciling the world to himself in Christ, not counting people's sins against them. And he has committed to us the message of reconciliation.

Father Gregory even quoted a portion of the Easter homily of Saint John Chrysostom in English, perhaps for the benefit of foreigners like me in the audience.

> Come you all: enter into the joy of your Lord. You the first and you the last, receive alike your reward; you rich and you poor, dance together; you sober and you weaklings,

celebrate the day; you who have kept the fast and you who have not, rejoice today. The table is richly loaded: enjoy its royal banquet. The calf is a fatted one: let no one go away hungry.

At the Eucharist, few went forward to receive the wafer dipped in wine, as only a minority of those in the church had been baptized in the Armenian Orthodox Church or in other churches with which it was in communion. The Sarkissians and the Khourys went forward with Zulehka. Even from where I was in the back, I could note the special words and joy with which Father Gregory put the consecrated wafer into her mouth for the first time. Her face glowed with thankfulness, peace, and happiness as she came back to her seat.

At the end of the service, Father Gregory went outside into the courtyard and blessed and greeted everyone individually. He encouraged the Christians, and he thanked the Muslim officials and supporters for their graciousness in coming to the service. After about a half-hour in the courtyard, he invited Zulehka and Hakob, the Khourys, and Sarkissians to go with him into the same private small chapel we had used for Zulehka's baptismal services in order to celebrate Hakob's and Zulehka's wedding.

Ashti and I asked if we could also attend the ceremony along with Dilovan and Rihana in support.

"Of course, but it is important that you don't say anything about it, as it could get Hakob and Zulehka and our church into a difficult situation with the authorities."

Don't worry, Ashti said, "We will say nothing."

Before the actual wedding ceremony started, the Sarkissians said that they had brought some traditional items to make sure this was truly an Armenian marriage. Dikran Sarkassian smiled broadly and pulled out of a plastic bag two portions of lavash bread and put them on the shoulders of Hakob and Zulehka. Father Gregory translated his words in Arabic to English so we could understand. "This is so your marriage may be plentiful."

Dikran then took some honey from the sack and touched the lips of Hakob and Zulehka. "This is so your marriage will be sweet."

Finally, he put two clean dishes on the floor in front of them and asked them to step on them and break them. "This is so there will be no evil in your lives," he said. He and his wife Arpi then embraced them and kissed them on their cheeks.

After that, Father Gregory called Zulehka and Hakob before him to the altar and conducted the rest of the wedding ceremony according to the liturgical format. He blessed their rings and directed them to exchange their vows to each other and to God. He then read from scriptures and had them recite their beliefs together using the Nicene Creed. After that was done, he crowned them with two crowns to illustrate that they were rulers of their family and had them face each other forehead to forehead, a symbol of their oneness in Christ. As their foreheads touched, Dikran held the Terzian Cross over their heads. Each then sat separately in two wooden chairs by the altar—their thrones—while Father Gregory prayed. Finally, he offered them wine from a single cup, and they said the Lord's Prayer together. Zulehka and Hakob were now married. They rejoiced in laughter, and we rejoiced with them.

At the end of the ceremony, Father Gregory brought us all back to the reality of their situation by counseling us once again to say nothing publically about what had just happened and by advising Zulehka and Hakob to register their marriage only when they got to another country like Armenia or the United States. "What is legal here in Turkey," Father Gregory said, "is not necessarily advisable."

After the ceremony was over and we had expressed our congratulations and said our goodbyes, Ashti, Dilovan, and I left to return to Elazığ to catch our plane. For their part, Zulehka, Hakob, the Khourys, the Sarkissians, and Rihana left to celebrate the marriage in a local restaurant. Father Gregory was to join them later after he had disrobed and changed into normal clothes.

During our two and a half-hour trip back to the airport in Elazığ, Ashti and I described to Dilovan what we had learned following the deportation route, and Ashti read anew some of the passages from Karine's and the American Consul's memoirs to him at our brief stops in Maden and Lake Hazar. Dilovan was much astounded and grieved as he had never before known of the Consul's eyewitness report. At the lake, we decided to get off the main highway and follow the road over the mountain that the Terzian family had probably taken.

Arriving at the Elazığ airport an hour before our flight, I turned in the car without any problems. We then boarded the plane, grateful that we could all sit together and elated to have completed our journey so successfully.

Fulya was waiting for us when we got to the Sabiha Gökçen Airport in Istanbul and she embraced us all—especially me, whom she described as her adopted son. We all went to bed as soon as we got to the apartment, as Monday was to be a busy day for all of us and we were all tired.

At around eight in the morning, Dilovan and Fulya said their goodbyes to me and left early for work in Dilovan's car. Before going, however, Dilovan insisted on giving me $200 for any emergencies that I might have on the way home, given my lack of credit cards and cash. I thanked him and promised to pay him back as soon as I got back to the United States. For my part, I gave them an extra memory stick where I had copied for them the photos I had taken on the trip.

Despite my protests that I could take a taxi and bus, Ashti decided to call her boss at the hotel and tell him that she would only be able to go to work in the afternoon as she wanted to take me to the airport to catch my Turkish Airlines direct flight to Boston.

While I was grateful for the ride, I was even more thankful for the time to be alone with her—my first opportunity in the past eight days. "I will never be able to thank you enough, Ashti," I said as she drove me to the airport. "I can't imagine how I would have done the trip without you."

"And I thank you for suggesting and organizing it," she replied. "It has helped me to grasp who I am. And who knows? It may also be the start of a new career for me."

"You mean your idea of setting up a tourist agency for Armenians and others to come back and discover their Turkish roots?" I asked.

"Exactly, I think it would not only be profitable, but would be a helpful way to bridge past animosities and create understanding on both sides."

"If I can help, let me know," I said.

"Thanks," she said. Then with a grin, she added, "I also want to thank you for being such a gentleman throughout the trip—except for that one slip-up."

I laughed. "It was your fault. You are just too attractive!"

"That's not the way I want to be attractive."

I nodded. "Actually, you're attractive to me in a much deeper way than you might think. This will no doubt embarrass you and make you feel uncomfortable again as you say I often do, but I have to say it now or never. I think I have fallen in love with you, and I hope that somehow this trip together will be the start of an even deeper relationship between us.

Ashti said nothing but reached over and softly touched my hand. We then drove for another five minutes, both of us probably pondering that exchange. When we got to the airport, Ashti pulled up to the curb and put the car in park leaving the motor on, still seemingly deep in thought.

"Well, I guess this is it!" I said, breaking the silence, but not wanting to say goodbye yet.

"Be sure to e-mail me and keep us informed of your progress on your novel and articles," Ashti said. "And remember," she added, with another of her teasing smiles, "If for any reason I appear in your story, make sure that my mother and father will not be ashamed of your portrayal of me."

I laughed. "You will never have to worry about that!"

"Thank you, Peter," she said. Her eyes then twinkled as she looked at me. "There's one last thing before you go. I want to give you a farewell gift that comes from my heart." She then reached for my hands and leaned towards me kissing me gently on my lips.

"Wow!" I said, surprised and pleased.

"Peter, I heard what you said earlier about falling in love with me. I have not commented because I don't know what to say. You are dear to me, and I do know that for me also our relationship has deepened because of this trip. But as to where it is going, only Allah knows. Things are complicated. You and I will have to wait and see."

"I take that as an encouragement," I said.

"That is the way it was meant," she said.

CHAPTER 33

Asheville, North Carolina

I am writing this now on March 8, 2015, just three weeks shy of one year since the start of my trip to Boston and Turkey. It is also only a week before my thirtieth birthday and my self-imposed deadline for either getting a full-time job as an international correspondent or finishing the writing of my first novel. While I have not attained my first goal, I may just squeak through on the realization of the second goal—at least the first draft of a novel. It has been a very busy year.

On my return to the United States, I arrived at Logan Airport at five in the afternoon. After I had gone through customs, I called the Petrosians at their home in Watertown. I did not have time to visit them, but I did have thirty minutes to talk with them on the phone while waiting for the departure of my seven o'clock flight for Charlotte and Asheville.

"Praise God, you're back safely, and that everything turned out so well," Aunt Susan exclaimed when she answered the phone. "After Ashti called us to tell us of the ransom demand, we were on our knees and on the phone almost without stop, trying to determine what we should do. It was terrifying!"

Although they had already spoken with Father Gregory several times now by Skype since our escape, the Petrosians were unaware of the role the Terzian Cross had played in the rescue of the Khourys and Zulehka.

Nor did they know of their son's extraordinary selflessness in offering to exchange his life for Zulehka's and mine. Father Gregory would never mention it to them, but I certainly wanted to. "Between seeing his and Zulehka's bravery, escaping with our lives, and meeting the grandson of Altay," I joked, "I will have to rethink my past opinions on Divine Existence and Providence."

When my flight finally landed in Asheville from Charlotte, it was a few minutes past eleven at night. I expected the airport to be mostly empty except for Mother and a few other people who had come to meet the last plane of the day and to take us weary passengers to our homes to sleep. To my surprise, that was not the case. Some fifty people were waiting at the passenger exit with banners, balloons, and cameras. To my astonishment, they were waiting for me!

My half brother, Frank, was the first to greet me with a huge grin and warm hug from his wheelchair, and my mother and stepfather were right behind him. Then other friends came up to me and welcomed me home. Some were teachers and friends from Warren Wilson College and others from Black Mountain, Montreat, and Asheville. Some of the greeters, I did not even recognize. I found out later that they were friends of my parents and members of their church who had been praying for me. A newspaper photographer and reporter were there as well.

After this unexpected reception, we drove to my parent's home where I had left my car. Rather than go directly to my apartment in Black Mountain, I decided to spend the night in my old bedroom at my parent's house. It took me a while to fall asleep, as I was still amazed at what had just happened at the airport—that people cared enough for me to come out that late at night to welcome me home.

The next morning, after Mother made me my favorite breakfast of French toast with mayonnaise on it, I told them the details of what had happened since leaving for Boston. My stepfather had cancelled all of his appointments for the morning and my brother had taken off a day from school so that they could be with me.

I also learned from my family what had happened in Asheville once they had found out from Ashti that I was being held for a million dollars in ransom. "We were absolutely frantic," Mother said. "The first thing I did was to call the Petrosians and ask them what we should do. They did not know, but that they said that they were looking into borrowing money on their assets to pay the ransom for their son. We did the same thing. Your father immediately got in touch with our bank to see how much they would be willing to lend us with our house and business as security. We had just enough. I also contacted the editor of the newspaper, as I knew that you were sending him articles. He advised us that we should expect no real help from the government as its policy was against negotiations with terrorists. In fact, he said, we could actually get into legal trouble if the government found out that we paid a ransom." She then added, "Our pastor and our church were our best support. They set up a prayer team for you and even started to collect contributions to help us."

"You were willing to do all of that for me?" I asked astonished. "Take out a loan on all your assets and compromise your livelihood and retirement to free me?"

"Of course," my stepfather said. "You are our son."

I was ashamed. I was ashamed at my past judgments of my parents and for putting them at such financial risk. "Thank you" was all I could say.

Later in the morning, I drove my old Toyota to the garage apartment that I was renting in Black Mountain. After calling my credit card company to get a new card and sending off a check to Dilovan to pay him back for his loans, I sat down at my desk, which looked out at the mountains, and began to plan and write.

In the next few weeks, I worked day and night writing up three new articles for the Asheville paper to add to the first one I had already sent in on Taksim Square. The first one was the longest and served me as the basis for my novel. In three parts, I told my own story: my attempt to understand my own identity as a Turk and Armenian; the discoveries that I made on the trip to Boston, Turkey, and Syria; and my capture and escape in Syria. The second article I wrote was about Hasankeyf and its imminent destruction, and the third was the story of Hakob and Zulekha. While I was paid for these pieces, and a couple of them even were picked up by other publications in the Gannett family of newspapers, none of them landed me a regular job as a reporter. Instead, I was encouraged to continue to send in articles as a freelancer.

I was discouraged but not devastated as my chief aim was not to be a journalist but to become a novelist, and I still had ten months left to write my book. My main problem was how I was going to pay my bills now that my inheritances from Karine and Noah were exhausted.

Through the summer and fall, my solution to that problem was to write during the day and work evenings as a waiter in one of the Black Mountain restaurants that cater to conference-goers and tourists who came to enjoy the mountains and fall colors. When winter came, however, both tourists and work diminished, and I needed to look elsewhere for a job. That was when my mother's pastor thought of a solution.

"The homeless shelter we help has a difficult time finding two volunteers each night to cover the midnight to seven in the morning shift," he told Mother. "Our church would be willing to pay Peter a minimum wage if he agreed to fill one of those spots five nights a week from November through March."

For me this was the perfect solution. Except for doing some laundry for shelter users, putting out breakfast materials in the morning, and dealing with occasional health and discipline problems, I had many free hours to write and surf the internet. At the shelter, I also came face-to-face with interesting characters and situations that I could describe in future novels. During those quiet hours, when the only sounds were snoring and the whistling cold wind outside, I had a lot of time to ponder who I was and where I was going with my life.

I learned many things about myself during my trip to Turkey. One of the most painful of these was my realization that I was not as noble and strong a person as I had previously imagined. I had a definite dark side of lusts and selfishness. My ancestor Altay and I were not so different after all, and Father Gregory, Zulehka, and Ashti far surpassed me in their courage and selflessness.

Constantly during those months, I remembered what Dilovan had said in the car about the type of person he wanted as a son-in-law—a truth seeker, a good provider, and a compassionate person who loved Ashti. Except for loving Ashti, I felt that I was none of those things that he desired.

What embarrassed me most was that I was not really a truth seeker or a truth teller. I, a person who loved to be frank with others, was actually a fake. If I were to fault the government of Turkey for not recognizing the truth of what happened in 1915 to the Armenians and Syriacs, I also needed to face my own denial of the truth of what happened that night on the Blue Ridge Parkway, which caused the paralysis of my brother.

Bringing myself to make that confession was the hardest thing I ever did in my life, but I finally did it. It happened at a family gathering at our house on New Year's Eve. Mother had made a nice dinner for us all, and then afterwards we sat in the living room and shared with each other our resolutions and goals for the coming year. After Frank shared that he had decided he wanted to stay in Asheville and study computer programming at the local community college, it was my turn.

"Of course I want to finish writing my novel and to get it published by the hundredth anniversary of Armenian genocide," I said. "But I also want to be more truthful, less selfish, and a better son and brother."

"You're already a good brother," Frank said.

"Thank you for saying so, Frank, but I'm not. Nor am I a good son," I replied. "I have always done just what I wanted to and haven't thought much of your desires and needs." I paused to gather my courage and looked at my parents to measure their reaction. They seemed very surprised because I had never talked like this to them before. "I also haven't been truthful with you, but I am determined to change that tonight," I said continuing.

All three of them looked at me quizzically. "What do you mean, son?" Mother asked.

"I mean that I lied to you and to the police about what happened the night of the accident when Frank was so badly injured. I said that I fell asleep at the wheel. The truth is that I was wide-awake, but I was texting a message to a friend and took my eyes off the road just as a mountain curve came up. I drove right through the barrier over the cliff. I did something that I knew I shouldn't do and look at the results," I said, pointing to Frank in his wheelchair. "I am so ashamed and deeply sorry."

After a moment or two of stunned silence, I braced myself for their anger. Finally my mother spoke. "Why didn't you tell us the truth right away?"

"I knew your view of me as a spoiled brat who only thought of himself and never of the consequences of his actions on others," I said. "I knew that you were fed-up with my lack of self-discipline and having to get me out of scrapes with the law. If I had told you the truth back then, I would have confirmed your bad opinion of me, and I was too proud to do that."

"What's different now?" my stepfather asked.

"I guess that after my trip to Turkey and Syria, I have come to value truth now more than pride. Like my great-grandfather Altay, I need to recognize my evil and try to do better. Life is short. Life is precarious. Life is precious. I want to live the one I have well."

My parents were silent again for a long time. Then Father got up from his chair and came over to me on the sofa where I was sitting and hugged me. He said nothing. He did not have to. Tears came to my eyes.

"It's all right, Peter," Frank said from his wheelchair, "Whether you were texting or sleeping, it was still an accident. And the truth is that I'm even more to blame for what happened to me that night than you because I decided to unbuckle my seat belt." He smiled and then added, "And don't feel so sorry for me for not having the full use of my legs. It isn't so bad. I will never have to get up to give someone else my seat, and when I need to, I can use my disability as an excuse for other failings!" He laughed at his own joke. "And the truth is that my condition will make absolutely no difference to my becoming a computer programmer or software developer. In fact, it may even help me stand out from the competition and get a job."

"Thank you, Frank," I said. I then got up and hugged him and then my mother. What I had dreaded as a moment of humiliation and anger directed at me had turned out to be instead a moment of forgiveness and grace.

The outcome that night on a personal level, so unpredictable and unexpected, gave me hope, not just for myself but for others as well. I even began to hope for reconciliations on a much larger scale—among Turks, Armenians, and Syriacs and among Muslims, Christians, and Jews. A similar reconciliation between whites and blacks had happened in South Africa because of the Truth and Reconciliation Commission initiatives. Would it not also be possible that an admission of past guilt by Turkey could also turn out positively for that proud and accomplished nation?

That night of confession and forgiveness changed me, and I began to have a new and deeper relationship with my family. Since then, I have been able to get out of myself more and more and become more interested and aware of their needs, especially those of my brother, Frank. Besides helping drive him to classes and appointments more often, I also put him in touch with our new relative Mehdi in Syria, who like him, is very interested in computing. They often communicate by Skype and e-mail, and we hope one day to bring Mehdi here to Asheville.

My opinion of working with my father at the family real estate firm also changed. Before, I felt that I was just too good for this sort of work. Now, I see its practical potential. The real estate firm had generated the income to support me growing up and the collateral to guarantee my ransom. My working there would also please my parents and would allow them more time to travel. It would also provide me with a steady income. I could still write if I so desired.

One of Dilovan's criteria for a husband for Ashti was that he be a good provider. That automatically eliminated me as I had lived most of my life on the largesse of others. Now maybe it was time for me to find a practical alternative to create wealth so that I could support myself and my own projects and also lend a helping hand to others like Father Gregory, Ashti, Mehdi, Hakob and Zulehka.

Speaking of Hakob and Zulehka, they just arrived two months ago to Nashville, Tennessee, to finish their medical studies at the Meharry Medical College in that city. Father Gregory had gotten them and the Sarkissians temporary visas to Armenia and then worked with his father, Aram, to see if he could get student visas and scholarships for Hakob and Zulehka to come to the United States to study medicine. Uncle Aram had used his contacts with the Armenian community and with medical schools and had been successful in getting them into Meharry with a full scholarship. "Your newspaper article on them helped me tremendously," Aram told me. During their spring break in April, Hakob and Zulehka will be coming to Asheville to visit us.

As for Ashti, we have kept in close touch, and she has created her own tourist agency, which she named *Come Home*. She resigned from her full-time job as an event organizer at her hotel, but she continues to work on a part-time basis. Although Fulya continues to teach at the university, Dilovan also retired from his job in order to travel and to help Ashti.

Together with her father, Ashti has already set up several historical itineraries for Armenians to choose from when they visit Turkey. One of them includes Harput, Lake Hazar, Diyarbakir, and Mardin. As part of the tours, she has arranged lectures and visits to the homes of Turks and Kurds in the region. She has even managed to put together some volunteer opportunities for Turks, Kurds, Armenians, and others to work side-by-side to restore a few former Armenian and Syriac churches, cemeteries, and monasteries. In the spring, she and Dilovan will be coming to the United States to promote their tours as well as to visit the Petrosians in Boston and us here in Asheville while Hakob and Zulehka Sarkissian are here. It will be the first time that she and Dilovan have met my family, and I hope that it will be the start of a long and meaningful relationship between them and us. Maybe I will even be able to launch my new novel while they are here.

I am determined to get the book out by April 24, 2015, the hundredth anniversary of the Armenian genocide. In order to do so, I will not have enough time to get an agent and then shop it around to traditional publishing houses. Given the high probability that my story would be rejected by them anyway based both on its lack of literary merit and potential for making them money, I have decided to publish it myself. Uncle Aram agrees, as timing to him is more important than prestige. He also insists on providing the funds for the printing since he says that my book is his family's story as well as mine.

It is strange this whole concept of timing. When Father Gregory, Zulehka, and I were captured in April of last year, ISIS was barely known outside of Syria. Now it is known and feared all over the world. Soon after we helped Zulehka and the Khourys flee from Deir ez-Zor, ISIS took over most of the city, and in September, they blew up the Armenian Memorial and Church that we visited. As for Karim Eminyan, Father Gregory is still unsure what happened to him, but he fears that he has now joined the thousands of other Armenian and Syriac martyrs of that city. History in this area of the world continues to repeat itself for Christians.

ISIS, or ISIL, or the Islamic State as they now prefer to be called, have made other rapid advances through the rest of northern Syria and into Iraq, capturing even Mosul, the second largest city of the country—the former Nineveh of the Bible. Their only effective opposition so far have been the brave Kurdish YPG and Peshmerger soldiers like Bakur, Loran, and Mehdi, who fight them in order to protect their own lands and people in Syria and Iraq.

Wherever ISIS is in control, they put in place the strictest versions of Sharia Law and show no mercy to the infidels they find in these places, whether Christians, Yazdis, or even people of their own religion whom they feel do not follow the literal teachings of the Koran and of their Prophet as interpreted by their own religious scholars.

"This cannot be my religion," Ashti wrote to me in her last e-mail, speaking of ISIS. "My parents and I are so ashamed. Thank Allah that so many Muslims are now standing up against them. We cannot tolerate any more their disregard for basic human rights in their desire to spread their version of Islam. Thank Allah for those Muslim political and religious leaders who have the backbone to stand up against these evil people." She ended her letter by saying, "Islam is at war with itself. May Allah bring victory to those on the side of mercy and truth!"

When I read Ashti's e-mail, I realized that her wish was my wish, and I hope that this story of my journey to Boston, Turkey, and the land between the two rivers will be of help in achieving that victory. I hope that it will remind people of the great suffering of so many forgotten Armenians and Syriacs a hundred years ago and help put flesh anew on their scattered dried bones in the desert. I hope that this story will also bring to the reader's attention the fact that the persecution of Christians in the Middle East continues today. Finally, I hope that something new and radical will take place that will change this paradigm. One such thing would be for the great nation of Turkey to admit to the sins of their ancestors and ask forgiveness for them. Another would be for Armenians and Syriacs to grant that forgiveness and admit to their own failings and not insist on reparations. As Father Gregory said in the car going from Batman to Diyarbakir, permanent change will only come in the Middle East when all of the children of Abraham realize that they are brothers and sisters to each other and to the rest of humanity. We were all created and are loved by the One God, whether he is called Allah, Yahweh, or Lord.

When I read Ashti's last e-mail, I also realized how much I loved and respected her. I can hardly wait to see her again in the spring here in Asheville. The truth is that I want to marry her despite the many obstacles that we both know are in that path. To me, such a union would symbolize the final reconciliation of my Turkish, Armenian, and American backgrounds. That is my hope, but whether it happens or not is another story. As Ashti said, "Only Allah knows!"

Map of Turkey and Neighboring Regions

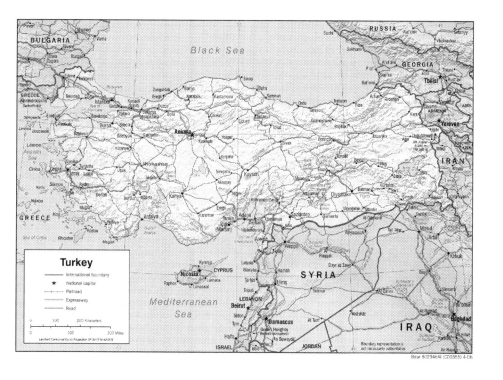

The Route of Peter Johnson
in Turkey and Syria

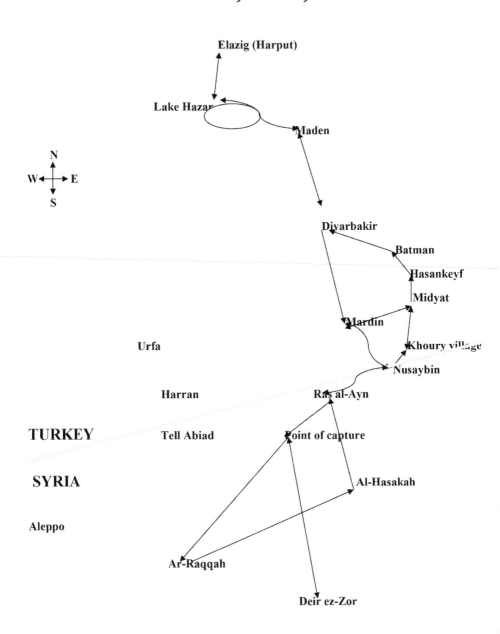

Elazig (Harput)

Lake Hazar

Maden

N

W ← → E

S

Diyarbakir

Batman

Hasankeyf

Midyat

Mardin

Khoury village

Urfa

Nusaybin

Harran

Ras al-Ayn

TURKEY

Tell Abiad

Point of capture

SYRIA

Al-Hasakah

Aleppo

Ar-Raqqah

Deir ez-Zor

Family Tree of Peter Johnson and Ashti Kaya

First Generation:

Garabed Terzian: A Turkish Armenian professor at the Euphrates College in Harput. He is the husband of the Turkish Syriac **Talitha Davut Terzian.** They have three children: Karine, Margarit, and Lazar. (Garabed and Talitha Terzian are the great-great-grandparents of Peter Johnson and Ashti Kaya.)

Second Generation:

Karine Terzian Petrosian: The eldest daughter of Garabed and Talitha Terzian. She is the mother of Noah with **Altay Aslan,** and with her husband, **Nigol Petrosian,** she is the mother of Aram and Margaret. (She is the great-grandmother of Peter Johnson.)

Margarit Terzian: The second daughter of Garabed and Talitha Terzian. She was kidnapped, forced to convert to Islam, and to change her name to **Zara**. She becomes the second wife of the Turkish Kurd **Egid Kaya**. She is the mother of Diyari Kaya and three other children who died before they married. (She is the great-grandmother of Ashti Kaya.)

Lazar Terzian: The youngest son of Garabed and Talitha Terzian who is killed as a young boy.

Third Generation

Noah Ross-Terzian: The son of Karine Terzian and the Turk gendarme Altay Aslan. Noah was adopted by Americans James and Grace Ross. With his wife **Elizabeth,** Noah is the father of Thaddeus and Mariam. (He is the grandfather of Peter Johnson.)

Aram Petrosian: He is the son of Karine Terzian Petrosian and Nigol Petrosian, and with his wife **Susan,** is the father of Richard (Father Gregory) and Nina. (Aram is the great-uncle of Peter Johnson.)

Diyari Kaya: He is the son of Margarit (Zara) and Egid Kaya, and with his wife **Kejal,** is the father of Dilovan and Rihana. (He is the grandfather of Ashti.)

Fourth Generation:

Thaddeus Ross-Terzian: The son of Noah and Elizabeth Ross-Terzian who never married. A friend of Peter's father, Brent Johnson, he dies in an airplane accident with Brent.

Mariam Ross-Terzian: The daughter of Noah and Elizabeth Ross-Terzian. With her first husband, **Brent Johnson,** she is the mother of Peter Johnson. With her second husband, **Bill Daniels,** she is the mother of Frank Daniels.

Richard (Father Gregory) Petrosian: The son of Aram and Susan Petrosian who becomes an Armenian Orthodox priest. (He is a first cousin, once removed, of Peter Johnson.)

Dilovan Kaya: The son of Diyari and Kejal Kaya and grandson of Margarit (Zara) Terzian Kaya. He is married to **Fulya** and is the father of Ashti. (He is a second cousin, once removed, of Peter Johnson.)

Rihana Kaya: The daughter of Diyari and Kejal Kaya who is the mother of Loran with her Turkish Kurd husband, **Bawan Yasin.** (She is Ashti Kaya's aunt.)

Fifth Generation:

Peter Johnson: The son of Mariam and Brent Johnson, grandson of Noah Ross-Terzian, great-grandson of Karine Terzian and Altay Aslan, and great-great-grandson of Garabed and Talitha Terzian. He is also the stepson of Bill Daniels and a third cousin of Ashti Kaya.

Ashti Kaya: The daughter of Dilovan and Fulya Kaya, great-granddaughter of Margarit (Zara) Kaya, and great-great-granddaughter of Garabed and Talitha Terzian. (She is Peter Johnson's third cousin.)

Loran Yasin: The son of Bawan and Rihana Yasin. He is Ashti Kaya's first cousin and Peter Johnson's third cousin.

Disclaimers

I have written this book as a first-person account, but the truth is that Peter Johnson and Tom Frist have little in common other than their interest in Peter's story and that they live near each other. This is a work of fiction. While similar events described in the book happened to real people, all of the characters, names, and events, as well as all places, incidents, organizations, and dialogue in this novel are either the products of the author's imagination or are used fictitiously.

I would also like to stress that while I have tried to be accurate and consistent, some readers may dispute my use and spelling of the names of ethnic groups, towns, and individuals in the novel. I have found that in this region of the world, such names change often and vary depending on ethnic background and political situation.

Acknowledgments

In this book I have quoted extensively from *The Slaughter House Province, An American Consul's Report* by Leslie Davis, an eyewitness account of those terrible years in the Harput Province of Turkey described in this novel. I greatly thank Ariste Caratzas, the publisher, for permission to do so. I have also used *The Burning Tigris* by Peter Balakian as an excellent source of background information on the events of those years.

I would also like to acknowledge here some of the individuals who have helped me in my research. My friend Hank Ackerman provided many important suggestions, and others assisted me, like Dr. Jeffrey Wickes, Fr. Daniel Findikyan, Fr. Samuel Rith-Najarian, Leith Tate, and a number of Turkish friends who do not want their names publicized given the sensitivity of the subject matter of the book. Thanks finally to my wife, Clare, and to my daughter, Lisa, for their contributions in practical matters related to the manuscript and website. While the help of all of these individuals has been very valuable to me, I want to make clear that any errors in the book are my own responsibility and not theirs.

Printed in the United States
By Bookmasters